The Last Long Night

Book # 5 in The Bregdan Chronicles

Sequel to Dark Chaos

Ginny Dye

The Last Long Night

Copyright © 2013 by Ginny Dye
Published by A Voice In The World Publishing
Bellingham, WA 98229

www.BregdanChronicles.net

www.GinnyDye.com

www.AVoiceInTheWorldPublishing.com

ISBN 1507886225

Printed in the United States of America.

For Bruce – my brother, the dream maker...
Thank you!

A Note From the Author

My great hope is that *The Last, Long Night* will both entertain and challenge you. I hope you will learn as much as I did during the months of research it took to write this book. Though I now live in the Pacific Northwest, I grew up in the South and lived for eleven years in Richmond, VA. I spent countless hours exploring the plantations that still line the banks of the James River and became fascinated by the history.

But you know, it's not the events that fascinate me so much – it's the people. That's all history is, you know. History is the story of people's lives. History reflects the consequences of their choices and actions – both good and bad. History is what has given you the world you live in today – both good and bad.

This truth is why I named this series The Bregdan Chronicles. Bregdan is a Gaelic term for weaving: Braiding. Every life that has been lived until today is a part of the woven braid of life. It takes every person's story to create history. Your life will help determine the course of history. You may think you don't have much of an impact. You do. Every action you take will reflect in someone else's life. Someone else's decisions. Someone else's future. Both good and bad. That is the **Bregdan Principle**...

**Every life that has been lived until today is a part
of the woven braid of life.
It takes every person's story to
create history.
Your life will help determine the course
of history.**

**You may think you don't have
much of an impact.
You do.
Every action you take will reflect in
someone else's life.
Someone else's decisions.
Someone else's future.
Both good and bad.**

My great hope as you read this book, and all that will follow, is that you will acknowledge the power you have, every day, to change the world around you by your decisions and actions. Then I will know the research and writing were was all worthwhile.

Oh, and I hope you enjoy every moment of it and learn to love the characters as much as I do!

I'm already being asked how many books will be in this series. I guess that depends on how long I live! My intention is to release two books a year, each covering one year of history – continuing to weave the lives of my characters into the times they lived. I hate to end a good book as much as anyone – always feeling so sad that I have to leave the characters. You shouldn't have to be sad for a long time!

You are now reading the fifth book. *Carried Forward By Hope* is waiting for you, and then just check Amazon to see what else has been released! If you like what you read, you'll want to make sure you're on my mailing list for my Blog and updates at:

www.BregdanChronicles.net. I'll let you know each time a new one comes out!

Sincerely,
Ginny Dye

Chapter One

Would it be today?

Carrie Borden turned away from the Chimborazo Hospital building and tents crowding the plateau as she crested the steep hill and moved to the edge of the cliff overlooking Richmond and the James River shimmering below. She pushed black, wavy strands back into her bun and tried to block out every noise in the overcrowded, bustling capital of the Confederacy. She was listening for just one thing...

The sound of battle.

Three years into the Civil War, there was no doubt that there would be another attempt to take Richmond. *On to Richmond* had been the Union battle cry from the beginning. Every spring there was vicious fighting that tore at the heart and soul of what had once been a united country. Every spring the buildings behind her filled with horribly wounded men who would never live the life they had known before—*if* they survived their wounds.

But it was just one man who held Carrie's heart. Just one man who had kissed her goodbye a few days before and headed out with General Lee's Confederate troops to meet the massive, hundred thousand-man Union Army waiting to attack on the other side of the Rapidan River.

Carrie's husband of one year, Captain Robert Borden, was once again on the battlefield. Carrie took deep breaths, trying to calm her nerves and focus her mind. Everyone knew the battle would start soon. *Today. Tomorrow.* And then it would begin all over again, the constant worrying and wondering of whether Robert had made it through another battle.

Sounds of battle would also trigger wagonloads of wounded men pouring into the hospital and into medical wards and homes all over the city, which were set up to handle the tens of thousands of men that would need them.

Carrie stared into the distance, her green eyes glistening with tears. She took one final deep breath and turned to stride into the nearest tent.

Battle would come. She had work to do.

"Good morning, Carrie," Dr. Wild called, his smiling green eyes glancing up at her from under his cap of curly, rust-colored hair.

The sound of his cheer, no matter how forced, made Carrie feel better. And it made her realize how thankful she was to be able to make a difference. She was the only woman working as a true medical assistant to a doctor at Chimborazo Hospital. Dr. Wild had been the first to give her a chance to use her skills. Now, they worked as a team.

The years of battle had sickened her, but they had also left her even more certain she would become a doctor when the war ended. The ridicule she suffered from so many when she had first arrived at the hospital had done nothing but steel her determination.

"Good morning, Dr. Wild," she called out, glancing down the rows of what was mostly an empty hospital ward. Most of the soldiers wounded in earlier battles had already been sent home or back to the battlefront.

"Will you check all the drug supplies?" Dr. Wild asked. "I've had the women stock everything they have made so far. I'm afraid we've got little but what has been created."

Carrie nodded. The blockades of the Southern coastline by the Union Navy had been grimly successful, blocking out the drugs and medicines so desperately needed to treat patients. Once again, Carrie sent deep waves of gratitude to Old Sarah, now dead, who had taught her the magic of the herbs that filled the Virginia woods. All spring, Carrie had directed groups of women in collecting plants and turning them into the herbal medicines and treatments that would be the only relief many of the men would have.

"I checked everything before I left last night. We've got a good supply of the most important medicines. The women will continue making them. They've become quite good at it."

"They're angels," Dr. Wild agreed. "All the beds are ready." He walked to the open door and stared north. "Now, we wait."

Carrie moved forward to stand beside him. The air was still. The whole city held its breath as it waited for the inevitable. Though the sun shone hot and bright, she could feel the heavy, dark clouds that had settled over the entire country. Storm after storm had wrought tremendous damage, but they weren't done yet.

The worst was yet to come.

Carrie shook her head to dispel her gloomy thoughts and smiled when she saw Janie striding up the hill. Carrie had finished breakfast with her friend an hour earlier, but she was already in need of Janie's steadiness.

Janie looked over and veered off her course to come join them. She took her position at the door and gazed north, just as Dr. Wild and Carrie were. "Will it start today?"

"I don't know," Dr. Wild said. "We've been told to be ready, but there is no definite word on whether General Meade has begun to move his troops. I suppose that, like always, we'll know when the wagons start rolling in."

He looked at Carrie with deep sympathy. "Any word from Robert yet?"

"No, but I didn't expect there to be. Both he and my father believe this will be the hardest fought battle for Richmond yet."

"Because of General Grant." Dr. Wild wasn't asking a question.

"Because of Grant," Carrie agreed. "He doesn't have the cautious nature of the generals who have come before him. Robert believes we've been lucky. There have been so many times the city could have been taken, but the generals didn't push forward. They gave up and left." She shook her head sadly. "But not before they injured or killed thousands of our men."

"But those generals weren't fighting against General Lee," Janie protested.

"That's true," Carrie agreed, "but Robert told me General Lee doesn't have enough men to stop them. His troop numbers are much smaller, and the soldiers are in much worse condition."

"We may not look so good, but we're tougher than them Yankee boys any day!" One of the few soldiers left in the ward had heard them talking. His voice rang out in protest. "I'll be out of this bed soon, and then I'll be back fighting. Them Yankees ain't coming down to take our country!"

Carrie and Dr. Wild exchanged a somber look. Both of them knew the soldier from Georgia wouldn't ever go back into battle. They had barely saved his life, but they had not been able to save his leg.

He seemed to read their thoughts. "Don't be worrying 'bout this missing leg of mine. I reckon I can strap on a wooden one and still aim a gun! I ain't going down without a fight!"

And that, Carrie thought as she smiled encouragingly at the soldier, was exactly why this war was still destroying lives. Neither side was willing to give in. There was no chance of peace. The war would simply have to burn itself out.

Janie changed the subject. "I tried to get information about Eddie again."

Carrie turned to her eagerly. She had been trying for two years to find out what happened to the man now languishing in Castle Thunder Prison. Opal, one of her father's slaves, had moved to Richmond from Cromwell Plantation to be with her cousin Fannie and work at the state armory munitions building. Opal had been so happy there. That is, up until the day Fannie was killed in an explosion at another munitions plant, and her husband, Eddie, had been thrown into prison for treason when he was caught as a spy.

Opal had returned to the plantation with Fannie and Eddie's four children, now her sole responsibility, and was determined to stay there until his release.

"Any luck this time?"

"I'm afraid not," Janie said. "Captain Alexander doesn't feel compelled to share anything about the inmates."

Carrie tightened her lips. "He is a hard man. His time in a Union prison before he escaped has given him no sympathy for anyone at Castle Thunder. I've heard conditions there are cruel and deplorable."

"Unfortunately, that is very true," Dr. Wild agreed, "which will make things that much harder for one of the newest Castle Thunder guests."

Carrie and Janie turned to him with questioning looks.

"Both of you probably missed the news a couple weeks back about Dr. Mary Walker."

"*Dr.* Walker?" Carrie asked in disbelief.

"A *woman*?" Janie gasped.

"There is a small ward for women," Dr. Wild explained, "but Dr. Walker is a rather unconventional woman." He smiled at Carrie. "I think you would like her."

Carrie smiled and waited for him to continue.

"Dr. Walker is one of the country's first women doctors. She graduated from Syracuse Medical College almost ten years ago. She married a fellow student, but I understand the ceremony didn't include a promise to obey. She didn't take his name, and she wore trousers and a dress coat to her wedding."

Carrie and Janie both laughed in disbelief.

"Neither the marriage nor their joint medical practice lasted long," Dr. Wild said. "She is quite the champion of women's rights and dress reform."

Carrie grinned. "You're right. I believe I would like her very much."

"They captured her as a spy," Dr. Wild continued, "though if my source is correct, she crossed our lines to treat civilians, not to spy."

"But to be in Castle Thunder," Janie said with a shudder. "It's such a horrible place."

"I wouldn't wish it on my worst enemy," Carrie responded, unable to forget the memories of her friend Matthew sick and gaunt after many months in Libby Prison. She could only hope he had been able to make it all the way to Fort Monroe and gain the protection of the Union Army.

"I hope she'll be released in a prisoner exchange quickly," Dr. Wild agreed.

Thoughts of Matthew made Carrie turn and stare east toward the coast and Fort Monroe. Had Matthew made it? Had he found Rose? Was she still teaching at the contraband camp? Even that tiny morsel of information about her former slave, who was closer than any sister could be, had fed her starving heart when Carrie and Robert helped Matthew escape several weeks before.

Janie, feeling her frustration, reached out to take her hand. Carrie absorbed the courage it offered.

Captain Robert Borden was weary to the bone. Not from fighting—the battle had not yet started. He was weary of the war and had lost all confidence in ultimate victory. Before the first shot was fired, he knew the outcome would be the slaughter of thousands of men, with the distinct possibility he would be one of them. Whether they won or lost, this particular battle didn't seem to really matter.

He settled back against the cunningly built earthworks that created a natural fortress the Union could not breach. The sparkling waters of the Rapidan River, flowing placidly below the high hills of the southern bank, had become the unofficial boundary of the Union and the Confederacy. The setting sun cast a golden glow that could almost make one believe there wasn't really a war going on.

Robert closed his eyes and let Carrie enter his thoughts, though somehow it seemed wrong to bring her fresh beauty and vibrant energy onto the battlefield. It was the only thing that kept him going. He was no longer fighting to win a war. He was fighting to protect his beautiful wife in the city the Union was determined to destroy.

"Hey, Captain!"

Robert opened his eyes and looked at who had crawled over to him. His heart ached when he saw a boy, barely sixteen, with his gaunt cheeks and exhausted yet defiant eyes. "Yes, Jimmy?"

"You reckon the battle will start tomorrow? The fellas are getting plenty tense."

Robert shook his head. "I don't know, Jimmy. I believe it will be soon, but we haven't gotten any orders yet."

"You really think we got a chance against Meade's army? I hear we're outnumbered pretty bad." Jimmy's face was much too old for someone his age.

Regardless of what he really believed, Robert knew it was his job to send his men into battle with confidence. "Of course we're going to beat them! It's not the first time we've sent a much bigger army running. They won't know what hit them when they run into us." He made his voice strong and reassuring and was rewarded when confidence replaced the fear on Jimmy's face.

"We're going to make them Yankees run like all the other times!"

Robert gazed at the boy. "Where are you from, Jimmy?"

"My folks got a place down in Georgia, Captain Borden. I ain't never been farther than a few miles from the farm until this war started. I reckon I've seen more of this country than anyone else in my family," he boasted.

"What do you want to do when the war is over?" Robert knew it would help Jimmy if he stayed focused on the future by having something to pull him forward through the hard times.

Jimmy shrugged, smiled slightly, and looked down for a moment before he raised his eyes. "I want to go back and start my own livery. I reckon I love horses more than anything. I've always dreamed of having my own place."

"There's nothing like a good horse," Robert agreed.

"Like that gray Thoroughbred you ride. I think that might be the finest animal I've ever seen. Where'd you get him?"

"Granite belongs to my wife," Robert said, already wishing the beautiful horse was far from the battlefield, safe in his stall on Cromwell Plantation.

"He's really something."

"That he is," Robert said. He looked more closely at Jimmy's shining eyes. "Would you like to take care of him tonight?" He was used to doing it himself, but he could tell the boy needed something to distract him.

"You bet!"

Robert was silent for a moment before he continued. "Hey, Jimmy, if something happens to me, will you take care of Granite? Make sure he gets back to Richmond?" He hated to diminish the boy's confidence, but he didn't want Carrie to lose her husband *and* her horse.

Jimmy's eyes widened as his shoulders straightened. "Yes, sir! I would consider it an honor, sir."

Robert smiled. "Thank you. Now go join the men and have something to eat." He didn't bother to acknowledge that the meager food the men had was far from sufficient. The odd mixture of wheat bran and beef closely resembled glue when it was cooked, and it did little to satisfy the men's hunger.

Hunger was as much a part of army life as fighting was. Only one railway line still operated, and it wasn't enough to get food to the men or fodder to the animals. Robert spent time every day gathering fresh spring grass for Granite. The horse was still thin, but he looked better than most of them did. That, at least, he could do for Carrie.

Jimmy rose to leave but turned back with one final question. "Hey, Captain, are there more men coming up to help us?"

Robert knew his men had been waiting for reinforcements, hoping for help. He shook his head but didn't want to go into the truth; that the South was out of men. All the available men were killed, wounded, or had deserted. "We're not going to need them," he said confidently. "Lee has them off fighting in other areas because he knows his army can handle anything the Yankees throw at us."

Jimmy gazed at him for a moment and seemed to draw strength from what he saw in his captain's eyes. Once more, he straightened his shoulders. "You got that right. We're going to send them Yanks running again. One day, they'll get tired of losing, and they just won't come back!" Jimmy crawled back to his group and went in search of Granite.

Robert closed his eyes again as the sun faded and darkness fell on the woods. He knew that even if it did not happen tomorrow, the battle would happen soon.

Carrie leaned back in the wagon seat and looked around at Richmond. It never ceased to amaze her how much the city had changed for the worse since the war began. Gone was the genteel elegance. Gone was the prosperity. Gone was the confidence.

Richmond's privilege of being the capital of the Confederacy brought with it the harsh reality of overcrowding, poverty, crime, prostitution, hunger and the ever-present fear that Union troops would capture the city.

Carrie had learned to block most of it out by focusing on caring for her patients. For now, she had done everything she could do at Chimborazo. She was on her way down to the hospital in the black part of town.

"I don't reckon there will be any trouble today," Hobbs said. "With a battle this close, I don't think anyone will try to stop us."

Carrie shrugged as Janie nodded her head. She had quit wondering what *would* happen and decided she would deal with whatever *did* happen.

She knew Hobbs took his job seriously, though. He was only three years her junior, but he seemed much younger. Hobbs had served under Robert until he almost lost his leg in the same battle that had nearly taken Robert from her—and had him missing for nine months. The boy remained fiercely loyal to his lieutenant. Unable to fight anymore because of his wounded leg, he was now Carrie's assistant at the hospital and helped provide security for her when she went into the most dangerous part of the city. Carrie had grown to love the redheaded boy with intense, shining brown eyes and unfailing enthusiasm.

"I think you're right, Hobbs. I don't think it will take us long to take care of the patients today, unless more have come in since we were last there."

Hobbs patted the rifle that sat across his lap. "We'll be fine, Miss Carrie," he promised. He knew of the times groups of men had tried to stop Carrie and Janie from going to the hospital, incensed that the "niggers" were getting help from white women.

"I think the boy be right, Miss Carrie," Spencer agreed. "I ain't got word of no trouble."

Carrie smiled warmly at her driver. Spencer was a free black who had been working for her family for nearly three years. Their bond, forged by the challenges they had faced together, was strong. "I'm not worried," she said. She leaned back to smile at Janie. Both of them were content to ride in silence, letting the late afternoon air wash away the fatigue from the day.

Pastor Anthony was waiting for them at the door of the hospital. The kindly man with warm blue eyes was such an important part of her life, and had done so much for her, including opening the door for her to operate as the sole doctor for the black hospital. She wished, though, that she could shake the disappointment she felt everytime she looked at him now. *Not even Janie knew...*

Carrie shook her head impatiently. Now was not the time to think about it. She had work to do. "Hello, Pastor Anthony," she said, jumping from the carriage. "How are our patients today?"

Not waiting for an answer, she and Janie moved into the simple wooden building. It was rustic and plain, but it was clean, and the patients had primitive wood slat beds that kept them off the ground. It was a huge improvement from what she and Janie had found when they first arrived more than a year ago, and discovered all the patients lying on the ground with coarse blankets their only bedding.

Carrie took comfort from knowing the back room held shelves of herbal medicines she had made while on the plantation and managed to smuggle into Richmond. She brought them to the black hospital because the people in this part of town had no way of getting to the woods to collect plants. As long as they were careful, there would be enough to last through another summer and winter.

Carrie made her rounds of the beds and was glad to see most of them were empty. Spring meant renewed activity at Chimborazo because of battles, but it also meant relief for people in the black section of town who suffered so much from the bitter winter cold. This hospital had not lost even one patient that winter, but Carrie knew serious illness could break out at any time.

She smiled when she got to Johnny's bed and knelt down to meet him at eye level. "Hello, Johnny." She was glad to see that the six-year-old's dark eyes, glistening with fever the last time she was there, were now clear.

"Hello 'dere, Miss Carrie! I be feelin' a heap much better."

"It sure looks that way, Johnny," Carrie agreed. "Are you eating?"

"Yessum."

"Drinking?"

"Enough dat I figur' I gonna drown in it!"

Carrie laughed as she looked up at the nurse—one of the women who volunteered at the hospital—and got her nod of agreement.

"Well then, I figure a boy like you would rather be out playing in such fine weather."

Johnny's eyes widened. "You mean I get to go home? I gets to leave?"

"Don't be so happy," Carrie teased. "I'll think you don't like me."

"Oh no, ma'am," Johnny cried, suddenly alarmed. "I didn't mean nothin' like dat!"

Carrie laughed and pulled back the covers of the bed. "I'm only teasing you. I'm thrilled you get to go home. One of the nurses will take you back to your parents." Her voice turned stern. "You are not to overdo it. Take it easy for at least another week, or the fever could come back. Do you understand?" She waited for his eyes to meet hers.

Johnny nodded his head vigorously. "Yessum. I be real good. I fo' sho don't want to be comin' back here!"

Carrie gave him a hug and watched as he disappeared out the door. Johnny's pneumonia had almost taken his life. She would never tire of the knowledge she could help people get well.

Janie moved over to stand beside her. "There are no new patients. Spring is helping everyone."

"Everyone but the soldiers waiting to fight." She forced a smile. "Let's go home. We can still make it in time for dinner."

Carrie and Janie were laughing and talking when they walked into the house with Hobbs. "We made it in time for dinner, Father," Carrie called, turning to head up the stairs to wash.

She stopped dead in her tracks at the sight of their unexpected guest.

Chapter Two

Carrie recovered quickly, dismayed to see the uncomfortable flush on their guest's cheeks because of her shocked stare. She moved forward and took his hand. "Jeremy Anthony! What a pleasure to have you here," she said warmly. "I'm so sorry for my surprise. I've just spent the afternoon with your father and was thinking about all my patients." She chose to ignore the disbelieving look on Janie's face, but knew she would have to dodge questions later.

"To what do we owe the pleasure of your visit?" she asked, still trying to gain her balance and knowing there was not one person in the house who could know why she was struggling.

"Jeremy is my guest." Thomas Cromwell strode into the room and placed his hand on Jeremy's shoulder. "I met this fascinating young man several weeks ago when we were working on a budget for the city, and I've developed profound respect for him. I convinced him to join us for dinner tonight, but I didn't realize you already know each other."

Carrie smiled at her father and turned back to Jeremy. "I'm so glad you're here. I haven't seen you since the day I met you down at the hospital." She answered her father's unspoken question. "Jeremy is Pastor Anthony's son. We met briefly some time ago."

"Why, I had no idea," Thomas exclaimed. "Your father has been here as a guest before. He's quite a remarkable man. That helps explain why he has such a remarkable son." He waved Jeremy into the dining room. "May almost has dinner finished. Let's have a drink while we wait."

Carrie moved toward the steps. "If you'll excuse me, I'll go and wash up. It was rather a dusty carriage ride. I'll be back down in a few minutes."

She wasn't surprised when Janie followed her up the stairs and cornered her as soon as the door was closed.

"Why were you so shocked to see Jeremy?" she demanded.

Many possible responses ran through her head, but Carrie knew Janie would see right through all of them, so she merely shook her head. "I'm afraid I can't tell you," she said. She had not given Pastor Anthony her word, but she *had* told him she didn't know what she would do with the information she had gained. She owed it to him to go to him first once she had decided.

Janie looked at her for a long moment, then nodded her head and turned around to wash her hands.

Carrie wrapped Janie in an impulsive hug. "Thank you." It was so wonderful to have a friend who wouldn't press for information. Hardly a day passed that she didn't feel immense gratitude for the friendship that had developed when she helped save Janie from a drunken soldier early in the war.

"You're welcome," Janie responded. "If you ever need to talk about it, you know I'll listen."

Thomas and Jeremy were deep in conversation when Carrie and Janie joined them at the table, along with Hobbs and five other men, all her father's associates, who were living with them because of Richmond's crowded condition. There was hardly a home in Richmond that was not also operating as a boarding house.

Thomas had bought the elegant, three-story brick home before the war began, thinking it would be a haven for his family if it were ever needed. After his wife's death, it had become *his* haven from the painful memories of the plantation, and he had buried himself in Virginia politics.

Conversation continued as Carrie and Janie took their seats and reached for the platters of simple food that was now their steady diet. Everyone was tired of beans and cornbread, but few complained because there were many more who had nothing at all. Thousands had died from malnutrition during the winter.

"Things can't be as bad as all that," Stiles, one of the boarders, protested, his round face flushed with disbelief, his wide-set eyes flashing with indignation.

Jeremy shrugged. "Richmond's finances are dire, as are the finances of Virginia and the entire Confederacy. When we decided to become a nation, we were not planning on three years of war. We also hadn't planned on losing the income from most of our crops because of the blockade."

"What do you know?" Stiles scoffed. "You're only a boy."

Jeremy merely looked at him and smiled, making it obvious he was used to being dismissed because of his age, and that he had ceased to let it bother him.

"This *boy*," Thomas said, "has the fullest confidence of our government. Governor Letcher counted on him until he left office. Now Governor Smith does the same."

"I've found that age has nothing to do with it, as long as one has the skills and talents for the job." Carrie spoke into the quiet, well aware she and Jeremy were only weeks apart in age. "Since Jeremy has been serving Virginia for the last three years, obviously he is well qualified."

"But we have all the munitions plants here," Stiles protested. Realizing he was getting no sympathy or support, he had decided to change the subject.

"That's true," Thomas conceded, "but right now there are too many drains on the money for that to make up for the losses."

"People in Richmond are starving," Janie said darkly, "but it's mostly because of the speculators."

Jeremy nodded. "Sadly, that is completely true. The speculators are greedy and ruthless. It's not that food isn't available—it's not being *made* available. Speculators are buying up huge quantities of flour, sugar, bacon, salt and other supplies, but they are merely storing them in warehouses."

"Knowing the longer they hold on to them, the higher they will go in price," Carrie said with disgust.

"President Davis has tried to stop it. Governor Letcher abhorred the practice, and now Governor Smith is making an attempt to stop it," Thomas said, "but the greed is too great."

"People are afraid there will be nothing left after the war, so they're making all the money they can now," Janie observed.

"Not realizing that if their greed means we lose the war, their money will have no value whatsoever," Jeremy said.

"People like that don't look at the long-term effects of their actions," Thomas replied. "It's enough for them to live the high life right now. They don't realize that every choice they make has an impact on someone else, usually *many* others."

Carrie remembered something she had seen coming through town. "I thought you said a law had been passed this winter against the importation of nonessential luxuries, Father? I'm sure I saw new gowns in some of the store windows."

Jeremy nodded. "Your father was right. Unfortunately, it is very often Richmond's leading citizens who are engaged in the importation of things like perfumes, silk stockings, dresses and liquors. The profit is rather enormous. We haven't found an effective way to stop them."

"Perfumes and silk stockings," Janie mused. "While our men are in agony because we can't get medicine and drugs."

Silence fell over the room as they absorbed the irony and the impact of people's choices.

Daring to broach the subject all of them were avoiding, James Crater, another of the boarders, broke the silence. "Dare I ask if we stand any chance against the hundred thousand Union troops sitting on the other side of the river?"

Thomas scowled. "General Lee has worked miracles before. I have hopes he can do it again."

"With an army that is outnumbered, underfed and exhausted?" Crater asked.

Thomas shrugged. "Those soldiers are fighting for their homes. I can only determine the Confederacy has lasted so long in this war because we are fighting *for* something, not against something."

Carrie pondered that for a moment. "I daresay the Union would say they are fighting *for* the continuation of our country."

"That is true," Thomas agreed, "but so far, very few of their soldiers have had their homes and family destroyed or threatened. That reality brings out a passion that is hard to conquer."

"How long, though," Carrie protested, "can we afford to lose tens of thousands of men in every battle?"

Thomas settled back in his chair. "I don't know," he admitted with a deep sigh. "It can't continue. We are running out of men, and there is no one else to fill the troops."

"I know General Lee proposed that slaves be recruited to fight, in exchange for their freedom when the war is over," Janie said.

"It's a ridiculous idea!" Crater snorted, his blue eyes shooting sparks of disdain. "Arm the slaves? We might as well give up the fight right now. We're fighting for the right to keep our slaves, and now we're going to arm them and promise them freedom. Preposterous!"

Carrie sat back, waiting for her father to reply. She knew it would do no good to point out to Crater that if the South lost the war, all the slaves would go free anyway. She also didn't have the energy to defend her belief that all the slaves *should* be freed now. She was quite sure Crater was aware of her beliefs anyway. She was used to being a topic of discussion in Richmond. It had long ago ceased to bother her.

Thomas shook his head. "I know Lee believes it would be a good thing. I also know there is far too much opposition for it to happen. At least for now—"

"It will quite simply *never* happen," Crater stated.

When Thomas did not reply, Crater looked at him more closely. "It will never happen, right?"

Thomas shrugged. "I don't know. There have been so many things that have happened since the beginning of this war that I could never have imagined. I've given up trying to read the future. I find that getting through today is enough."

Carrie gazed at her father, took his hand, and gave it a gentle squeeze. She knew how far he had come to let go of the bitterness and anger that seemed to swallow him for the first three years of the war. Her heart swelled with love for the man who had always supported his headstrong daughter.

The war had exacted a heavy toll from him. He was still tall, handsome and distinguished, and his eyes were still a glorious blue, but his salt and pepper hair was now solid silver, and his face was heavily lined. Carrie knew that, in spite of the conversation, his mind was solidly with the men lined up to fight Grant's army waiting on the other side of the Rapidan.

She was relieved when all the boarders pushed back from the table, leaving her, Janie, Jeremy and her father.

No one said anything for several long minutes while the warm spring air pushed through the curtains and caused lantern light to dance around the room. It was far from a peaceful feeling, but for a moment there was stillness and even relative quiet in a city that seemed to be collectively holding its breath.

Thomas finally turned to Jeremy. "I'm sorry, but I shouldn't have expected our meal would be any different. Everyone has their opinions lately, and I find I disagree with many of them."

Jeremy smiled briefly, white teeth flashing from his tanned face topped with blond hair, and lit by vibrant blue eyes.

Carrie stared at him, stunned by his good looks, and wishing she could...

"It was more than enough to have a good meal," Jeremy said cheerfully.

"You call beans and cornbread a good meal?" Thomas asked with disbelief.

"It's more than what my father has right now. Everything I take home, he pours back into his congregation."

"Do you resent it?" Thomas asked.

"Not at all," Jeremy replied. "The free blacks of Richmond have so little, and the war has made it even harder. Carrie helped them get through the winter by insisting they all plant gardens, and by turning the land behind the church into a huge garden, but it's run out. It will be a while before the new gardens will produce."

Carrie's heart warmed as she listened to Jeremy and saw the genuine caring on his face.

"My father has given his life to his congregation," Jeremy continued. "The least I can do is give a few meals."

Thomas smiled at Jeremy. "Your father is a lucky man."

"As are you, sir," Jeremy replied. "Carrie is well loved by many people who owe their lives to her. And to Janie, too."

"I'm well aware how lucky I am," Thomas agreed, his face lighting with a genuine grin. "I hope you'll join us more often."

"I would like that, sir. Now that the days are getting longer, my father is usually off working with his parishoners. I eat most meals alone."

"It must be lonely for you," Carrie observed. "All the men your age are fighting."

Jeremy shrugged. "I suppose I get lonely at times, but I also find it rather positive to have a skill that keeps me from being someone's target. I never agreed with this war from the start, so I'll admit I'm glad I don't have to fight."

Thomas smiled. "I see I have several young people in my home who have no trouble speaking their minds."

"Does that bother you, Mr. Cromwell?" Jeremy asked.

Carrie's fondness for Jeremy was growing.

"Not at all!" Thomas responded. "I have discovered that I find complacent people who go with the flow rather tedious." He smiled over at Carrie. "My headstrong daughter has probably shortened my life from fear many times, but she certainly has made it less boring."

Thomas leaned back in his chair and lit his pipe, something he saved for special occasions because of the tobacco shortage. "There *is* one thing that bothers me, though, Jeremy. I know I'm old enough to be your father, but I have already gained tremendous respect for you. I would appreciate it if you would call me Thomas. Perhaps it is my awareness of my age that wants me to bypass the Mr. Cromwell label."

Jeremy grinned. "I'd be happy to, Mr—I mean, Thomas. I have tremendous respect for you, too."

Carrie watched them, her insides churning with her secret. She pushed back her chair and stood. "I hope you all don't mind, but it's been a long day, and I suspect tomorrow will be even longer. I'm going to say goodnight." She leaned over to give her father a kiss on his cheek.

"Of course, dear," Thomas said. His expression said he knew something was troubling her, but he probably assumed it was the impending battle and her worry about Robert.

"It was wonderful to see you again, Jeremy. I hope you'll return soon."

"Goodnight, Carrie," Jeremy responded. "Thank you for a wonderful evening."

Janie smiled at her. "I'll be up in a little while."

Carrie smiled back and let her eyes show her gratitude. She knew Janie was giving her time to be alone in the room they shared when Robert was away fighting. Both of them appreciated the comfort it provided, but Janie would know Carrie needed time to think.

~ ~ ~ ~ ~ ~

Carrie sank down onto the windowseat, grateful for the soft spring air wafting in that could almost block out the carriages, trains and industry that kept the city awake twenty-four hours a day. So much was racing through her mind and heart.

Carrie's mind flew back to the day when she had discovered that Rose—the slave she had grown up with, and who had become her best friend—was actually her *aunt*. The result of her grandfather raping Old Sarah, Rose's mother.

That same day, she had discovered Rose was a twin. But her brother, born white, had been sold by her father to protect her grandfather.

Carrie and Rose had found paperwork that said to whom he had been sold. They'd been surprised to also discover he was taken to an orphanage and adopted by a white family who would raise him as a white boy.

Carrie, on the plantation the winter before, had discovered old family paintings and realized Jeremy Anthony was the spitting image of her grandfather at that age.

When she had brought the picture to Pastor Anthony, he had admitted he knew all along and asked her to keep it secret. He asked her to promise she wouldn't reveal Jeremy's true identity. He was afraid of what it would do to the young man who had grown up white. He didn't want his son to face the prejudice and hatred he saw aimed at his congregation every day.

Knowing how desperately Rose wanted to meet her twin, Carrie had tried to change the pastor's mind, but to no avail. In the end, she had told him she didn't know what she would do, but she thought he was underestimating his son. Jeremy deserved to know the truth.

She felt she didn't have to make a decision yet because the war still separated her from Rose. She had helped Rose and Moses escape through the Underground Railroad, sending them to Aunt Abby in Pennsylvania. Now Rose was in the contraband camp. Carrie knew she wouldn't see her again until this crazy war ended.

To walk in and find Jeremy in her parlor had been quite a shock. The mutual respect and affection he shared with her father was amazing. Only *she* knew they were actually half brothers.

Everything in her wanted to reveal the truth. She had promised her father never to lie to him again about *anything*. But then, Pastor Anthony's fearful eyes as he begged her to keep the secret rose in her mind. Carrie pressed her forehead against the window as her feelings battled in her heart.

She shook her head and looked north. She didn't have to make the decision tonight. All she wanted was to send her love and thoughts to Robert tonight.

Her brave, wonderful husband was part of an army that was woefully outnumbered and pitifully equipped. She already knew thousands of men would die or be horribly mutilated. So far, Robert kept coming home to her. Would he make it through another battle? Carrie groaned and clenched her fists, her heart reaching out to fill Robert with her love. It was all she could do, but it left her completely dissatisfied.

Her mind turned to Moses. Rose must be worried sick for her own husband as well. Was Moses still a spy? Was he now fighting like the tens of thousands of free blacks and former slaves that swarmed into the Union Army after the Emancipation Proclamation? Would he and Robert try to kill each other tomorrow or the day after?

Carrie groaned and pushed away the tears flowing down her cheeks. She heard the door open and close, and then she felt Janie's hand on her shoulder. "It's starting again," she said brokenly.

"I know," Janie said. "But we've learned how to do this, Carrie. We can't look beyond this moment, and then the next moment. We'll simply deal with whatever comes."

Carrie nodded, gaining comfort from her friend's strength, while knowing Janie was saying it as much to herself. Whether it was tomorrow or the next day, the battle would start, the hospitals would fill, and they would once again give their all to save lives.

Janie settled down with her on the windowseat, and they both looked north. *Would tomorrow be the day?*

Chapter Three

Moses yawned and stretched, his tall, muscular body much too long for the blanket to cover him adequately. Since the sun was just lighting the horizon, and there had been no call for his men, he could only assume the big battle wasn't going to start today, either. That was fine with him.

He'd only been back with the Union Army a couple of weeks since returning from the failed raid with Dahlgren against Richmond. He'd had no trouble making it to Fort Monroe after most of Dahlgren's men had been killed or captured in the ambush that left Dahlgren dead.

It hadn't been so easy, however, to rid himself of the recurring nightmares and haunting images of the terrified black spy that Dahlgren had hanged when he unknowingly led Dahlgren's raiding troops to a James River crossing that was impassable. Dahlgren's rage at the black Union spy hadn't surprised Moses, though he wished it would have.

Black men, both free and former slaves, had joined the Union Army after the Emancipation Proclamation, but they fought prejudice and hatred from their fellow soldiers every day. Moses knew it would take a long time for that reality to change. He had learned some things recently that only made that more obvious.

"Mornin', Moses."

Moses smiled easily. "Good morning, Pompey." His love for the elderly former slave had grown throughout the campaigns they had shared.

"You reckon it gonna be today?" Pompey asked, settling on the ground beside him.

Moses shrugged. "It doesn't feel like it, but things could change at any time."

"You ready for more fightin'?"

"Do I have a choice?"

Pompey stared at him through narrowed eyes. "You ain't been de same since you done come back from dat raid."

Moses shrugged again. He wasn't about to tell Pompey or the rest of his men what had happened. They would each have to deal with the reality of being a black man in a white man's army, but he wasn't going to throw more of it in their faces. He was sick to death of fighting, but he hadn't lost his desire to do whatever it took to guarantee freedom for his people.

If it meant fighting, he would fight. If it meant losing Rose and his little boy, it was a price he would have to pay. There was nothing that said he had to like either of his options.

Pompey let the silence sit between them for a while. "De boys be pretty heated up, Moses."

Moses looked at him sharply. Pompey's voice expressed much more than his impassive face. "About?" He knew he was about to find out the real reason Pompey had sought him out that morning.

"You done hear 'bout dat Fort Pillow?"

Moses groaned inwardly, but he felt his face tighten with anger.

"I reckon dat be answer 'nuff," Pompey replied, his own face blazing with fury. "It be true what dey be sayin'?"

"I'm afraid so."

"Dey really killed all our boys after dey done surrendered?" Pompey asked in disbelief.

Moses shook his head. "I wish I could say I was surprised." He groped for words as fury spun through his entire body.

"What be de story?" Pompey asked. "I dunno we heard de right thing."

Moses was silent for a long moment but decided the truth was always best. "There were two regiments of black soldiers—about half of the six hundred soldiers who were stationed at Fort Pillow. Fort Pillow was a Confederate fort that we took over a couple years ago in Tennessee. The Rebels decided they wanted it back.

"There was a battle about three weeks ago. We were rather outnumbered. Anyway, the Rebels took the fort, and the Union troops surrendered."

"Dat's what we done heard," Pompey said. "Dey should hab been took as prisoners!"

Moses nodded his agreement even while his face twisted. "The South isn't real keen on having former slaves as prisoners of war."

"So dey really did kill dem all?" Pompey asked heavily.

Moses groped for words and finally nodded, sick at heart. How could words possibly communicate the horror of the massacre he had been informed took place at Fort Pillow? All but twenty of the three hundred black soldiers there had been executed after they surrendered. General Forrest, knowing the fort had no real significance to the Confederacy, had abandoned it an hour later, leaving behind all the corpses to rot.

Rage and sorrow engulfed Pompey's face. "I reckon de boys gonna be out for some revenge," he said flatly.

"I have a feeling it will make all of us fight harder," he agreed. A sudden stirring among his men a hundred feet away caught his attention.

Pompey glanced over. "What dat white man doin' ober dere?" he asked. "That ain't one of de officers."

Moses shrugged but stood. "Let's go find out."

As he got closer, he couldn't contain the broad smile that spread across his face.

⁘⸎⋆⋅⋆⸎⁘

Matthew Justin couldn't help being relieved that a battle didn't seem scheduled for that day. He had long ago grown weary of covering battles, but he never grew tired of discovering the people wearing the uniforms, especially the black soldiers that were increasing by such vast numbers.

It was also possible Lee would start the battle, but Matthew didn't think that was the Confederate plan. They had dug into an impregnable defense system on the banks above the Rapidan, and he knew Lee had less than half the men the Union did. It wouldn't be the first time the Confederate general surprised them, but something in his gut said it wouldn't be today.

As Matthew sauntered around looking for the men he wanted to interview, he couldn't say he was back to one hundred percent after his imprisonment at Libby Prison, but he had gained back a lot of weight in the weeks since his escape. And the *Philadelphia Inquirer* was eager to have its leading war correspondent back in the field. He had spent the last week writing the story of the prisons and the men languishing there. Now, he had a battle to cover.

Matthew was also quite certain he would do whatever it took not to be taken prisoner again. He knew he wouldn't survive another turn in Libby Prison, and he doubted the other Confederate prisoner-of-war camps were any better. In fact, he'd heard others were worse. He couldn't control the shudder that coursed through his body as the memories, still so fresh in his mind, swarmed through him.

It was time to quit thinking and start working. He stopped and decided to speak with the group of men he was standing in the midst of. The fact that it was a black regiment was all the better. He wanted to tell their stories and bring them to life for his readers. There was one black soldier in particular whom he wanted to meet, but he knew better than to expect he could find him in the tens of thousands of men spread out on the river banks.

"Good morning, men," Matthew called out.

"Mornin'," several of them responded, before going back to cooking their bacon over the glowing campfire. He wasn't in uniform, so it was obvious he wasn't an officer.

Matthew knew the black men were curious. He smiled and settled down on his heels. "My name is Matthew Justin. I'm a journalist for the *Philadelphia Inquirer*."

The soldiers continued to watch him. He didn't feel any antagonism from them, just caution. He knew they had every right to feel that way. Over one hundred thousand black soldiers were now fighting in the Union Army, but there were still many white soldiers who didn't believe they belonged there, and they took every chance they could to let them know it.

"I just spent time in the contraband camp at Fort Monroe," Matthew said, instantly aware many of the men were watching him more closely now. "I recently escaped from a prison in Richmond and made my way to Fort Monroe."

"I heard 'bout dat escape from Libby Prison," one of the men acknowledged. "There was a whole bunch of us prayin' all you would make it."

"Thank you. We didn't all make it free, but most of us did." Matthew suppressed a shudder as he thought of the treatment the captured escapees must surely be enduring.

"It be true that some of you dug a tunnel all the way out from dat prison?" one of the men asked.

Matthew nodded, not wanting to relive the experience.

"Welcome to freedom, man!" one of the soldiers said, giving Matthew the first real smile he had received since joining them. As he expected, that one acceptance loosened the ice. Everybody relaxed and lost their cautious looks.

Matthew smiled back. "All of you who were slaves know exactly how glad I was to get out of that prison. I only had a taste of what you've experienced, but it was enough to last me my whole life. I would do anything to keep from going back to prison."

"That be about how we feel," one man responded, stretching his lean body back against a log. "I done spent thirty years as a slave. I ain't neber goin' back to it, and I want to help all dem that are still stuck down there. I reckon dat's a good enough reason to fight."

Matthew gazed around the campfire as the rest of the men nodded solemnly. "I had a chance to talk at the school down at Fort Monroe. It's so wonderful to see the children learning for the first time in their lives. I have a friend who is a teacher down there."

"Dat be so?" another one of the men asked. "I know one of the teachers down there, too. When she started out, she be the only black teacher down there. Don't know about now."

Matthew stared at him. "You know Rose?"

"Miss Rose? Rose Samuels? Why, most of us be knowing Miss Rose."

"Miss Rose be Moses' wife," another offered.

Matthew gasped. "This is Moses' unit?" he asked incredulously.

Moses had been listening for a while, but now he stepped forward with a loud laugh. "Matthew Justin! I didn't figure there were many lanky, redheaded journalists around here, so I figured it had to be you even before I heard what you said. I don't know how you managed to find me in all this chaos, but I sure am glad you did."

Matthew rose to his feet and reached out to clasp the hand Moses held out to him. "I can't believe it's you, Moses." He fell silent as the two men stared at each other.

Moses was the first to speak after he cleared his throat. "I reckon I owe you more than I can ever repay you," he said gruffly. "Rose told me how you saved her from Ike Adams, and what a good friend you were to her when she was with Aunt Abby."

"This be dat journalist fella Rose done told us about?" one of his men demanded.

"He is indeed, men!" Moses said, sweeping his gaze over the one hundred and fifty men in his regiment. "I imagine he wants to tell some of your stories. Let him. Every chance we get to show white people we are no different from them, we should take it."

Moses turned to see Matthew still staring at him.

"I saw Rose just a few days ago," Matthew said. "I'm so glad to finally meet you. I had almost decided you were a figment of everyone's imagination, but someone as big as you can hardly be a figment."

Moses joined in on the laughter, while he tried to swallow back the longing for his wife and son that threatened to choke him. When everyone had quieted, he turned back to Matthew. "Go ahead and talk to my men. When you're done, we'll take some time for ourselves."

Matthew shook his head decisively. "It's a miracle I found you in all these men. We both know an order could come through any minute, and then the chance of my finding you again in this war would be about impossible." He swept his gaze over the men staring at him. "I would, indeed, like to talk to many of you, but if you don't mind, I'm going to talk to Moses first."

"You two go right ahead," Pompey said. "Me and the boys gonna hab us some grub. We be right here when you wants to talk to us."

Moses smiled and motioned Matthew over to his spot. They were still surrounded by tens of thousands of men and animals, but for that moment they felt as if they were alone.

"Carrie sends her love," Matthew said.

"You've seen Carrie?" Moses demanded. "When?"

"About a month ago. She helped me escape from Libby Prison."

Moses settled back on his heels. "Sounds like you got a story to tell."

Matthew grinned. "You can read it in the paper—all but the part about the wife of a Confederate captain, and the Confederate captain himself, who helped me escape. I thought it best if I left that part out."

Moses whistled. "Carrie Cromwell—I mean Borden—is a special woman."

"That she is," Matthew agreed. "She's doing well, at least as well as can be expected in a city that is under constant attack and where almost everyone is going hungry."

"Carrie is starving?" Moses asked.

"No," Matthew said quickly. "I'd say all of them are tired of the simple diet they have, but they're not going hungry. Thomas still has enough money to pay the ridiculous prices." He took a sip of the hot coffee Moses held out to him. "I saw her only for the one night, but she's happy. You knew she and Robert married?"

Moses nodded. "I stopped by Cromwell when I was doing a raid through the countryside with my men last fall. Carrie had been there, so Sam was able to fill me in on everything."

"I was on the plantation for a couple weeks during the escape," Matthew said. "Sam and Opal were wonderful, filling me with enough food to almost make up for months of starvation." He smiled. "I still miss Opal's apple pie." He took another sip of coffee. "Sam didn't say anything about you being there."

"Raiding the countryside with a regiment of black soldiers is not exactly something to broadcast. I asked Sam not to tell anyone we were there."

"Makes sense," Matthew agreed. "Robert is a different man," he said quietly. "He was wounded badly during a battle. Almost died. Someone took him to a black family, though, that saved his life."

Moses saw no reason not to reveal the truth. "That was me."

Matthew stared at him in astonishment. "What?"

Moses told him the story. "I couldn't let him die without trying to help. Robert *or* Granite. I did it for Carrie." He stared out over the smoke from campfires in every direction. "I'm glad he made it, and I truly hope he's good enough for Carrie now."

"He knows owning slaves is wrong."

Moses whistled. "That's a big thing. Of course, his slaves have probably all run away by now, but I'm real glad he knows a man shouldn't own people."

Matthew, knowing they didn't have a lot of time, changed the subject. "Your wife is quite an amazing woman."

"That she is."

"And your boy will be as big as you."

"Looks like it," Moses said, trying once again to swallow the heaviness in his heart.

"You miss them terribly."

"More than I ever thought possible," Moses agreed, clearing his throat. "I chose to join the army, and I know Rose is as safe as she can be at Fort Monroe, but every second I'm away from her hurts." He shook his head. "I know I'm surrounded by men who feel the same way I do."

"You're lucky to have someone you love that much."

Moses pulled his thoughts away from Rose. "You're not married." It wasn't a question. "Does Carrie know how you feel about her?"

Matthew flushed bright red and stared at him. "It's that obvious?"

Moses shrugged. "Your secret is safe with me."

"Robert knows," Matthew admitted. "He also knows I'll never do anything with my feelings. He knows he can trust me."

"Hard not to love Carrie," Moses said. "Only time will reveal what will come of your feelings."

Matthew searched for a way to change the subject. "I was with Aunt Abby a couple days ago."

Moses grinned. "How is she? Some of the best memories I have are the months Rose and I lived with her in Philadelphia. It was like some kind of fantasy to live in her fancy house. Add to the fact, she is one of the most remarkable women I know and..." His voice trailed off.

"That she is," Matthew agreed. "She took me in and finished fattening me up when I got back from Libby Prison."

Moses eyed him keenly. "And helped heal you from the memories," he added.

"You always know what other people have in their hearts?"

"I know what it's like to carry a load of hurt and anger. Rose's mama, Sarah, was the one who helped me work through mine. I about let bitterness and hatred eat me up. She taught me how to let it go, but I know how to see it in other people."

Matthew gazed at him for a long moment. "I'm still working on it," he admitted. "I'm mostly angry for the men who escaped and then got caught again. I can imagine the hell they are living in right now." He took a deep breath. "I wouldn't have gone back," he said. "They would have had to kill me. *I wouldn't have gone back,*" he whispered.

Moses said nothing, waiting for Matthew to get control back. He knew time was the only thing that could heal his pain and anger.

Matthew took another deep breath. "Aunt Abby is moving to Washington, DC for a while, though she'll always have her own in Philadelphia."

"What?" Moses asked in surprise. "What's she going to do in Washington?"

"Business demands are calling her there, but she also wants to be closer to the action—both with the war and with her fight for abolition and women's rights. She could have sent someone else, but she's decided to go herself."

"Will she be safe there?" Moses asked. "Rose told me she's been making some enemies in Philadelphia. She told me about the dead chicken on her doorstep."

"There are men who will be threatened by women having equal rights. There are some that also resent all she is doing for the abolition movement. I worry about her, but I also know nothing will stop her from doing what she believes is right." He paused for a long moment. "I won't be around to help her this time, though. Not that I'm in Philadelphia much anymore, but at least I was able to drop in when I could."

A courier appeared at the fire. "Captain Jones is asking for you, Moses."

Moses nodded and stood. He grasped Matthew's hand and stared deep into his eyes. "You're a good man, Matthew Justin. Thank you for everything. I look forward to spending more time with you when this war is over. My men will talk to you as long as they are able."

Matthew gripped his hand just as strongly. "I'm grateful for the chance to meet you, Moses. I, too, look forward to the time when the war ends, and we can all be together in a country at peace. Perhaps we'll all meet in Richmond," he said with a smile.

Both their smiles disappeared when they considered what the fall of Richmond would mean to Carrie. Would she and Thomas survive? They stared at each other for a long moment, and then Moses turned toward Captain Jones' tent.

Aunt Abby was exhausted when she finally opened the door to her home and stepped inside. She was glad to take off the light jacket protecting her against the early spring chill as she headed for the kitchen.

She had time to warm up some soup before she heard a knock at her door. Stifling a sigh, she went to the door and hoped whoever it was would need only a minute of her time. All she wanted to do was eat, do some reading, and go to bed.

"Abigail Livingston?"

Aunt Abby smiled at the young woman standing on her step. "That's right. How can I help you?"

The young woman, who upon closer examination was clearly distraught, turned and called to a group of women standing under a gas lamp. "It's her, girls. We found her."

Aunt Abby thought longingly of the bowl of soup waiting for her in the kitchen and then watched the group cross the street. It must be important, or they wouldn't have gone to such lengths to find her. She held the door open. "Please come in."

The leader of the group, the same woman who had knocked on the door, stepped forward. "My name is Amanda." Dull blue eyes gazed at her from under a thatch of dark brown hair. Her clothes were rough but clean. "We were told you could help us."

"I'll try," Aunt Abby promised, warm gray eyes smiling out from under soft brown hair. "Why don't you tell me what the problem is?"

"The problem," one of the women said in a shrill voice, "is that we're not being paid what we should be. We're doing the same work as the men we replaced who are fighting in the war, but they don't pay us the same."

"And sometimes we don't get paid at all," another added bitterly. "I've got babies to feed now that my husband is off fighting, but I don't bring in enough money." She scowled from under long red hair. "I *make* enough money. I just don't bring enough money home."

"My husband came home," another stated, "but he lost both an arm and a leg. He'll never work again. I'm the only one bringing money into our home. We're not being paid enough to make it. My kids were cold and hungry all winter!"

"It's not right," Amanda cried. "We heard you are different, Mrs. Livingston."

"I've hired a lot of women since the beginning of the war. I pay them a fair wage. The same as what the men made, sometimes more." She was more than aware that wasn't usually the case.

The war had changed things drastically. Industrial development, already growing before the war, had tremendously accelerated. Equipping and maintaining large armies had brought about huge growth. Thousands of Northern women were forced to go to work when their husbands went to war, came home crippled, or didn't come home at all.

"What do you girls do?" she asked.

"We sew," Amanda responded. "All of us work in the factories that make uniforms for the soldiers. Why can't they pay us more?"

Aunt Abby sighed and tightened her lips. She had been talking about this same problem with a group of her friends that day. President Lincoln had decided to subcontract army uniforms. The contractors were well paid for the uniform orders, but then paid the women who actually did the work very poorly. They were getting rich while the women and their children were going hungry.

One of the divisions of Aunt Abby's business made uniforms, but she kept only enough earnings to create a reasonable profit, enabling her to pay a fair wage to the women who sewed the uniforms. She and her friends had been protesting the practice of employers withholding fair pay, but so far, there had been no change.

She gazed at the women. She knew an explanation wouldn't matter to them. They were simply concerned about feeding their families.

Amanda leaned forward and grabbed one of her hands. "Can you help us, Mrs. Livingston? We're desperate, or we wouldn't have hunted you down like this."

Aunt Abby kept hold of her hand and looked at the twelve women in her parlor. Twelve sets of determined and defiant eyes stared at her. She chose honesty. "There are women working hard to change things for you, but it's not easy, and we haven't been able to accomplish much. Until women have the vote, we are at the mercy of a system that is terribly unfair."

"The vote!" one woman snorted. "I don't care about the vote. I want to feed my family."

"You *should* care about the vote," Aunt Abby said sharply. Then she softened her voice with a gentle smile. "Until you are as passionate about having a say in what decisions are made about your life as you are about feeding your children, nothing will really change." She knew by looking at their pinched faces that their immediate need was greater than their ability to care about the future.

She reached for a sheet of paper on the table and wrote for a few minutes. Then she handed the paper to Amanda. "Go to this place tomorrow. The address is for one of my factories. All of you will be hired to work. You will be paid fairly, and my manager has been directed to pay you a week in advance so you can feed your families."

The women in the room gave an excited cheer. Desperate looks transformed into smiles. "How can we possibly thank you?" Amanda cried, wiping at the tears running down her face.

Aunt Abby smiled. "Do a good job. Our boys on the front are counting on you." She fixed them all with a steely gaze and said, "And when you have the chance to fight for the freedom to vote, do it. I can help the twelve of you sitting in this room, but there are thousands more women that need help just as desperately. The best way to show gratitude for kindness and opportunity is to offer it to someone else."

The room fell silent as they pondered her words.

"I'll do it, Mrs. Livingston," Amanda promised.

"Me too," added the one who had snorted that she didn't care about the vote. "I'm deeply grateful."

Solemn promises came from all the women in the room, and then they stood to leave. Aunt Abby waved goodbye and finally went to eat what was now a cold bowl of soup. She was simply too tired to warm it again, and she still had packing to do before she left the next morning.

⁘⁘⁘⁘⁘

Matthew was still talking to the men when Moses strode up purposefully. One look at his face, however, had everyone snapping to attention.

"I reckon you gots news for us," Pompey said.

Moses nodded. "All of you are to cook rations for three days."

The men, who had been with him through campaigns nodded, knowing instantly what his order meant. The new ones gazed at him with confusion. Moses didn't bother to go into details. The experienced soldiers would prepare the rookies.

"I reckon we gonna get dat chance at payback for Fort Pillow," Pompey observed.

Angry murmurs sounded all around the campfires.

"We gonna fight real hard," one man promised. "Dem boys at Fort Pillow ain't gonna be forgot."

"Got that right!" another added, his voice hard with anger. "They ain't seen fightin' until they see us fight now."

Matthew gazed at Moses. Moses nodded. "They know."

Matthew raised his voice so it would carry to all the men. "There is nothing that can make what happened at Fort Pillow right," he called. "But you need to know that Lincoln cares. A few days after the massacre, there was a demand made that, in the exchange and treatment of prisoners, black prisoners had to be treated identically to white."

"I bet them white boys didn't go too good for that," a soldier observed bitterly.

"No," Matthew agreed, "they didn't. But it doesn't end there. Lincoln already put an order into place last year that for every soldier in the United States Army killed in violation of the laws of war, a Rebel soldier shall be executed."

"You reckon that gonna happen?" Pompey asked. "Just 'cause an order be given, it don't mean nothin' gonna happen."

Matthew gazed at him and then swept his eyes over the men. "What I know for certain is that all of you are soldiers in the United States Army. You're here because we need you. You already know that not everyone wants you, but that doesn't mean they don't need you."

He watched as shoulders straightened and eyes, sparking with anger moments before, now flashed with pride. "When we win this war, it will be because close to one hundred thousand of you stepped up to fight for freedom and the country that now belongs to you!" Matthew knew anger could be a valid tool, but pride and self-respect would carry them much further.

"Yeah!" Pompey raised his fist to the sky and yelled out.

All around him, fists were raised into the air, and strong voices competed against the other sounds of a suddenly bustling army.

Matthew exchanged a long look with Moses and smiled slightly at the gratitude he saw there. They clasped hands for a long moment, and then Moses turned to his men. Matthew strode off, knowing he must get back to press headquarters.

The spring campaign was about to begin.

※※※

The sun was barely over the horizon when Aunt Abby's driver pulled the carriage up in front of her house the next morning. He loaded her two trunks, helped her into the carriage, and clucked to the horses. "Move on!"

Aunt Abby leaned back against the seat and took a deep breath. She was on her way to Washington, DC. She had decided in the last few weeks that the nation's capital was where she belonged for the time being. There was certainly much she, as a widow, could achieve with the business she inherited from her husband in Philadelphia. But her decision to go came from a belief that she could accomplish more in the nation's capital in the fight for complete freedom for the slaves and for the fledgling women's rights movement.

She allowed her thoughts to wander until suddenly the carriage jolted to a stop, and the horses threw their heads up in protest.

"What do you think you're doing?" her driver said to the group of men who had stepped into the road.

"We need to have a little discussion with Mrs. Livingston here," a slight, narrow-faced man snarled.

"I have an appointment to keep," Aunt Abby snapped. "We need to move on."

"I reckon we'll say when that happens," another man piped in, his eyes cruel and hard.

Aunt Abby reached slowly under her seat. "What do you men want?"

"We figure we need to come to a meeting of minds."

"I'm quite sure my mind will never meet with men who accost women in the middle of the street," Aunt Abby said with disdain. She had learned that to show fear would only make things worse, but she longed for Matthew to appear and save her as he had in the past. She knew, though, that this time she was on her own. The certain knowledge somehow fueled her courage.

The slight man snarled and his eyes turned even crueler. "It's this way, *Mrs.* Livingston. You're messing up things for me and the boys by paying those broads who work for you too much money."

"Is that so?" Aunt Abby had heard rumors that many weren't happy with her business practices.

"It needs to change," the man snapped.

"Or what?" Aunt Abby demanded, staring at him boldly, well aware her driver was terrified.

"Or we figure this whip will be used for more than stopping your horses."

Aunt Abby had heard enough. She took deep breaths to calm herself so that her voice wouldn't betray her terror, along with her anger. She reached beneath her seat and pulled out the pistol that she carried everywhere. She stood and pointed the pistol right at the man's heart.

"Whether it's you or another in your group that pulls out a whip, this bullet is going straight through your heart," she said. "And then I'll make sure the rest of the bullets are put to good use."

"You're bluffing," the man whined, a look of fear settling on his face.

"Try me," Aunt Abby said, almost enjoying herself now that she was the one with the power. She silently blessed Matthew for giving her the pistol before he had left town a few days before. She had protested at the time, but he had been so right. "You're in my way, and I have places to go. Now move!"

There was muttering, but all the men cleared the road.

"Let's go," Aunt Abby said to her driver.

He complied while Aunt Abby remained standing and kept her pistol trained on the group until they disappeared around a bend. "Continue on to the station," she said calmly.

"Would you have really used that thing?" her driver asked as he stared at the pistol.

"I don't know," Aunt Abby admitted, her voice shaking now that the moment had passed. "I've never shot a pistol in my life. I'm quite glad I didn't have to find out."

The driver stared at her with admiration and then increased the horses' speed. "I'll have you to the station on time, Mrs. Livingston."

Aunt Abby nodded, settled back in her seat, and longed for the day when things would change for women in the country she loved so much.

Chapter Four

It was past midnight when Robert felt movement beside him. He sat up quickly.

"It's going to happen today, ain't it, Captain?"

Robert nodded but realized Tabor, a young man from Alabama, couldn't see him. "Yes."

"The fellas said you got called away tonight. Anything you can tell us?"

Robert believed the men had every right to know what he did. He would never reveal battle plans, but what he knew wasn't going to be a secret much longer. Orders would ring out any minute. "I was part of a group General Lee called up to the top of Clark's Mountain."

He paused, remembering the overwhelming feeling that had engulfed him when he looked down at the vast army of men in blue spread out on the opposite riverbank. There was no need to talk about any of that. Every Rebel soldier knew they were woefully outnumbered.

"What did you see, Captain?" Tabor asked.

Robert knew the calmness in his voice had come from the experience of many battles. "They're preparing to break camp," Robert said. "I believe it will happen today. General Lee is very sure he knows exactly where they are going."

"So we're going to meet them there?"

Robert hesitated before deciding to tell him a little more. "Not exactly. We're going to let them come a little further. General Lee's plan is to lure them into overconfidence and then strike them by surprise when they are least expecting it."

Tabor didn't ask where because he knew Robert wouldn't tell him even if he knew. "I reckon the general has a good plan. Me and the boys will give it our all."

As he had many times in the past, Robert felt deep gratitude at the loyalty Lee inspired in his army. Loyalty was surely the only thing that had kept them alive this far into the war. "I know you will, Tabor. We're going to lick them again."

Robert didn't intend to tell him what General Longstreet—whose troops would remain in the background so they could fall back to protect Richmond—had said. He had learned that Longstreet was the best man at General Grant's wedding to a cousin, and therefore, knew their new Union opponent quite well. What he had said still rang in Robert's head. *"That man will fight us every day and every hour 'til the end of this war."*

Robert suspected Lee hadn't been very daunted by the statement. He wondered whether that fact would create even more danger for them, but he wouldn't say any of that to the men trusting him to give them confidence.

There was a long silence before Tabor melted back into the darkness. Robert stared up at the stars and let his thoughts drift to Carrie. As with every battle, he wondered whether he would see her shining green eyes again. He had embedded every detail of her into his mind and heart. As in the past, he knew it was what would carry him through the days ahead.

Thousands would die or be horribly wounded. Would he be one of them?

~ ~ ~ ~ ~

Moses and Pompey moved through the men, inspecting haversacks by the campfire light as they went. The new recruits always over-packed for a campaign. Moses found another haversack stuffed with clothing. He calmly reached in and began to pull things out.

"You have too much." He cut the bag down to a change of underclothing, three pairs of socks, a pair of spare shoes, three plugs of tobacco, a rubber blanket and a pair of woolen blankets.

"That's it, sir?" the recruit asked, staring at the much larger mound Moses had tossed aside.

"Yes," Moses replied. "Do not pick up anything except food and tobacco while you are on the march. Get hold of all the food you can. Cut haversacks from dead men.

Don't look at clothing or shoes or blankets. You can get those items from the quartermaster."

He knew other men were listening in. "Stick to your gun through thick and thin. Don't straggle. Fill your canteen at every stream we cross and wherever else you get the chance. Never wash your feet until the day's march is over. If you wash them, they will surely blister."

His men listened solemnly.

"It's today, ain't it, Moses?" one asked.

"Yes," he said. "Be ready when you hear my order. We'll be moving before the sun comes up."

Twenty minutes later, Moses walked back into camp and barked his order. "Let's move, men!"

Matthew was with General Grant and General Meade when they crossed the Rapidan at Germanna Ford and established their headquarters in an old farmhouse on a bluff overlooking the river.

"Can you believe Congressman Washburne is with him?" Peter Wilcher asked.

Matthew shared a cryptic look with the man he had escaped Libby Prison with. He had been thrilled when Peter found him hours ago. "Perhaps we should tell him the story of Congressman Ely—how he did the same thing and found himself a guest of Libby Prison," he said. "We could share with him exactly why he doesn't want to be there."

Peter nodded. "I know Congressman Washburne has been instrumental in Grant's rise to the top. I guess he wants to watch what he feels he is responsible for."

"He might want to wear something besides all black. It won't be long before the heat gets to him," Matthew observed.

Peter snorted with laughter. "I heard some of the men asking if Grant had brought his personal undertaker."

Matthew chuckled but fell silent when a reporter called out to Grant. "How long do you think it will take to reach Richmond?"

Grant, in a good mood, paused in smoking his cigar. "About four days. That is, if General Lee approves the agreement. If he objects, the trip will undoubtedly be prolonged."

Matthew turned around to talk to Peter, but a courier dashing up and handing the general a message interrupted their conversation. Grant's face tightened as he read the words. Then he whipped around and snapped out an order.

Matthew drew closer and listened carefully until he could determine what was happening. He returned to where Peter was waiting. "General Lee is on the move, moving much faster than Grant anticipated. He's ordered General Burnside to join the troops."

"I thought he was going to leave Burnside and his troops on the north side of the Rapidan to protect the railroad?" Peter said.

Matthew nodded. "He changed his mind. It's not the first time Lee has had this effect." He knew Peter had spent most of his time covering the war in Mississippi until Vicksburg fell. "Lee very seldom does what you would expect him to do. That's why his army is still alive. He can't be taken for granted."

"You sound like a fan," Peter said,

"I wish he was fighting for the Union. This war would have ended a long time ago."

〜━☆・ぅ・☆━〜

Robert gazed out over his men and knew they had earned the exhausted looks on their faces. They had marched all day down the Orange Turnpike until they moved past the old fortifications at Mine Run and then moved quietly through the dense woods they called "the Wilderness," where they positioned themselves for a daylight attack.

Robert had just returned from a briefing. He knew they were to attack early in the morning. The Union troops were completely unaware of the Confederates' close proximity. General Longstreet's army and the backup they could provide were still a full day away, but

Lee felt he had no choice. If Grant got through the Wilderness unscathed, the full brunt of the Union would have a clear path around Lee's southern flank to Richmond. If that happened, the war would be lost.

Attacking immediately would at least give the Confederates a fighting chance.

"This is it, Captain?" Tabor materialized and spoke quietly, staring into the dense woods.

"We fight in the morning."

"What if we lose?"

"We're not going to lose," Robert spoke what he knew was in Lee's mind. "If victorious, we have everything to live for. If defeated, there will be nothing left for us." He paused and let the words sink in. "It's simple, really. We can't lose."

Tabor stared at him, nodded, and slipped away. Robert knew the young soldier would spread the word. The men had every right to be afraid and nervous, but he knew they would fight with everything they had.

Moses felt the same as what he saw on his men's faces. An ominous dread had settled over the entire camp. Who could blame them?

After a day of steady marching, the Yankee troops were camped among the disinterred remains of the hastily buried Union dead at Chancellorsville.

His men had tried to make light of it by pointing out that the greenest grass and the brightest flowers were fed by Union blood. "This ground was made rich by our soldiers," one of his men stated. Most had merely stared at him, their faces tightening when one of them uncovered a bullet-shattered skull from a shallow grave and rolled it across the ground.

"De men are right scared," Pompey said, easing up to where Moses stood.

"Who can blame them?" Moses muttered. "They're seeing evidence of what is coming." His own stomach was doing flips, and he fought to steady his breathing as he stared into the deep woods. He could tell the next day would be hot. His men—former slaves used to the heat of the South—would be fine, but he knew it would be much harder for the out-of-shape Northern white troops, who had spent all winter eating and lounging about camp.

The next day dragged by slowly in the hot stillness. More and more Union troops marched in to join them, their line stretching for two miles on the Orange Turnpike. Suspense and dread hung in the air as thick as the humidity that threatened to strangle them.

"Moses?"

Moses shook his head at Pompey. "I feel it, too. This isn't going to be good." Knowing he had to focus completely on what was about to happen in the brambly cornfield they faced, he tried to keep his mind off Rose and John.

"You reckon dem boys of Colonel Ryan's know what a good target dey make?"

Moses glanced over at the gaily colored uniforms of the 140th New York Zouaves. He shook his head. "They sure will be easy targets." He couldn't help thinking those bright colors that would draw Rebel bullets would mean more of his own men would make it.

"It done been a real honor, Moses."

Moses whipped his head around. "What?"

Pompey's face was set, his eyes steady. "Iffen I don't make it out of dat cornfield, I be wantin' you to know it done been a real honor."

Moses stared at him and wanted to shout that everything would be okay, but he knew lying wouldn't serve anyone. Instead, he reached out and gripped his friend's hand. "I feel the same way, Pompey. You've become a real friend. If I don't make it, I want you to know how much I appreciate and love you."

Pompey held his hand and gazed into Moses' eyes for a long minute. Then he nodded and turned back to stare at the cornfield.

～✼･」･✼～

Robert and his men were concealed in the trees on the western edge of a bramble-choked cornfield. Holding their positions, the Southern army had been watching the Union buildup all day.

Robert knew the heat was choking his men. He also knew his unit had a real advantage against the Union troops. His troops were used to it because they had been fighting in this kind of heat for three years. Robert would take any advantage he could get.

The order came at one o'clock in the afternoon.

Robert watched the blue wave moving into the cornstalks, and then he closed his eyes for a moment, raised his rifle, and began firing.

The lines of blue began to melt away like snow.

"Let's get them, men!"

Moses and his men began running the minute the order came, straight into the cornfield thick with thorns. They fought to break through the dense cover. Wild yelling, fortified by determination, broke the fearful silence.

Moses struggled through the brambles and tried to ignore the screams of agony that replaced defiant shouts. His men disappeared as if the ground had swallowed them. Then the musket smoke settled in and obliterated almost everything. Moses could barely tell where *he* was, much less where his men were. He embraced the thought that these conditions would also make it harder for the Confederate sharpshooters to pick them off.

"Retreat! Retreat!" Moses yelled. He knew there was no way anyone would make it across that field, and he saw no sense in more slaughter.

Moses' body was drenched with sweat and covered with splattered blood from men shot down around him when he stumbled back behind the lines. He stared around, numb with shock, then gazed back at the cornfield. He knew that at least half of his men would never make it out. Tears pooled in his eyes.

He caught sight of Colonel George Ryan, the commander for the soldiers clothed in the bright uniforms. The colonel, weeping, peered through the dense smoke for some sign of his men. "My God," he cried, "I'm the first colonel I ever knew who couldn't tell where his regiment was!"

Moses knew most of them lay dead or wounded in the ragged cornfield.

"Hey, Moses."

Moses looked at one of his men, covered with as much blood as he was himself. The soldier seemed uninjured except for the glassy-eyed shock that consumed him. "Yes, Jasper?" he asked wearily, knowing he could receive an order again at any moment to advance.

"Pompey," Jasper whispered, tears filling his eyes.

Moses' shoulders slumped as he relived Pompey's handclasp. It had been minutes ago, but it seemed like an eternity. He turned and stared into the cornfield. He would look for Pompey when the battle ended. Pompey might only be wounded. There was a chance, as there had been with Robert.

Jasper read his mind. "They shot him in the head, Moses. He was gone real quick."

Moses closed his eyes in defeat, grateful Pompey hadn't had to suffer.

Robert watched the wave of blue coats halt and then retreat. He settled back against the tree, wiped sweat from his face, and waited for it to start again.

"Captain Borden!"

Robert stood to attention. "Yes, sir!"

"Move south with your men to support Jones' Virginia brigade. They're being hit hard."

"Yes, sir!"

Within moments, Robert's men were on the move.

They arrived as Jones' men stumbled back in confusion. Robert's men took their positions and opened fire. As soon as Jones' men realized they had help, they found the courage to rush back into battle. "Get them!" they yelled.

The woods were a bedlam of noise so loud Robert could no longer hear the sound of his rifle, but only feel its recoil on his shoulder. He kept aiming and firing, knowing his men were taking serious losses but sensing the Confederates still held the advantage—at least for now.

The Union troops surging forward faltered and fell back. Hopelessly entangled in the vine-choked wilderness, they took flanking fire on two sides.

Robert watched as the Yankees staggered back to their lines in a complete rout.

Suddenly his eyes widened in astonishment. "What in the…"

He watched as the North's commander wheeled and rode back into the open field, blood trickling from his scratched face.

"Surrender!" boomed a Rebel voice from the woods just to the right of Robert's position.

Robert watched as the Union officer shook his fist defiantly and spurred his horse across the field. A barrage of bullets crashed into the animal and sent it somersaulting to the ground. Robert groaned at the senseless waste while understanding the cheers that rose from the watching Rebels.

"I can't believe it," one of his men cried. "Look!"

Robert watched as the officer crawled out from under his horse and hobbled toward his lines with bullets whizzing around him, somehow missing their target.

For over an hour, blistering crossfire between the forces piled heaps of men, clad in both blue and gray, across the fields and woods. Unable to move forward or backward, those who were wounded buried their faces in the dust and prayed for the fighting to end.

And then it happened…

Brushfires, kindled by bullets striking the breastworks soldiers had mounded for protection, erupted on all sides, filling the air with the unmistakable, sickening stench of burning flesh. Ominous, muffled popping sounds marked the explosion of dozens of cartridge belts tied around wounded soldiers' waists, sending deadly shards of tin slicing through their bowels.

"My God," one of Robert's men muttered. "Those poor devils."

Robert stared, knowing God must surely be weeping now. The firing stopped on both sides as soldiers stared at the horror and listened to the shrieks of burning men. Then the firing started again, but this time it was sporadic.

"What—"

Robert shook his head heavily. "They're committing suicide," he muttered. "They would rather die by their own hands than be burned to death."

⁓⊱⊰⁓

Matthew and Peter, safe behind the lines, could only hear what sounded like an incessant peal of thunder. They could see massive clouds of smoke lying thick above the ground. Matthew already knew what the scene would look like when it finally ended.

His face grew grim as he watched General Grant nervously whittling pieces of wood into formless shavings. That was his only portrayal of emotion.

"Will he call them back?" Peter asked.

"He can't," Matthew stated simply, answering Peter's questioning stare. "He had all but one of the bridges across the Rapidan torn down after the troops crossed them. There will be no turning back."

⁓⊱⊰⁓

Carrie, as well as all of Richmond, had heard the sounds of battle all day, had seen the heavy smoke filling the horizon. She spent the day in endless prayers while she worked at the hospital, and now she expected the wounded would begin to roll in that night.

She and Janie had just arrived home, nighttime finally silencing the battle, when her father stepped through the door.

Everyone in the parlor ceased talking, waiting to hear what he would say. Thomas stood in the hallway and stared at all of them, weariness creasing his face with even deeper lines.

"Lee sent a telegram. He reported the enemy crossed the Rapidan yesterday. A strong attack was made upon Ewell, who repulsed it. The enemy subsequently concentrated upon General Hill, who resisted repeated and desperate assaults." Thomas took a deep breath. "Lee ended the telegram by saying that by the blessing of God, we maintained our position."

Carrie listened numbly, then turned and climbed the stairs to snatch a few hours of sleep before the ambulance wagons started to roll in. She knew it was too soon for a list of wounded and dead. She had no idea whether she was still a wife or whether she had become a widow. What she did know, was she would be needed as soon as dawn announced a new day.

Janie followed closely behind her. Neither said a word as they got ready for bed. They walked to the window, stared north, and clutched each other in an embrace that said far more than words possibly could.

The battle had come.

Their work would begin in the morning.

Moses stared into the cold ashes of the fire, too tired and beaten to stir them into a fresh flame. All around him, his men lay silently, exhaustion engraved on every face, eyes numb with horror. More than half of them had not returned from the day's battle. Eighty men who had laughed and joked that morning would not see another sunrise.

Moses shifted and gazed up at the sky, or at least what would have been the sky if it hadn't been obliterated by smoke. He had already received orders that his men were to march out again at four thirty in the morning. He knew that was only a few hours away. He should be sleeping, but every time he closed his eyes the nightmare of the day would begin to play. It was far easier to stay awake and wait for whatever came next.

Pompey...

Moses sighed heavily. He would miss every man he had lost, but Pompey held a special place in his heart. He would miss his steady friendship and wisdom so much.

Moses closed his eyes for a moment and shuddered as the smell of burning flesh haunted his mind. His eyes sprang open, and his breath came in gasps as fear swallowed him.

"I can't do it, God," he whispered. "I can't do it." The very idea of leading his men back into battle—if that's what anyone could call the slaughter in the cornfield—was more than he could bear. Tears filled his eyes and his broad shoulders shook silently. He was grateful for the dark that embraced him, and the silence that swallowed his bitterness and pain.

As he wept, his mind traveled back to Old Sarah, Rose's mama. He could see her clearly and hear her voice just as though she was still alive. *"Give God dat anger and pain, Moses. Ain't nobody but him be able to take it. Keep it locked up inside and it gonna eat you alive. Let it go, boy. Let it go..."* He could almost feel her hand stroking his head. *"Let it go, Moses..."*

He wasn't sure how long he cried, but he was well aware when peace replaced fear and horror. Tomorrow would come. Whatever it would bring, he was not alone.

Moses rolled over and slept.

Chapter Five

Carrie and Janie could already hear the sounds of battle when they reached the top of Chimborazo Hill at six o'clock. Heavy smoke, pushed by southerly winds, still hung over the city from the day before. It would get worse before the day was over.

They had received word that the first wave of ambulance wagons was en route. Dr. Wild and Matron Pember stood side by side near one of the hospital wards. They merely nodded when Carrie and Janie came to stand beside them.

Matron Pember was the first to break the heavy silence. "It's too soon for official numbers, but—"

"It's bad," Janie finished, her voice hard and flat.

"It's bad," Dr. Wild agreed. He took a deep breath. "We're ready for them."

Carrie fought to control her trembling—fought to control her desire to scream out that she would never be ready for wagons full of mutilated boys and men who would never live the lives they had dreamed of before this horrible war. She clenched her fists at the thought of the new mountain of amputated arms and legs that would grow in the stifling heat, attracting swarms of flies to feed upon the flesh. She struggled to control the fear that one of the wagons carried Robert, or worse, that he had been buried in a makeshift grave.

Janie reached over to take her hand, allowing Carrie to take a deep breath. Actually, she would be glad when the first wagon appeared. Only then would the nightmares, the wondering and the questioning be swallowed by endless activity and duty.

A distant rumbling told her the wait was almost over.

Matron Pember tried to distract them all. "I finally got rid of the Robinson clan," she announced with forced cheer.

Carrie and Janie looked at her blankly.

Dr. Wild chuckled. "I don't think these two know the story. Let me fill them in before you tell us how you accomplished the miracle." He turned to Carrie and Janie. "There was a family—parents, wife and two siblings—that came down from the western Virginia hills to be with one of our patients. Private Robinson was recovering from typhoid fever."

"That was good of the family," Janie offered.

"It would have been," Dr. Wild agreed, "except that they refused to leave the ward. They sat by his bed smoking pipes and getting in everyone's way. They left only after Matron Pember ordered a nearby patient to change his underwear in their presence."

Janie snorted with laughter.

"The family demanded food and lodging. Even when the private returned to the battlefield, they refused to leave, saying he might get wounded and return."

"That's what happened a week later," Matron Pember snapped, taking over the story. "Imagine my surprise when I arrived at my ward to discover the private had given up his cot to his wife and newborn baby, who had come the night before."

Carrie stared at her in amazement. "She had a baby?"

"When one of our surgeons suggested the mother be moved to another ward and fed tea and toast, she said she would rather stay right there and have bacon and greens."

"Oh my," Janie murmured.

"They were quite content to let us feed the whole lot of them for as long as we were willing. Last week, I finally sent the family away with free rail tickets, food and baby clothes made by Richmond women," Matron Pember said.

"How wonderful for them," Carrie said.

"Except that the woman left the baby behind," Dr. Wild finished.

Both Carrie and Janie turned to stare at him with disbelief.

"She left her baby here?" Carrie wasn't sure whether to laugh—whether her *desire* to laugh indicated she was finally about to go over the edge. A glance at Janie's face reassured her. If she was losing grip on her sanity, at least she wasn't the only one.

Matron Pember nodded grimly. "I arranged to have Private Robinson sent home yesterday on furlough. He took the baby with him. I, for one, hope to never see *that* family again."

Carrie allowed her laughter to come, grateful for anything that distracted her from the sight of the first ambulance wagons pulling up the hill.

Robert was growing more anxious by the moment. Men were asleep all around him, their rifles stacked in rows. They had been promised relief by fresh troops before daylight, but none had appeared as of yet. Though the sun hadn't risen, was not even lightening the sky, everything in Robert told him something was about to happen.

He had woken his own men, but there was no sense of preparation going on around him. They were looking to him for direction, but Robert had none to give them. All he could do was grip his rifle, stare into the darkness, and pray that today would not be as horrific as the day before.

Perhaps they had beaten the Union troops so badly they were already on the other side of the Rapidan licking their wounds like earlier armies had. Then he remembered Longstreet's words about Grant, gripped his rifle tightly, and tried to penetrate the smoky gloom with his eyes. He knew it was futile.

"Sir?" Tabor materialized beside him.

"I don't know, Tabor," Robert admitted. "I don't know if any replacements are coming."

Tabor stared into the darkness. "You reckon they're out there?"

Robert wanted to deny it, but knew the truth was best. "I don't know. All I know is that we're going to be ready."

"What about all them men sleeping?"

"I think their wake-up call will be a rude one when it comes," he said.

Tabor chuckled softly and then swore when the first gunshot cracked through the morning air.

"Prepare yourselves, men!" Robert yelled, watching as sleeping men all around him sprang up and grabbed for their rifles. Many of them never had a chance to reach them.

The woods erupted with gunfire and loud battle cries as the blue coats exploded from the trees, their positions betrayed only by the flash of their muskets. The barrage of bullets was relentless. Wounded men's screams joined the enemy's yelling.

Robert stared around him and knew it would go badly, but he was proud of his men, who stood their ground and kept firing. The men caught sleeping who had not been killed simply turned and ran, convinced it was impossible to hold their position. Robert could hardly blame them, but he tightened his lips, raised his rifle to his shoulder, and fired again.

As the sun finally began to lighten the smoke, he stared in astonishment at the action on his right. Another unit of Rebel soldiers had run out into the onslaught, grabbed up wounded Union soldiers, and propped them against the trees.

Robert heard one of them shout, "This will stop the Yanks' shooting so we can get out of here."

The lull in firing did indeed give the Confederates a moment's rest. Robert looked around for more troops, but could see nothing except the drastically reduced Rebels left to face what looked like a sea of Union blue. His own men looked at him with wild eyes. Knowing the blue coats would work their way around their wounded men and resume the onslaught, Robert knew what he had to do. He would not sacrifice any more of his men for a futile cause.

"The game is up, men. Retreat!" Robert grabbed his rifle and joined his men as they ran back toward their lines. He would fight hard, but he wouldn't submit his men to slaughter, especially when it seemed he and his unit were on their own. He hadn't seen one other commanding officer since the firing began.

Robert's troops had been crashing through the vines and brambles for close to thirty minutes when they heard the Rebel's yell split the air.

Reinforcements!

Robert's men stopped in their tracks, hope replacing the defeat frozen on their faces.

"Push them back, men!" The yell came from a colonel charging forth on his horse, his sword lifted high in the air.

Robert and his men yelled, turned around, and charged back into the smoke. The battle was not over yet!

Moses watched in disbelief as a swarm of Rebels yelling at the tops of their lungs burst from the woods. The Rebels had carried the advantage of an entrenched position yesterday, but now Moses and *his* men had taken protection within the trenches Lee's men had built.

He aimed and fired, watching as gray coats fell in waves across the field. The few shots the Rebels managed to get off flew high while his men and the other units blasted away at point-blank range in comparative safety.

Even though Moses prized his men's success today, it in no way diminished the revulsion he felt at the slaughter spread before him.

"Finish them!"

Moses gripped his rifle, sprang from the protection of the trenches, and charged forward. The blue wave crashing down on the already demoralized Confederates broke the last of the resistance. He watched as the entire line of gray turned and ran, crashing back through the woods they had swarmed out of minutes before.

"We got 'em!" his men yelled in wild exuberance.

"Look at 'em run!" another yelled.

Moses understood how they felt after the terrible beating they had taken the day before, but he also suspected this long day had only just begun.

Robert stumbled out of the woods into camp, fell onto the ground, and reached for the water someone handed him. He nodded his head, too exhausted for words, and guzzled the liquid.

He didn't need anyone to tell him things had gone badly, and that the final charge had been nothing but a crazed death wish by someone who believed they could penetrate an impenetrable position. Robert was grateful to be alive, but heart-weary to know many of his men were dead or wounded.

How long before there was no one else to protect Richmond? How long before the entire army was destroyed?

He could only hope Grant would pull his troops back and give them a chance to lick their wounds.

Working their way around piles of dead bodies, Matthew and Peter walked grim-faced through the bloody fields. Neither had said a word for over an hour. The horror of what they were seeing made words seem pointless.

Nothing could be said to express it.

Peter finally stopped, took several deep breaths, and turned to Matthew. "What will happen now?" he asked hoarsely.

Matthew stared at him with bloodshot eyes and wiped a hand across his dust-caked face. "Grant received a message yesterday from one of his officers that Lee was at it again—that Lee would beat our troops in the Wilderness just as Stonewall Jackson did last year."

Peter stared at him and waited for the rest.

"Grant told the officer who brought him the news that he was heartily tired of hearing what *Lee* is doing. He said that some of them tremble, thinking Lee will suddenly turn a double somersault and land on our rear as well as on both our flanks at the same time. Grant ordered the officer to go back to his command and devise his own plan, instead of quaking over what Lee would do."

"So you don't think he'll pull back?"

Matthew shook his head. "I've been studying Grant since I got out of prison. I also heard of his promise to President Lincoln, that there would be no turning back in this campaign. He will not repeat the mistakes of the generals who came before him."

"But so many of our troops have been killed in this battle," Peter protested. "It has to be close to twenty thousand men!"

Matthew's face was white and set as he shrugged his shoulders. "Grant is known as 'the butcher.' There is a reason he has that nickname," he said grimly. "He figures mathematics are on his side."

"Mathematics?" Peter echoed.

"The more men he loses, the more men *Lee* will lose, and we have more. The numbers are all on our side," Matthew said as they stepped around another blackened and bloated pile of Union and Confederate soldiers twined together, united in death.

"So he continues to sacrifice men because he has more of them?" Peter shook his head in disbelief.

Matthew nodded heavily. "He has already started moving men southeast, heading for Spotsylvania Courthouse. It's not over."

***

Carrie pushed back her hair and wiped at the perspiration streaming down her face. Her ward was completely full. She was taking a few minutes in between assisting Dr. Wild in surgery to check on some of the patients. "Hobbs! Bring this soldier some water."

"Thank you, ma'am."

Carrie gazed down at the man who stared up at her, his face flushed with fever. His bandaged right arm revealed where his limb had been removed above the elbow that morning. He had finally woken up, but now the pain would set in with a vengeance. "You're welcome," she said.

"I reckon I'm glad I didn't lose a leg," he whispered through clenched teeth. "I think I can still handle a plow with one arm, at least with my kids helping me."

"You have children?" Carrie knew talking would help him keep his mind off the pain.

"Yes, ma'am. I got four kids down on the farm in Alabama. They're being a big help to their mama right now. My oldest boy is twelve." He gasped as a bolt of pain shot across his face. "I pray to God he won't have to fight this war."

Carrie reached for his hand and held the glass of water to his lips. "I'm praying the same thing, soldier."

He took several gulps and then passed out from the pain. Carrie eased him back down. It was better this way. She hoped he would sleep for a long time, because he would only awaken to more pain.

The thing that amazed her, though, as she gazed across the ward, was the difference three years of war had brought. Though there were horribly wounded men filling the beds, she had heard very little complaining. These were hardened soldiers, not fresh-faced boys off the farms who thought the war would be a lark, and they would laugh as the soft boys of the North ran back to their easy factory jobs.

"You reckon you can get me back out on the field again soon?" one of the patients asked, reaching for her arm. "The general needs me."

Carrie looked down at the soldier, a delicate-featured young boy. He was either a new recruit or one of the soldiers who lied about his age when the war started. He could hardly be sixteen. "What's your name, soldier?"

"George Frasier, ma'am."

Carrie looked at the soldier closely. There was something not quite right. Then she pulled in her thoughts, knowing it had been a long day, and smiled. "I know you've had to wait a while, but the surgeon will see you soon." She pulled back the bandage and examined his arm. "If we're lucky, we'll be able to save it."

"I know other fellas were hurt a lot worse than me," George said, trying to sound casual through his pain. "I don't really reckon I need a surgeon. Why don't you bandage it up for me, and I can head on back to camp."

Carrie stared down at him. "I don't think so," she responded firmly, wondering at the fear stamped on the soldier's face. It seemed to be about more than his arm.

George seemed to struggle with something as he gazed around to make sure the soldiers in surrounding beds were either asleep or occupied. Then he beckoned Carrie closer.

Mystified, Carrie leaned down.

"I can't go in there to that surgeon's tent," George whispered, his blue eyes opening wide. "They'll find out."

"Find out what?"

George hesitated a long minute and then cursed quietly. "I should have known I wouldn't make it all the way through the war, but I've managed it for almost three years," he said proudly.

Now Carrie was thoroughly confused. "Managed what?" she demanded.

George looked around again and lowered his voice even more. "My name is not really George. It's Georgia."

Carrie stared, completely speechless, for a long minute. She had known something wasn't quite right. She finally found her voice. "You're a woman?"

George—Georgia nodded wearily. "I can't go into that operating room. They'll find out."

Carrie stared at him...*her*, took a deep breath, and struggled for words. She would deal with the reality of a woman soldier later. Right now, she had a patient to save.

"If you don't go into the operating room, you're likely to come down with a raging infection, and then you can be quite sure you will lose that arm," Carrie said. "Is that what you want?"

Georgia shrugged. "I don't know that it really matters. I ain't got anything to go back to." Bitter sorrow shone in her eyes before she turned her head away.

Carrie's heart caught at the sheer misery she saw on Georgia's face. The most important thing a patient needed was hope. She thought quickly and leaned down to speak quietly.

"We'll hold your examination for last. Dr. Wild is a close friend of mine. We will keep your secret."

Georgia stared up into her face. "Why would..." She stopped, obviously at a loss for words.

"I know what it's like to be a woman going against what everyone expects of her," Carrie responded with a slight smile.

She knew from the sheen on Georgia's face that her fever was rising. She would keep the soldier's secret, but Georgia needed help soon.

<hr/>

Dr. Wild looked at her in astonishment. "George is really a woman?" He shook his head. "How?"

"I don't know," Carrie replied. "Today wasn't the time to find out how she managed to enlist in the army. Now is not the time either. Her fever has risen all day, but she was so desperate to keep her secret. I promised her."

"And now that everyone else is gone, you and I can take care of her," Dr. Wild finished.

Carrie shrugged, knowing Dr. Wild was as exhausted as she was. "Something like that," she admitted, forcing a smile.

Dr. Wild stared at her for a long moment and grinned tiredly. "Life is never boring with you around," he stated. "Let's bring her in."

Carrie motioned for Hobbs and another man to carry the remaining soldier into the operating room. She could tell by the look on Hobbs' face that he knew something was going on, but she also knew he wouldn't ask.

Once the curtains had closed around them, they went to work. Carrie cut away the shirt that was shredded on Georgia's arm, and winced at the angry red fingers of infection that had grown during the long, hot day. "It's infected."

Dr. Wild nodded. "I don't know whether we can save it. If I'd seen her earlier..."

"Her secret is evidently more important than her arm," Carrie whispered helplessly. "We have to at least try."

Dr. Wild exchanged a long look with her. "She ended up with the right person," he finally said. "I bet her story is as good as yours."

Carrie grinned. "I have a feeling you're right." She knew if anyone could save Georgia's arm, Dr. Wild could.

Silence fell on the operating room as they worked.

Thomas met Carrie at the door of the house. "I was so worried. I expected you to be late, but not this late." He grabbed her close. "Janie was home hours ago."

Carrie nodded, relaxed into his warm embrace for a moment, and then moved back. "We had one final surgery." She stepped outside and beckoned to Hobbs.

Thomas watched in speechless astonishment as Hobbs, along with another orderly, clumped up the stairs carrying a stretcher.

"Take her up to my room," Carrie said. "Put her in my bed."

Thomas stared after the stretcher. "*Her?*" he asked. "I thought civilians were being treated in other hospitals."

"They are," Carrie said.

Carrie stepped forward and grasped her father's hands. She was glad Janie had appeared on the steps and would also hear her. "I didn't have time to find out her story, but Georgia is a soldier and has been fighting with our men for almost three years. She goes by the name of George."

"How in God's name—" Thomas demanded.

Carrie interrupted him. "I don't know. I do know I promised to keep her secret, and I know Dr. Wild and I were able to save her arm. She needs a place to recuperate, and I didn't know where else to take her." Her voice had risen with weary desperation.

Janie joined her then. "You brought her to the right place, Carrie. We'll take care of her, and May can help when we're at the hospital."

Thomas nodded helplessly. "I suppose."

Carrie kissed his cheek warmly. "Thank you."

Thomas shook his head as he stared up at the staircase to Carrie's room. "Things are never boring..."

Carrie managed a slight grin. "That's what Dr. Wild said, too."

That earned a slight chuckle from her father. "I imagine he did."

As Carrie moved to climb the stairs, she turned back to her father. "I can tell by your face that things went very badly today. I can't take any more bad news tonight, so if you don't mind, I'll wait until tomorrow."

She followed the stretcher to her room. Once she was satisfied Georgia was sleeping soundly, she moved to where Janie was curled on the window seat taking advantage of the breeze that brought welcome coolness.

Janie grasped her hand as Carrie rested her forehead on the window and stared north.

Neither said a word as Carrie sent all her love flying to Robert.

Chapter Six

Carrie and Janie were too exhausted to talk as they trudged down the long hill, thankful for the evening rain that had cleansed some of the awful smoke permeating the capital.

For the first time in a week, there seemed to be a lull in the barrage of constant gunfire before darkness swallowed the battlefields. There had been no such lull in the flow of hideously wounded soldiers streaming into the city, many of them coming to Chimborazo.

Both of the women worked heroically when they were in their hospital ward, but whenever the two left Chimborazo, they allowed their exhaustion to numb the horror. They chose to neither think nor feel. They walked home, ate a simple meal, crawled into bed, and then repeated the routine the next day. It was the only way Carrie and Janie knew to survive it.

Carrie did allow her mind to travel down the hill to where Georgia still lay. She had not woken for more than brief moments in the week she had lain in bed. May had been with her each time, giving her a small sip of water before she lapsed back into unconsciousness.

"Georgia should be awake," she muttered, frowning.

"Perhaps she doesn't *want* to be awake," Janie said. "Who can blame her?"

Carrie nodded, thinking back to the complete misery stamped on the woman's face when she said she didn't have anything to live for. She was more struck, however, by the defeat in Janie's voice.

Carrie reached down and grabbed her hand. "Every day has been awful, but did something especially awful happen today?"

Janie turned bleak eyes to stare at Carrie, and then her face dissolved into tears. "I don't know how much more I can take," she whispered.

Carrie stopped walking and gently took Janie's hands. She knew the emotions needed to come. Janie was always her strength, but even Janie had her limits.

They stood for several long minutes before Janie took a deep breath and wiped away the tears. "It was nothing in particular," she said slowly. "It has just all added up. I thought the hospital had been crowded before." Janie shook her head. "It's nothing like now. Every bed is full, but so is every floor space. And I can't keep them off..." Her face twisted with revulsion.

"Keep them off?" As soon as Carrie asked the question, she knew the answer.

"The rats," Janie whispered, not able to control the shudder. "We can keep them at bay during the day, but they come at night. They chewed right through the bandages of several of the men on the floor last night." Tears filled her eyes again. "Every time I close my eyes, I see it...think about it. Those poor men."

Bile rose in Carrie's throat. She still dreamed of working in a hospital that was clean and sanitary, but she almost couldn't imagine it anymore. Overcrowding, shortages of medical supplies, many drugs not available at all... Just when she thought it couldn't get worse, it got more horrible than even *she* could have imagined. What amazed her was that with all the disadvantages, Chimborazo lost only about ten percent of its patients. Vast numbers would never live the life they had known, but they still had a life to live.

Janie gasped and grabbed Carrie's shoulders, turning her to the east. The setting sun, glimmering through the remnants of the squall, painted a glorious rainbow across the sky. It seemed to stretch over the entire battlefield hiding behind the waves of forest.

"Oh my," Carrie whispered, her eyes absorbing the sight, her soul drinking in the hope it held out to her.

"God is still God," Janie whispered. "He can still create rainbows." Hope trembled in her voice as the pain etched on her face eased.

Carrie grasped Janie's hand more tightly and watched until the rainbow started to fade. All around them, people had stopped to do the same. Rainbows had always been little miracles to her. Even after she understood the science behind their existence, it didn't erase the magic for her.

"Robert is still alive," she whispered suddenly, a light bursting into her heart.

"I know," Janie agreed. "He hasn't been on any of the lists."

Carrie shook her head. "No. The rainbow...it's a sign. He's still alive. I know it." She took long breaths as a deep knowing filled her heart with renewed strength and courage. She turned to Janie. "More horrible things will happen, but it's going to end," she said urgently.

Janie stared at her, obviously at a loss for words. "Carrie?"

"This war has been like an unending night of utter darkness. But God is still God, like you said, Janie." Carrie stared at the last remnants of the rainbow. "The night always ends. God always shines light into the darkness. *Always.*" Her own hope took wing and soared as she spoke. "This year will be an awful last, long night, but it *will* end. We have to hold on to that."

Janie watched as the rainbow disappeared. She took a deep breath and shifted so she could watch the golden orb of the sun slip beneath fluffy, purple clouds perched on the horizon. Finally she nodded. "You're right. It will end. Nothing lasts forever—neither the good nor the bad."

Carrie smiled. "That's what Old Sarah used to tell me. That no matter how bad something was, it wouldn't last forever. And that no matter how good something was, it wouldn't last forever. She told me I had to endure the bad times but suck all the goodness and joy I could from the good times."

"Is it okay that I can hardly wait for the good times to start again?" Janie asked, her voice breaking.

"I think we would both be absolute idiots if we didn't feel that way," Carrie said with a small laugh. "I know one thing for sure," she said as she wrapped Janie in a hug. "You're one of the best things in my life, and I intend to make the most of every single moment we have together."

Janie laughed softly and turned to swing back down the hill. "Let's go have some dinner."

Neither said a word when the sound of battle once more lifted over the trees.

Carrie wasn't surprised this time when she saw Jeremy sitting in the parlor. "Welcome again, Jeremy," she said sincerely, almost surprised to find she meant it. Regardless of what she would ultimately decide about her promise, she was glad to get to know her uncle better. She caught herself before she shook her head at the irony of the situation.

"Hello, Carrie," Jeremy responded, claiming her hand. He took hold of Janie's as well. "How are you, Janie?"

"It's been a long day," she said. "If you'll excuse me, I'll run up to get ready for dinner."

Carrie chose to stay, wanting a few minutes alone with Jeremy. She smiled as she settled herself onto one of the chairs. "My father?"

"He should be here any moment," Jeremy answered. "He was going through a document that arrived just before we were to leave. He told me to come ahead and let you know he might be a little late."

Carrie nodded. She had scarcely seen her father in the last week, and she knew little of what was going on outside the hospital. She had wanted it that way, because she was convinced she couldn't handle anything more than what she faced each day. She waited for her father each night to be assured Robert's name wasn't on the list of wounded or dead before she escaped to her room, but suddenly she found herself wanting to know more.

"I've not wanted to hear any of the news," she confessed. "Would you be so kind as to fill me in on the events of the last week?"

Jeremy frowned. "I'm afraid I have nothing but bad news."

Carrie smiled slightly, holding on to her certainty that the war would end. "I hardly expected there to be good news," she said. "There has not been a single break in the stream of ambulance wagons. That tells me there has not been a break in the fighting, either." She remembered her father's hope that Grant would fall back. "I take it General Grant is not behaving the way we hoped he would."

"That is true," Jeremy said. "After the two days of fighting in the Wilderness, he simply moved his men and headed down to Spotsylvania Courthouse."

"How many?"

When Jeremy looked at her questioningly, she persisted, though she was quite certain the answer would make her sick. "How many did we lose?"

Jeremy's face turned white and hard. "We lost close to eight thousand men." His voice held no triumph when he added, "The Union lost eighteen thousand."

"Twenty-six thousand men?" Carrie thought of Georgia upstairs. "*And women,*" she added silently.

"That was just in the Wilderness," Jeremy stated. "We don't have the final numbers in from Spotsylvania yet. The Union will have higher numbers than us again, but *any* Rebel soldier wounded or killed is a waste."

Carrie looked at him closely. "You hate this war as much as I do."

"If even the thought of it makes you sick, then yes, I hate the war as much as you do."

Carrie took comfort in knowing that someone who was undeniably connected with her felt the same way. "Are they still fighting at Spotsylvania?"

"The last I knew," he said. Then he changed the subject. "Your father is a remarkable man."

Carrie smiled. "I've known that my entire life," she agreed. "Why do *you* feel that way?"

Jeremy seemed to search for the right words. "Your father is a voice of reason. Oh, I know he believes in the war, and that he wants us to win, but I find I can talk with him about anything and he will listen. I don't see the same bitterness in him that I see in almost everyone else."

Carrie thought back to the bitter shell her father had been only months ago, before he was able to embrace a truth that released him from the bitterness. "My father is one of the few who realize that even if the South loses the war, there is still much to live for. He finds comfort in that." She thought further about what Jeremy had said. "You don't want the South to win?"

Jeremy stared at her a moment and shrugged. "I don't want things to go back to the way they were."

"Meaning slavery," Carrie interjected.

"Yes. No one is meant to live in slavery, but..."

Carrie waited quietly for him to go on.

"I thought it would be simple if the North won the war," Jeremy finally said.

"And you don't think that anymore?"

"I don't know what to think, but I do know nothing will be simple. This war became something no one envisioned, so I'm quite sure no one really knows what will happen when it ends."

A stomping on the stairs ended their conversation. Thomas pushed through the door and slumped down into his chair.

May appeared at the sound of his entrance. "You be ready for dinner, Master Cromwell?"

Thomas shook his head. "Give me about twenty minutes please, May." His voice was hoarse and strained.

"Yessuh." The door swung shut as May disappeared back into the kitchen.

Carrie and Jeremy waited for her father to speak, and only nodded at Janie when she slipped into the room. The rest of the boarders had eaten hours before. No one else would be joining them.

Carrie could tell by the broken look in his eyes that the news wasn't good—not that there was a chance of good news at this point. She reached over and took her father's hand.

"Jeremy said you received a new document before you left the Capitol," she said gently, praying it wasn't a new list of dead that had Robert's name on it. She took deep breaths while trying to hold the image of the rainbow in her heart.

"Yes," Thomas said. "General J.E.B. Stuart has died."

Carrie's eyes filled with tears as she thought of the dashing young cavalry commander who had won the hearts of the entire Confederacy with his flamboyant attitude, accented by the long, black, swooping plume he always wore on his hat.

Thomas shook his head and focused his eyes on Carrie and Janie. "This is the first chance we've really had to talk since the fighting started up again."

"I'd like you to give us a basic idea of what has happened," Carrie said.

"I'm afraid it's all bad news," Thomas admitted. "The fighting in the Wilderness was basically a tactical loss for Grant, but we lost almost eight thousand men to make it happen." He paused for a long moment and stared out the window. "Instead of leaving, Grant took his troops and headed to Spotsylvania Courthouse. Lee figured that's what he was doing and beat him there, getting his army into the trenches before Grant arrived."

Carrie felt a moment of gladness that Robert had the safety of the trenches to protect him, for she was quite certain he was right in the midst of the fighting.

"They've been fighting ever since. The Union is taking much heavier losses than we are, but our losses are more devastating," he finished.

Jeremy scowled. "Grant knows he has a bigger army. He can afford to let more of them die."

Thomas stared at him wearily. "That's true. We're simply running out of men."

"What happened to General Stuart?" Janie asked, her face white and set.

"He was sent out with his troops to stop a cavalry raid of close to ten thousand men led by Sheridan. They met at Yellow Tavern...." His voice trailed away, and then he straightened his slumped shoulders. "Stuart has pulled off miraculous feats before, but I don't think he had a chance with this one. He was outnumbered two to one, and the Union Army has those new rapid-fire repeating carbines I've heard about. Most of our boys were killed." He stared out the window at the magnolia tree in full bloom. "Stuart was wounded. They brought him here, but they couldn't save him. He's gone."

He's gone...

The words echoed through the parlor. Carrie knew they reflected the loss of more than just a popular Confederate officer.

They reflected the loss of more hope, the ebbing away of the belief that the South might somehow win this war after all. The three years they had already lived through under siege had been horrible, but eight days into the spring campaign of 1864 made it clear they had not seen true horror before.

Carrie could only imagine how many more men had died in the five days of fighting at Spotsylvania. The steady stream of ambulance wagons said the number would be higher than she dreaded. She fought to contain the groan that slipped out anyway.

Thomas gazed at her with sympathy, but he wasn't done yet. "There is a force of close to thirty thousand men who are coming up the James River under General Butler."

"I leave to join them tomorrow," Jeremy said.

Carrie and Janie gasped as Thomas shot a look at him. "You're not a soldier," he protested.

"Neither is much of the army now being commanded by our General Beauregard," Jeremy retorted. "He's had to pull in every teenage boy and old man who can hold a rifle. I seriously doubt Grant thinks Butler can take the city, but it will certainly take some of the pressure off him at Spotsylvania."

Carrie watched Jeremy closely. He didn't say it, but the gray pallor of his skin indicated he was terrified. Her heart grew tender. He had wanted to spend the evening with them before he left. "Does your father know?" she asked.

Jeremy shook his head. "I'll tell him tonight." He looked at Carrie. "I'm worried about him."

"Is he sick?" Carrie demanded. "I haven't been able to go to the black hospital since the fighting started."

"He's not sick exactly..." Jeremy paused. "It's something I can't put my finger on. He doesn't have the energy he used to have. The light seems to have gone out in his eyes."

"You're afraid he's going to get sick," Janie stated.

"Yes. If any disease starts to spread, I don't think he'll be able to fight it off. He spends so much time in the hospital."

"We'll send some food home with you tonight," Thomas said. "Make sure he eats it. I know his congregation needs food, but they need your father more."

"I'll try," Jeremy murmured gratefully.

Silence reigned around the table as they ate the food May placed before them. Thomas had bought May shortly after he bought the house in Richmond. Carrie hated that the woman was still a slave, but she knew it was a matter of time before the South lost and all the slaves would be free.

As she looked at Jeremy heaping beans on his plate, she could admit to herself that she hoped the South would lose quickly so no one else had to die. Robert. Jeremy. Her father. She knew if the danger was close enough, her father would be called into action, as he had been weeks before. She was sick of losing people she loved.

She also allowed herself a small quiver of excitement to think of what it would mean when the war was over. Rose. Moses. Aunt Abby. Matthew. People whom she loved dearly, those been ripped away from her, would once again be a part of her world, and her country.

If they lived.

Carrie looked up as May headed up the stairs with a pitcher of fresh water. "Has there been any change?"

"Not a sound outta that woman today," May said. "I been dripping water in her mouth like ya tole me, but..."

"We're doing all we can," Janie said. "Sleep is probably the very best thing for her. The infection has disappeared from her arm, and she seems to be resting better. She'll wake up when she's ready."

Carrie couldn't help thinking of Robert. It had taken him two months to come out of his coma after he had been wounded. Georgia had been unconscious for only a week. Carrie had to wonder whether the girl had the will to live—whether she had anything to wake up for.

"The other day she be mutterin' in her sleep," May said. "Kept sayin' the name Jimmy ober and ober, tossing around like de James in a storm."

Carrie and Janie exchanged looks. They were sure Georgia had a story to tell. Only time would reveal it.

May turned and trudged up the stairs.

"Miss Carrie!" May appeared at the top of the stairs moments later, her eyes wide with excitement. "Dat Georgia woman be awake. She be askin' fer you!"

Chapter Seven

Carrie and Janie pushed away from the table and ran up the stairs, then walked more slowly to the room so they wouldn't alarm Georgia. May was standing next to the bed with a wide grin on her face.

Georgia stared up at Carrie when she walked in. "I didn't dream you up," she said weakly, her blue eyes staring up at her from beneath short red hair.

"No, you didn't," Carrie agreed with a smile as she placed her hand on Georgia's forehead, glad to see she was completely fever free.

Georgia gazed around in confusion. "Where am I?" she murmured.

"In my father's home," Carrie said. "I thought it was better that I bring you here rather than leave you in the hospital."

"How long have I been out of it?"

"A week. Your body needed rest and time to get rid of the infection. Your fever is gone."

"They know?"

"No, they don't," Carrie told her quickly.

Georgia looked relieved and then glanced down at her arm.

"We were able to save it. I don't know how well you'll be able to use it, but it's still there. It will take some time for it to heal. Then we'll know more."

Georgia nodded. "Thank you."

Carrie nodded at May, who slipped from the room to fix the sick girl some soup, and then she introduced Georgia to Janie. "You can trust her," she said.

"It's so strange to be called Georgia," she said, her voice still weak. "I've been George for almost three years."

Carrie was bursting with questions, but she knew Georgia needed to get her strength. "Try not to talk right now. May went down to get some soup. We'll have to feed you little bits at first, but your strength will return sooner than you think."

"You ain't going to ask?"

"Well," Carrie admitted with a grin, "I certainly can't say I'm not curious, but now is not the time. You need to build your strength back up."

Janie stepped forward. "I'm dying to hear your story," she said, "but Carrie is right, I suppose. I imagine it won't kill me to wait."

Georgia managed a weak laugh. "I reckon I got real lucky when I ended up in your hospital ward." She gazed up at Carrie. "Are you really a doctor?"

Carrie shook her head. "Not yet. But there is such a dire need for people with medical experience, that I'm allowed to act as one. Officially, I am Dr. Wild's assistant, and even that is strange for a woman."

"You're filling a need," Georgia said faintly. "That's what I did."

Carrie and Janie stared at her but didn't have time to ask anything before May rushed into the room with soup.

The small bowl Carrie fed Georgia worked wonders. Color started to seep back into her cheeks, and her eyes lost some of their dullness. Carrie was sure, given time, Georgia would recover fully.

"We'll give you some more soup in a little while. Pretty soon you'll be as bored with beans and cornbread as we are."

"I reckon it will take me a while to get bored. Sure sounds a heap better than what I've been eating, especially for the last year or so."

Carrie knew how poorly the troops had been eating. It was almost impossible to get supplies to them. Georgia's thin, pinched face was not all due to her illness. Carrie kept trying to block images of Robert, exhausted and hungry, out of her mind. Her sleep would be filled with him, but for right now she needed to focus on Georgia.

Carrie and Janie were sitting on the windowsill talking softly when Georgia woke up again.

Carrie fed her some more soup and was satisfied with the life she saw flowing back into the woman's face. "How old are you?" she asked.

"Twenty. I started fighting when I was seventeen. I know I look younger." She paused, and a deep sadness engulfed her face. "I enlisted with my brother, Jimmy."

Carrie exchanged a look with Janie. That's who she had been calling for in her sleep. "What happened to Jimmy?"

Georgia's eyes filled with tears that she tried to blink back. "He's dead," she said woodenly. "I saw him shoot himself right before the flames reached him back in the Wilderness. He'd been wounded. I figured I could go back for him when the fighting started, but I never got the chance." Her voice cracked. "The fire got him first. He didn't want to die that way, so he shot himself."

Carrie shuddered with horror and locked eyes with Janie. No wonder she had slept for a week.

"How?" Janie asked bluntly

Georgia interpreted Janie's question. "How did I end up in the army?" She shrugged. "Jimmy had to fight, and I didn't want to get left alone. He was all I had. Me and Jimmy were orphans. It'd been just the two of us since I was ten years old. We didn't have any family. We took care of each other." She paused, remembering. "Jimmy was a year older than me. He made a big deal out of being the big brother," she said with a small smile.

"But how did you get past the recruiters?" Carrie asked. "They're supposed to check every man who enlists."

"Supposed to," Georgia agreed. "What they actually do is a different story. Can't say as how I blame them. The South has been desperate for soldiers almost from the start. Ever since those fancy boys figured out this would be a real war that wouldn't end in a few weeks." She made no effort to hide her disdain. "Anyway, all I did was show up dressed like a fella, tell them my name and age, show them my hands—which were pretty rough from working the farm—and they let me in."

"Hasn't it been horrible?" Janie asked in amazement.

Georgia thought about it and shook her head. "Can't really say it has been horrible. At least not any worse than what my life would have been like if I'd stayed behind. I couldn't have worked the farm on my own without Jimmy. There ain't no opportunity for women to make any real money, especially women like me. Why, I've been making more money as a soldier, than I ever could have made as a maid or whatever other pitiful job I could have found. The best I can tell, women left behind on the farms are starving right along with their kids. I reckon that would be worse than soldiering."

"Didn't anyone guess?" Carrie asked. Now that she knew Georgia was a woman, she couldn't believe others hadn't seen her delicate features and known right away. Her hands may have been calloused, but she certainly didn't look like a man.

"They saw what they expected to see," she said. "Wasn't nobody looking that hard anyway. I held my own, fought when I needed to fight, and didn't complain. I was just another soldier."

"Are you glad to be a woman again?" Janie asked. "At least with us?"

Georgia thought about it briefly and shook her head. "No. I reckon I'll go back to being a man once I get out of here. Even once the war is over, if I can get away with it."

"Why?" Janie gasped.

"It's easier." She gazed at Carrie for a minute. "I don't know anything about doctoring, but I know you're the first woman I've ever seen doing it. That means you're going against a lot of people who figure you shouldn't be able to. That ain't easy. If you were a man, they would accept you. You would go to school, and you would be a doctor. Ain't that right?"

Carrie nodded.

"Well, I like being treated with respect. I ain't got to fight people's stupidity over my being a woman, and men thinking I can't do the same things they can. I figure it will be a real long time before women have it easier. Why not live life as a man?"

Georgia laughed suddenly. "I wish you two could see your faces. I ain't the only one, you know. There ain't a lot of us, but I wasn't alone. I fought right along with other women, all hiding like I am. We just know how to see past the secret." She smiled slyly. "We see a whole lot more than them men we fight with!"

Carrie laughed, realizing she liked her unexpected roommate.

Janie was still struggling to understand Georgia. "But what about marriage? Children?"

Georgia shrugged. "Ain't seen many women who had much of a life once they made that choice. It seems like they become somebody else's property. I don't remember my folks much, but what I do remember ain't good. My mama got beat up pretty good, and my daddy drank all the money away."

"Not every man is like that," Carrie protested.

"That's probably true," Georgia agreed. "And I can always change my mind at any time and decide to have all that. It wouldn't be any big deal to go somewhere and live as a woman again." Her face puckered in thought. "I don't see it happening, though."

Georgia gazed down at her arm. "This arm gonna work again?"

Carrie almost wished she could say no so that she could keep Georgia off the battlefield, but time would reveal the truth. "It may not ever be the same, but it will work again."

Georgia nodded. "I'll head back to General Lee when I'm well enough. In the meantime," she added, gazing around the room, "I reckon I'm in a pretty good place." She looked at Carrie. "I'm real grateful to you, but you can take me back up to the hospital any time you want."

Carrie stared at her while she searched for words. "We don't need to make any decisions tonight," she finally said.

Georgia nodded and a moment later was sound asleep.

***

Carrie knew she and Janie should be asleep as well, but neither one of them could get the astounding conversation out of their minds. The two sat on the windowsill talking quietly.

"I can't imagine carrying that kind of secret around," Carrie whispered, not wanting to wake their patient and be overheard.

Janie nodded and seemed to grope for words.

Carrie looked at her more closely. "You're carrying your own secret," she said. "I've seen something in your eyes the past few days, but we haven't had time to talk."

Janie smiled. "I promise you my secret is not that I'm a man."

Carrie chuckled, then reached out and grabbed her hand. "What is it?"

"I think I'm in love."

"What?" Carrie's voice rose before she remembered their patient. She lowered her voice to an excited whisper. "In love? With whom? When? How did I miss this?"

"Do you remember the patient I had over the winter who was from my hometown of Raleigh?"

"The lawyer from North Carolina who caught a bullet in his chest? Clifford Saunders? The two of you talked about home for hours." Carrie nodded. "Of course, I remember."

"He showed back up in my ward the first day of fighting last week," Janie said. "The minute I saw him, I felt my heart swell."

Carrie smiled, recognizing the feeling immediately. "What happened to him?"

"Two bullets in the arm," Janie said. "The doctor had to take his arm."

"Oh, Janie," Carrie cried, reaching out to grab her other hand. "I'm so sorry."

"Don't be," Janie said decisively. "He'll never have to fight again. He is recovering well and is already planning to go back to his law practice when he is ready." She paused and stared out the window. "He has asked me to marry him."

"How wonderful!" Carrie whispered. She hesitated as a conflicted look crossed Janie's face. "Isn't it?" she asked.

Janie looked at her helplessly. "I want it to be wonderful, but I'm not sure it's the life I want." She searched for words. "Clifford was a very prominent attorney. I know what life is like for wives of prominent men. They are expected to maintain their place in society. That kind of life is about entertaining and making their husbands look good."

"And that's not what you want."

"Everything is different now," Janie agreed. "The war has changed me. Being on my own has changed me. Knowing I can do something meaningful has changed me."

"And you don't think Clifford knows that?" Carrie asked. "Didn't he fall in love with a strong woman who is doing meaningful work in the midst of horrible circumstances?"

Janie stared at her for long moments and then nodded slowly, a smile starting to spread across her face. "I guess he did," she whispered.

"You talk to your Clifford," Carrie urged her. "You might just find your way to each other."

Janie grabbed her in an impulsive hug and pulled Carrie over to the bed they were now sharing.

Within moments, they were sound asleep.

Tomorrow would come.

Chapter Eight

Rose walked out onto her tiny porch and stared west toward Richmond, as she did every morning. She took a deep breath, shifted John more solidly on her hip, and headed to school. Her heart would be with Moses all day—wondering if he was dead or alive—but her mind would be in the little white schoolhouse packed with her students.

Rose gave thanks every day for being able to do what she loved best, teaching her students and caring for little John. "Of course," she chuckled softly, "you're not very little. I sure am praying you walk soon, because you're almost too heavy for me to carry, little man." She thought longingly of the baby carriage Aunt Abby had sent, but banished it from her mind. She would never have accepted a gift that would distinguish her so much from other former slaves in the contraband camp.

"Miss Rose! Miss Rose!"

Rose stopped and waited for eleven-year-old Carla to catch up with her, smiling as the little girl's braid bobbed up and down as she ran along the hot, dusty road. "Good morning, Carla. You're in an awfully big hurry this morning."

"Yes, ma'am. I told that man I would run as fast as I could," she gasped, her eyes wide with excitement.

"What man?" Rose asked with a smile. She was used to being called to help in all kinds of situations.

"He's a real big man with red hair. He said his name was..." Carla's face puckered as she tried to remember.

"Matthew?" Rose gasped.

"Yes! Matthew be his name!"

"Matthew *is* his name," Rose corrected, her eyes scanning the road.

"That's what I said, Miss Rose," Carla said impatiently.

Rose didn't take the time to clear up the misused verb. She didn't have long before school started. "Where is Matthew, Carla?"

"He's down at the fort, Miss Rose. He said he knows you have class, but that he needs to speak with you for a minute." She paused, her face growing serious. Her eyes said she had seen more than an eleven-year-old girl should have seen. "He told me it was about Moses."

Rose made her decision. "Come on, Carla." She ran the rest of the way to the schoolhouse, deposited John on the floor with instructions for Carla to watch him, and to tell everyone she would be a little late. Then Rose lifted her dress and ran as fast as she could to Fort Monroe.

Matthew was on the outskirts of the fort watching for her. Rose ran up to him and grasped his hand. "Moses?" Her heart was beating with fear. "Is he..." She couldn't bring herself to say the word that invaded her dreams every night.

"He's fine," Matthew assured her. "I'm sorry you were so frightened. I shouldn't have sent Carla for you that way, but I don't have much time."

Rose nodded, her heartbeat slowly going back to normal. She stepped forward to hug Matthew. "How are you?" He had regained his lost weight since she had seen last him nearly two months ago, after his prison escape, but there seemed to be fresh lines engraved on his face, and his eyes were heavy.

"I'm good," he assured her, his smile helping to wipe away some of the strain. "So is Moses. At least he was when I last saw him," he said teasingly.

Rose gasped. "You met Moses? How?"

Still amazed he had found Moses in an army that huge, Matthew told her the story. "He is quite a leader," he finished. "His men love and respect him."

"It comes naturally to him," she agreed. Then she frowned. "There have been a lot of battles since you saw him on the Rapidan. I heard last night that Grant lost eighteen thousand men in the Wilderness, and now he is fighting at Spotsylvania," she sighed. "Anything could have happened."

"That's true," Matthew said, "but when he gave me this note a few mornings ago, he was alive and well. At least, as well as anyone can be under those circumstances."

Rose reached for the envelope eagerly but looked deeply into his face. Matthew returned her gaze. "It's been bad, Rose. He's lost more than half of his men."

Rose thought of the men she had met the couple of times they had been through Fort Monroe. "Pompey?"

Matthew shook his head. "He died the first day of the Wilderness battle."

Rose made no attempt to wipe away the tears flowing down her face. Pompey had been both a friend and a father figure to Moses. "He was a good man," she whispered.

"All of them are," Matthew said fiercely, anger blazing in his eyes.

Rose stared at him. Matthew was usually so calm, but now she could feel the rage rolling off him in molten layers.

"Most of these battles are more like slaughter than fighting," Matthew said. "Trying to break the lines behind these entrenchments is nearly impossible. Lee can build them faster than our men can attack them. Men are dying on both sides, but we're losing a lot more of our soldiers."

Rose listened, her heart burdened with sadness, but knew there was nothing she could do to change the war. All she could do was pray every minute of every day that somehow, God would allow Moses to come home to her and John. "Where are you headed?" she asked, not wanting to think about senseless slaughter any more.

Matthew understood instantly and reached for her hand. "I'm sorry," he said. "I shouldn't have said any of that."

Rose shook her head. "I'm not naïve. I know it's awful." She forced a smile. "Have you seen Aunt Abby?"

"She's doing fine. She should be in Washington by now." He told her what he had told Moses of Aunt Abby's move to the capital. "You know her. It won't be long before she's making as much of a stir there as she did in Philadelphia."

Rose smiled, fighting back tears as she thought of the woman who had become like a mother to her. The ache of missing her real mother, and now Aunt Abby, never seemed to go away. She supposed the uncertainty of the war made her especially vulnerable, wishing she had someone strong to lean on when she was carrying so many others.

She forced her thoughts to something more pleasant. "You should see John. He'll be walking any day now. He's crawling all over the place and pulling up every chance he gets. I expect him to walk across the house to me tonight," she chuckled. "He loved watching the parade of boats going up the river a few days ago." Rose sobered as she thought of Carrie in Richmond.

"General Butler's forces."

"Yes. I understand they are going up to take Richmond."

Matthew nodded, but his eyes were skeptical. "I wouldn't be concerned about Carrie from that threat," he said. "Butler is a fine lawyer, but he is most definitely not a soldier."

"He's done many good things for those of us here in the contraband camp," Rose said. "He's helped me when no one else would."

"I didn't say he was a bad man," Matthew said, "just that he's a bad soldier." He shook his head. "He's really nothing more than a political appointee of President Lincoln. I know Grant wishes he could have anyone else to lead those thirty thousand men up the James River."

Rose looked up the river, remembering the line of two hundred boats ten miles long, each one sending a spiraling column of smoke into the clear May sunshine. "The men seemed to believe in him," she mused. "They were quite confident."

"I hope they have reason to stay that way," Matthew said. "Only time will tell. So far he's done nothing but fail miserably, with very little action taken at all." He frowned as he looked up the river. "He got as far as

Bermuda Hundred and dug solid entrenchments to protect his troops."

Rose looked at him in confusion. "From what? I don't know a lot about this, but I understood most of Grant's army is fighting in Spotsylvania, and Butler had orders to attack Richmond because they don't have much defense on the river."

"You obviously understand it far better than General Butler does," Matthew retorted. "I've learned that it's best not to try to figure out what goes on in his mind. I do, however, have to report on it, so that's where I'm headed now. I suppose I'm grateful, for I'm quite certain this army won't see a lot of fighting."

Rose lifted her head as a bell started clanging. "I have to get back. School is starting."

"Of course," Matthew said. "I just wanted to see you for a few minutes."

Rose hugged him again, grasping the envelope from Moses and knowing she would wait until that night to read it. "Thank you so much for bringing this. I look forward to the time Moses can get to know you better. I like the idea of my two favorite men becoming friends."

She stepped back but couldn't resist the impulse to hug him again. She had no idea when she would see him next. It was a reality of war she had learned to deal with, but would never accept. "Please be careful," she whispered, tears once more swelling into her eyes.

Matthew grinned and hugged her back. "I imagine I'll see you soon. I'll have to come back through here before they send me somewhere else. Take good care of that boy."

Rose watched as he disappeared into the fort before she turned to fly back down the road toward school.

⁓✦⸱⊹⸱✦⁓

Aunt Abby had been in Washington less than a week, but was quite sure she would never get used to its utter chaos. Philadelphia was a busy city, but it had grown into itself gradually and was maturing gracefully. When she had been in the capital briefly before the war, it had been a rather modest, semi-rural city of a few thousand people.

To say war had changed it would be putting it mildly.

The Civil War had transformed Washington into an urban center of national importance. A few thousand had exploded to seventy-five thousand, with government, infrastructure, and both public and private buildings to support all of it—or at least on the way to supporting it. So much work remained to be done.

Abby's friends had been concerned about her moving so close to the fighting. She had laughed it off. Now that she was here, she was more certain than ever that she was safe. McClellan may no longer have been a general in the army because of his lack of results on the battlefield, but the evidence of his thoroughness in protecting Washington was everywhere.

An extensive line of entrenchments and fortifications completely encircled the city. Sixty-eight forts had been built, along with twenty miles of rifle pits. Fifteen hundred artillery guns, including mortars, were ready to use at any moment. She was living in one of the most heavily defended cities in the world. Abby was confident it was almost unassailable by any force of men.

She frowned as her thoughts turned to the South. She knew the constant siege of Richmond was exacting a heavy toll on the Confederate's capital. Was Carrie still safe?

What about Moses? Rose? Matthew? She was able to communicate fairly regularly with Rose so she felt better about her, but the reality of Moses and Matthew on or near the battlefield was a constant weight on her heart and mind.

Abby sighed heavily as her thoughts spun in the spring heat.

"That was a mighty heavy sigh, Mrs. Livingston," her driver observed, turning to smile back at her.

Abby managed to return the smile. "I suppose it was, Damon. I have a lot on my mind." She had developed a solid liking for her driver. He had escaped a plantation in Mississippi, and found his way to the capital in 1862 when the city outlawed slavery, even before the

Emancipation Proclamation. For the first couple of years, he worked on the fortifications until he had enough money to buy a horse and carriage. Now he transported the endless stream of people flowing in and out of the city.

"Are you glad to be here, Damon?"

"I reckon I am," he said easily as he gazed around. "I know this city still be pretty rough. Not enough of the streets be paved, and I know things don't smell so good because they don't collect the garbage enough, but I reckon it's better than being a slave."

Not to mention the swarms of mosquitoes breeding in dank canals and sewers, nor the poor ventilation in most public buildings, Abby added silently as she gazed around at the struggling city.

Damon clucked to the horses and continued. "I reckon I got things a whole heap easier than all them men fighting this here war. Them hospitals seem to be full all the time, and I hear things didn't go so good for our boys down around Richmond."

Abby grimaced. She'd heard the numbers, too.

"It be true about that amendment to the Constitution?" Damon asked, his intense eyes belying his casual tone.

"Well, I can tell you the process to make the Thirteenth Amendment part of our Constitution has begun," Abby said, bringing her mind back to the main reason she was willing to endure this season in Washington.

"It really gonna ban slavery?" Damon asked hopefully.

"Yes," Abby said. "Lincoln is solidly committed to the abolition of slavery."

"Yessum," Damon agreed, "but do you reckon Lincoln gonna be president again? If he ain't, do you still figure that amendment gonna happen?"

"That's the question of the day," Abby admitted. "Lincoln is a good man. I hate to think what will happen in our country if he's not reelected, but the war is going badly, and people need someone to blame."

"You don't blame him?"

"No," Abby replied. "I blame all the non-thinking hotheads on both sides that made this happen far before Lincoln became president. I'm sure he's made mistakes along the way, but he was thrust into a war no one ever imagined would be the horror it has become."

"So you don't think he'll be president again?"

"I don't know what to think, but I do believe it's too early to know. People are sick of the war. They're sick of losing so many of our boys and men. They're sick of what it means for their families. But people are funny. If we start winning this war, feelings will change. Men will still die in horrific numbers, but if we start *winning* and the end is in sight, people's feelings will change. Lincoln will stand a chance then."

"You know about that thing that happened out in Montana, Mrs. Livingston?"

Abby looked at Damon sharply. "How in the world did you hear about all that?"

"I learn all kinds of things driving this carriage around," he said with a smile. "Some of it I know better than to repeat. But that whole thing about Montana wanting to be a state, but being told they had to let the black man vote first sure did get my attention."

Abby nodded. "It did seem a little silly to me since there *are* no black men in Montana, but I know it's about more than that. The country is trying to find its way forward in ending slavery and making you equal."

"What you think about the black man having the vote?"

"I think it absolutely should happen," Abby responded. "You should be free, you should be a citizen, and you should have the right to vote and have a voice in this country."

"Don't that bother you none?" Damon pulled up to the building where Abby had her meeting and turned to her. "I mean, women been free from the beginning, and you a citizen, but you don't get to vote. Don't it bother you that someone like me might get to vote before you?"

Abby took a deep breath. "It's wrong for you not to be able to vote. It's also wrong for women not to have the vote. To take it from you because we want it first would also be wrong. To hold it from blacks would do nothing to ensure women would get it." She smiled up at him. "We'll continue to fight for *both* of us to have the right to vote. I can only hope that when it has happened, every woman and every black person will take advantage of the power it gives us."

"Why, nothing would keep me from voting iffen I had the chance," Damon protested.

"I agree with you, but there are too many people who want to criticize what is happening without being involved in the process. Take this war. The people of the United States let a handful of hot-tempered men decide their future, and now we are paying the price." Abby stared off into the distance where men were finishing the dome of the Capitol building. "If more people had stood up and let their voices be heard, could we have stopped the death of so many of our nation's men and boys, the destruction of so much of our country? We'll never know, but I believe it would have been different."

Abby glanced toward the door of the building, saw a group of women going in, and quickly gathered her things. "My greatest hope is that when this war is over, the people of this nation will not sit back and let others dictate their future. The reunion will be every bit as difficult as the war."

"Say what?" Damon asked. "How you figure that?"

Abby shook her head sorrowfully. "However this war ends, there will be a deep bitterness on both sides. I'm afraid people will simply want revenge, and that even if the armies go home, people will continue fighting." She stared off into the distance. "They'll just find another way to fight."

She shook her head again and stepped out of the carriage. "I'll be here for about two hours. Will you pick me up later?"

"Yessum, Mrs. Livingston. I be here." Damon hesitated. "Thank you."

"For what?" Abby paused as she headed up the sidewalk.

"You done made me do some thinking. I don't want to be one of them people who lets things happen. I reckon

I'm gonna find a way to let my voice be heard in this country, no matter what happens with that amendment, but I sho gonna pray it goes through."

"Thank you, Damon." Abby reached out and touched his arm. "You give me hope for the future." Then she turned and joined the other women on the building's porch.

Abby nodded greetings to all the women on the porch and moved inside. "Will Dorothea be here today?" she asked the woman closest to her.

"I know she's going to try, but the new influx of patients from the fighting in Virginia is occupying most of her time."

"Of course." Abby was hoping to meet the famous Dorothea Dix she had heard so much about. She'd been aware of the woman's pioneering work in setting up hospitals for the insane before the war. Abby hadn't been surprised when Dorothea showed up to offer her services in the capital right after the war began. She had been rebuffed at first because everyone, including all government officials, thought the war would be short-lived. It hadn't taken them long to change their minds and accept the help she offered.

Abby's attention was called to the front of the room when one of the women stood up and turned to address them. "Dorothea sent a message that she will be late, but she will be here."

Abby smiled. One of her goals for this trip to Washington was to make connections Carrie would need after the war. Three years of war and distance had done nothing to diminish the love she had for the spirited girl who had come to her home before the war began.

Abby had drilled Matthew for information about Carrie when he returned from his time in prison. Carrie was now a young woman being tempered by the reality of medical service in the war. Abby was determined to do everything she could to lay the foundation for Carrie's dream of becoming a doctor. Meeting the superintendent of nursing was near the top of Abby's list.

One of the women standing close to Abby touched her hand. "Is it true that this is the first time in our nation's history that our army is being cared for by women, and that Miss Dix is the superintendent of women nurses?"

"Yes, it's true," Abby replied, "but not everyone has been happy with it." She smiled as she thought about what Dorothea had accomplished. "She started with a completely volunteer corps of nurses, but she was able to set up a system of compensation so all the women were paid by the government. Now close to fifty thousand women take care of our soldiers."

"Oh my!"

Abby frowned. "Not everyone reacted as enthusiastically as you. Far too many doctors and surgeons were quite put off with the power Dorothea Dix held over their hospitals."

"What happened?"

"They passed new laws that keep the women nurses from being paid, and they've given the power back to the senior medical officers of each hospital. Dorothea has lost a great deal of her power and influence," Abby said. Then she smiled. "Not that it has slowed her down any."

Another woman leaned in. "Did you hear about what happened at the Battle of Antietam?"

Both Abby and the other woman shook their heads.

"Dorothea was out on the battlefield, right in the midst of the fighting. She was holding the head of a wounded soldier in her lap so she could give him water. He was lying right there in her lap when he jerked once and died."

"From what?" Abby asked, her heart pounding from the image she could see so clearly.

"A musket ball hit him directly in the head. Dorothea stood up and took her water to the next soldier who was down."

Abby's eyes filled with tears. She knew nothing could stop that kind of compassion and caring. Regardless of Dorothea's rank or position, she would continue to serve every way she could. "What does she need from us?"

Just then Dorothea walked into the room. Applause welcomed her, but she held up her hand impatiently and walked to the front of the room. Dark hair carefully pulled back into a bun framed a strong, caring face.

"Thank you all for coming. I can only stay a few minutes because the wounded from Richmond are flowing into the city." She gazed around the room. "All of you are women of influence from other cities. I need your help to mobilize the women in your city to sacrifice even more to take care of our soldiers. We need everything..."

She motioned to two women standing on the side of the room. "I've asked these women to prepare a list of what we need. I pray you all will take it and do what you can to get the supplies."

She moved toward the door as if to leave but then turned back to scan the room. "Is there an Abigail Livingston here?"

Abby stepped forward immediately, mystified as to why she was being singled out. "Yes, I'm here."

"Will you please walk out with me?"

Not caring what had created this small miracle, Abby fell into place beside her. "What can I do for you?"

"I wanted to thank you," Dorothea said warmly. "I've heard you single-handedly sent down more barrels of goods—including medical supplies—to the contraband camp at Fort Monroe than all the other people combined. You are obviously a very powerful woman." She smiled broadly. "And I like to surround myself with powerful women. It gives me hope for the future."

Abby laughed and reached down to squeeze the woman's hand. "I feel the exact same way. I will send a letter to the women of Philadelphia as soon as I get back to my room."

Dorothea nodded. "I was quite sure of that. Now, what can I do for you?"

Rendered speechless for a moment, Abby stared at her.

Dorothea smiled. "We all need to stick together. I know more about you than you realize, Abby. You have touched so many lives. Is there anything I can do for you?"

Abby's heart swelled with gratitude. "Not right this moment, but as soon as the war is over," she said, "there is a young woman who's like a daughter to me who has a passion to be a doctor. She is working in Richmond at Chimborazo right now. When this war is over, I want you to meet her and help her connect with the medical colleges for women."

Dorothea smiled. "I would be honored," she said. "Bring her to me at any time." She squeezed Abby's hand. "And now I have to go. Thank you so much for everything."

"The same to you, Dorothea," Abby whispered. She reached out to embrace the older woman in a warm hug. "God bless you."

Rose walked slowly down the dusty road back to the cabin she shared with Moses' sister June and her baby boy, Simon. One of the other women had brought baby John home earlier, but it was time for Rose to feed him. She knew he would be demanding his mama very soon. The image brought a soft smile to her face. She loved her baby with a fierceness that surprised even her, and she hoped the day would come when she could have more children with Moses. She gently touched the envelope in her pocket.

It had been a long day, but the advances her students were making filled her heart with such joy. All of them, even the youngest, were now reading and writing and absorbing all the books Aunt Abby was sending down in the barrels that arrived every week.

Rose took deep breaths of the soft spring air. If not for constant worry about Moses, nothing would have marred the happiness she experienced as a teacher. It was everything she had ever dreamed it would be.

Rose knew the war would come to an end. She already had so many plans for how she would help her people, as well as how she would continue her education.

She was steps from their cabin when the door flung open and June ran out onto the porch. "Rose! Come quick!"

Rose's heart sprang to her throat as she ran up the stairs. "John? What's wrong?" Her alarm was lessened by the smile spreading on June's face. "What's going on?"

"You don't want to miss the first one," June said simply, motioning her inside.

When Rose walked inside, her baby John had pulled himself up next to the chair, his hand grasping it with a look of determination she recognized instantly. It was the same one Moses got when he was about to do something important.

John looked up, saw her enter the cabin, and gave her a big smile. "Mama!" he sputtered, then held out his arms to her, and tottered across the floor. He took only three steps before he fell, but his grin never wavered. "Mama!"

Rose scooped him up and held him close. "What a big boy!" she cried. "You walked! Won't your daddy be so proud of you when he sees you again?" She forced down the tears that threatened to come because Moses had missed his son's first steps, and instead she focused on celebrating.

"Walk," John babbled, kicking his feet.

Rose laughed, lowered him to the floor, and joined June in cheering as John practiced his new skill.

The house had grown quiet, with John and Simon tucked into bed and June in her chamber, before Rose opened the envelope she had carried in her pocket all day. She had not wanted to share this moment with anyone.

> *Dear Rose,*
> *You're right. Matthew is a good man. I'm so glad I got to meet him, and I'm glad I can get a letter to*

you through him. But I can't help wishing I was the one who could bring it to you.

There are times I fear this war will never end. Pompey is dead, as are many of my men. There are times I want to run away and come back to you and John.

Rose wiped at the tears streaming down her face.

But then I remember why I'm doing this. I remember my daddy. And your daddy. And your mama. I remember I've got to go back and find Sadie and my mama. I have to help them build a new life. I can only do that if we are all free. So I will continue to fight.

Mostly, though, I will continue to hold close the truth of how much you love me. It means everything to me, Rose. It's all that keeps me going most of the time. You and John. I will do everything I can to come home to you. I love you so much.

Moses

Rose grasped the letter to her heart, listened to John's even breathing in his crib, and finally slept.

Her dreams that night were all of her husband fighting to survive in the midst of death, flashing guns and burning smoke.

Chapter Nine

Carrie was upstairs in her room washing off the dust from the streets and changing her dress, when she heard her father's voice boom throughout the house.

"Jeremy! It's good to see you, son!"

Carrie smiled, glad to know Jeremy had come home safely. She had daily scanned the list of dead and wounded for him, grateful she had not found his or Robert's name on that hated list. It was not conclusive however...

"Aren't you going on down?" Georgia asked. "I'll be fine."

Carrie shook her head. "I'll give my father some time with Jeremy. It will be a little while before May has dinner ready." She turned back to Georgia. "I wanted to talk to you anyway."

Georgia nodded. "I'm doing right well. I reckon it's time for me to go back to the hospital. It shouldn't be long before I can go back to fighting."

"That's not what I wanted to talk to you about," Carrie responded. "Although, I am pleased you're doing so well."

"My arm is getting better every day. I'm even starting to use it a little."

"Ready to shoot a gun with it?" Carrie asked.

"Well..." Georgia hesitated and then admitted, "My aim might not be so good."

Carrie nodded decisively. "Exactly." She settled down on the edge of her bed. "What do you want to do when this war is over?" She had put off this discussion for a while, but it was time.

Georgia stared at her and shrugged. "I haven't looked much past being a soldier."

"I know you may continue to pass as a man," Carrie said gently, though she had doubts Georgia could pull it off when people were paying attention and not seeing a soldier. Now that Georgia was putting on some weight, her true beauty was shining through. Carrie had decided she didn't need to voice her skepticism, she just needed to offer Georgia an opportunity. "This war won't last forever."

"Things going bad?" Georgia asked.

"Right now General Lee is holding Grant back, but things are going badly around the rest of the country." Carrie took a deep breath. "It's only a matter of time, Georgia. The South doesn't have enough men, or guns, or money to win this war."

Protest sparked in Georgia's eyes, and then she closed them for a moment. "Why are you telling me this?"

"Because I genuinely like you. You may go back to fight when you're well, but when the war ends, you will have to figure out how to live in a brand new world." Carrie reached out to take Georgia's hand. "Do you know how to read?"

"Read?" Georgia echoed. "Now you got me totally confused. What's reading got to do with anything?"

"Do you know how to read?" Carrie repeated.

"Never saw no use for it," Georgia said defiantly. "Didn't need reading to plant crops and bring in a harvest. Me and Jimmy never had a chance to go to school, but we did fine."

"Janie and I want to teach you how to read," Carrie responded, holding up her hand before Georgia could protest. "Whatever you decide to do after the war, reading will help you. It will help you if you decide to live as a man. It will definitely help you if you decide to live as a woman because it will open doors you can't imagine right now."

"I don't see no reason—"

Carrie interrupted her. "My father had to fight my mother for my education. I broke all the rules and taught Rose how to read. Then Rose had a secret school in the woods on the plantation, so she could teach our slaves how to read and write." She paused and stared into Georgia's eyes. "Reading opens up a whole new world, Georgia. It means that no one, neither man nor woman, can take advantage of you because you're ignorant."

"Why are you willing to teach me how to read, Carrie?" Georgia asked. "Ain't that a lot of work?"

"You're smart," Carrie said with a smile. "I don't think it will take too long, but it's more than that..." She stared out the window for a minute. "I don't believe anything happens by accident. You were meant to end up in my ward. I was meant to know your secret and bring you home. And I believe we're meant to help you learn how to read while you're here."

"Amen!" Janie strolled into the room and headed straight for the water pitcher. "I couldn't have said it better myself." She washed off her face, drank a large glass of water, and turned to Georgia. "I still remember the thrill of learning how to read. I was a teenager before I learned."

Carrie gasped. "I didn't know that."

Janie nodded. "My father wasn't strong enough, like your father was, to fight my mother. She believed education would make me less desirable to the boys she thought I should marry. I finally took things into my own hands when I was fifteen, and found someone to teach me how to read in secret. It was the greatest thrill of my life when all the letters finally made sense."

Georgia smiled. "I reckon it would be nice to have the letters make sense," she murmured, nodding her head. "When do we start?"

Carrie and Janie laughed and replied in unison, "Tonight!"

"After we have dinner," Carrie added, propping Georgia up.

"May will bring it to me soon," Georgia replied, her eyes confused again.

Carrie shook her head. "You're well enough to join us downstairs. You're part of our family now. Let's go eat some dinner."

"I ain't got no clothes," Georgia gasped. "Just this gown from the hospital."

"Sure you do," Janie said, grinning. "I got you some the other day."

"I ain't putting on no dress," Georgia protested, her eyes flashing.

"A dress would look strange on a man," Janie agreed calmly as she reached into the wardrobe and pulled out a pair of pants and a shirt. "They might be a little large, but I think they'll fit pretty well."

Georgia grinned and reached for them. "Why are you two doing this for me?" she asked. "Most women would be appalled that I'm living as a man. They sure wouldn't be giving me men's clothing."

Carrie turned serious. "How you live your life is up to you, Georgia. All I've ever wanted is for people to give me freedom to live my own life without making me feel bad about my choices, no matter how much they may disagree. "

Janie nodded her agreement. "I sure am hungry. Can we go eat now?"

Minutes later, the three of them entered the dining room.

⁙⁘⁙

The table was crowded with people since all the boarders had joined them for dinner. Georgia looked panicked, only relaxing when Carrie instantly introduced her as George and let everyone know *he* was convalescing in a spare room in their wing of the house until he could return to the army. Thomas, Janie and May were the only ones who needed to know the truth. There was hardly a house in Richmond that didn't have a wounded soldier.

Carrie headed straight to Jeremy after the introductions and gave him a warm hug. "I'm so glad you're home safely."

"Was it horrible?" Janie asked, her gaze including three of their boarders who had also been called to duty when Butler headed up the James River.

"Well, the food wasn't too good," Jeremy replied, "but other than that, we could probably have all stayed home and Richmond would have been fine."

"So it's true," Thomas said with a chuckle.

Jeremy nodded. "If every Union general was like their General Butler, we would have won this war a long time ago."

Thomas answered Carrie's unspoken questions, addressing the whole table. "General Butler headed up the river with thirty thousand men. If he had come straight through and attacked, he probably could have taken the city, or at least opened the way for Grant to sweep in. We quite simply didn't have enough men to stop him."

"Why didn't he?" Janie asked.

"We may never know the answer to that," Thomas replied, "but we can all be grateful."

"I never even got to fire a rifle," Jeremy complained, but then smiled his delight. "By the time Butler's men got around to trying to do anything, General Beauregard had arrived. He managed to pull together twenty thousand veteran soldiers and sent us all home."

Carrie glanced around the table at the three other boarders who had been called up. All of them looked as relieved as Jeremy. Their years in Richmond's government offices had done nothing to prepare them for fighting.

"Did Butler finally have enough guts to put up a fight?" George demanded.

"Two days ago," Thomas informed him. "I can't say he was the one to put up the fight, though. Beauregard went after him pretty hard and pushed him back to Bermuda Hundred. Butler's troops took heavy losses."

"So did we," Carrie added, determined the whole story be told. "Beauregard's men were successful, but I treated several of them today. One of them was with a brigade that suddenly stumbled into a whole trap of telegraph wires strung all over the field."

"Telegraph wires?" George echoed. "You mean they set up a booby trap?"

Carrie nodded. "Nobody could see them because the fog was so heavy. Our men fell over them. When they tried to stand back up, they were shot down." She took a deep breath. "The man I treated this morning lost his right leg."

Silence settled over the table as her words reminded them any good news came with a solid dose of bad news and reality.

George was the first to break it. "Has Lee driven the Yankees away from Spotsylvania yet?"

"From what I can tell from the reports, Grant is still hanging around, but after the Bloody Angle, he is surely going to decide he can't win there either," Jeremy responded.

"The Bloody Angle?" George asked.

"Grant decided to go after our army when they were solidly in the entrenchments. From what we can tell, it was the longest sustained fighting of the war—close to twenty-four hours of hand-to-hand combat," Thomas explained. "Our lines held, but there was a heavy price to pay."

Carrie pressed her lips together and exchanged a long look with Janie. Ambulance wagons were still arriving with men from that battle.

"I think this fighting has taught the Yankees some lessons," Thomas said grimly. "I believe Grant has learned the futility of winning a battle against us in an untracked forest. I also believe he is figuring out that he cannot take Lee in trench warfare once our general, who is also an excellent engineer, has gotten our troops dug in."

"So General Lee is winning?" George asked hopefully.

Thomas took a deep breath and seemed to choose his words carefully. "As much as I would like to say he is, I don't think I would go that far."

When he hesitated again, Jeremy added, "I think the best you can say is that, at this point, we seem to be reaching a stalemate. Neither side can truly say it has won or lost."

Carrie flushed angrily. "How can you say that?" she exclaimed, her green eyes snapping fire. "Over twelve thousand soldiers are either dead or wounded. More than eight thousand have been captured or are missing. I hear the numbers are even higher for the Union side." She allowed her scathing look to touch everyone at the table. "I believe I would say both sides have indeed *lost*."

She couldn't hear any more. Her attempts to hang on to the promise of the rainbow that she had tucked into her heart were failing. Blinking back hot tears, she pushed away from the table and fled up the stairs.

Chapter Ten

Moses shifted his body and stretched out his exhausted legs. He and his men had been marching in blistering heat all day. He'd heard that men who arrived earlier attacked the trenches, briefly overran them, and then were pushed back by a strong counterattack.

"Hey, Moses?"

Moses managed a smile for the wiry boy he had discovered was only seventeen. Having run away from his plantation in Georgia, he had come north, determined to fight. "Yes, Clay?"

"You know where we be? These here woods and fields are all startin' to look de same to me."

"The word is that we're near Cold Harbor. General Sheridan's cavalry took it yesterday."

"If they done took it, what we doin' here?"

"I imagine Grant figures he can cut around Lee's army and open the way for us to move into Richmond."

"You figure he's right?" Clay asked.

"I have no idea," Moses answered honestly. "I sure hope he is, though." He didn't add how much he wanted the war to be over.

"We don't seem no closer than when we started," Clay said dubiously.

That brought a chuckle from Moses. "I'd say you're right. The one thing I know, though, is that we can't see the big picture from where we are. Grant and the generals know things we have no way of knowing. We have to trust them and follow their orders," he said, knowing the best gift he had to give his men was confidence—whether it was justified or not, and whether he believed it or not.

"I reckon that be the truth," Clay said. He paused and stared out into the rapidly approaching darkness. "When you reckon the next orders comin'?

"They'll come when they come," Moses responded. "The best thing you can do is get some rest. When they come, we'll have to be ready."

The boy turned to move away, but Moses stopped him. "Make sure you and the rest of the men have tagged your jackets."

Clay nodded soberly. He knew what that meant. Those who could were to write their names on slips of paper, and sew them to their coats so they could be identified if there was a need.

⁑⋘⋙⁑

The Union orders came about thirty-six hours later, while darkness and dense fog lay over the ground. During those thirty-six hours, what had been a small force of Rebel infantry was able to reinforce their position and bring more troops in.

"Get your men ready, Moses!"

Moses snapped to attention when Captain Jones rode up in the foggy darkness. "Yes, sir!"

The captain rode closer and hesitated.

"Something else, Captain?"

"It's been a rough month for your men."

"Yes, sir." Moses tried to block out the faces of almost one hundred men who had not made it out of the battles.

"They've fought well. Please let them know I'm proud of them."

Moses straightened a little more. "Thank you, Captain. That will mean a lot to them."

"We're going to win this thing, you know."

Moses smiled grimly. "It's what keeps us fighting, Captain. We've *got* to win this war."

Captain Jones hesitated again.

Moses gripped his rifle. "Is there something you want to tell me?" he asked quietly.

"I'm not feeling good about today," Captain Jones finally admitted.

"It's going to be a bad one," Moses agreed.

"You feel it, too?"

"Have ever since we arrived. We've already learned what happens when we go against Lee's entrenchments. Combine it with hilly, woody terrain..." He shrugged his massive shoulders. "I think it's going to be a very bad day."

Captain Jones said nothing, but reached down and gripped Moses' hand for a long moment. "I'll see you when it's over."

Moses managed a smile. "Yes, sir!"

The order to attack came moments later.

Moses and his men raced straight into Hell.

⁙

Matthew struggled to breathe, torn between fury and sickening pity for the soldiers lying in piles on the field stretched out before him and Peter.

"But... aren't they going to help them?" Peter gasped. "The army can't leave them there. It's been two days..." His voice trailed off, fatigue and misery etched into every line of his face.

"Seems Lee didn't like the way Grant worded his letter requesting a truce, so he denied it," Matthew snapped.

"But those men..."

"Grant sent a letter requesting a truce. He tried very hard to make it sound as if both sides needed time to retrieve their casualties. Lee responded that he didn't have any."

"But—"

Matthew turned around and glared at Peter. He knew he was directing his anger at the wrong person, but he had to vent it somehow. "As long as there is fighting, Grant won't send anyone out there to get those men. More will be shot!"

"But listen to them," Peter protested. "There are thousands of men who have been crying out for water and help for the last two days. I can't even imagine how they're suffering."

Matthew's stomach rolled as the cries continued unabated. His dreams the last two nights had been full of confused eyes begging someone to help them, not to leave them out there to suffer and die.

"The whole thing should have never happened," he said hoarsely, his eyes burning from the heat and smoke and stench of decaying bodies. "They never stood a chance."

"Do you think the numbers are true?"

Matthew nodded grimly. "We lost eight thousand men in less than an hour, most of them in the first ten minutes. I can't bring myself to call it a battle."

"It was a slaughter," Peter said heavily. "I've seen horrible things in the last three years, but I've never seen anything like this." He stared out over the field. "I hope to never see anything like it again."

Matthew was still furious. "I wish the men who ordered those poor soldiers to attack the entrenchments were out there with them. Instead, they stay far behind, knowing they have plenty of men to sacrifice for the cause." He made no attempt to hide his bitterness. He finally dropped his head into his hands. "I hate this war!"

⁙⁘⁙

Two hours later, when darkness had swallowed the sight of the suffering soldiers, if not their cries, Matthew was startled by steady movement out on the battlefield. "Who goes there?" he called, hating the job that made it necessary for him to document such atrocities.

"We's goin' out to get our friends," came a quiet voice. "We figure we gots a better chance in the dark."

Matthew held up his lantern and stared at the black soldier, really nothing but a boy, looking back at him. "No one has called a truce."

"No, I reckon they ain't, but that ain't stoppin' their sufferin' none," the soldier replied. He peered closer at Matthew. "You're that journalist fella I met back on the river," he said.

Matthew nodded. He had met hundreds of soldiers.

"Moses know you up here?"

Matthew straightened. "You're one of Moses' men?"

"Yessuh." He turned to stare out onto the field. "Moses already be out there. Said he's sick of losin' his men and aims to do what he can to save some of them. I reckon I be goin' to help."

"But there are thousands of men out there," Peter protested. "How are you going to find them?"

"We knows 'bout where we made our attack. We's gonna look in that area. Ain't so many black. It make it a mite easier to find 'em. We reckon anyone we hauls outta there be real grateful."

Matthew nodded and made up his mind. "I'm going with you."

Peter was already headed in the direction the black soldier had pointed. "Me too." He turned to the soldier. "What's your name?"

"Clay. I lost me a bunch of friends out there durin' that fight. I aim to help as many of dem as I can."

"Then let's go find them," Matthew said.

Five hours later, they had hauled close to fifty soldiers, both black and white, off the battlefield while praying sporadic gunfire from the Confederate entrenchments wouldn't find their mark. As soon as they got the wounded behind the lines, willing hands carried them to the medic tents.

Matthew took a deep breath and turned back around for one final trip. He knew he would never forget the sight of the bloated, blackened bodies seeming to float over the ground in the moonlight, but he would also never forget the wide-eyed looks of gratitude when he held water to a soldier's lips and carried him to safety and medical care.

A hand on Matthew's arm stopped him.

"You can't go back out there."

"I've got to," Matthew said desperately. "I might be able to save someone else." The horror of the night suddenly rose in waves and threatened to overwhelm him. His breath came in short gasps as he pulled at the arm holding him. "Let me go! I can save someone else."

The arm held him tight. "Rose will never forgive me if I let something happen to you."

Matthew gasped and turned around. "Moses!"

"Clay told me what you did. He said you helped bring twenty of my men off that field. Me and my boys got some more. They're pretty bad off, but at least now they stand a chance." Tears glistening in his eyes, Moses let go of Matthew's arm and grasped his hand. "Thank you."

"We might be able to get some more," Matthew said urgently, turning to stare over the field.

"The sun is about to come up," Moses replied. "You can't go back out there. Getting yourself killed isn't going to help any of those men, and being out there in sight will make the Rebels fire at you. Instead of saving someone, you could be the reason they get shot again."

Matthew took a deep breath and nodded, watching as black heaps turned into recognizable forms and the sun turned the smoke into a misty haze. "You're right," he said.

He turned back to Moses. "I'm glad you're alive." He'd been about to say he was glad Moses was okay, but one look at the tortured expression on his face told him Moses was far from okay. Matthew knew there were no words that could comfort that kind of pain and agony, so he simply laid his hand on Moses' shoulder.

Both of the weary men stared into the field of death and waited for what the new day would bring.

***

Carrie was not sure she could take one more day of not knowing whether Robert was dead or alive. She tried berating herself for her feelings and knew women all over the country were suffering. Then she tried telling herself she should be glad Robert wasn't on the list of soldiers who had died. She was certainly grateful, but the ache inside grew, fueled by the pain and suffering she faced every day at the hospital.

She stared off to the northeast toward Cold Harbor. Her father had told her the night before that Grant had taken his army and moved. No one was quite sure where he was going yet, but there were no illusions that he was simply going away. He would rear his head again, and more suffering would follow.

Carrie gazed at the horizon, longing for a rainbow to appear in the sky again to infuse her with the hope that had slowly drained from her heart over the last month. She tried to bring it forth in her mind, but nothing materialized. All she could see was thick smoke hovering over the trees in the distance. All she could hear was the sound of more ambulance wagons creaking through the city, competing with the sound of funeral wagons as they wound their way to Oakwood and Hollywood Cemeteries.

She had helped save over a dozen soldiers today. She could certainly be glad about that, but the pain of not knowing still threatened to swallow her. "God..." she whispered brokenly, fighting back hot tears and forcing herself to take deep breaths.

Carrie had been here many times before. The last three years had been one long string of pain and not knowing. Yet, she sternly reminded herself, the years had also been full of good moments. Moments when love won. When miracles happened. When good triumphed. She knew she had to hang on to those moments.

She stood where she had stopped in the road. Gradually, her heartbeat slowed and her breathing became easier. Today had been a hard day, but it would end. Tomorrow would be a new day that held hope and the promise of better things.

A breeze picked up and cooled her hot cheeks. The breeze also carried a whisper...

The culmination of every day, no matter what it holds, carries the promise that tomorrow will bring the rest of your life. Embrace what has come before. Embrace what is before you. In so doing, you will learn the joy of living.

The joy of living...

Carrie pondered the words that drifted into her heart. Could it be possible to find joy in the midst of such horror? As her breathing slowed, she remembered the gratefulness on a soldier's face when she told him his leg had been saved and he would be able to farm again. She remembered the laughter of a small child when he had climbed onto his daddy's lap to smother him with kisses.

She even managed a small smile when she remembered the huge pile of roasted meat the men in her ward had consumed that day, and their cheering when they learned they were eating the very rats that crawled through their ward at night.

You have to look for the joy, Carrie. You have to choose to find it in the midst of the pain. You have to choose...

Choose.

Once again, Carrie chose to be stronger than the horrors in her life. "Okay, God," she whispered. "I choose joy."

Carrie felt suddenly eager to have dinner and continue with Georgia's reading lessons. Georgia had already come so far.

Her smile became genuine as she made it down the hill.

"Your smile is the thing that keeps me going, Mrs. Borden."

Carrie let out a laugh and flung herself into Robert's arms, as he stepped off the porch to meet her.

Robert grabbed her close and spun her around, then held her as if he would never let her go.

Carrie knew without looking that his face and eyes were haunted. She stepped back, held his face close in her hands, and poured all the love she could into his eyes. Slowly, very slowly, the pain ebbed away and a smile began to light his eyes. Carrie knew the pain would return, especially in his dreams, but for as long as he was with her she would give him all she could to carry him through, knowing these moments would also carry *her* through.

"How long?" she whispered.

"I have to leave tomorrow," Robert replied. "General Lee is sending me and my men into the Shenandoah Valley to join up with Jubal Early."

"I'm glad you'll be out of Richmond," Carrie said. She knew it also meant it would be longer before she had a chance of seeing him again, but nothing could be as horrible as the battles to take the capital.

Robert nodded but pulled her close again. "I hate the thought of being so far from you...of leaving you here." He groaned as he buried his face in her hair.

"We have to choose joy, Robert," Carrie said.

"Joy?" Robert's eyes and voice left no doubt what he thought of that.

"Yes," Carrie insisted, sharing what she had learned on the way down the hill. "I will hate every minute we are apart, but I can also choose to find joy in the midst of it. We have the power to choose."

Robert shook his head as he smiled. "I'll try, Carrie. I can't imagine it right now, but I'll try." He pulled her up onto the porch. "Janie has given us her room tonight."

Carrie gasped, thinking about Georgia. Robert read her thoughts.

"I already know about Georgia...or George...or whatever she wants to be called. I will admit the whole thing seems preposterous to me, but with only one night to spend with my wife, I simply don't have the energy or desire to think about it." He began to lower his head. "Can we leave that conversation for another time? We have this one night."

Carrie lifted her lips, her hands pulling his head closer. "Well then, Mr. Borden, I suggest we make it a night to remember," she whispered, smiling when he grabbed her hand and pulled her up the stairs past a dining room of smiling faces.

Chapter Eleven

Robert settled down in the shade of an oak tree and gulped water from his canteen. As much as he wanted to wash off the dust caking his face, he knew better than to waste a single drop of the precious fluid. Summer heat this intense could kill a man quickly. The number of men suffering from heat exhaustion was increasing.

"You reckon we're going to do anything but march, Captain?"

"That's a good question," Robert replied, managing a small smile as he answered Alex, a veteran soldier from Virginia who, at twenty-two years old, had many battles under his belt.

"I was kind of hoping we would stay down in the Shenandoah and take out some more of them Yankees. I hadn't figured on marching straight up into Maryland."

"I'm sure there's a reason. You'll find out soon enough."

Alex settled back on his heels and stared at him from under greasy, dusty black hair. "You were called into a meeting last night," he said. "Did they tell you nothing?"

Robert shrugged.

Alex leaned in closer. "Me and the boys would sure like to know what's going on."

"That the reason they sent you over here?"

Alex smiled. "Could be."

Robert laughed. "I can't tell you anything about General Early's plans. What I *can* tell you is that the marching is about to stop. At least for a while," he added.

"We figured maybe something would happen after we whupped them Yankees back there outside of Frederick."

"That was a solid victory," Robert agreed, though he was also quite sure Early's army couldn't stay north of the Potomac for too long.

"How come Early didn't destroy Frederick?" Alex asked. "Me and the boys figured he would set us loose."

Robert shrugged. "They paid a two hundred thousand dollar ransom to save their city. Early decided the Confederacy could use the money more than a burned town."

Alex nodded. "That makes sense. That's a lot of money."

Robert nodded, but his thoughts were spinning through what he had learned the night before. The original plan had been for Early to create enough of a crisis that Grant would have to send troops, thereby relieving the pressure the Union was putting on Lee at Petersburg, where Grant had settled into what looked to be a long siege.

Early had been so successful that the plans had expanded. Still hoping to wear the North out, Confederate leaders wanted the offensive action north of the Potomac to shock the war-weary North in an election year, assuring Lincoln would lose the presidency.

But that was only part of the plan. Lee had directed Early to capture Washington if he could—to destroy rail and telegraph communications around Baltimore, and free the thousands of prisoners held at Point Lookout in southern Maryland. Along the way, he was to gather much-needed supplies.

Robert knew it was a tall order that depended upon speed, deception and—to some degree—the weather.

"When you figure we gonna stop marching?" Alex asked. "We're ready to fight!"

Robert stared at him and was brought back to the present. "March hard today, Alex. Tell the boys we'll be done marching for a while tomorrow." He paused but saw no reason to avoid filling in one more gap. "We'll be on the outskirts of Washington."

Alex gasped, his eyes growing wide. "Washington, DC? The capital?"

Robert nodded. "I can't tell you anything else. March hard and drink a lot of water."

"Yes, sir!" Alex responded, his eyes alight with excitement as he walked away.

Robert knew he would spread the word.

Robert was on his way to the command tent when drunken laughter and loud talking split the early evening heat.

"You're looking at the soldiers that raided Montgomery Blair's house today," an officer explained, casting a sardonic look at the inebriated cluster.

Robert stared at the besotted men. "There are hundreds of them!"

"The cellar was rather full of whiskey barrels."

"Montgomery Blair? Isn't he a member of Lincoln's cabinet?"

"Yes, and his father was real big in politics until he retired and founded Silver Spring, Maryland."

"Were they captured?"

"No," came the disgusted answer. "Seems the entire clan left a few days ago for their annual summer retreat in Pennsylvania." He chuckled. "Let's just say their estates won't look quite the same when they get back!"

Robert smiled and ducked his head to enter the tent.

Early was waiting for them, his face flushed with frustration. "I had planned on launching an attack this afternoon, but our troops are too exhausted from the heat and the long march."

"Not to mention they're drunk as skunks," another officer muttered.

Early sighed. "That, too," he admitted.

"Are we attacking in the morning?" Robert asked.

Early hesitated and then shook his head. "It's too risky. We don't know how many soldiers are in that fort. I've decided to take another day for reconnaissance before we go after them."

Robert frowned but didn't voice his concern. The troops had already been delayed on their march. Waiting one more day might not matter at all...or it might mean the difference between defeat and victory.

Abby was deep in a meeting regarding her business when bells began to clang all over Washington. She ran toward an open window. "What in the world? I thought the bells were supposed to ring only when the capital was under attack." She whirled around to stare at her business associate, Mr. Patrick Hill.

"That's true, Mrs. Livingston," Patrick snapped, stuffing papers into his briefcase. "I believe it would be prudent to find out what is happening."

Minutes later, Abby was out on the porch staring around at the wild chaos surrounding her.

"The Rebels are about to attack!" she heard several women scream.

Men dashed around with white, set faces.

"Grant was so certain the South would never dare come to attack our capital," Patrick said angrily. "Now they seem to be here, and to the best of my knowledge, we have hardly any troops to stop them."

"But what about all the fortifications?" Abby protested.

"They are no good without men in them to fight," Patrick said. "It takes forty-five thousand men to fill all those forts and rifle pits. I am quite sure we have only a few hundred."

"Hundred?" Abby gasped, suddenly very frightened.

"I must go see where I can be of use." Patrick readied himself to go. "Do you have a way to get back home? When is your driver scheduled to arrive?"

"I'll take her home."

Abby turned at the sound of the familiar voice. "Matthew!" She nodded to Patrick. "I'll be fine. You go ahead. My prayers are with you." She turned into the hug Matthew had waiting for her. "What are you doing here? How do you always manage to save me?" She laughed as tears of relief filled her eyes.

"I was hoping to find you before you grabbed a gun and went off to fight." Matthew said.

"Hardly!" Abby retorted. "But, Matthew, is it really as bad as Patrick made it sound?"

"It's not good," Matthew admitted, his bright blue eyes shadowed with concern.

"How did Rebel troops get so close to Washington? I thought I was in one of the safest cities in the world."

"Well, you would be, except that it never crossed Grant's mind that Lee would be bold enough to send twenty thousand men into the North."

"Twenty thousand?" Abby gasped. She looked around, trying to make herself stay calm. "What will happen if they take the city?"

"Our soldiers are on the way now," Matthew assured her. "I came in on the boats with thousands of men. More are on the way."

"But why has Grant waited so long? Someone must have known twenty thousand Confederate soldiers were crossing Maryland."

Matthew nodded. "Grant received word from many people that General Early was invading the North, but with each message, he blindly wired back that General Early was still with Lee in Richmond. Grant refused to take it seriously."

Abby was flabbergasted. "But—"

Matthew held his finger to his lips. "It's best not to try to understand it. I've been trying for the last two months to make sense out of this war, and I still can't. I report the facts, but I can't pull anything out of them that creates a picture I can understand."

"You don't think Grant is a good general?"

Matthew shrugged. "I'm not sure what to think. I know he promised President Lincoln he would not repeat other generals' mistakes, and that he would not leave Richmond until the job is done. He's still there. He's a fighter. I'll give him that."

"But..."

"But he seems to treat our troops as if they are expendable numbers on a chart," he said. "The Rebels mow them down when he sends them into impossible situations. Then he just sends in more soldiers."

Abby looked deeply into Matthew's eyes and saw only sorrow and pain. "I'm sorry." She grasped both his hands. "This will all end, Matthew," she said. "Nothing lasts forever. No matter how horrible the war is, it will end. And then all of us can go about the job of healing our hearts and our country."

"I know," Matthew murmured. He shook his head, his weary eyes saying he didn't really know anything anymore. "It's not over yet, and I have a job to do, but not until I get you home safely."

"We'll walk," Abby said. "Trying to get a carriage through all this mess will take more time than walking."

"It's so hot," Matthew protested.

"I'll hardly melt," Abby laughed, not at all certain that was true. Hot humidity had settled on the city, along with an oppressive air of fear threatening to smother everything.

She forgot her discomfort as they walked through the clusters of people clogging the streets and sidewalks, their excited talk intensifying the chaos. Wagon after wagon full of families rolled by with belongings bulging from every possible nook and cranny.

"Refugees from the surrounding areas," Matthew explained. "They're bringing in reports of what is going on out there. Every family who saw the Rebels advancing has escaped here for safety."

"But you need to talk to them," Abby said urgently. "I'm keeping you from doing your job."

"My most important job right now is to get one of my favorite people in the world to a place of safety."

"Will there *be* a safe place if the Rebels take the city?" Abby asked. She paused in thought. "Richmond is like this all the time, isn't it? Carrie has to live with this fear every day," she murmured, her eyes wide with compassion and sudden understanding.

"I wouldn't say she's living in fear," Matthew replied. "She's ceased letting it bother her, and instead puts all her focus on the patients in the hospital. She told me that if the Union took the city, she would still have patients to care for. She's scared for Robert, but she's not scared for herself."

Abby turned and gazed south. "How I would love to see her..." The longing was so strong it was an ache that swept through her.

"Moses sends his love," Matthew said.

Abby gave a cry of delight. "Moses! He is still alive then. I've been so afraid for him. How in the world did you find each other?"

Matthew told her the story as they walked the rest of the way to the boarding house where she was staying. "I don't like how close this is to Fort Stevens," Matthew said, a deep frown bunching his eyebrows. "That's probably where they will attack."

Abby shrugged. Her fear had disappeared with his words about Carrie. "If the Rebels take the city, they take it. I will deal with whatever comes. In the meantime, I'm going to join some of the other women in making more bandages. I'm sure we will need them. It's not much, but it's all I can do right now."

She lifted her chin bravely and smiled at Matthew. "Go do your job, Matthew. If you find you can see me again while you are here, I would love that. If it's not possible, know that my thoughts and love are always with you."

Matthew hugged her again, and after a long and meaningful look, turned and strode rapidly away.

Abby watched him until he was out of sight.

⁘

"Why are we all just sitting here, Captain?" Alex asked, coming over to sit down beside Robert.

Robert had just returned from a briefing. "General Early is still trying to determine how strong the Union force is." He decided not to include the detail that every moment they delayed gave the Union more time to reinforce their troops. Robert knew he had no way of knowing what was really going on behind the walls of the fort, but he couldn't see how waiting would do them any good.

All of Washington was on alert, with bells clanging wildly all through the day and night. He knew what would have happened in Richmond if bells rang continuously that way. He couldn't imagine the citizens of the Union capital would simply wait and let the Rebel forces waltz in when they were ready.

"Why aren't they attacking?" Peter asked. "For that matter, what made them sit there all day yesterday? We wouldn't have been able to stop them if they had attacked."

Matthew shook his head. "That seems to be the question throughout this entire war. I believe Richmond could have been taken many times in the beginning of the war if the generals leading the troops had pushed their advantage and taken action."

"I think I've learned a big lesson from covering this war," Peter said.

"Such as?"

"I've spent too much of my life hesitating instead of boldly taking action. I've sat back and let life happen around me, only taking action when I thought I could be sure of success." He paused. "Not only can we never be sure of success, we can lose so many amazing opportunities because we're too afraid to act. I don't ever want to live that way again."

"I know what you mean," Matthew agreed. "When we escaped Libby Prison, I promised myself I would live to the fullest. I decided I wouldn't let life happen to me—I would go out and make life happen."

"Will you still be a correspondent when the war is over?" Peter asked.

"My dream is to find a small town somewhere and have my own newspaper," Matthew responded, a smile on his face as he envisioned it. "I've traveled around this country all I care to, and seen things I never want to see again."

Suddenly his attention was pulled away, and he turned to inspect what had distracted him. Matthew put down his field glasses after a long moment and faced Peter, who was lowering his own glasses in astonishment. "Is that President Lincoln coming up the road?"

Peter nodded his head. "Looks like it," he murmured in disbelief. "Is he really coming out onto the battlefield?"

A passing soldier overheard them and laughed. "We won't let anything happen to the president. The Rebels won't get past us," he boasted.

Matthew decided not to comment on the naiveté of the soldier's boast. The only thing certain about a battlefield was that one could never be certain of anything. He took a deep breath, knowing his job was simply to report on the events. He determined, though, to stay close to the president so he could report whatever happened.

Matthew watched as President Lincoln climbed to the top of Fort Stevens' parapet to get a clear view of the skirmishing armies. "He's crazy," Matthew muttered. "It would only take one bullet from a Confederate sharpshooter to kill him. What is he thinking?"

He and Peter gasped at the same time when a Union surgeon, standing to the side of the president, slumped to the ground with a bullet through his leg.

From somewhere close came an angry shout, "Get down, Mr. President!"

President Lincoln ducked down but didn't leave his position.

Matthew shook his head. "I wonder whether he has any idea that he's making their job harder. They don't have just an invading army to worry about, now they have to protect the President of the United States."

"I have nothing but respect for Lincoln," Peter stated, "but I agree this is ridiculous. He seems to be enjoying it!"

"Right now it's still a game to him," Matthew agreed. "I wonder whether he'll still be here when they're hauling blackened corpses off the field." Matthew knew he was losing patience with any aspect of the war. "I wonder how he would feel then." Shouts in the distance caught his attention and brought a sigh of relief.

"Here come more of our troops!" Peter exclaimed.

Dust rose from the long columns of troops marching down the road. "Finally, they're here," Matthew said with relief. "Now let's see what happens."

A sharp call from within the fort moments later sent several brigades from the Army of the Potomac marching out onto the open field. It was all military precision—flags flying, lines straight.

Matthew, carefully watching the president, could tell Lincoln loved it. Matthew shook his head but supposed he could understand. For most of the last three and a half years, the war had been all on paper—reports of victories and losses, hospitals filled with the wounded, and one problem after the other for the president to solve. Now here was an example of Union strength. The president was determined to experience it and perhaps revel in the power it revealed. Who could blame him?

Then reality sank in as hundreds of the attacking Union soldiers went down under heavy fire as the Rebels rushed out of their camp to fight. Matthew lost sight of the president as he positioned himself for a clearer view of the battlefield.

The battle was sharp and furious but relatively short-lived. By afternoon, things seemed to be at a stalemate again. Sporadic gunfire continued, but there was no sustained attack the rest of the day.

The next morning, Early was gone. He had slipped away under the cover of darkness.

⸎

"What now, Captain Borden?"

Robert looked up from pouring his coffee. "We're getting out of here," he said. "It's time to go home."

"That's it?"

"The game's up," Robert replied. "We put an awful scare into them, but we don't have enough men to do more, and Lee needs us back in the Shenandoah. A lot of the summer is still ahead of us."

He smiled up at Alex and then stood to address his men. "You can all be proud. We may not have done everything we came to do, but we did more than anyone thought was possible, and we gave Richmond a reprieve by forcing Grant to send thousands of his troops back to Washington. We showed everyone the South isn't done yet!"

"Yeah!" his men shouted loudly, their faces lighting with pride. "We showed 'em, all right!"

Robert wasn't done. "We've collected valuable supplies that will go back with us, we've got money to sustain the Confederate government, and," he paused and smiled, "we're eating better than we've eaten in a while. All in all, I think we did a good job. Hold your heads high, men!"

He smiled as all around him his men did just that. These were good men who had suffered a long march through hideous heat without complaint. They were toughened soldiers who were willing to give their all. Robert might be sick of the war, but he was proud to command these men.

Now, all they had to do was manage to get out of Maryland and cross the Potomac before anyone caught up with them.

Matthew sat on the porch with Aunt Abby and watched as groups of citizens talked quietly. The panic was gone. Relief was as thick as the humidity.

Abby fanned herself and turned to Matthew. "What did all this really mean?" she asked.

"I believe only time will tell the whole story, but I've heard many different things. London newspapers proclaimed the Confederacy seems more formidable an enemy than ever. They rightly observed Grant was caught off guard and nearly lost the capital by neglect."

"Just one day would have made such a difference," Abby murmured.

"The Rebels may never realize how easily they could have taken the city," Matthew agreed. "Their hesitancy gave our troops enough time to get here."

"How different things would be if Lincoln had been shot standing up there on the top of the fort."

Matthew nodded. He had told Aunt Abby what had happened. "Again, we'll never know what that would have meant, but I shudder to imagine it."

Abby gazed at him for a long moment. "Do you think Lincoln can be reelected?"

Matthew frowned. "I would say that right now, his political fortunes have sunk to a new low. People are sick of the war. To have almost lost the capital is more than some of them can comprehend. They are afraid this war will go on forever, destroying their loved ones and ripping families apart. There are many who believe things will change only if we have a new president."

"Do you believe the same?" Abby asked.

Matthew took a deep breath and stared out over the dome of the Capitol in the distance. "I think it's only a matter of time before the war ends, regardless of who the president is. The South will simply run out of everything at some point and have to surrender. They have hopes that if someone other than Lincoln is elected, that perhaps the South will be let go to form another country."

"You don't believe that."

"No. Too many people have paid too high a price. This war will not simply fade away with time. It will continue to burn itself out with fighting and agony. It's what comes afterwards that has me concerned about the reelection."

"Me too," Abby said fervently. "Lincoln, like any man, is not perfect, but he genuinely wants freedom for the slaves, and he genuinely wants to create a way for the country to come back together after the war is over. I don't see that same passion in any of the other candidates, nor in much of our Congress. Without Lincoln at the helm, rebuilding our country after the war could be an overwhelming task."

"I agree with you," Matthew said. "Things will have to turn around in the next few months, though, for him to have a chance. "

⁃⁌⁘⁙⁘⁌⁃

Word came two weeks later about the burning of Chambersburg, Pennsylvania. Renewed fury swept through the Union as the details filled the papers and passed from mouth to mouth.

Twenty-eight hundred Rebel cavalrymen on their way back to the South entered the town and demanded a ransom of five hundred thousand. When the town failed to raise the ransom, it was burned. Flames destroyed more than five hundred structures and left more than two thousand homeless. To make matters worse, many drunken soldiers looted homes and abused civilians.

It made no difference that good samaritans in the Rebel ranks helped some of the citizens escape, saved their valuables, and even helped douse the flames. The damage had been done.

The attack inspired a national aid campaign and renewed the battle cry to win the war.

The Union was sick of the war, but by God, they were going to win!

Chapter Twelve

"It's going to be a beautiful day," Carrie announced, throwing back the draperies so sunshine could stream into the room and bring with it a cool breeze. "When Richmond has a cool August morning from a rainstorm that lasted all night, but disappeared in time for a sunny day, we know God must be smiling on your marriage."

Janie tucked her knees to her chin and smiled broadly. "I can't believe this is happening. I'm really going to marry Clifford."

"Even though you're a strong woman?" Carrie teased. "I guess I was right after all."

Georgia laughed loudly. "Which is something you love to be!"

"Right?" Carrie asked. "Of course it is. It's a good thing it happens so often." She grinned and spun around the room. "I love weddings." She was determined to hold back thoughts of Robert. Their wedding...How long it had been since she'd seen him...

Janie saw through it and stood up to grab her hands. "It's okay to miss Robert on a day like this. Of course it's going to bring up memories. I'm so glad he is alive and back from the raid on Washington, DC. At least he's on the Confederate side again."

Carrie nodded, tears stinging her eyes. "Last night, after Father brought home the letter Robert sent from the Shenandoah Valley, it was the first night I haven't had horrible dreams." She shook her head. "Not another word about the war," she proclaimed.

She winked at Georgia and smiled at Janie. "You are not to come downstairs until the ceremony is about to start. I will come get you. Until then, you are to do nothing but pamper yourself."

"I have time to go check on my patients," Janie protested weakly, her eyes revealing her longing for a day to herself without reminders of the war.

"I told you she would say something that dumb!" Georgia sputtered.

"Good thing I know her so well," Carrie replied. She turned to Janie. "Dr. Wild and Hobbs are taking care of your patients this morning. You'll see them soon enough. May will be up shortly with your breakfast and enough hot water for a bath. And you will wear this."

Smiling broadly, Carrie reached into her closet and pulled out a dress she and her father purchased the week before. She had been appalled at the price, but nothing would stop her from giving Janie a wedding day to remember.

Janie gasped and clapped her hand to her mouth. "It's beautiful," she whispered, her hand stroking the pale yellow gown softly.

"There are no wedding gowns to be found in Richmond," Carrie apologized, "but I thought this came close. You will be beautiful!"

Janie wrapped her in a hug. "Thank you so much." Tears spilled down Janie's cheeks. "I can't believe I'm getting married without my family, but having all of you here is just as wonderful. They will get to meet Clifford when the war is over," she said.

"Yes, they will," Carrie agreed. "I'm still trying to decide, however, whether I will forgive Clifford for taking away my roommate." Her grin said she was just fine with it.

"What about me?" Georgia protested.

Carrie smiled, thrilled the three of them had become so close. "You? You're going to leave of your own accord and go back to fighting," she teased. "Even after having two such wonderful women for roommates, you're actually going to return to posing as a man." She rolled her eyes at Janie and laughed.

An instant later she grew serious, concern for Georgia outweighing the laughter. "I'm so tired of having people I love shot at!" She slapped her hand over her mouth. "I'm sorry...I said no talk about the war."

Janie smiled. "I'm not so naïve as to think I'll get through this day without war talk," she said. "Grant is pounding away at Petersburg. Sherman is camped on the doorstep of Atlanta, and who knows what is going on in the Shenandoah Valley. I'll just be content to get to the end of this day and be married. That's all it will take for me to be deliriously happy!"

Georgia reached down to pull something from under her pillow. "I reckon I have a wedding gift for you," she said shyly.

Carrie grinned, knowing what was coming. "You've been so excited about your wedding that you've missed a few things," she teased.

Janie cocked her head and eyed the book Georgia was holding. "Like what?" she demanded. "Is that a book I've wanted to read?"

"Like you're going to have time to read for a while," Carrie snorted.

Georgia laughed and opened the book. "This here was written by Elizabeth Barrett Browning." She cleared her throat and began to read.

How do I love thee? Let me count the ways.
I love thee to the depth and breadth and height
My soul can reach, when feeling out of sight
For the ends of being and ideal grace.
I love thee to the level of every day's
Most quiet need, by sun and candle-light.
I love thee freely, as men strive for right.
I love thee purely, as they turn from praise.
I love thee with the passion put to use
In my old griefs, and with my childhood's faith.
I love thee with a love I seemed to lose
With my lost saints. I love thee with the breath,
Smiles, tears, of all my life; and, if God choose,
I shall but love thee better after death.

Not a sound was made when Georgia finished reading. Her words hung in the air and then swirled with the breeze, dancing joyfully through the room. "I reckon you love Clifford that way," Georgia finished.

Janie struggled for words while tears streamed down her cheeks and a smile as bright as the sun illuminated her face. "You're reading," she finally managed to say.

"And reading beautifully!" she cried as her voice returned all the way. Jumping up, she embraced Georgia in an affectionate hug. "Thank you so much. What a wonderful wedding present!"

Janie took the book and read the passage again. "Elizabeth Barrett Browning is one of my favorite poets, and I've always dreamed of having a husband I could feel this way about. I finally do," she whispered, her face glowing. She glanced up at Georgia. "I'm so proud of you."

Georgia flushed bright red, but nothing could dim the glow of pride on her face. "Once you get the hang of it, reading is right easy," she said modestly, but then shook her head with frustration. "It's the talking thing I'll have to work on some more. If I could just read everything I say, I wouldn't have to worry about whether I sound right."

"Oh, Georgia, you've come so far," Carrie replied. "I told you in the beginning that it wouldn't take you long to learn because you're so smart. Anyone intelligent enough to fool the army for as long as you have can do anything. You remember that."

May entered the room with a breakfast tray. "You two girls get out of dis here room," she scolded. "Your breakfast gettin' cold down on the table and Miss Janie needin' pamperin' time."

Georgia moved to leave, but then turned back around. "You know how to read, May?"

May stared at her in astonishment. "Where I gonna learn how to do a thing like dat?" she demanded.

"I've been learning," Georgia said eagerly. "I reckon it will be a few more weeks before I get cleared to go back to fighting. I could teach you how," she offered.

May's eyes lit up, but she shook her head. "Can't be doin' nothin' like dat," she muttered, not meeting Carrie's eyes.

"Of course you can," Carrie said. "It's only a matter of time before you're free, May. Those stupid laws about slaves not reading are just that—stupid! You need to know how to read to live in this new world."

She turned to Georgia. "It would be wonderful for you to teach May everything you're learning. She'll have plenty of time in between household chores."

May stared at Carrie with something approaching awe. "Thank ya, Miss Carrie. I reckon readin' be a mighty fine thing." She paused and smiled slightly. "I suppose it be okay for me to teach Micah what I learn?"

Carrie laughed and nodded. "That would be perfect." She was no longer concerned about her father objecting, and she knew both May and Micah would not let it get in the way of their work.

She grabbed Georgia's hand and pulled her toward the door. "Let's go while Janie's food is still hot, and while there is still any food on the table for us!"

Laughing, they made their way to the dining room.

Pastor Anthony arrived shortly after the noon meal. "Is Janie still determined to get married in the hospital ward?"

Carrie nodded, alarmed at the pasty pallor of his skin and the dullness in his eyes. She pulled him forward to sit down in a chair and then sent May to bring a cold drink and some cornbread. "Are you okay, Pastor Anthony?" she asked, leaning down to put a practiced hand on his forehead.

"I'm fine," he insisted, his voice no longer strong and robust.

Carrie's thoughts flew to the concern Jeremy had expressed a couple months before. The few times she had made it to the hospital, Pastor Anthony hadn't been there. She opened her mouth to ask more questions, but he waved them away.

"She's still determined to get married in the hospital?"

Carrie nodded. "She wants her patients to be a part of it. So does Clifford. He's going to be released today, but all his fellow soldiers have watched the romance between him and Janie. He doesn't want to cheat them out of the actual wedding."

Pastor Anthony nodded. "Those patients need all the good moments they can get, and they need to see that sometimes love wins." He thought back. "I thought the same thing when I performed the ceremony for your other friend at the hospital."

"Yes, Louisa Blackwell." Carrie smiled as she remembered. "We almost lost her husband, Perry, but he pulled through. I'm convinced Louisa's care for him played a big part in it."

"They moved down around Atlanta?"

"Yes," Carrie said with a frown. "I'm worried about them."

"You should be. Sherman's men have Atlanta under siege."

Heaviness seemed to blow in the window. "There is nothing I can do about that right now. What I *can* do is make sure Janie has a wonderful day. That's what I intend to do."

"Still determined to hold on to the good things," Pastor Anthony said lightly.

Carrie stared into his eyes and was disturbed by the dullness she saw there. She silently berated herself that she hadn't taken Jeremy's concern more seriously. Pastor Anthony was not well. Something was sapping his spirit.

"More determined than ever," she replied. "I'm learning it's my choice how I live my life, but it's also my choice how I see my life. I'm doing everything I can to choose to live each day looking for all the joy I can. Sometimes I have to look pretty hard, but I always find something to be grateful for."

Pastor Anthony stared at her, a brief spark igniting in his eyes. "Choice," he murmured. "Yes, I suppose all of life is about choice."

Carrie moved to the door as Spencer pulled the carriage up to the house, and then she went up to get Janie. Carrie found the bride-to-be whirling in front of the mirror, her arms spread wide with a glorious smile on her face. Now was certainly not the time to share her concerns about Pastor Anthony.

Carrie clapped her hands as she moved into the room. "You look absolutely beautiful!" She took Janie's hands in her own and gazed at her lovingly. "You're radiant. Clifford Saunders is a very lucky man."

Janie grinned. "I'm the lucky one. I still can't believe he loves me."

Carrie snorted. "Every man in your ward is in love with you. Clifford just got lucky." She pulled Janie toward the door. "Your magic carriage awaits you, Miss Winthrop. When you return in it, you will have another name."

"And another room," Janie said demurely, her eyes sparkling with excitement. "I'm so glad one of the boarders left. It was kind of your father to give us the room."

"Kind? He knows I would have never forgiven him if you had to leave this house," she said with a laugh. "He was simply being wise." She sobered and pushed aside the thought of Janie's eventual departure at the end of the war. Today was a day for joy. It was a day for *choosing...*

Laughing, the two friends went down the stairs. Carrie gave a cry of delight when her father stepped in the front door. "You're home! I thought you wouldn't be able to make it."

Thomas smiled and pulled Janie into a hug. "I told the State Department they would have to do without me, because my beautiful second daughter is getting married and I need to give her away."

Janie brushed at the tears in her eyes. "Thank you," she whispered. "It means so much..."

Thomas tucked her hand into the crook of his arm and led her out to the carriage. Carrie, a broad smile wreathing her face, followed with Pastor Anthony.

~·❦·~

Cheers and congratulations rang inside the hospital as Pastor Anthony announced Clifford and Janie man and wife.

"You finally got her, old man!" one patient yelled.

"I can't believe she was crazy enough to take your name!" another recuperating soldier teased.

"When you get tired of that ugly mutt, I'll be here waiting," a young man promised Janie with a laugh.

When the newlyweds reached the door of the tent and Clifford turned around, the men suddenly stopped talking. An awkward silence fell over the building. Clifford stood still, his deep brown eyes sweeping over every man in the building. "Thank you," he finally said. "I wouldn't have made it through these last months without all of you."

Carrie gazed around the room and watched emotions play over the faces of every man there.

One man finally broke through the emotion. "Well, you remember that when I need a lawyer after the war and come knocking on your door!"

"I figure we at least deserve family rates," another shouted, bringing a fresh wave of laughter.

Clifford and Janie, laughing and waving, moved out to the carriage and headed back for the house. Privacy for newlyweds was an unheard of luxury in crowded Richmond, but at least the two would have several hours in their wing of the house before the rest of the boarders came home from work. Then, there was a plan in place to keep those men in the parlor as long as possible. Carrie had done all she could do to give the couple some time.

Carrie took her father's arm and reached over to put her other hand through Pastor Anthony's. "I'll have the two best escorts in town to take me back to the house," she said. She had been about to say she would like to swing by her ward to check on her patients, but the strained look and the sheen of sweat on Pastor Anthony's face, in spite of a cool breeze, forced the words back. Her concern flared up anew for him.

"I must head back to the church," Pastor Anthony replied. "I have much to do."

"And it won't wait for you to have some lunch?" Carrie asked. When he opened his mouth to protest, she stopped in the middle of the road and put both hands on her hips. "This is not a matter for discussion, Pastor. I am the doctor at your hospital. Right now, I am giving you doctor's orders. You are not going anywhere until you have some food. If you get sick, everyone in your congregation will suffer."

"I'm fine," Pastor Anthony protested, but tucked her hand back in his arm and continued to walk down the hill toward the house. "I suppose I can eat some lunch."

Carrie exchanged a long look with her father. She could tell he was as concerned as she was—that he, too, was remembering what Jeremy had said.

May bustled around the kitchen and came out with a tray of fresh collard greens, cornbread and sliced tomatoes. Carrie was so grateful for the large garden she had created in the backyard. Everyone took turns in the garden, and they also took great pride in it. It was going a long way in providing healthy food for the many people in their house. Any extras were sent to the black hospital.

Last year, there had not been enough for canning. The garden was now twice as big, and May had already set aside a large supply of filled canning jars for the winter. Carrie sensed it was going to be a hard winter. More than that, Old Sarah had taught her to read the signs at the same time she'd taught her how to use the herbs and plants. The husks on the corn were thicker than usual, and the dogwoods were heavier with berries than she had seen in a long time. Both of those things indicated a long, cold winter. She would do the best she could to prepare for it.

"Thank you, May," Pastor Anthony said, his eyes lighting up when he bit into the juicy tomato.

"You welcome, Pastor," May responded. "Does a body good to see her food ate. You do right good work down at dat church. I be honored to feed you."

Pastor Anthony smiled warmly and cut into another piece of cornbread.

Silence reigned over the table while the food was enjoyed. Sounds of trains, carriages and wagons rolled in through the windows, but there was also peace.

Thomas was the first to speak. "Will I be shot if I speak of war news?"

Carrie smiled, knowing the question was directed at her. "Janie is married and with her new husband. You have my permission to talk about anything you want."

"I fear for Atlanta," Thomas said.

Pastor Anthony finished the last of his tomatoes and looked up. "I had heard the Confederate cavalry was holding Sherman's army back."

"So far," Thomas agreed. "Now Sherman has changed his tactics. He seems to know he can't take the city in a direct assault, so he has taken his entire army and is swinging them in a broad flanking maneuver to the west."

"For what purpose?" Carrie asked, renewed concern for Louisa and Perry sharpening her tone.

Thomas gazed out the window for a long moment. "No one will really know until he actually does it, but there is speculation he is heading for the railroad tracks around Macon. Once Hood's supply lines are completely severed, our troops will be forced to leave the city." His voice sharpened. "They simply must hold it. Atlanta is an important rail hub and industrial center for the Confederacy. If we lose it..."

Carrie reached out to take her father's hand when his voice trailed off, though she remained silent. There was nothing she could say. There was no need to say she was certain the war was coming to an end and that it would mean defeat for the South. Let her father hold on to hope. Reality would come soon enough.

"Any word from the Shenandoah?" Pastor Anthony asked.

Thomas frowned again. "General Early has been holding his own since he brought his troops back from Maryland." He scowled. "Our troops that burned Chambersburg were ambushed by Union cavalry and badly defeated. Everyone is back in Virginia now."

Carrie barely listened. She had lost all interest in the war or its battles unless they directly involved Robert. She knew he had not been with the cavalry that destroyed Chambersburg. She was confident he was safer than if he was behind the lines in Petersburg trying to hold off Grant. She would have to content herself with that.

"I've heard Grant is replacing General Hunter up in the Shenandoah with General Sheridan."

There was something in her father's voice that caught Carrie's attention. "What does that mean?"

Her father avoided her eyes as he looked out the window again. He seemed to choose his words carefully. "Sheridan has the reputation for being very aggressive. He was the one who led the raid that resulted in the death of J.E.B. Stuart." Thomas paused. "Grant has chosen him because he intends to destroy the Shenandoah Valley," his voice quiet with controlled anger.

"You believe that?" Pastor Anthony asked.

Thomas nodded heavily. "I believe he'll move slowly because Lincoln has not been reelected yet, but it's going to be a brutal campaign."

"Lincoln was nominated by his party," Pastor Anthony pointed out.

"Yes, but the North is still sick of the war. It's our only hope..."

"That Lincoln won't be reelected?" Carrie asked, thinking about something Robert had said earlier in the spring.

"Yes. It's possible that if we can hold on through the fall, and if the North refuses to elect Lincoln again, that they'll decide the cost is too high and give us our freedom."

Thomas' words hung heavily in the air as the three contemplated what it might mean.

༄ ༄ ༄

Carrie was happy to have an evening free to go to the black hospital. She was grateful for this year's thriving vegetable gardens that kept most sickness at bay. She had most of the volunteer nursing staff canning vegetables from the garden and teaching others throughout the community to do the same thing. She knew what a hard winter would do if the people were also hungry.

Only a handful of patients needed her help tonight. She smiled easily as she dispensed herbs and listened to their talk.

"Miss Carrie! Miss Carrie!"

Carrie looked up in alarm as Bella, one of the volunteer nurses, ran into the hospital, her eyes wide with alarm. "What's wrong?" she asked, taking her arm.

Bella gulped, leaned double and fought to get her breath before finally straightening. "It's Pastor Anthony. Somethin' be real wrong. Jeremy sent me for you."

Carrie grabbed her bag and headed out the door. "Come with me, Bella."

Spencer was already in the carriage waiting for her. "I heard 'bout Pastor Anthony. We'll be at his house in a couple minutes."

Carrie swung out of the carriage and ran up the walk before it had even stopped.

Jeremy met her at the door. "I'm not usually home during the day, but something..." He looked into the bedroom where a simple bed was the only piece of furniture. "My father is very sick. He has a burning fever and is having trouble breathing."

Carrie nodded and pushed past him.

Pastor Anthony managed a very weak smile. "I guess you were right."

"I'd rather not be right," Carrie said gently, alarmed by the bright flush on his face and his rapid breathing. "Are you hurting anywhere?"

"My chest," Pastor Anthony whispered weakly. "The pain has been coming and going for a while, but this time it's really bad."

"You've been hurting like this for a while?" Carrie gasped. "Why..."

Pastor Anthony held up his hand to stop her. "You don't have to tell me I was unwise..." His words broke off when he gasped. His face whitened as a new wave of pain swept through him, and he fell back against the pillows gasping for breath.

"Carrie..."

Carrie shook her head at Jeremy. "Not now. Give me my bag." She pulled out the stethoscope, held it to Pastor Anthony's chest and listened carefully, trying to hide her grave concern for Jeremy's sake.

She turned to Bella and was glad she had thought to bring her. "Bathe his face with cool water. If he wants water, give it to him. Do *not* let him move out of this bed." She stared down at her patient and turned back to Bella. "Do you think you can do that? He can be rather stubborn," she said.

"You leave him to me, Miss Carrie. That man only gonna be movin' over my dead body!"

Carrie's lips turned into a quirk of a smile before she motioned to Jeremy and led him outside the house to the street.

"It's bad," Jeremy said quietly.

Carrie nodded. "It's his heart."

"Can you do anything?"

"I will try, but he may have waited too long," she admitted, berating herself that she had let this happen.

Jeremy read her thoughts. "It's not your fault, Carrie. I tried to get him to tell you he wasn't feeling well, but he refused. You know how stubborn he can be. He even hid it from me most of the time. He made me promise not to say anything. I was afraid refusing would create even more stress."

Carrie did indeed know about Pastor Anthony's demanded promises. Her mind turned to solutions. "I'll mix up a solution of Lily of the Valley. It strengthens the heart, but it's also important he not get too much. I'll teach Bella how to give it to him. No one but her is to administer it," she ordered. "Is that clear?"

"Certainly," Jeremy agreed, "but isn't there something I can do?"

Carrie hesitated and gazed at him.

"It's that bad?"

Carrie knew the truth was best. "I'm sorry. His heart is in very bad condition. I will do all I can, but I think the best thing you can do for your father is keep him quiet and spend as much time with him as you can."

"Visitors?"

"Only one at a time and only a few a day. Not seeing his people will only cause him more distress." She didn't add that it would be their chance to tell him goodbye. Her voice softened as she saw the misery in Jeremy's eyes. "God still works miracles," she said gently. "I see them every day. If anyone deserves a miracle, it is your father."

Jeremy forced a smile and moved back toward the house. "I'll tell Bella you'll be back soon with the Lily of the Valley mixture."

Neither Spencer nor Carrie said a word as the carriage moved through the night toward the house. Alone with her thoughts, Carrie could admit how damaged Pastor Anthony's heart was. *The long hours... The skipped meals... The burden of caring for his congregation...* It had all taken its toll on his tender, giving heart.

Tears blurred Carrie's vision as she leaned her head back against the carriage seat.

All she could do was try.

Chapter Thirteen

"Perry Appleton, you are not going to fight again! I simply won't have it." Tears filled Louisa's blue eyes as she took her stance in front of the door to their white clapboard house, her blonde hair lit like a halo by the sun streaming through the windows. She looked every bit like an avenging angel. "You're all I have left," she gasped. *"You're all I have left..."*

Louisa could hardly breathe as pain ripped through her heart. She had lost her home, her father, her beloved brother. And now her mother, an empty shell of her former vibrant self, lay wasting away in a bedroom upstairs. Louisa had fought not to give up on life, not to give in to bitterness. Her love for Perry, along with his love for her, had saved her.

She gripped his hands as she pleaded. "Don't you understand? I love you so much. I simply can't lose you. I can't..."

Perry gazed down at her with deep love in his eyes, which were as vividly blue as hers. His dark blond hair curled just above his collar. He gripped her hands tightly. "Louisa, I have to go. The Yankees will take Atlanta."

"They can have this old city," Louisa cried. "They can have every building, every round of ammunition, every morsel of food. They *cannot* have my husband!"

Her protests were drowned out by more mortars falling into the city. Explosions rocked the house, but still she refused to move.

"And your mother?" Perry asked, still trying to be reasonable. "Will you allow the Yankees to blow the house up?"

"Putting yourself out there to be killed is not going to stop the Yankees," Louisa argued, knowing she was right. "You know that as well as I do. It's only a matter of time before they take Atlanta," she yelled over the noise. "I'm sorry we left the farm and came here." Images of their charming little farm tucked away in a mountain valley danced before her eyes. For all she knew, it was already destroyed.

Perry and Louisa had joined the thousands who streamed into Atlanta looking for refuge. But because it was not safe to move her mother again, they had not followed the thousands who then fled the city when it offered no safety. Atlanta had become a city under constant bombardment.

Perry stared down at the floor. "I thought you and your mother would be safer here," he muttered.

"Of course you did. Both of us did," Louisa said instantly, raising his head with hers to meet his eyes. "And we will be fine here—as long as you don't go off to fight." Her voice became defiant again. "I won't hear of it." She stopped short of ridiculing his desire to go back to battle with only one leg. Every man had a right to his pride. Even though Perry was quite adept with his wooden stump, there were limits.

She stepped closer and laid her head on his chest. "Please don't leave me. I need you. Our baby and I need you." She knew she was fighting dirty when she put her hand over her newly swelling stomach, but she also knew she would do anything to keep him home. "If something were to happen, how would I get Mama out of here? How will I take care of our baby?"

"But all the men are fighting!"

Louisa hid her smile. She knew she was winning this battle. He was still protesting, but his protestations had lost all their fire. "Then let them fight. You have paid all you're going to pay for this war. You gave them your leg. You will *not* give them your life." She could tell the instant he gave in by the look of relief on his face.

She and her husband never talked about the horrid nightmares that covered him with soaking sweat every night. She never told him how many nights she went without sleep and stroked his head so he could rest. Perry never acknowledged, and she never pressed him to talk about, the pain that still gripped him from his injury.

Carrie Borden, her childhood friend, had saved Perry's life and then allowed her to care for him until they could marry. Louisa's love for Perry had saved her. She hid her sigh of relief as she led him into the kitchen for a glass of water. Now that he had given up the insane idea of fighting, she wanted to know more.

"What is Sherman doing now?" she asked calmly.

"I was wondering how long it would take for one ugly, red-headed journalist to make it down to the real action!" Matthew laughed as he settled next to Peter. "They sent me down to Petersburg for a few days but decided the same news about a stalemate wouldn't be flattering for Lincoln. They sent me down here instead, hoping something more promising would happen."

"How is the siege of Petersburg going?" Peter asked, taking a sip of water from his canteen as he cooked bacon over the fire. The end of August in Georgia was brutally hot.

"I wouldn't call it a siege," Matthew said. "Petersburg is not surrounded, and its supply lines aren't cut off. The Confederates are still getting supplies in from the Shenandoah Valley through Richmond. They're hurting, but they're still very much alive."

"Must be driving General Lee almost mad," Peter said with a smirk. "He's used to calling the shots, but now his army has nowhere to go and no way to maneuver. I wonder whether he knows it's just a matter of time."

"If he knows it, he'll never admit it," Matthew observed. "As long as there is one chance in a million, the man will fight. It's in his genes."

"What's happening there?"

"Oh, Grant is trying to breach Lee's entrenchments," Matthew said. "He's having about as much success as he's had all summer. So now he's digging his own. They just keep getting longer." He shrugged. "It's not a bad plan, and it will wear out the Confederacy in time, but I know it's not the glorious victory Grant hoped for."

"He's general-in-chief of the Union forces," Peter replied. "He'll have a glorious victory to report soon. You were about to miss all the excitement."

"Yeah? What's happening down here?"

"Well, from the looks of things, both armies are lying still, like two savage dogs watching one another to see how and where the other will attack."

"From the *looks* of things?"

"Yes," Peter said with a grin. "Everything looks the same from the Rebels' view, but they're not seeing a big chunk of this army that has moved way back and is circling around to cut the railroad around Macon. Sherman has most of his army on the move."

Matthew whistled. "That will completely cut off the Confederacy's transportation link and all their supplies."

Peter nodded.

"So everyone is just sitting here?"

"Oh, they're making the Rebels think we might still attack at any time."

A mortar whistled overhead. Matthew threw himself onto the ground and heard the whistle as it passed overhead. He heard it explode about a hundred feet away and looked up to see the smoldering remains of a tree. What astonished him the most, though, was seeing Peter lounging in his chair and laughing at him.

"You think that's funny?" Matthew sputtered. "We both could have been killed! Does that go on all the time?"

"Pretty much," Peter said easily. "We've learned how to read the music. That wasn't one to worry about."

Matthew stared at him, wondering if the strain of the war had finally made his friend lose his mind. "Read the music?"

Peter laughed harder, then took a breath, and explained. "We have been hearing those shells ever since we got here. I finally figured out the whistle of the shells vary through an entire octave. If it's traveling very fast, it sounds in a high key. If it heads our way more slowly, then it gives you a bass note. Listen to it tonight. You'll hear a whole tune from *do* to *ti*, with sharps and flats now and then."

"Fascinating," Matthew muttered, certain Peter had finally lost it. "And this is important why?"

Peter grinned. "That shell that went over was playing on the higher notes. I knew it would pass right over us. It's the ones that strike a bass note that you have to worry about. That means it's going to fall short or land right among us."

"What do you do if you hear the bass?" Matthew asked.

"Pray."

Matthew looked at him and managed a smile. "I believe I'll start praying now that I hear only high notes."

"That would be good," Peter said calmly. "The bacon is ready. Want some?"

Matthew looked around as they ate. "Everyone seems pretty relaxed."

"They are. They've had two pitched battles that produced casualties for both sides, but for the most part everyone is sitting around while they lob shells at each other." He gave a deep sigh. "Oh, some of the shells do their job. We've lost more men than I care to think about, but you learn how to block it out and live your life." His eyes said the strain was getting to him, but the smile on his face said he wouldn't give in to the fear.

Matthew decided to change the subject. "How did the battles go?"

"The Confederates lost heavily each time. Sure, we lost our share, too, but it's nothing like what went on up at Richmond."

"I hope to God not," Matthew muttered.

"It was a long three-month campaign for these soldiers," Peter continued. "They did a lot of marching. They're pretty happy to be in camp for a while. They need a rest."

"You're sure Atlanta will be taken?"

"Hood isn't Lee," Peter said, "and Sherman is nobody's fool. I predict the city will fall within the next couple days. You can't tell by looking around, but when that railroad is cut, Hood won't have much of a choice. He'll have to surrender or leave."

"You sure you want to go out there?"

Matthew stared out at the picket lines and then looked over at the soldier, still a teenager, carrying his rifle and a smug grin. He knew his editors would love a story from the trenches surrounding Atlanta, but he could admit to second thoughts.

"It ain't that bad, Mr. Justin."

"What's your name?" It wouldn't hurt to ask some questions while he was making up his mind whether he wanted to risk his life again for a story.

"Brady Kremer. I'm from up in Massachusetts."

"How you handling the heat down here?" Matthew asked, grinning.

"Once I get back to Massachusetts, I don't intend to *ever* spend another second in the South."

Matthew laughed. "The summers are brutal," he agreed, feeling suddenly embarrassed that a pimple-faced kid was telling him he didn't have to be afraid. Fear or not, he still had a healthy ego. Nodding toward the pits, he said, "You ready?"

Brady grinned. "Keep real low and jump into the pit right behind me. We wait until night so we won't be such a good target, but there can't be more than twenty feet or so between us and the Rebel pits. You want to move real fast."

Matthew was glad Brady couldn't see his face go white. *Twenty feet?*

"Move!" Brady said quietly as he leaned over and dashed through the darkness.

Matthew was right behind him and dropped instantly into the same pit he saw Brady disappear into. He started to take a breath of relief until he felt himself sucked into mud and water up to his thighs, which made him crouch at his waist to keep his head below the edge of the pit. "What in the?"

"*Shh...*" one of the soldiers cautioned him. "Won't be too good if you give away our position. We can talk down here, but we find it works best if we whisper. You're more likely to stay alive that way."

"Do you always stand in a lake?" Matthew whispered back, glad that at least the water was warm.

Brady chuckled quietly. "We've had some rain," he admitted. "It ain't got nowhere to go because of all this good red Georgia clay, so it fills up our pits."

Matthew stared around at the five men sharing his pit. "You can't stand up. You can't sit down. What do you do?"

"We scrunch," Brady offered. "It ain't the most comfortable thing, but it's better than getting shot."

Matthew decided getting a story would take his mind off how uncomfortable he was. Whispering, he asked the nearest soldier, "What's your name?"

"Paul Maltz." Anticipating Matthew's next questions he added, "I'm from a small town up in Vermont. I have a small maple syrup farm up there. I signed up at the beginning of the war."

"You re-enlisted in June?"

"Yes. I've stayed alive this long. I figure I want to be a part of it ending," he said, his voice confident. "Me and the boys don't figure it can last much longer, especially with General Sherman and Grant running things." The soldier stared out into the darkness and then turned back to Matthew. "The last three months have been real rough, but we've done what we set out to do."

"How do you feel about slavery?" Matthew asked, suddenly deciding to take the story in a different direction.

"Slavery?"

Matthew could tell the question puzzled the soldier. "The slaves will all be freed when the war is over if the Union wins. You're serving in an army with over one hundred thousand black soldiers. Does that play a role in how you think about the war?"

Paul shrugged. "I can't say it does. I never thought much about slavery because we never owned any, and I never knew anyone who did. We always did what needed doing ourselves. I joined up at the beginning of the war because I believe in the United States of America. My granddaddy was just a boy during the Revolution. He lost his father and his brother. I figure if having the country was worth fighting for, that it only made sense to keep it."

Everyone jerked to attention when a spatter of gunfire kicked up the dirt around their pit, but they relaxed when quiet returned. Matthew could tell the men were used to it, so he focused on hiding his fear by keeping his breathing steady.

"Slavery?" Paul continued. "It's not why I started to fight, but I suppose everyone deserves to be free. The black soldiers I've been fighting with are good soldiers. I've heard all those arguments about blacks being less than whites, and not being able to take care of themselves without white people. I figure that's a bunch of hogwash."

A murmur of agreement gave Matthew hope for the future. One lone voice caused him concern.

"I don't reckon they oughta be slaves," one man growled into the darkness, "but that don't mean they're the same as us. When this war is over, they've got to know their place."

"Their place?" Matthew asked.

"They might be free, but they will never be equal," he stated. "They should not be allowed to have the same freedoms we do. They might be able to take care of themselves, and I reckon they can fight pretty good, but white people will always be better than them. That's the way it is."

His sentence broke off when a shell whistled over their heads. Matthew listened carefully, recognized the bass note, and tensed, poking his head up a little to look back toward the lines. He watched the shell hit one of the supply wagons and explode on impact. Screams indicated more than the wagon was hit.

Cheers from the Rebel side of the lines rent the night but faded as soldiers popped up from muddy pits all around and fired at the Rebel side, yelling taunts as they did. Matthew ducked down, grateful for the pit full of mud and water that kept him from becoming a Rebel's target.

A figure emerged from the shadows, leaned down to whisper to Brady, and sprinted off, melting into the darkness once again.

Brady exchanged quiet words with the pit leader and grinned down at Matthew. "Having a good time, Mr. Justin?"

Matthew managed to grin back. "I figure I have the easy job here, Brady."

"I reckon you do." Brady fired a few more rounds and crouched beside him again. "There probably will be a lot more firing, so I don't know that you'll be able to talk to many more men. I hear we're supposed to keep things hopping tonight."

"Why?"

Brady shrugged. "That would be a question I wouldn't expect an answer to," he said. "The order came down, so I figure Sherman is up to something, but he won't bother to tell me about it."

Brady glanced around at all the men during a brief lull. "I figure Matthew needs to get back behind the lines, fellas."

The soldier turned back to Matthew. "We will rip at the Rebel lines to give you some time to get back behind our lines. When we stand up and start firing, you run like crazy."

Matthew nodded, waited for Brady's hand signal, then crawled out of the muddy hole and took off running.

⁂

Thomas Cromwell strode through the door and tossed a paper onto the dining room table where everyone was seated. "There is hope," he announced with relief.

Carrie waited for him to explain, wondering if his news would give her more information about Robert in the Shenandoah.

"The Atlanta defenses are strong." He pointed at the paper. "The *Richmond Enquirer* reports Sherman is in bad shape and unable to get past our defenses. Atlanta will hold."

"Wonderful!" one of the boarders exclaimed. "At some point he'll get tired of losing, just like Grant will get tired of hammering away at Petersburg, and they will leave us alone."

Thomas nodded. "Lincoln's campaign is in trouble. If McClellan wins the election, we believe there is a great chance he will end the war and let us have our freedom. We have to hang on. If we can make it to the election..."

Louisa was startled when Perry burst through the door. The sound of exploding shells had covered the sound of his stump on the porch. "What is it?" she asked, looking up from where she was rolling biscuits.

"I'm afraid it's over," Perry exclaimed. "Hood was aware Sherman would try to destroy the railroad at Macon, so he sent out General Hardee with two corps." His mouth tightened.

Louisa watched him carefully, knowing the next news would not be good. She thought briefly of the idyllic years she spent as a child on Blackwell Plantation. She had been so certain secession would solve all Southern woes. Louisa was convinced it would be a short war, and ridiculed Carrie when she suggested the war would be a horrible thing. The last three years had taught Louisa many bitter lessons.

Perry was silent so long she felt compelled to say something. "It didn't go well?"

"Sherman had almost his entire infantry with him. They smashed Hardee's army and completely destroyed the railroad. They melted railroad ties in big bonfires and wrapped them around trees."

Louisa forced herself to take a deep breath. Panic would do no good. They could not leave without her mother. "What happens now?"

Perry looked at her with admiration. "You've become a very strong woman," he said.

Louisa smiled. "Circumstances seem to call for it. My greatest prayer is that I will not give up on my life as my mother has."

Perry gave her a tender look and then answered her question. "Hood is evacuating the city tonight. It's either evacuate or surrender his army. He's leaving with the hope that he can pull Sherman away from the city to fight again."

"I see..." Louisa waited, knowing there was more.

"He's opening all the stores to distribute any supplies he has left so Sherman can't have access to them. I hired a wagon to bring us bags of flour and some other supplies. There are already long lines of people."

"You think Sherman will let us stay in the city?"

"I don't know." Perry hesitated, his expression saying he knew his next words would upset her. "Hood has ordered the train cars and ammunition depot be set ablaze."

"He's going to blow it all up?" Louisa cried. "What will happen to the people who live near there? It will kill them!"

"He's ordered an evacuation of everyone within a half mile of the depots," he hastened to assure her.

"So instead, they'll lose their homes and everything they can't carry," Louisa said. "How kind!"

"If it helps to know, everyone handled it well."

Louisa looked at him sharply.

"I was part of the team sent out to tell residents they had to leave. Some of our troops passed by while they were packing, but everyone stopped to come out onto the streets and cheer them."

Louisa nodded. "I do know our soldiers did everything they could to save the city," she said. "Are there plans to control the burning, or will the whole city be left to go up in flames?" she asked, determined to remain calm.

"There will be men to control it," Perry assured her.

※ ※ ※

The explosions began late that night. Reverberations could be heard for miles. Nearby homes were destroyed. Windows were blown out of every home within a half-mile radius. Hood's entire eighty-car munitions train was completely destroyed. The only remains were metal wheels that glowed strangely in the wild orange flames and reflected back the terror of the night.

Louisa stood on the porch, Perry's arm wrapped around her tightly.

"Your mother?" Perry asked.

Louisa glanced at him sadly. "When I told her what was happening, she merely looked away and said nothing. She gets thinner every day. Her face is taking on the look of a starved person. I can barely get her to eat or drink."

"She gave up a long time ago," Perry murmured.

Louisa wiped at her tears. "I so hoped I could bring her back to life—that a new beginning would make her care about life again."

"The only life she cared about was Blackwell Plantation," Perry said gently, pulling her even closer. "Your mother doesn't have your strength, Louisa."

"She was calling for Daddy and Nathan in her sleep last night," Louisa admitted. "There was even a happy look on her face for a few minutes. It's the happiest I've seen her in so long...and she was asleep."

Perry remained silent, holding her.

"We can't leave the city, you know," Louisa said. "Mama would never survive the move."

Perry nodded. "I know. We'll figure it out."

"Will Sherman allow anyone to stay?"

"We don't know yet. The mayor is going out tomorrow to surrender the city. We'll find out more soon."

Matthew finished his wire and settled back to stare at Peter. "It's sent."

"Mine, too."

Atlanta has fallen and is now in Union hands. Story to follow.

Matthew stared off into the distance. "This will save Lincoln's election," he said quietly. "Sherman didn't do everything he set out to do..."

"Like destroy Hood's army?"

"Right, but he has secured Atlanta for the Union."

"The thing Sherman probably cares the least about. He's the most apolitical man I know. All he cares about is winning the war," Peter replied.

Matthew shrugged. "Whether he cares or not, the fall of Atlanta will be the kind of news people want. It's something positive that says this whole war effort is worth it."

"You sound less than enthusiastic," Peter observed.

Matthew gazed at him. "I really don't know what I am," he finally murmured. "I'd like to say I think all of this has been worth it. I'd like to say that when this war is finally over, things will go back to normal."

Peter held up his hand. "Say no more. I'm with you. When this war finally does end, it's not really going to *end* anything. Most people don't want to acknowledge it, but it's simply going to open a new chapter of struggle and change."

"I wonder how many more people have to die before it's over," Matthew said. "How many more towns will be destroyed? How much more of our country will be decimated before it is done?" He paused. "The only good I can see from all this is the reelection of Lincoln. I still believe he's the only man who can lead our country out of this mess and into a new beginning."

***

Perry pushed through the door as Louisa made her way down the stairs.

"I'm afraid I have terrible news," he said, reaching for her hand. "Sherman is demanding all citizens leave the city. There are to be no exceptions."

He paused, but Louisa still just looked at him.

"I appealed to the mayor and told him about your mother, but he reaffirmed there are to be no exceptions." He took a deep breath. "We'll figure it out. I'm sure we can find a way to transport your mother from the city."

Louisa's complete silence finally registered. As did the blank look when she turned to stare out the window.

"Honey?" Perry reached for her hand, shocked to find it slack and cold. "Louisa," he said more urgently, turning her to face him. "What is it?"

Louisa glanced at the stairs briefly and then stared up at him. "Mama," she whispered. "You won't have to worry about moving her." She gasped and allowed the tears to fill her eyes. "Mama is dead, Perry. She's gone to be with Daddy and Nathan."

Perry drew her close as sobs wracked her body. He said nothing, rocking her silently and letting her sob out her grief.

When her tears finally stopped, he lifted her chin so her eyes would meet his. "We're going home, honey. We're leaving Atlanta, and we're going home. We'll deal with what we find when we get there.

"Home," Louisa whispered, her hand resting on her belly. "Home."

Chapter Fourteen

Rose could barely contain her happiness. She grasped the letter in her hands, hurried back to the cabin, and laughed when she saw June on the porch. *Wait until June found out!*

"It's way too hot to walk that fast," June observed, wiping her face with a cloth as she hid from the sun under the narrow overhang of their porch covering. Both boys were asleep on a blanket she had laid on the porch to escape the stifling heat of the cabin. She peered at Rose harder. "You don't seem too upset, so it must not be bad news."

Rose waved the envelope in the air. "I got a letter from Moses!"

June smiled broadly. "How's that brother of mine doing?"

"He's doing fine," Rose said joyfully. "The hard fighting for Richmond is over right now. Our soldiers have Richmond under siege. The conditions aren't pleasant, but they're better than they were."

June stared at her and cocked her head. "And that makes you happy? What about Carrie?"

Rose nodded and frowned. "I absolutely hate to think of Carrie having to survive in Richmond right now, but there's another reason this letter makes me so happy..." She paused, her eyes twinkling, and let the silence stretch out.

"You planning on telling me sometime today?" June finally demanded.

Rose shrugged, enjoying the game she was playing, but knowing she wouldn't hold out much longer without blurting it out. "It's good news," she admitted as she waved the envelope and fell silent again.

"You gonna make me jump down off this porch and take that letter?"

"Going to," Rose corrected automatically. She laughed when she saw June's eyes narrow with threat. "Okay. Okay. I can't wait another second to tell you anyway!"

Rose flipped the letter to the second page and began to read...

We had a new batch of soldiers join us yesterday. I spent some time talking with them to get to know them. One of them, a big fellow, told me he had been hired out by his owner to work on the fortifications around Richmond.

She heard June's gasp, but Rose kept reading.

He said he escaped when he found out about the North taking on black soldiers. Evidently, his escape is quite a story, but he made it and then joined up. He said it was the only way he knew to reunite with his wife, who was still a slave on a plantation outside Richmond.

Rose, it's Simon! June's husband, Simon.

"Oh my God," June whispered, tears streaming down her face. "Is there more?" she demanded in a broken voice.

Rose turned back to the letter.

You should have seen his face when I asked him if he was June's husband from Millstone Plantation. We both danced around like lunatics when I told him I was June's brother and that June was safe with you in the contraband camp. My men thought we were both crazy until they got the whole story. We stayed up and talked for hours.

"Simon...Simon..." June kept repeating his name, her tears falling in a cascade of joy.

You tell June her husband is safe and well, and that he can hardly wait to see his little boy. We will watch after each other until both of you have your husbands back.

Rose finished reading and leapt onto the porch to give June a big hug. "Your Simon is okay. He's with Moses."

June took a deep breath and finally the smile broke through as she gazed tenderly at her sleeping son. "It's been so long...more than two years... I was about to decide I had dreamed him up, but then I would look at little Simon and know our love was real—that my man was real."

Simon woke up and raised his arms. June scooped him up and cuddled him close. "Your daddy is alive, Simon. He's alive!"

Simon leaned back to stare at his mama's glowing face. "Daddy?"

"Yes! Your daddy!"

Joy suffused June's face as she looked at Rose. "He's alive!"

Rose knew the reality was still working its way into June's heart and mind. "That he is, June." The same penetrating joy danced in her heart. "I'm so happy for you. For you and Simon." Rose reached down and lifted John when his eyes opened and he looked up at her in sleepy confusion. "He and Moses will take care of each other. Moses has felt so lost without Pompey. Now he'll have his brother-in-law with him."

June nodded as Simon buried his face into her chest. "I reckon we've got some celebrating to do."

Rose looked at the cabin and tried to imagine walking into the heat to cook some food. "Anyone bring food by today?" she asked hopefully.

"What do you think?" June asked, laughing. "There isn't a day that goes by that your students don't bring you food."

"Any celebrating food?"

June cocked her head and considered. "Only if you figure two blackberry pies and the sweetest cornbread you ever imagined are celebration foods. And that's after we eat the collard greens and corn that is still piping hot on the table."

Rose laughed happily, her eyes shining with joy. Both their men were alive, and June finally had word from Simon after two years. This was a day to celebrate. "Let's go eat under the Emancipation Oak," she said suddenly.

"That's a perfect idea," June agreed. "You take the boys over. I'll bring the food and a blanket for us all to eat on. It'll be a sight cooler under that big oak tree."

Rose grabbed both boys by the hand and walked to the tree while staring up at it with wonder. The huge sentinel oak never ceased to awe her. This was the tree that Mary Peake, the camp's first black teacher, had taught under before there was a schoolhouse. It was also the tree where everyone had gathered to hear the Emancipation Proclamation read. She couldn't help wondering how many generations of her people would stand under its mighty branches. Would they be able to grasp the power it had because of the stories it had seen unfold?

June walked up beside her quietly.

"I hope it stands here for centuries," Rose whispered. "I hope generations of black children will stand under this tree and understand the price that was paid for their freedom."

June let the solemnity wrap them for a few minutes and then clapped her hands. "The generations will come, but right now we have some celebrating to do." She broke away and danced a crazy jig around the tree, both boys staring at her in wonder. "My Simon is alive and well!"

Rose laughed happily, her own joy about Moses sweeping through her in a huge wave of thankfulness. She lifted up the hem of her dress and joined June in her wild dance. Then the two wives laughed even harder when both boys stood and started jumping up and down.

A voice broke into their celebration. "You and Miss June sure seem real happy, Miss Rose."

Rose looked down and saw Carla, her face a study of puzzled delight. She grabbed the girl's hands and pulled her into the dance. "That we are, Carla!"

Within minutes, children appeared in mass under the tree, all of them dancing wildly without a thought of why.

It was enough that there was happiness to celebrate. Finally, everyone collapsed on the ground laughing.

Rose was the first to speak. "It is way too hot for this kind of craziness," she gasped.

"I reckon y'all gonna need some water after all that dancin'." Deidre, Carla's mother and the midwife who delivered John and Simon, appeared with a bucket of cool water from the well and a tin dipper.

"Thank you," June gasped, still doubled over to catch her breath.

The children all crowded forward and drank their fill, before Rose and June satisfied their burning thirst.

"You gonna tell me what this be all about?" Deidre asked.

"Once you ask us correctly," Rose replied. She was determined every person in the camp would be as well-equipped as possible for the new life that drew closer every day.

"Don't you ever get tired of teaching?" Deidre demanded. "I'm a midwife. Wasn't my bringing your baby boy into the world enough for you? Are you forever going to pester me about the way I talk?"

Rose cocked her head and smiled at Deidre. "Want to know why we're dancing?"

Deidre scowled, but her dancing eyes gave her away. "Are you going to tell me what this is all about?" she said.

Rose grinned, patted the blanket next to her, and told Deidre the story while the children drifted away into the shade on the far side of the tree to play.

Deidre gave June a huge hug. "You must be happy enough to pop!"

June nodded. "I'll pop with relief when I have him in my arms again, but knowing he is alive and with Moses is enough joy to carry me for a long time."

Rose's heart swelled with emotion. She couldn't imagine going two years without hearing anything at all about Moses. Two years of no news...of fear...of single parenthood... "You're a strong woman, June," she said. "Such a strong woman."

June shrugged and filled a plate with food. "We're all strong women. It's not like we have a lot of choice. Tough times bring it out in you."

"Sometimes it does, and sometimes it doesn't," Deidre said quietly. "I see lots of women who fold up and fade away in hard times. They quit believing in life, and it sucks all the color away. They walk around in a gray fog, and their lives get swallowed up in bitterness."

All three women fell silent and stared off at the horizon.

June was the first to speak. "It's a miracle, you know."

Rose read her thoughts. "Us all being together?" she asked. "I know. For all of us to have family in the midst of all this horror is indeed a miracle. I have to believe miracles will keep happening." Her gaze shifted toward Richmond.

"Carrie," June stated.

"Yes, Carrie. I hold her in my thoughts every second. We're so close in distance, but we might as well be a million miles away." Rose couldn't stop the tears that filled her eyes as she wondered whether Carrie experienced any joy at all in the besieged capital. She knew that her friend was married now, and must worry for her husband as much as Rose worried over Moses.

Deidre reached for her hand. "It ain't gonna last forever," she assured Rose as she shifted her eyes toward Richmond. "I can see the dark clouds that have settled down over that city, but they ain't gonna be there forever."

Rose stared at her, knowing the look in Deidre's eyes. The wise midwife could see more than most people could see. She was that close to God.

"The end is coming, Rose. There be some more suffering, but the end is coming. You hold on to that."

"Is Carrie okay?" Rose whispered, not sure if she really wanted to know.

Deidre nodded. "For today she's doing fine." Her eyes sharpened. "But you know that already. Your hearts are twined together. You look in your own heart, and you'll know how Carrie is doing."

Rose nodded. "I can feel her," she said softly. "I figure that as long as I can feel her, as I can with Moses, that she's okay."

Deidre nodded. "You hold on to that and live your best life right now."

"It's been so long," Rose whispered. "She won't be the same."

Deidre snorted. "What about you? You ain't the same either. You were girls when you last saw each other. Now you're women—women who have been forged by fire and hard times. But your hearts are the same. Don't you worry about when you gonna see her again," she scolded.

Rose nodded, took a deep breath, and brought her thoughts back to the celebration under the oak tree. She smiled and handed a plate of blackberry pie to Deidre.

The afternoon passed in a haze of laughter and talk as a breeze kicked up from the nearby ocean, bringing welcome coolness as the leaves fluttered over their heads.

✦

Louisa gripped the sides of the wagon and gritted her teeth against the jostling. She turned her head and gazed back at the city and the charred Atlanta depot standing stark and black against a gray sky that threatened rain.

"Do you think there is anyone left?" she asked Perry as she scanned all the wagons crowding the road.

"I'm sure there are some that can't leave, but anyone who is capable has left, or is leaving. Sherman has made it clear that Atlanta is now only a place of occupation for his forces. It's a military city now."

"Fine," Louisa announced, tossing her blonde hair to show her disdain of the Union forces. "Let them have it. They have to leave at some point. They can hardly stay there forever."

"That's true," Perry agreed.

Caught by something in his voice, Louisa turned to stare at him. "What aren't you telling me?" she demanded.

Perry turned to gaze at the city and then brought his attention back to the team pulling the wagon full of the belongings they had brought when they fled their farm.

"Perry!" Louisa grew more alarmed by the shadow in his eyes.

"I don't think much of Atlanta will be left when Sherman is done," he said. "There is a lot of talk. Sherman believes the best way to win this war is to break the South's spirit by destroying as much as he can."

Louisa stared at her husband and then turned around to watch the city until it disappeared around a curve. "You think he'll destroy Atlanta?"

"I think he'll do as much damage as he can."

Louisa pondered his words and set her hopes forward. "There is nothing we can do," she said finally. "We're going home. We're thirty miles east of the city. His troops will have to go back the way they came—west—or they won't have any supplies."

"Our best chance is on our farm," Perry agreed. "Not even Sherman is crazy enough to break loose of all his supply routes. How could he feed his men and animals?"

The miles passed pleasantly, a soft breeze keeping the humidity at a minimum. It was too soon for the bite of fall, but the stranglehold of summer had loosened. Louisa sighed and leaned back against the seat, relieved when the wagon turned onto a less-used road and the jolting evened out.

Perry glanced down at her. "How are you and the baby?"

"I think our child is much happier now that he or she isn't bouncing around like a ball," she retorted, suddenly flooded with happiness. "We're going home, Perry. We're going home."

"We're going to miss your mama," Perry said tenderly.

Tears filled Louisa's eyes. They had laid her mama to rest the day before in a very simple ceremony. "It's better," she said softly. "Mama is with Daddy and

Nathan again. That's what she wanted. She was so tired, Perry. So very tired."

The happiness rolled through her again. "I will always miss her, but she's in a better place."

The look Perry gave her said he understood. The burden of caring for her mama had become more than her heart could handle at times. No matter what Louisa did, or how much love she showed, her mama ignored everything and chose to live in her darkness.

Louisa put her hand in Perry's. "I don't know what will happen with this war, but I believe we'll be okay. We have each other, and we have a child coming soon. That's a lot of happiness."

Perry grinned at her. "I wish there was a way to let Carrie know," he said.

"As do I. I was horrid to her for so long, and still she saved your life, made it possible for us to be together, and was my matron of honor." Louisa stared down the road. "She was a true friend."

Silence fell on the wagon, leaving both of them with their thoughts. Louisa rested her head on Perry's shoulder. When she woke, she was startled to see the sun had sunk below the horizon. "We must be almost home!" she exclaimed.

"Just about," Perry agreed, his smile making him even more handsome.

"That's the big maple on the edge of our property," Louisa gasped. She tensed, wondering what they would discover when they rounded the last bend. "What if..." She closed her eyes tightly and buried her face in Perry's shoulder, not wanting to know whether the worst had happened.

"We're home!" Perry shouted. "And everything is just as we left it."

Louisa opened her eyes and allowed the tears of relief to roll down her face. Her eyes drank in the sight of their sweet little cabin tucked up against the woods, their fields spreading out on either side of their land. It was a far cry from the splendor of Blackwell Plantation, but she had never loved a place as much.

"Home," she whispered.

It was past dark when Thomas arrived home. Carrie, knowing he would need to talk, had waited to have dinner with him. She understood the deep lines on his face when he walked in without saying a word and sat down at the table. Carrie settled down next to him and smiled when May placed plates of hot food in front of them.

"Thank you," she murmured.

May cast a worried look at Master Cromwell and hurried from the room.

Carrie remained silent. A breeze ruffled the curtains and caused the chandelier to tinkle gently, the gas lamp flickering shadows throughout the room. Nothing ever silenced the incessant rumble of wagons, nor the blast of the whistles as trains rolled in and out of the station. But the rest of the city was gripped by uncommon quiet as news rolled in from the South.

"I was so sure Sherman couldn't take Atlanta," Thomas finally stated. "The newspapers were so sure..."

"It's true then?"

Thomas nodded. "Sherman's troops have moved into Atlanta."

"Hood's army?"

"They evacuated." Thomas shook his head. "His troops fought three major battles for Atlanta. There were heavy losses each time. Our forces were simply too weak to stop Sherman. Hood evacuated, but not before he blew up the train depots and more than eighty train cars full of munitions."

Carrie tensed as all the blood flowed from her face. "Atlanta? Is it still standing?"

"For now. The citizens still there knew what would happen and were able to put the fires out. The mayor went out the next day, surrendered, and asked for protection for the people still in the city." Thomas clenched his fists and scowled. "Sherman refused. He demanded every person leave the city."

Carrie's thoughts were with Louisa and Perry. Getting no news from them was the hardest. Left to her own imagination, she could easily dream up horrible scenarios. "I see," she said.

"The worst part," he said angrily, "is not what Sherman did, but what Hood said about his troops. After all the effort his troops gave, he dared to say his troops had been so long confined to trenches, and had been taught to believe that entrenchments cannot be taken, that they attacked without spirit and retired without proper effort." Thomas scowled. "Those were his exact words."

Carrie gasped. "I saw the casualty number from those battles," she protested. "How could he blame them and say they weren't willing to fight?"

"Seems that losing twenty thousand men wasn't enough to make him think his men had fought with spirit and effort," Thomas said. "And yet he is still in charge of that army," he said with disbelief.

"What will he do now?'

Thomas shook his head. "I don't know that it matters," he muttered, staring into the flames of the gas lamp.

"You think there is no chance of victory?"

"Lincoln losing the reelection was our only real hope. I've known for a long time that we simply don't have the power to defeat the North. Our only hope was that the North would grow so sick of the war, they would finally let us go."

"And now?"

"The North is ecstatic about Sherman's taking Atlanta. It has become the symbol for Lincoln's party. As long as Atlanta could hold out, the war was a failure. Now that Atlanta has fallen, the North has taken it as visible proof they will win." Thomas sighed and ran a hand through his hair, his eyes shadowed with grief and worry.

"We're going to lose everything, Carrie."

Carrie reached over and took both his hands. "Not the things that are most important, Father. You'll never lose those."

Thomas stared into her eyes until the shadows began to fade. He managed a small smile. "No, not the important things," he agreed.

Carrie drew a breath of relief. She never wanted to see her father consumed with bitterness and anger again. "Will the South surrender?"

Thomas shook his head. "Davis will never consider it. He is convinced if we hang on, the North will eventually let us go peacefully. While I admire his tenacity and perseverance, I doubt his confidence."

"So what happens now?"

Thomas stared at her for a long minute. "I guess only time will tell. Hood has sent word he's going to try to force Sherman to leave Atlanta and come after him. General Early is still holding his own in the Shenandoah. And so far we are holding Grant back at Petersburg."

He reached down and took a long drink of the cool water May had brought him. "There is still a lot of this summer left, and I have a feeling fall and winter will not bring relief. We can only wait to see what each day brings."

Carrie was startled by loud banging on the door. Micah hurried to the door and appeared moments later with Spencer by his side.

"Pastor Anthony?" she asked, rising immediately from the table.

Spencer nodded. "I'm afraid it's real bad, Miss Carrie."

Thomas paled. "It can't be safe to go down there so late at night."

Hobbs appeared at the door with his rifle. "She won't go on her own, sir."

Carrie reached for the bag May held out to her and brought out her pistol. "I think we'll be able to persuade anyone that tries to stop us."

"You'll have even more assurance," Thomas said grimly, reaching for his own rifle. "I'm going with you."

Chapter Fifteen

The ride through the dark streets of Richmond proved how disheartened the town had become from the news of Atlanta's defeat, and the constant noise of gunfire and shelling from Petersburg. The roads were almost completely deserted. Porches had been abandoned. The whole city appeared to have drawn in on itself.

No one said a word. Thomas and Hobbs held their rifles in a ready position as Carrie tried to prepare for what she would find.

The last two times she had visited Pastor Anthony, she could tell he was getting worse, but his spirits were still good. There was a steady stream of parishioners flowing into his house, bringing food and all the love they could share with the good man who had done so much for them. Jeremy had taken a leave from work to help care for him.

Carrie jumped from the carriage as soon as it reached his house. She nodded her greeting to the large mass of people who had defied the curfew and gathered outside their beloved pastor's home. She ran up the walk, squeezed Jeremy's hand, and headed for Pastor Anthony's room.

She could hear him even before she reached his room, his labored breathing causing her heart to break. "Hello," she said gently, taking his hand.

He gazed up at her, his eyes saying he knew there was nothing she could do. Then he looked at Jeremy, who watched from the doorway. "Please give us some time alone," he wheezed.

"But..."

Pastor Anthony's eyes stopped Carrie from saying anything else.

Jeremy nodded reluctantly and closed the door behind him.

Pastor Anthony beckoned her to come closer. "You were right," he whispered, his voice broken by the wheezing.

He held up his hand when Carrie started to say something. "Please..."

Carrie nodded, understanding what this effort was costing him.

"You haven't told Jeremy?"

Carrie shook her head, hope springing forth in her heart. "No."

Pastor Anthony's face twisted with pain. "Thank you." He fought to regain his breath. "He deserves to know the truth."

Tears sprang to Carrie's eyes as pain robbed him of his ability to speak again. "Pastor Anthony..."

He shook his head weakly. "My dresser," he gasped. "The top drawer...a letter...for Jeremy." He fell back against the pillow, a blue tint beginning to form around his lips.

Carrie placed a finger against his lips. "I will get it to him," she promised. "My father and I will be there for him. I promise you he will not be alone."

Relief flared in Pastor Anthony's eyes. For a moment his breathing grew easier. "You're a good woman," he whispered. "Thank you."

"Thank *you*," Carrie said, tears falling freely now. "You've been such a good friend. You saved Rose and Moses. You brought me here to the hospital. I will always be grateful for having you in my life."

Pastor Anthony, able only to stare at her, slumped back against the pillow. Carrie had seen that same look many times.

She went to the door and opened it for Jeremy. "It's time," she said tenderly. "I'll leave you alone with your father."

Jeremy grabbed her hand. "No. Please stay."

Carrie understood. Death could be such a scary thing. She nodded and settled down in the chair beside the bed. When Jeremy pulled one up beside her, she placed his father's limp, cold hand in his own strong, tanned one. "Just be with him," she whispered.

Jeremy stared down at his father. "I love you so much. Thank you for the life you've given me. Thank you for everything you've done for me," his voice broke off, clogged with tears.

Pastor Anthony stared back, unable to speak, but all his love shone through his bright blue eyes. Long minutes passed, the only sound in the room was the rattle of his labored breathing.

Suddenly, Pastor Anthony's eyes cleared as he reached up to hold his son's face. "I love you, Jeremy," he said, his strong voice ringing through the room. "I am so proud of you and always will be."

Jeremy, hope springing forth in his eyes, gasped with wonder and looked at Carrie.

Carrie shook her head sadly. She had seen this before. Just before death, some men became so infused with God's spirit that they were able to say what was most important.

"I love you, too," Jeremy cried.

Pastor Anthony smiled and relaxed back against the pillows. He opened his eyes again, a light of wonder shining in them, and raised his arms to the ceiling. "They've come for me," he whispered.

He lay back and closed his eyes, peace settling on his face like the calm on a stormy sea.

Jeremy looked at Carrie wildly. "Is he sleeping?"

"He's gone," Carrie murmured.

Jeremy moaned and put his head on his father's chest. "Goodbye," he whispered.

Carrie slipped out of the room to give him some privacy. She nodded to her father to let him know it was over, and then stepped out onto the porch. Almost one hundred faces stared up at her.

"You can go home now," she said. "Pastor Anthony is with God."

Silence greeted her announcement, and then, one by one, mourners faded away into the darkness, silently slipping back to their homes. These were people accustomed to death and grief.

As Spencer drove her, Janie and Thomas through the dusty streets to attend Pastor Anthony's funeral, Carrie stared off toward Petersburg thinking of all the men who had died during the war. She knew that most soldiers who died on the field would never rest in their family plots. Casualties were typically buried where they fell. Alone.

The rate of wounded soldiers dying in the city had altered the funeral process from a carefully followed ceremony to something much less elaborate. Usually, a handful of Confederate women, determined not to let even one of their "boys" be buried alone, attended the funerals, watched them be laid to rest, and then wrote letters home to the families.

Pastor Anthony's congregation was determined their beloved leader would leave them with the love and respect he deserved. When Carrie filed in with Janie and Thomas, over two hundred people already filled every nook and cranny of the small church. Children sat on laps. People lined the walls.

What amazed Carrie was how many white faces were interspersed among the black ones. The sight filled her with hope. She and Pastor Anthony had often talked about what it would take to bring the two races together.

"He would be pleased to know his death brought all these people here," she murmured.

Thomas nodded. "Many of Jeremy's colleagues are here to show their respect. Many didn't know his father, but they know Jeremy and want to give their support."

Thankfully, this early September day still carried the coolness that had enveloped the city the night before. No one doubted an Indian summer would heat things up again, but they were grateful the tiny church was not as stifling as it usually was in summer.

The service began when Pastor Michael George, a white pastor from a small Richmond church and a longtime friend of Pastor Anthony, stepped to the podium.

"We will do things a little differently," he said, smiling down at the earnest faces staring up at him. "A few weeks ago, I talked with Pastor Anthony about his service. He knew he didn't have much time left."

Carrie and Janie exchanged looks and smiled. Neither was surprised today's funeral would follow no one's expectations. One reason their friend had made such a difference was that he had never cared what others thought. His only goal was to serve God.

"Your pastor requested I let all of you speak," Pastor George continued. "Oh, he knew I could be eloquent," he said with a smile, "but he wanted all of you to share your memories. He plans on smiling as he listens."

The congregation gasped and looked upward as if they expected to see Pastor Anthony's kind eyes gazing down at them.

"Who would like to begin?" Pastor George asked as he stepped back from the podium.

A young mother, two small children in tow, stood up first. "Pastor Anthony be like a father to me. My husband died right after my youngest be born, and I lost a daughter when the Tredegar Iron Works exploded. I sho 'nuff didn't see any reason for living." She paused and looked toward Jeremy. "Your daddy be the finest man I know. He come to see me most every day and prayed for me. He made sure I had food, and he got other church folks to plant me a garden. He knew I didn't have nothin' in me to fight with."

The church was silent as she told her story.

"The day finally come, like he said it would, when I felt a mite better. I realized I still had me two fine young'uns to love, and I best get around to doin' it." She gazed around the room. "I'm gonna miss Pastor Anthony a powerful lot, but I know he be in a good place now. I figure God done have real special places in heaven for people like him."

One by one, people stood and told their stories of Pastor Anthony's love and care. Tears flowed freely and love wrapped the church in its embrace.

Carrie smiled when a lanky man stood.

"I didn't think too much about God for a right long time. Not till I got beat up by a bunch of white men." He paused and stared right at Carrie. "I reckon I would have died—me and the other fellas—if Pastor Anthony hadn't started that hospital, and if Miss Carrie and Miss Janie hadn't come down here to help us."

Everyone in the church turned to smile at Carrie and Janie.

"I was beat up real bad. Both arms was broke, most of my ribs was caved in, and Miss Carrie had to put a whole lot of stitches in to put me back together." He took a deep breath. "I reckon I wanted to die, but Pastor Anthony convinced me I had a reason to live. Miss Carrie fixed my body, but Pastor Anthony fixed my soul." Nodding solemnly, he sat back down.

Carrie stood and gazed around the room. "I have lost a very special friend," she said. "All of you have lost your pastor...your spiritual leader. I know you feel lost right now, but Pastor Anthony has given you what you need to move forward. He taught you about God, but he also taught you how to take care of each other. None of us lives alone in this world. He taught us how to come together as a family. He taught you to grow gardens for each other. He taught you to care for each other in the hospital. He taught you to teach your children what he taught you."

She stopped and smiled at all the intense faces. "Pastor Anthony taught you to love. That will never die. His greatest legacy, and his greatest hope, is that you continue to love one another."

She paused again and thought about the conversations they had in the last few weeks. "Pastor Anthony was ready," she said. "His only regrets were that he had to leave Jeremy and all of you. He loved you all so much," she said. Her eyes shining, she glanced toward the ceiling.

"Pastor Anthony was ready to go home. He told me once that when he died, he thought God would reach down to give him a big hug. He planned to raise both his arms and give God a hug right back, and then God would take him home."

She heard Jeremy's gasp and met his eyes across the church, knowing both of them were remembering Pastor

Anthony's final moments when he raised both arms and whispered, *"They've come for me..."*

"When he knew there was nothing that could be done to save him, he was so excited to go home to be with God. He's always felt that way—that being here on Earth was being away from his true home. He was determined to live his life the best he could, but he's always longed for his true home. He could hardly wait to see God." She smiled as tears streamed down her face. "His prayers every day for the last few weeks have been for all of you. He loved you all so much."

Silence enveloped the church when she sat down.

Jeremy was the last to stand. "Thank you, Carrie. It helps to think of my father smiling with God." He turned to the congregation. "It was just as my father wanted it to be," he told them. "At the end, with a glorious smile on his face, he raised both his arms toward heaven and whispered, *'They've come for me.'*"

"I know my father is happy," he said with a smile. "Now it's up to all of us to live our best lives. Your decision to do that will be the best thing you could possibly do for my father." He took a deep breath and blinked back his tears. "I will do the same thing. I had the best father in the world. I will miss him every single day, but I'm determined to make him proud."

When he sat down, a group of women came forward to sing softly while Pastor George finished the funeral.

The sun was below the horizon, with its glorious rays turning clouds purple and red, before Jeremy walked up onto Carrie and her father's porch.

"I'm sorry I'm late," he said. "People needed to talk."

"Of course they did," Thomas said. "They loved your father so very much. His death will leave a huge hole in their lives, but time will heal it." He put an arm across Jeremy's shoulder. "Just like it will for you."

Carrie gazed at her father and knew he spoke from experience. She knew he still missed her mother, still thought of her every day, but the loss had faded enough to let joy back into his life.

Jeremy looked into her father's eyes for a long moment and finally nodded. "I hope so," he murmured.

Carrie led the way into the dining room. May had done everything she could to fix a special dinner for Jeremy. Summer's bounty had the table almost groaning. A plate of steaming corn on the cob was surrounded by sliced tomatoes, fried squash, peppers, piping hot green beans with fatback and two blackberry pies.

Carrie's mind flew to the plantation. She had a brief moment of regret that her plans to provide food for people in the city had been cut short by the Union Army. She longed to know how Sam, Opal and the kids were doing, but she knew she was where she was meant to be.

Jeremy laughed and looked around the room. "Is there an army joining us to eat all this food?"

Carrie laughed with him. "May was determined that you know how much she thought of your father."

Silence fell on the room as they consumed the food. Carrie knew Jeremy needed quiet after the long day he had experienced.

Pain was heavy in his eyes. "Have you ever known anyone who was adopted?" he asked.

Carrie stared at him. "Only you," she admitted. "What's it like?"

"When I got adopted by *my* parents, it's like I was the luckiest person in the world," he said softly, "but..."

"But what?" Thomas prompted after the silence had spread.

Jeremy shook his head and made no attempt to hide his tears. "I feel so alone now. And I can't help wondering..."

Silence filled the room again.

"You can't help wondering whether there is another family out there?" Carrie asked, her heart beating harder.

Jeremy hesitated and then nodded. "Is that horrible?"

"Of course not," Thomas said. "I think if it were me, I would feel the same way."

Carrie remained silent, but she could feel excitement taking wing in her heart. The time had come.

When Jeremy looked at her, he was obviously startled by the smile on her face. "Carrie?"

"I've been waiting a very long time for this moment," she said. "I'll be right back." She ran up the stairs, reached into her dresser for the letter, and ran back to the dining room.

"This is for you," she said. "It's a letter from your father." She paused. "You may want to read it alone. Father and I can leave."

"No," Jeremy protested. "You two have become like family to me. I want you to stay."

Carrie sat down again and stared at her father, wondering how he would take the revelation.

Silence reigned in the room for several long minutes as Jeremy read his letter and then read it again, disbelief sharpening his features. He gazed up at both of them several times, and his eyes jerked back to the letter, his breath coming in short gasps.

"Son?" Thomas reached over to touch Jeremy's arm. "Are you okay?"

Jeremy looked up and managed a shaky smile. "I guess that should be *brother*," he replied. He turned to stare at Carrie. "You knew?"

"Since last winter," she admitted. "I promised your father I wouldn't tell you." She took a deep breath. "It was a hard promise to keep."

"Is someone going to tell me what is going on?" Thomas demanded.

Carrie gazed at Jeremy. "Perhaps you should read the letter aloud, if that's all right. I don't know what it says either. Your father told me about it the night he died, and asked me to give it to you."

Jeremy stared at Thomas, took a deep breath, and began to read.

Dearest Jeremy,
You're reading this letter because I've gone home. You can be sure I'm happy with God, but I want you to be happy, too. It's time for me to do

*something I should have done a very long time ago,
but I was too afraid.*

  *Please know I wasn't afraid for me. I was afraid
for you—afraid of what it would mean for your life.
I'll also confess, I wondered whether you would
believe me. Carrie told me I was underestimating
you, but I asked her to promise to keep my secret.
She agreed to for now, but said when the war was
over, she didn't know what she would do. I'm glad
she doesn't have to make that decision.*

Thomas glanced at Carrie but remained silent as
Jeremy continued to read.

  *Jeremy, I've never told you about where you
came from. It's time. You have a rich heritage and
have been surrounded by more of your family. You
just didn't know it. Before I tell you, please try to
understand that I kept the secret only because I
thought it would be best for you.*

Jeremy's voice faltered and tears filled his eyes. He
stared at Carrie wordlessly and then handed her the
letter.

Carrie found her place and continued.

  *We adopted you after you were sold as a slave
from Cromwell Plantation.*

Carrie heard her father's shocked gasp, but she
continued to read. This letter would tell him what he
needed to know.

  *Your mother was a slave woman named Sarah.
Carrie has told me many wonderful things about
her. I'm sorry to tell you she died two years ago.
She was raped by Thomas Cromwell's father.*

  *This is so hard to write now. You are a twin,
Jeremy. Your sister, Rose, was born black and was
raised on the plantation. Rose is Carrie's best
friend.*

Thomas, not wanting to sully his father's reputation, took you from the plantation the same day you were born and sold you. The woman at the plantation you were sold to didn't want to have a white slave, so she sent you to the orphanage in Richmond.

That's when your mother and I received the greatest blessing of our lives. Having you as our son has been nothing but pure joy. Your mother was determined to raise you without your knowing about your black heritage. I went along with it. Even after she died, it became easier not to tell you.

Now, I know I made a mistake. You are half black, Jeremy. I didn't want you to have to deal with that in the white world we are a part of, especially in the South, but that is no longer my decision to make. You are a man. You deserve to know.

You deserve to know the rest of your family. You deserve to know where you come from. You deserve to know that you could one day father a black child.

In a small way, I'm relieved that I'm going to die soon. I should have told you before. Now, I don't have to see the disappointment in your face. I suppose I am a coward.

Please know how very much I love you. Being your father was the greatest honor of my life.

Carrie looked at her father.

Thomas stared back at her with stunned eyes, turned to gaze at Jeremy, and then stared back at her. "How did you find out?" he asked.

"I found an old family album last winter when I was home on the plantation," she explained. "When I saw a portrait of Grandfather as a young man, I knew I was looking at a mirror image of Jeremy. I had met Jeremy only once before." She looked over at Jeremy. "I went to Pastor Anthony, and he told me the truth, but begged me not to tell."

Thomas turned around to stare at Jeremy again. "How could I not have seen it? Carrie is right. You look just like my father when he was younger. He changed so much when he got older that I had almost forgotten what he looked like as a young man."

"You weren't looking for him," Carrie said gently. "I was. After I knew about Rose's twin, I looked for him everywhere. It wasn't until I saw the picture that it all fell into place."

Silence blanketed the room as feelings swirled, collided, entwined and then swirled again.

Thomas was the first to break it. "Do you hate me?" he asked Jeremy hoarsely. "I won't blame you."

Jeremy shook his head. "It's all so new," he murmured. "But no. I can't imagine what I would have done in the same situation. I may question it at some point, but the truth is, it would be wrong to judge something I've never experienced."

Jeremy shook his head as he continued to gaze at Thomas. "So you're my half-brother. We have the same father."

"I knew there was a reason I liked you so much," Thomas said. His lighthearted tone released the vise that had gripped the room since Jeremy began to read the letter.

Jeremy turned to Carrie. "You're my niece?" he asked in a disbelieving tone.

His eyes widened as everything sank in. "I'm black? I have a twin?" he whispered. "I have a sister? She's your best friend?"

Carrie laughed, happiness filling her as truth spun through the room. "Rose is the most wonderful person in the world!" she exclaimed. "Father made sure we grew up together in our home. He made life easier for her because of what his father had done."

"No," Thomas said. "If tonight is about truth, it should be about the entire truth." He turned and faced Jeremy. "I made Rose's life easier because I felt so guilty. I know what I did was the wrong thing, but I didn't know what else to do. And I didn't understand that black people are as human as I am. I thought you were a possession I could do with as I chose." He turned a tender look to Carrie. "Your *niece* has taught me differently."

Thomas reached for Jeremy's hand. "Will you please forgive me?"

Jeremy threw back his head and laughed. "There is nothing to forgive, but if it makes you feel better, yes!" The laughter seemed to release something in his soul. "I've had a wonderful life, and I didn't have to work in the tobacco fields. I received a wonderful education and had the best father a son could hope for. I'd say I came out on the good end of this."

Jeremy jumped up to pace the room. "And now I find out that a man I greatly admire and respect is my brother. And a woman who is one of my favorite people on the planet is my niece, though I suppose our ages will steal the *uncle* privileges from me," he teased.

Carrie jumped up and ran over to give Jeremy a big hug. "I'm so happy you know! I've hardly been able to keep from telling you."

Understanding dawned in Jeremy's eyes. "That's why you were so startled when I came for dinner the first time."

Thomas shook his head. "I know you're good at keeping secrets, but this one must have been really difficult for you."

"You have no idea," Carrie murmured.

"And I have a twin," Jeremy said again, looking overwhelmed. "Tell me about her."

"Rose is amazing," Carrie proclaimed, so happy to be able to tell him. "She is beautiful and one of the smartest people I know. She is also kind and wise, and the best friend anyone could hope for. I miss her every single day."

"Is she on the plantation?" Jeremy asked, his face hopeful. "Is there any way..."

Carrie shook her head. "Rose is married now. I helped her and Moses escape the plantation three years ago. Moses is a Union soldier, and Rose teaches school at the contraband camp at Fort Monroe."

She paused and took Jeremy's hand. "One of the reasons Rose decided to escape was so she could come back after the war and find her twin brother. You're all she has left now of her family, and she so wants to meet you."

It was time for total truth. "She was afraid you might not want to know her," Carrie admitted, "and I didn't know what to tell her. She was afraid that because you had grown up white, you wouldn't want to know you had a black sister."

Jeremy stared at her. "And that's what my father was afraid of?"

"He knows how hard it is for black people in America. He saw the oppressive nature of it every day in his congregation. He didn't want you to go through the same hardships they did." Carrie squeezed his hand. "Your father loved you so much. He only wanted the best for you."

Jeremy nodded, the dazed look returning to his face.

"Move in with us here," Thomas said suddenly.

"What?"

"Move in with us here," he repeated. "I recently had another boarder move out, so we have a room. It would be wonderful to get to know my brother." He smiled. "That will take a little getting used to. I've come to think of you as a son, so it will take me a bit to absorb the fact that you're actually my brother."

Thomas stood and walked over to Jeremy. "Please move in here," he said again. "I know you have your father's house, but wouldn't you like to be with family?"

"*Family,*" Jeremy repeated, seeming to roll the word around on his tongue to get used to it. He turned to stare out the window, nodding. He swung back around, a wide smile on his face. "I would like to move in here," he agreed. "I've wondered what I would do. A family from the church can live in the house for now, and I'll move in with you. Thank you."

Carrie laughed with delight and moved to stand next to him. "Don't think you get to tell me what to do now, uncle or no uncle," she warned playfully.

"Trust me," Carrie's father said. "That would be a total waste of your time. This is a woman who does what she wants to do."

"One of the reasons I love her," Jeremy said quietly. "Rose is like that?"

"Perhaps more so," Carrie said. "Rose held a secret school in the plantation woods because of her determination to help other slaves read. I can assure you, you'll have two very strong-willed women in your life."

Jeremy fell silent. "I know this is all going to take time to process, and I know we have so much to talk about..."

"But you need some time alone," Thomas finished for him. "I totally understand. I rather feel the same way." He put his arm around Jeremy's shoulder again. "Your room is ready for you when you're ready. *Brother...*"

Chapter Sixteen

"Philadelphia certainly smells better than Washington. I imagine you're glad to be home," Matthew said as he entered Aunt Abby's house and greeted her with a hug.

Aunt Abby nodded. "I was glad to go, but I was even happier to return home," she admitted. "Washington is becoming a formidable city, but the growing pains are rather difficult to endure. I'm sure everyone there is breathing a sigh of relief that fall is almost here. It will push back the mosquitoes and cool things down."

"Did you accomplish what you went for?"

"Even *more* than I went for," Abby said with a smile. "I garnered several business contracts that are allowing me to hire even more women. I put seventy-five more women to work in the last couple weeks."

"I know they are grateful," Matthew said. "Especially with winter on the way." He reached out to take her hand. "How has the business community reacted? And I want the truth, please." Abby had told him about the threatening group of men who had stopped her carriage.

"Everything is fine," she assured him. "Oh, I won't pretend there aren't people who are upset with my actions, but so far the connections I made while I was in the capital seem to have provided a shield of protection. No one has approached me."

"You mean having lunch with President Lincoln gave you some status?" Matthew asked with a grin.

"That seems to be true," Abby agreed with a laugh, her gray eyes lit with amusement.

"That was quite an honor," Matthew observed.

"It was indeed," Abby said. "I never dreamed I would ever meet the president, much less share a meal with him. Not that I was the only one there of course. There were five other women." She clasped her hands together. "It's a day I will always remember."

"What did you talk about?"

"The president brought us in to thank us for our service to the soldiers and the contraband camps. It seems he'd received word of how involved I've been in getting supplies to the contrabands."

"Involved?" Matthew snorted. "You've been a one-woman supply depot for Fort Monroe. The last time I was there, Rose told me how well supplied her school is."

Abby smiled softly. "You know I would do anything for Rose."

"I wish other contraband camps had someone like you."

"Yes, I hear some of the other camps are not very pleasant."

"Not very pleasant?" Matthew frowned and settled back in his chair. "They're terrible," he said bluntly. "People are sick, they're hungry, and many of them have no shelter at all." He shook his head. "But there is really nowhere to place blame. It's not that the Union doesn't care, it's that no one was ready for the tens of thousands of slaves that would go to the camps. There was no real plan, in addition to very little organization."

"Is there no improvement at all?"

"Yes, improvements are being made, but the flow of new slaves into the camps is not slowing down. Slaves are lured by freedom, but too many leave situations that are much better than the squalid conditions at the camps."

"Are you suggesting they should continue to live as slaves?" Abby asked with disbelief.

"No," Matthew replied, "but most of them are living on plantations where little is being done and there is no oversight. At least on the plantations, they have a home and food until the war is over, but there is no way to let them know that, and so they continue to come. Many of them think it's their only chance."

"They're afraid of what will happen if the South wins the war."

"Definitely. They're willing to pay the price for freedom now." Matthew reached forward and selected one of the sandwiches Abby had laid on the table. "Thank you," he mumbled as he took a big bite.

"Are you not getting fed on your assignments?" Abby asked with a laugh.

"Oh, they're feeding me," Matthew replied, "but everything tastes better here. Did I smell an apple pie when I walked in the door?" he asked hopefully.

"You might have," Abby said playfully, "but you'll only get it if you bring me up to date on the politics in Washington. I know the *Inquirer* sent you there before you came home. Have things really turned around for Lincoln as much as I hear they have?"

"You hear correctly," Matthew confirmed. "How much do I have to tell you before I earn my apple pie?"

"You talk. I'll decide when you've earned your pie," Abby said, her eyes laughing.

Matthew grinned and reached for his coffee. "Lincoln was almost positive in the summer he would not be reelected. Sentiment against the war had risen, which practically guaranteed the voters were against him. There was talk of calling another convention and nominating a new candidate to take Lincoln's place."

"Then things changed?"

Matthew nodded. "The fall of Atlanta was huge, but it seemed to be only the beginning. We haven't had any major victories around Richmond, but neither has there been a major defeat. In the people's eyes, it means we're winning. It was Sheridan's victory in the Shenandoah, however, that has made people believe we will actually win the war."

"I was still in DC when they did the one hundred-gun salute to celebrate Sheridan's victory at Opequon."

"The people definitely needed something other than bad news. There was also what happened down at Mobile Bay in August."

"The port town in Alabama?'

"Yes," Matthew agreed. "It didn't seem like much of a victory back then. Admiral Farragut took control of the port, but we lost the monitor *Tecumseh*, and we suffered more than three hundred casualties." Matthew sipped his coffee thoughtfully. "Mobile was the last important Gulf of Mexico port east of the Mississippi that remained in Confederate possession. Its closure was the final step in completing the blockade in that region."

"People didn't see it that way back in August," Abby observed. "The casualties were piling up so high that's all anyone saw."

"That's true. Things have changed now. In addition, the victory in Atlanta, and Early's army being routed in Opequon, have certainly turned around people's attitudes."

"And the way they see the election," Abby finished.

"Republicans are celebrating," Matthew confirmed. "They're jeering that Farragut, Sherman and Sheridan knocked the bottom out of the Democratic platform."

"It's rather hard for Democrats to run on a peace platform when their own candidate, McClellan, writes a letter saying the war must go on until it's won," Abby said. "Especially when the Democratic platform demands armistice and a peaceful settlement."

"Precisely," Matthew replied. "The tide has turned for Lincoln. I believe he will be reelected. It would take a massive loss to change national opinion, and I don't believe that will happen."

"Because all the generals are being told to be cautious until after the election," Abby stated.

Matthew gazed at her with admiration. "I don't know how you manage to stay so well informed, but you are absolutely right."

Abby shrugged. "What would have been the point of being in the capital, if I hadn't taken advantage of it?"

"And what would be the point of my coming to your home and not taking advantage of that wonderful apple pie I smell?" Matthew replied.

Abby threw back her head and laughed heartily. "I suppose you have earned it," she said, leading the way into the kitchen.

When both of them had finished a warm piece of flaky pie, Abby gazed over at him. "I accomplished more than just building my business and helping the soldiers," she said.

"Such as?" Matthew asked, reaching for another piece of pie. "I learned a long time ago not to be surprised by anything you do."

Abby settled back with a fresh cup of coffee. "This war will not last forever. So I made connections for Carrie."

Matthew tensed as the thought of Carrie exploded in his mind. Aunt Abby knew how he felt about her, though, so he had nothing to hide. He could only hope that in time, the pain of longing he felt whenever he thought of Carrie's gleaming hair and shining green eyes would fade.

Abby took his hand but remained silent.

After long moments, he was able to smile naturally. "What did you do for our favorite Southern belle?" he asked lightly.

"I told you about meeting Dorothea Dix," she said. "I also had the honor of meeting Dr. Elizabeth Blackwell."

"I've heard of her," Matthew said, leaning forward with interest. "She was the first woman to receive a medical degree."

Abby nodded. "She also graduated first in her class. What she has gone through to achieve her medical training is an amazing story. She's an astounding woman."

"How did you meet her?"

"Can you believe she showed up at my office one day?" Abby asked. "Dr. Blackwell has been responsible for the medical training of the nurses Dorothea hired. When she arrived in town, Dorothea told her about me and about Carrie. She came by my office to tell me she would do whatever she could to help Carrie receive her medical training. She also told me of a medical school for women started by Quakers, right here in Philadelphia."

"That's wonderful!" Matthew exclaimed. "I hope I'm in the same room when you tell Carrie."

Sudden tears filled Abby's eyes. "Oh, Matthew, please tell me it will be soon. I can't stand the separations this war is causing. I'm so very grateful to see you when I can, and I'm thankful for the letters I'm able to exchange with Rose, but the complete separation from Carrie breaks my heart."

Matthew stood and gathered her in a warm hug. "It will end, Aunt Abby." He searched for a way to reassure her, but all he could come up with was, "The South can't hold out much longer." Then he took a deep breath.

Abby looked up at him knowingly. "You're leaving."

Matthew nodded. "The *Inquirer* is sending me to the Shenandoah Valley."

"To cover what Sheridan is doing?"

"Yes," he said heavily. Abby stared at him until he added, "Grant lost all patience with what was happening in the Shenandoah after General Early's troops burned Chambersburg. That's why he sent Sheridan down. He's known to be much more aggressive. Grant believes he will get the job done."

"Which is to burn out the lovely Shenandoah Valley and destroy all the food," Abby said, her face tense and white. "I know about it. My family lives there. So far, their home seems to be removed from the actual fighting, but it's another thing I have absolutely no knowledge about and no control over." Tears brimmed in her eyes once again.

"I hate this war," Matthew said as he reached forward to grasp her hand in sympathy, "but I'm afraid I agree with Grant's belief that only complete destruction will make the South give up."

"And what then?" Abby asked softly. "When there is complete destruction...when an entire society's spirit has been crushed...what then?"

Knowing there was no answer to her question, Matthew stared off into the distance. The question had been reverberating in his own heart and mind for months.

What then?

⁙

Matthew was happy to see Peter settled in a chair by a blazing fire. October in the Shenandoah Mountains brought frigid nights. "Hello, old man," he called, moving up to rub his hands over the flames. Matthew had arrived at the camp an hour ago, reported in, and then went looking for his friend.

"Who you calling an old man?" Peter scoffed. "You've been hanging out in the plush splendor of Philadelphia while the rest of us have been out here working!"

Matthew laughed and grabbed his hand. "It's good to see you." He couldn't see Peter without vivid memories of their months at Libby Prison. Memories, too, of the escape that gave them back their freedom.

Matthew took some time to look around the camp. "This isn't too shabby for army life," he commented. Row after row of white tents gleamed in the waning sun. Aromas of frying bacon and simmering coffee scented the air. Chairs and tables were scattered around. Troops played cards and relaxed while they laughed and talked.

Peter shrugged. "They earned it."

"So Early is completely defeated?"

"The Rebels were beaten so badly at Fisher's Hill two weeks ago that they ran and kept on running. They're hiding out somewhere down in the shadows of the mountains. There is no way they could pull together enough to mount another offensive. They're beaten," he said decisively.

Matthew listened and believed, but he couldn't ignore his sense of unease. "This is General Early you're talking about," he observed. "You believe a man who had enough guts to attack Washington, DC is really done?"

"He's done," Peter insisted, laying a pan of bacon on the stones next to the fire. "Want some cornbread with dinner? We even have butter," he said with a grin. "Courtesy of the fine farmers of the Shenandoah Valley."

"Is it as bad as I've heard?" Matthew asked as he thought of Aunt Abby's family farm somewhere in the Shenandoah. He suddenly remembered Robert's plantation was somewhere in this vicinity as well.

"Bad, sir?" asked a soldier crouched nearby. "What we're doing is saving the Union!"

"By burning all the farms and crops?" Matthew asked, deliberately keeping his tone casual.

"You bet," he said proudly. "We're making sure Lee and the rest of them Rebels won't keep getting food from this valley. We're burning every barn and crop we can find." With that final boast, he sauntered off.

"So it's true?" he asked Peter.

"It's true," Peter confirmed. "It's a good thing, Matthew."

"Is it?"

"This war will never end if we don't break the South's spirit. Lee will continue to hold Richmond as long as he can get food from the Shenandoah," Peter protested. "Surely you don't want the war to continue dragging on?"

"No," Matthew agreed, deeply troubled. "But I can't help thinking about what will come afterwards. Sheridan is sowing seeds of hatred in the valley that will continue long after the war. What then?"

Peter shrugged. "The South should have thought of that before they started this war."

Matthew gazed at him thoughtfully. "You didn't used to be so hard."

Peter met his gaze levelly. "My editor asked me to cover wounded soldiers for the next editions. I've seen far too many men who will live without arms and legs. Those are the lucky ones. The unlucky ones are buried in a mass grave in the middle of nowhere, with no place for their loved ones to visit. I'm sick of it."

"The Rebels are facing the same things," Matthew said quietly.

"They are the ones who started it," Peter said bitterly. "This war must end." He stared off at plumes of smoke in the distance. "If it takes burning this entire valley, then that's what it takes."

"Robert Borden's plantation is around here," Matthew said, wondering whether Peter would agree that burning the plantation of the man who had helped them escape from Richmond, after their break from Libby Prison was just part of war.

Peter's lips tightened as regret shot through his eyes. "I'm sorry for that," he said, "but..."

"You would condone burning the plantation and home of the man who saved your life?"

Peter stared at him, closed his eyes, and shook his head. "I hate this whole war," he said. "I've seen so much horror I hardly know *what* I think anymore. Sometimes I don't even know if I *am* thinking. I'm just reacting to what I see at the moment."

Matthew nodded with understanding. "I know. It's as if the human spirit can only take so much suffering. At some point, our minds shut down. We stop registering the reality of what we're experiencing, and we look for a way to make it stop."

"Yes," Peter said heavily. "I want it to stop." He pulled the bacon from the fire and stared at it. "I want to go home to my wife and kids. I haven't seen them in three years. I want to stop having nightmares. I want to sleep through a night without gunfire—without wondering whether a mortar will blow me up." His voice was broken when he finished, his eyes gleaming with tears.

Matthew put a hand on his shoulder but said nothing. There was nothing to say after all. All anyone could do was try to survive.

A long silence wrapped around them, the sinking sun bouncing off the famous blue mist that gave the Blue Ridge Mountains their name.

This lush, productive region along Virginia's western border was one of the Confederacy's cornucopias. Unlike the scarred terrain of eastern Virginia, the Shenandoah Valley had not been much trampled by armies until now. The battles fought in the beautiful valley had been few and relatively small.

The Shenandoah had remained in Confederate hands throughout the course of the war. It continued to produce food supplies that sustained the Rebel Army. For the South to lose its bounty now would be a disaster. Losing the valley would also mean cutting vital lines of communication with Richmond. But perhaps the worst result would be opening a door for the Federal forces to strike a blow against Lee's left flank when he was woefully unprepared to face it.

"I know there is no good answer to this. No matter what is done, or how it is done, people will be hurt."

Peter nodded, the defiance gone from his eyes. "And the results will echo down through generations."

He and Matthew exchanged a long look, both realizing how much truth they had spoken.

✾

"You reckon we're finished, Captain?"

Robert looked up from a letter he was writing to Carrie and frowned. "We haven't run back to Richmond have we, Alex?"

"No, sir," Alex said as he leaned against a towering oak tree, "but we ain't doing nothing either. It's been more than two weeks since we got beat so bad at Fisher's Hill." He gave a long look north. "The boys are figuring maybe we're done."

Robert couldn't blame them. "Sit down, Alex." He stared into the flames for a long moment. "I can't tell you anything," he said, "except this... We're not done yet."

Alex sucked in his breath and released it with a grin. "I told the boys Early wouldn't give up."

"Sheridan has gone too far," Robert said grimly.

Alex nodded. "All the smoke we been seeing. He's burning things."

"Seems like he's set to burn the entire valley."

"Some of the boys told me you have a plantation in these here parts. That right?"

Robert nodded heavily.

"You reckon it's burned?"

Robert ground his teeth and shook his head. "I don't know." The not knowing was killing him. Robert was only eight miles from Oak Meadows, but it might as well have been a thousand. He couldn't leave his unit. He had asked for permission, but it had been denied because of the uncertainty of his battalion's plans.

"You know this area pretty good?" Alex asked.

"Like the back of my hand," he admitted. "My brother and I have ridden just about every square inch of this county training our horses."

"You don't raise tobacco?"

"No. We raised horses." Robert decided not to mention that for many years they had also made money breeding slaves. That was a life and an attitude he deeply regretted. Sometimes he wondered how he could ever pay for the wrong he had done.

"Bet you have a right nice place," Alex said.

Robert was silent, envisioning the verdant green pastures of Oak Meadows. For the last few days, he had been tortured by thoughts of early mornings on the plantation when the sun would shimmer off the mist, horses running and playing, foals dancing beside their mothers. He could smell the drying hay and see the mountains framing the fields with their embracing beauty. He and his brother had spent the last ten years developing bloodlines that made his horses some of the finest in Virginia.

"You got one of them fancy plantation homes?" Alex asked.

Robert shrugged. "There are much nicer," he replied, but his heart longed to see the sprawling brick house with the long, columned porch. It was certainly not as opulent as Cromwell Plantation, but his mother had turned the house into a showpiece all the same.

Robert almost ached when he thought of his mother. Was she still there? Was she in danger of being harmed by the Federals? What would she do if they came and burned her out? He knew every soldier had someone they had to leave behind that they worried about. He knew the war was changing every man. He suspected women, left to their own devices for survival, were also undergoing massive changes.

He had felt okay about not being there when almost all the fighting was far from home, but now that the valley was in flames...

He clenched his jaw and gritted his teeth. He had thought many times of disobeying orders and riding out to discover the truth for himself. Only his responsibility to his men kept him in place.

"Captain Borden!"

Robert snapped to attention as a courier strode up. "What can I do for you?"

The courier shrugged. "General Early told me to give you this, sir." He handed over an envelope, saluted, and strode off.

Robert opened the envelope and gasped.

"Bad news, sir?"

A smile spread across Robert's face. "Feel like going for a ride, Alex?"

"I reckon I wouldn't mind," Alex said easily, his eyes revealing how excited he was to be doing something other than sitting in camp. "Where we going?"

⚬⚭⚬

Robert breathed deeply as he turned Granite down the long driveway that led to Oak Meadows. Towering oaks lined the drive as it meandered its way through fence-lined meadows tall with gently swaying grass. Before the war, the fields had been dotted with beautiful horses. Now the land was empty, but it didn't mar the beauty.

"It's beautiful, Captain," Alex said, envy ripe in his voice.

Robert nodded but remained silent, tense with the anticipation of what he might find when he rounded the last curve. It had been over three years since he had been home. He knew it was foolish to hope Oak Meadows was still standing, but it was so far off the main roads that it might have been missed.

Singing birds and chirping crickets blended with the whispers of wind blowing through the trees. It seemed wrong, somehow, that such beauty could still exist in the middle of such horror, but he could feel the old magic working its way into his heart. He loved Oak Meadows and had such dreams of what it would one day be.

Robert remained silent as creaking leather accompanied the thud of horse hooves on the dry road. Granite swung his head proudly as if he knew they were on a very special mission.

Robert heaved a sigh of relief as they rounded the last curve and the chimneys of his home appeared in the distance. "It's still standing," he murmured. He threw his head back and laughed loudly. "I'm home!"

He urged Granite into a gallop as he closed the last hundred yards. He had hoped the sound of his approach would pull his mother out onto the porch, but as soon as he stepped onto the white painted planks, he felt the house's emptiness. He stood still and turned toward the quarters. The same empty feeling welled up in him.

"There's no one here."

"It sure does seem deserted," Alex agreed. "You go on inside, Captain. I'll keep an eye out."

Robert nodded his gratitude and strode inside. No damage had been done, but a layer of dust said the house had been unoccupied for a long time. Gusts of wind swept in through the open door and shook the chandelier. Showers of dust sprinkled from the tinkling lamp and glistened as rays of sun shone through the huge windows facing the golden pasture.

Robert frowned. Where was his mother? What had happened?

Looking around, he saw a single envelope lying on the foyer table. He caught his breath when he discovered his name written in an obviously shaky hand. Pulling the stationery out, he read the letter.

Dear Robert,

I can no longer stay on the plantation. Your brother was called to the city months ago, and all our slaves have left. Federal soldiers took the horses two days ago. The last slaves who had stayed behind went with them. But at least they didn't burn our home. For that, I am thankful!

I cannot possibly stay here all on my own. I have moved into Winchester with your Aunt Emma as of early July.

I do so hope you find this letter when you are able to return.

I love you,
Mother

Robert scowled and gazed around. The plantation had been abandoned for almost three months. He tried to ignore the ache he felt when he saw empty pastures through the window. He hadn't really expected his horses to still be here, but he had harbored hope. Years of hard work that would have secured his and Carrie's future had been wiped out, but it was more than that. The empty fields were a reflection of all the South had lost.

"Bad news?" Alex asked through the open door.

Robert shrugged, bringing his thoughts back under control. "My mother left in July to stay with family in Winchester."

"Winchester? I wonder how she's handled armies running rampant through her city."

Robert stared at Alex and realized how right he was. Winchester seemed to always be in the middle of the fighting. The city had changed hands several times, like a massive tug-of-war rope, as Rebel and Federal forces fought for control since the start of Sheridan's campaign. So far, Winchester stood, but would that change? Had his mother fled to supposed safety, only to find greater danger?

Robert shook his head helplessly. "There is nothing more we can do here," he said, striding back out onto the porch.

"Don't you want to go through the house, Captain?"

"No," he said in a clipped voice, his eyes burning and his throat thick. He cast a look around the plantation, mounted Granite, and took off at a ground-eating trot.

"You okay, Captain?" Alex asked after a long period of silence.

Robert shrugged, not able to articulate the empty feeling that had swallowed him. All along, he had been fighting the war to protect what was his. Even though his home was still standing, all he had worked for was gone. He and his brother worked for years to breed some of the finest horses in Virginia. How could he start again, with no money and no foundation stock?

The emptiness faded, replaced by boiling anger.

When they were almost back to their encampment, Robert turned to Alex. "We're not done yet, Alex. You'll find out soon."

Robert swung off Granite and stared north. "No, we're not done yet..."

Chapter Seventeen

Robert's heart pounded with excitement as Granite picked his way carefully through boulders and around trees, night covering their presence. He knew there were five other men with him, but no one said a word.

Secrecy was paramount.

Word had come to them that Sheridan's army was encamped in what it believed was an impregnable position.

Impregnable perhaps to the softer Union troops, but not to the Rebel soldiers who called these mountains home.

Robert and several of his men had been chosen for this mission because they knew the area well. Orders had come that afternoon. They had set out after a hasty meal and ridden north toward Cedar Creek, staying carefully concealed on deer trails well off the road. He was grateful for the darkness that now gave them added protection.

Robert winced every time he heard a horseshoe strike a rock—the metallic ring sounded as loud as a gunshot in the thick silence—but he became confident there were no lookouts on this side of the mountain. Crickets and frogs provided the only other noise. Fireflies offered the only bursts of light. If the mission hadn't been so critical, he could've almost pretended he was out on a late-night ride with his brother.

Eventually, the grade became too steep to risk riding any further. He pulled Granite to a stop, signaled to his men, and dismounted. Robert tied Granite loosely so that the horse would have a chance of breaking free if he didn't return. Knowing his men were right behind him, Robert proceeded on foot.

As they continued to move forward, the trees thinned. Robert breathed a sigh of relief as the moon illuminated their way. He knew the light put them at greater risk, but the glowing orb was necessary for them to navigate the rest of their way up the mountain.

Heavy breathing from his men was the only noise as the steep grade forced all of them to crawl forward on their hands and knees, grabbing at bushes and boulders to keep from sliding backwards. A fall at this point would almost certainly be deadly.

Trees disappeared altogether as scrubby bushes fought for a place in the patches of boulders tossing back the reflection of the moon, flecks of mica sparkling like diamonds. Robert fought to keep his breathing even as he and his men scaled the mountain. He could tell the top was very near. Sweating profusely from nerves and exertion, he was grateful for the almost frosty October air.

When they broke out onto the top, he immediately turned east and continued down the ridge. He knew exactly what he was looking for. He and his brother had spent many afternoons there. Robert and his men hiked for another mile before a hand signal from him had them cutting left out onto a jagged precipice.

Robert took a moment to absorb the sheer splendor of the scene before him. The moon glimmered across the mountains, wave after wave disappearing into the distance until swallowed by the dark horizon. Far below, the silver ribbon of the Shenandoah River slipped through the valley, while Cedar Creek trailed away into the bosom of the mountains.

Robert took a deep breath and focused on why he was really there. The glow of thousands of campfires looked like tiny orange specks on a dark canvas. Sheridan's camp was spread out in stark detail below their position. Nearly every tent was visible in the bright moonlight. He stayed motionless, identifying the locations of Sheridan's cavalry, his artillery, his infantry and his wagon train.

Robert stared intently, noting where Sheridan's lines of entrenchments had been run, and where they stopped. He could see it all...the roads leading to the camp, the place where the Federals could best be attacked. The scene below was like a huge map showing him where to move, how far to go, and what to do.

He knew every man with him was documenting the same picture in their minds as the wind picked up and turned their sweaty bodies into shivering muscles. Finally, they turned away and headed back down.

Alex caught up to him and tapped him on the shoulder. Robert said nothing, but they exchanged a broad grin.

They were definitely not finished yet.

Grateful for the flickering fire flames, Matthew leaned back against his chair and stared up at the full moon. He pulled his coat tighter and let his thoughts roam.

"Today was fun," Peter commented.

Matthew grinned. "Who would have thought I would be playing baseball on a battlefield?" he snorted. "Of course, they change the rules so fast it's hard to know who is really winning."

Peter nodded his agreement. "It's fun, though. I wouldn't be surprised if the game becomes popular." He paused. "Sheridan should be back sometime tomorrow from Washington. I understand he's spending tonight in Winchester."

"He must be quite confident nothing will happen."

"Definitely," Peter replied. "The troops wouldn't be playing baseball if this was considered an active camp. Right now, we're biding time until Sheridan decides what our next move is. Early may be done, but I'm confident Sheridan will make another move toward Richmond when he's ready."

"He's basking in his glory."

"It's more like the Republican Party is basking in his glory. The election is less than three weeks away. Sherman is hanging out in Atlanta until the election is over, too. Nobody wants a defeat to upset the results of the election. Right now, it's almost certain Lincoln will win."

Matthew nodded again and fell silent, content to let the crackling flames embrace his thoughts. His mind traveled back to a night much like this one, when he and

Robert had camped in these very mountains on a break from school. He wasn't sure where Robert's plantation was, but he knew it must be fairly close.

He smiled as he remembered swimming in a frigid mountain stream and eating trout they caught, complete with berries they pulled from bushes. It had been an idyllic weekend. They had shared dreams and hopes, and spent hours in laughter.

Matthew's smile faded as the sounds of the army encampment reminded him he was at war against his friend. For all he knew, Robert had been wounded or killed since he'd last seen him eight months before, when his friend had saved him from being recaptured and taken back to prison. He only hoped the day would come when he could repay Robert.

Robert gazed around him, amazed that thousands of men could be this silent. He knew it was the only thing that had brought Early's army so close to Sheridan's camps. No alarms had been raised.

It was five o'clock in the morning on October nineteenth.

Sheridan had no idea what was about to befall him.

"Your men are ready?"

Robert snapped his head around when the quiet question sounded behind him. "Yes, sir," he replied, his voice barely audible. He exchanged a grim smile with General Kershaw.

Robert's men were stationed with General Kershaw. They were poised east of Cedar Creek, near the point where it formed a lazy loop in its southward course toward the North Fork.

Robert tensed his body and prepared for the signal to move forward. All around him he could sense coiled bodies ready to advance. He gripped his rifle tightly and thought of Oak Meadows' empty fields. He had lost everything he had worked so hard to obtain. Even the image of Carrie's smiling face wasn't able to diminish the anger coursing through his blood.

Up until now, he had been fighting to protect what was his. Now he was fighting to avenge what had been lost. The war had a face now—one hundred horses that would never be reclaimed.

When the signal came, he plunged forward down the trail. He began firing as soon as the first tents entered his field of vision, his lips tightening with satisfaction as screams and curses filled the air.

Within minutes, the part of Sheridan's camp under attack was in a complete rout. Men still in their night clothes ran wildly from their tents, their weapons and provisions left behind.

The need for secrecy was over.

Robert raised his voice in a wild Rebel yell and continued to push forward, jumping over bodies in his path and leaping over campfires.

"*Get them!*"

Matthew jolted up from a dead sleep and jerked at Peter's arm. "Wake up! We're being attacked!"

"You're crazy," Peter muttered, snuggling deeper into his warm blankets. "Go back to sleep."

"Get up, Peter!" Matthew dashed out of the tent. The musket shots grew louder, and the crazy Rebel yell echoed faintly through the valley.

Moments later, Peter's head poked from the tent. "What is going on?" His voice was as bewildered as his face.

"The army *that has no fight left* is attacking," Matthew snapped.

Suddenly, the camp swarmed with retreating men, all in night clothes, many bloodied and limping, their eyes wide with fright. Almost none had weapons.

"The Rebels are attacking!" dazed Union soldiers yelled. "They came out of nowhere!"

Officers appeared in the darkness and tried to regain order. "Prepare yourselves, men!" they commanded, trying to stop the stampede of soldiers to the rear. Most ran right around their officers and continued on their wild flight.

Musket fire and screams grew louder. Matthew was suddenly very frightened. He exchanged a grim look with Peter. They ducked back into the tent to grab their packs, and then they ran. Remaining in the middle of a battlefield with no defense was certainly not wise. He would *not* be captured again. Just the thought of it made him run faster.

⁓⚬⚬⁓

Robert yelled victoriously as Union men spilled from their tents and ran in fright. He watched as his men grabbed up new rifles, pulled shoes onto their bare feet, slipped into warm coats, and kept pressing forward.

"We got 'em running, Captain!" Alex yelled triumphantly, shaking his new rifle at the sky.

"Keep moving, Alex," Robert yelled back. "This day has only begun. We will drive this army back to the North!" He knew the element of surprise was gone. The Confederates' bellowing attack and booming guns had destroyed that. Now, speed was going to be their weapon. They had to press forward too quickly for the Federals to mount an effective defense.

His men yelled and pushed even harder. Robert couldn't know how other units fared, but at least in his area, victory appeared imminent.

Within moments, they burst out into another encampment. Open flaps revealed most of their enemy had fled, but they were met by sporadic bursts of gunfire.

"Fire!" Robert yelled, emptying his rifle in the direction of the rifle flashes and running straight for them.

Gunshots erupted all around him as his men yelled wildly and followed right behind him. A few more musket flashes lit the predawn before silence came.

"Looky what I got here, Captain!"

Robert looked up as several of his men appeared in the firelight, herding forward confused Federal soldiers, their eyes wide with sleep and fright. "Hold them as prisoners," he snapped and then motioned the rest of his men onward.

Morning crept forward. Daylight revealed how successful their surprise attack had been. Robert couldn't help laughing as his men continued to surge forward into absolute chaos. The fields behind the Union tents had become a living mass of men and horses fleeing for life and safety. Shoeless and hatless Union soldiers scurried like flightless fowl escaping their predators. Artillery guns were left deserted. Horses darted around madly, some cannoneers mounted bareback attempting to regain control. Panic hung in the air like a heavy cloud.

Chaos increased when Rebel cannoneers captured Union guns and turned them on their former holders, throwing shells—grapeshot and canister—into the fleeing fugitives. White flags of surrender flew from every Union entrenchment.

"Look at this, Captain!" one of his men yelled. "You ever seen such finery?" his voice mocked.

Robert looked into one officer's tent, set up as if he had been on a grand vacation and not on a battlefield. Robert's eyes narrowed as he absorbed the elegant scene before him. A small dining table perfectly set with china, shiny tableware, and even a vase of fresh flowers incited Robert's anger over his own men's hardships.

Opening his mouth to call his men onward, he stopped when his soldiers began to grab things. This bounty must look like the wealth of the Indies to his half-fed, half-clothed men.

It took them only seconds to grab slices of bacon and bread off a table, or to shrug into a warm overcoat, or slip on thick boots they hadn't seen the likes of since the beginning of the war. His men couldn't carry much, but at least for a while, they would be warm at night. How could Robert take *that* from them?

Moments later, order was restored and they continued to press forward, laughing at the victory that was obviously theirs.

⌇⚹⌇⚹⌇

Matthew stumbled forward, both mesmerized and horrified by the chaos surrounding him.

"You all right?" Peter grabbed his arm and held him upright.

Matthew couldn't breathe. He knew how easily he could be captured again. Sheridan's army was being badly beaten. The Confederates would take many prisoners that day.

"Matthew?" Peter shook him. "We have to keep moving."

"I won't be captured again," Matthew gasped. "No more..." Terror gripped him as memories of Libby Prison and the escape filled him. "They'll have to kill me."

"There will be no capturing and no killing," Peter snapped. "We're getting out of here." He pulled Matthew forward through a stand of trees and then jerked to a stop.

Matthew stared at the group of Federal soldiers being herded by laughing Rebel troops. "No," he whispered. He jerked free of Peter's arm and dashed away, searching for a way out. He was aware of Peter right behind him, but freedom was his only thought. Perhaps the soldiers hadn't seen them.

"Get those two that disappeared into the woods!"

A call from behind him destroyed Matthew's hope. He paused for a moment and raced headlong into a field of boulders and huge rocks, dashing through them and around them as fast as he could. His breath came in gasps, and he couldn't hear anything beyond the roaring in his head.

He was hugging a boulder, looking for a place above him to hide, when the ground seemed to open up and swallow him. He cried out as he slid down and came to a jarring halt.

Peter landed right beside him. "What-"

Matthew's hand clamped over Peter's mouth to silence him. "Not a word," Matthew whispered harshly. He gasped for breath and held it when he heard the scramble above them.

"They had to have come this way!" one of the men yelled. "They didn't disappear into thin air."

Moments later, another soldier's voice filled the silence. "I ain't worried about two more men since we got us close to one hundred back there. Let 'em go." A harsh, triumphant laugh rang in the air. "If they get away, they can tell about how Captain Borden's men destroyed their camp."

Matthew gasped again. Robert's men were pursuing him. If they caught him and Peter, even Robert couldn't get them out of trouble this time. He shrank into himself and prayed their hole would protect them. He would worry later about how to get out of it.

⁓⸎⊙⸎⁓

Robert was exhausted, but he laughed and joked with his men as the morning rolled on. Couriers from other divisions relayed the message that General Early's attack had swept the Federal forces off the field. Robert was certain Early would order another attack against their badly mauled enemy to finish them off.

He looked up expectantly as one of his commanding officers rode up. "Are we moving again?"

"No," came the clipped answer. "General Early has decided to hold what has been gained. We're to carry off all the captured and abandoned artillery, small arms and wagons."

Not sure what to say, Robert simply looked at him.

The officer shrugged. "The men are exhausted. They've been short of food and supplies for weeks." He leaned forward to add quietly, "Your men are in order, but in other areas, one third of the men have left their lines to go plundering."

Robert understood. These men had suffered so greatly. Still...

"Do you think they're finished?" Robert asked, looking north. "I doubt Sheridan will simply ride away."

"I guess we'll cross that bridge if we come to it," the officer replied.

Sheridan's response came that afternoon.

Robert and his men moved up to help form a final line. His troops stared uneasily, first at the Union force, and then at Robert, as the Federals gathered *en masse* across from them.

A messenger came through relaying that Confederate signalmen on Massanutten Mountain had sent warning of a Yankee buildup.

"Captain?"

"I don't guess it's over yet," Robert said as his eyes scanned the horizon.

"The boys are feeling right nervous," Alex muttered. "I reckon we celebrated a mite too early."

Robert remained silent, gripping his rifle tightly as he fought to breathe. His men wore their newly confiscated uniforms and shoes. Robert prayed these brave soldiers would live long enough to enjoy them.

Their waiting ended at four o'clock, when the Federals fought forward in a series of assaults. Robert watched the wave of blue coats teeming toward them. He knew even before the fight began that his men didn't stand a chance. He raised his rifle and fired, but in less than an hour, he heard the call to retreat, as men dropped all around him.

"Retreat!" Robert yelled, knowing he would have to run a long way to escape the Union fury.

"Don't you think it's time for us to get out of here?" Peter asked, staring up at the small hole above them. He had carefully selected footholds and handholds that would allow them to climb the twenty feet they had fallen.

"I don't know," Matthew said nervously. "Let's wait until dark. We don't know what's going on up there." He had become quite fond of the small cave they had fallen into.

Peter licked his lips. "No, we don't, but I know what is going on down here. We're about to die from thirst!"

"Better than going back to prison," Matthew muttered. He flushed when Peter's eyes softened with compassion.

He realized Peter couldn't possibly understand. All the prisoners at Libby Prison had suffered, but only Matthew had been relegated to Rat Dungeon for months. Nightmares continued to haunt him. His terror of going back there had stolen any strength and courage he'd once had.

"Let's wait a while longer."

Peter sat back down. "Okay. It's not like I have any idea what we'll do once we get out of here," he admitted. "If we're behind Rebel lines, I don't know how we'll escape."

His voice broke off as booms of cannon fire exploded in the distance. Another full-scale assault was under way, but they had no way of knowing which direction it came from. Were the Rebels finishing the job, or had Sheridan returned from Washington to rally Union troops?

Steady firing and booming of cannons thundered for over an hour. Then Matthew and Peter heard voices.

"Get out of here!"

"Retreat!"

"The Yankees turned the tables!" another called. "Run!"

Matthew and Peter cheered, knowing their voices couldn't be heard amid the chaos, and confident that Rebels in retreat wouldn't stop to capture prisoners. They settled back to wait. Soon, it would be safe to leave their unexpected refuge.

⁘⸎⟡⸎⁘

Within one hour of Sheridan's assault, every Confederate force nearby had been routed. The same chaos that had existed earlier in the day for the Union now belonged to the Rebels as they fled for their lives, giving up all they had gained and losing much of their artillery.

By the end of the day, Early's army had fallen all the way back to New Market, and was no longer a fighting force in the Shenandoah.

The battle for the Shenandoah Valley was over.

Robert stared at the remnants of his men huddled around a fire.

"We're finished now, ain't we, Captain?" Alex asked hoarsely, his eyes red with exhaustion.

Robert nodded. "We're finished," he admitted. "I imagine we'll be called back to Richmond, but the Shenandoah Valley is gone."

Heaviness and defeat settled over Robert as he lay down and pulled a new Union blanket over him. It provided no warmth as the cold reality sank into his bones.

The Valley was lost... Oak Meadows was lost.

Never had Robert felt so alone. He tried to pull the vision of Carrie's shining eyes into his heart, but all he felt was emptiness.

Chapter Eighteen

Matthew was more than ready to go home. Actually, he was ready to go *anywhere* other than where he was. He didn't think he could stand one more minute in the Shenandoah Valley. He stared off at the plumes of smoke clouding the horizon as far as he could see. Overhead, those black and white pillars of burning buildings and fields pointed down to heartache.

Peter rode up next to him. "You wouldn't think there was anything left to burn."

"You said you believed it would take total destruction," Matthew reminded him. "I believe it has been accomplished."

"Not this," Peter protested. "I don't think I understood what it meant... I know it's necessary to destroy the food supply for the Confederate Army, but not whole farms... Not homes..." He lapsed into brooding silence. After a long moment, he added, "The haunted eyes of those women and children will be with me as long as I live."

"You mean you don't think thousands of women and children should be left without a home or any food for the winter?" Matthew snapped. He turned to his friend. "I'm sorry," he said. "I know it bothers you as much as it bothers me."

"I feel sickened every day I ride out to cover it," Peter said wearily. "How many ways can I describe the massive devastation of what used to be one of the most beautiful, lush valleys in the United States?"

"Readers in the North are eating it up." Matthew sighed. "It's more proof we're winning the war—that *right* is on our side."

"You don't agree?"

"This war ceased to be about *being right* a long time ago. Now it's about nothing more than bull-headed stubbornness. Why doesn't President Davis accept that the Confederacy doesn't stand a chance, and stop all the destruction and suffering?" Matthew gritted his teeth and stared off toward Richmond.

"Does Davis still hope Lincoln will be defeated?" Peter asked. "I believe in hope, but I'm afraid Davis is living in a fantasy land. The election is just a few days away. There is not a chance McClellan can beat Lincoln."

"The entire South has been living in the fantasy that they may somehow get out of this war as an independent nation. By hanging on, they guarantee more destruction, dead soldiers and destroyed lives."

"They're also afraid of what comes after," Peter observed. "As horrible as this is, at least they feel they know how to fight. What about when it's over? They never considered defeat, so they surely have no idea how to live in it."

Matthew looked up when he heard a call. "They're waiting for me," he said.

"You're going with another raiding party?" Peter asked.

"Editor's orders," Matthew snapped. He shook his head. "I wish I could quit caring and just become numb to the whole thing."

"No, you don't," Peter replied. "It's when you quit caring that you have something to worry about. It was your passion and caring, your refusal to give up, that got us out of Libby Prison."

"And it almost killed me," Matthew said.

"But it didn't," Peter shot back. "You lived. You helped many others live. Look for ways to make a difference, Matthew. You'll find them. Even here."

Matthew gazed at his friend for a long minute, took a deep breath, and nodded his head. "You're right. I hate that you're right...but you're right."

<hr>

Robert lifted his head when his commanding officer rode up to his campsite.

"Good morning, Captain Borden."

"Good morning, Colonel Cartland." Robert nodded toward the fire and decided to play the politeness game, even though he couldn't feel one good thing about the day. "Care for some coffee?"

"No, thank you. General Early has received word from Richmond. He is leaving a skeleton force here in the valley. The rest of his troops, including you and your men, are to return to Richmond and join Lee's defenses at Petersburg."

Robert nodded. He had been waiting for the order. "When do we leave?"

"Not for a week." The colonel moved a little closer, glancing over at Robert's men.

Robert stood and walked over to stand next to the officer's bay gelding. "Is there something else, sir?" he asked quietly.

"Not much will happen for the next week. General Early thought you might have business in the area," his voice trailed off meaningfully.

Robert scowled, thinking of the empty fields at Oak Meadows. "I'm afraid I have nothing left to have business *with*," he snapped.

"There are raiding parties out," the colonel said slowly.

"And I'm to do something about them?"

"If it were my home, I would want to know," Colonel Cartland replied, his eyes saying he understood Robert's angry frustration. "Not knowing is sometimes worse than knowing."

Robert nodded. He had watched the plumes of smoke spoiling the horizon all week long. He'd also thought of his mother constantly, but with Winchester once again in Federal hands, there was nothing he could do.

"Is your place still standing?" Colonel Cartland asked.

"It was a few weeks ago, sir."

"You might stay lucky, Captain. There's only one way to know, though."

Robert realized the colonel was right. "I'll go alone. I know these woods, and I'll attract less attention."

Colonel Cartland nodded and nudged his gelding forward.

"Thank you, sir."

"You're welcome. Good luck to you."

Matthew was sick at heart when the raiding party he was with turned down yet another tree-lined drive. Chimneys in the distance said there was another target waiting to be fired.

"This will be the fourth one today, Captain!" one of the men yelled as he spurred his horse forward. "We're showing them Rebels they might as well give up!"

"I'll take the barn," another hollered. "The hay makes them burn hot and fast."

The soldiers dashed off, whooping and hollering, and Matthew followed them reluctantly, groaning when he saw a tight cluster of people standing on the porch. As he got closer, he identified a mother and four young children who clutched at her dress while gazing fearfully at the soldiers racing toward their barn.

"What are they gonna do, Mama?" a little boy cried, his blue eyes wide with fright below a mop of red hair.

Matthew's heart caught. That little boy could have been him twenty years ago.

The woman hushed him and pulled the children tighter behind her. "May I help you, gentlemen?" Her cultured, calm voice couldn't hide the panic in her eyes.

Captain Hill rode forward and tipped his hat. It seemed to Matthew that the man wasn't getting much joy from his mission—certainly not as much as his men were. "I'm sorry, ma'am, but you're going to have to move on. Your farm is now the property of the federal government of the United States of America."

"And where do you suggest I go with my four children?" she asked, clasping her hands tightly, bright eyes peering around from either side of her.

"I don't know, ma'am," Captain Hill responded. "I'm under orders to burn every place I find."

"Then I'm terribly sorry you found my place," the woman replied, a catch in her brave voice.

As Matthew gazed at the commanding officer, he was certain Captain Hill was sorry, too. He remembered hearing the captain had four children of his own. He must be putting his wife in this woman's position. Matthew saw him open his mouth, but then close it again in hesitation.

"We'll have the barn burning in no time," one of the soldiers yelled. "It's got a load of hay and grain in it."

"I don't reckon they'll be needing it since we'll be taking their cattle!" another snickered as he rode forward, leading three cows by their ropes.

"Mama, they can't have Lucie!" a little girl screamed, dashing out from around her mother before the woman could stop her. She ran down the steps and raced toward the cows. "Lucie! Lucie!"

"Matilda!" the mother cried. "You get back here, right now!"

Matthew swung off his horse and grabbed the little girl up before she reached the soldier.

"Let me go, mister," Matilda screamed, her blue eyes bright with tears and terror beneath golden curls. "They can't have my Lucie!"

Matthew held her tightly, tipping her chin up as he forced her to look at him. "Matilda," he whispered. "I'm so sorry, but there is nothing you can do." He glanced at the porch and saw the white-faced mother grasping the rest of her children. He tried to reassure her with his eyes that he wouldn't hurt her daughter. "Your mama is real scared for you right now. The best thing you can do is go back to her. I promise you I'll look after Lucie."

Tears poured down Matilda's face as she stared at him with desperation. "You promise you'll look after Lucie?" she whispered brokenly. "She's a real good cow. She gives us the best milk I ever had." She gulped. "I sit in the hay and talk to her every day. She's my friend..."

Tears stung Matthew's eyes as his throat thickened. "I promise."

Matilda leaned back in his arms and stared up at him. "You don't *seem* like a real bad man. How come you're doing this to us?"

Matthew had no answer for her. "I'm sorry, Matilda," he whispered again as he handed her to his mother.

Captain Hill sighed as he watched flames shoot from the barn, sparks flying up and catching the breeze, swirling in a crazy dance. Within minutes, the roar of burning hay drowned out every other noise.

"Ma'am, you have to get your children out of the house," he yelled.

"But, where?" Numbed confusion replaced fear on the woman's face as she herded the children under the shade of a tree away from the house. The children, terrified, screamed as they watched their farm go up in flames.

Their screaming died to stunned whimpers when the soldiers spurred forward and used their torches to set fire to the house. Roaring flames were soon accompanied by crashing glass.

The soldiers laughed and cheered as their horses galloped in circles, with the men setting fire to the outbuildings and the chicken coop.

Matthew clenched his jaw as he stared at the shattered family huddled beside the tree. He could only pray the woman had food stored away in a cellar that would help them get through the winter, though he already knew in his heart that starvation was a distinct likelihood for them.

"We're done here," Captain Hill snapped.

Matthew turned and stared at him. "How do you stand it?"

Captain Hill stared back at him defiantly before his shoulders slumped. "I want this war to end. Over and over, I'm told breaking the spirit of the South will make it happen." He shook his head and turned away.

"Let's go, men," he called, cantering back down the way they had come.

Matthew turned for a final look at the family. The woman was gazing right at him, her eyes saying she knew what he was feeling. He smiled sadly, lifted his hand in a final wave, and followed the raiding party down the road.

It no longer mattered what the *Inquirer* wanted. He was leaving the Shenandoah tomorrow and heading for Philadelphia. He could not watch one more family be destroyed.

Matthew rode side by side with Captain Hill as they moved down the dusty road. A late Indian summer had yielded to a sharp northern wind that made him grateful for his thick coat. The sun was barely skimming the tops of the trees as they headed back to camp.

"Hey, Captain," a soldier yelled. "There's a road up here on the left. I'm going to ride down it and see if I find us another place. I figure we got some daylight left."

Minutes later, the soldier came galloping back. "I knew it, Captain!" he yelled triumphantly. "There's another place back here. From the looks of the drive, it must be pretty fancy."

"I don't know," Captain Hill replied with a frown. "It's getting late. I think we've done enough for today."

"It won't take us long, sir," another soldier chimed in. "I hear we might be moving on from here pretty soon. I reckon we want to do as much for the cause as we can, sir."

Captain Hill nodded reluctantly. "Go on then." He leaned forward and urged his horse into a gallop.

Matthew had no choice but to follow. He gazed around in admiration as he rode down the drive, noting the carefully built fencing and the splendor of the oak trees lining the drive. The fields were empty, but the tall, swaying grass spoke of high quality.

As their raiding party broke out into the clearing, Matthew saw the sprawling brick house. Another beautiful symbol of the South was about to be destroyed.

Two women were standing on the porch when he rode up, their faces set with defiance.

Matthew got there in time to hear Captain Hill tell the ladies they had to evacuate the home.

"We most certainly will not," one of the women snapped, holding tight to the hand of the older woman beside her. "We have nowhere to go." She drew herself up to stand erect. "You are on private property, and I demand you leave," she said imperiously, her blue eyes startlingly bright beneath salt and pepper hair pulled back in an elegant bun. She looked to be in her late forties, though the strain of the war had etched lines around her eyes.

The soldiers waiting behind Captain Hill laughed.

"You must not be aware that the entire Shenandoah Valley is now under the control of the United States government," one yelled.

"I'm aware you men have been burning and destroying the only world I've ever known," the woman snapped. "You will not destroy my home."

Matthew leaned forward and fixed his eyes on the woman. Why did he feel he should know her? He was certain he had never seen her before, but there was something so familiar…

"I'm sorry, ma'am," Captain Hill repeated. "You have to go," he said firmly.

"Oak Meadows has been here for fifty years," the woman snapped. "I most certainly will not leave it for you to destroy. I've already run to Winchester, but you ran us out of there. My sister and I have nowhere else to go."

Oak Meadows! Matthew gasped, suddenly realizing the woman on the porch was Robert's mother. Captain Hill heard Matthew's gasp and turned to look at him with questioning eyes.

Matthew's mind raced as he thought through the options available to him.

Robert had ridden hard all day and now made his way through the woods north of the house. It would bring him out above the house where he could look down from a sheltered position. Granite wove his way through the trees, the wind creating a dance of red and gold leaves that swirled around them. How could so much beauty exist in the midst of such destruction?

Robert could see the beauty, but he couldn't feel it. All day long he had passed by smoldering barns and homes, the air rank with acrid smoke. Several times he had almost run into raiding parties. Only his intimate knowledge of the area had saved him.

He reached down to pat Granite's neck. "At least my mother isn't here," he murmured. "It would kill her to watch anything happen to Oak Meadows. It has been her life for so long. Even without the horses, at least she would have something to come back to if they didn't destroy it."

He moved the last hundred yards in silence and then swung down, tied Granite to a limb, and edged forward where he could see down on the house.

He groaned.

Robert watched as a party of Union soldiers cantered around his yard. He gasped when he saw two women standing on the porch. "Mother," he whispered, clenching his fists. "Why did you come back?"

Even as he whispered the question, he was sure she had fled Winchester in terror, and had come back to the only place she knew. His mind and heart burned with helplessness. The only thing he would accomplish by riding down to her was death or capture—neither of which would help her.

Images of what he had seen all day flashed through his seething mind. He knew what was about to happen.

⁙

Matthew fought to think clearly as the captain looked at him. He finally decided an honest appeal was his only solution. "I know the man who owns this plantation," Matthew admitted. "Robert Borden saved my life five months ago."

Mrs. Borden gasped and stepped forward. "You know my Robert?"

Matthew turned to look at her. "Yes, ma'am. Your son is a fine man and a good friend."

One of the soldiers scowled at him. "I heard Oak Meadows was owned by a captain in the Confederate Army."

Matthew bit back his groan. He had been hoping that fact wouldn't come to light.

"Is that true, Matthew?" Captain Hill snapped.

"Yes," he admitted reluctantly, his eyes meeting the captain's squarely, "but he also risked everything to help me escape Libby Prison last winter."

"I heard about that escape," Captain Hill said. He looked at Matthew more closely. "I also heard it was a journalist fellow who was largely responsible for helping so many of our officers escape. That man chose to live down in Rat Dungeon while he helped dig the tunnel. I also heard it was the stories he wrote after the escape that helped get the prisoner exchange moving again. Was that you?"

Matthew nodded, praying it would make a difference.

"That don't matter none!" one of the soldiers yelled. "So what if this here journalist fellow knows the Rebel who owns this plantation. It's our job to destroy it!"

⁙⁙⁙

Robert, looking down from his perch, caught the soldier's words as he yelled. *Matthew?*

A sudden flash of sunlight glistened off Matthew's red hair, and he turned just enough for Robert to recognize him.

Anger flared in Robert when he realized his friend was helping to burn the Shenandoah Valley. He could see Matthew talking to the officer standing next to the porch, but could only guess at what they were saying.

Helpless frustration created a roaring in his head as he frantically tried to come up with the right strategy.

⁙⁙⁙

"Be quiet, soldier," Captain Hill snapped. "The last I checked I was the one giving orders around here."

He turned to gaze at Matthew thoughtfully. "My best friend was one of the officers who escaped through that tunnel when you left word it was there. He had a rough time of it, but he was able to reach Fort Monroe."

"I'm glad," Matthew said sincerely. "Captain Borden snuck me and another journalist out of Richmond in his personal wagon. I don't think we would've stood a chance without his help. Peter was too sick to make it on his own. I owe the captain a deep debt of gratitude."

Captain Hill stared around the plantation and looked up at Robert's mother and aunt with stark compassion. "I'm under orders," he said finally, his voice full of regretful resignation. "I'm sorry".

Matthew saw the spark of compassion in his eyes. "What would you do if it were your friend?" he asked, knowing he had to fan the flames of compassion.

"Fight to protect it," Captain Hill responded.

Matthew managed to smile. "Since I don't have a gun, and I'm only one man, I sincerely doubt I could stop you and your men from destroying Oak Meadows, so I can only use the weapon I have."

"Which is?"

"Words," Matthew said as he prayed for wisdom. "We've got a war to win, but we also have a country to rebuild. If we toss aside all our humanity in a thirst for revenge, we will win the battle and lose the war. You and I both know the South will lose. It's only a matter of time."

Matthew paused, taking a deep breath to let his words sink in. He glanced up and somehow controlled his shock when he saw Robert standing on the knoll above him.

Chapter Nineteen

Matthew managed to keep his voice calm as he looked back at the captain. He could tell he was getting through to him. "Destroying the plantation of a man who saved my life, and who risked everything to help a *Northerner* in the midst of war makes no sense. When this war is over, our country will need acts of compassion to balance the acts of vengeance and destruction. You have a chance to be responsible for one of those acts of compassion, Captain. I predict the ramifications will reverberate down through our nation's history much longer than an act of destruction."

Determined not to look up and risk revealing Robert's position, Matthew stared into Captain Hill's eyes. He had no idea how Robert had gotten here, but he would not betray him.

"You going to let this yellow-bellied newspaperman talk you out of burning this place?" a soldier yelled angrily.

"Shut up!" the captain ordered and then turned back to Matthew. "You use your weapon well," he acknowledged. He gazed up at the two women waiting quietly on the porch, their backs ramrod straight.

"We're done here," he ordered brusquely, cutting off any soldiers' protest with a burning look. "I said we're done. Head back for camp."

The soldiers, muttering, turned their horses down the drive and headed out.

"Thank you, Captain," Mrs. Borden said softly.

Captain Hill nodded and tipped his hat. "I'm sorry to have frightened you, ma'am. Have a good day," he added, before he turned his horse and cantered away.

Mrs. Borden hurried forward to squeeze Matthew's hand. "My son is very lucky to have a friend like you," she said. "I know how much you risked to save our plantation. I will always be grateful."

Matthew held her hand tightly. "I wish you the best." Then he had a quick thought. "There is a family about a mile from here—a young mother with four children. They've lost everything today."

"Lily Champion!" Mrs. Borden's lips tightened as her eyes shone with unshed tears. "Her husband died in the first months of the war. I'll bring her and the children here. They will be safe for at least as long as we are," she added.

Matthew smiled, wishing he could stay longer, but knowing he was already pressing his luck with the captain. "Goodbye, Mrs. Borden. I hope we will meet again under more pleasant circumstances."

"Just about *anything* will be more pleasant circumstances," Mrs. Borden said, relief and gratitude shining in her eyes as she brushed away the tears.

Matthew tipped his hat and moved away from the porch before glancing up toward the knoll. Robert stood there in the same place.

The two men exchanged a long look.

Robert lifted his hand, and even from this distance, the sun glistened off his teeth when he smiled.

Matthew breathed a sigh of relief and urged his horse into a gallop to catch up to the captain.

꒷꒰ꂦ꒱꒷

His heart pounding wildly, Robert remained where he was until Matthew disappeared from sight. He knew exactly how close he had come to truly losing everything. Suddenly, the loss of the horses didn't seem so huge.

Yes, he would have to start over again, but at least he had a home to return to. Most importantly, his mother and aunt still had a home to live in, at least for today.

Tomorrow might change all that, but for today, Matthew's courage had saved everything important to Robert. Bitterness ebbed from his heart, leaving gratitude to take its place.

Robert knew he should turn and disappear back into the woods. He longed to spend time with his mother, but darkness was coming, and he should return to camp. He yearned to spend just one night on the plantation, but he knew if he was discovered, no amount of talking would dissuade the Union from destroying the home of a Confederate captain.

The best thing he could do was leave his mother and Aunt Pearl safe on the plantation, and pray another raiding party didn't make its way to Oak Meadows. He made his decision, then turned Granite and headed straight for the house. He couldn't be this close and not visit his mother and aunt.

He saw his mother tense at the sound of hoofbeats when Granite broke out into the clearing. Robert was grateful for the protection the rapidly approaching nightfall offered. He stopped and sat quietly for several moments, listening for sounds that would say the raiding party was returning, but only hooting owls interrupted the quiet.

His mother moved forward to the edge of the porch and peered into the shadows. "Who is out there?" she called.

Robert smiled. "Mother," he called back, walking out from the shadows.

"Robert?" His mother leaned further forward. "Robert? Is that really you?"

Robert laughed as he leapt onto the porch and swept his mother up in his arms. "It's me. It might be a good idea to go inside." He wrapped his arm around her, drew his aunt close with his other arm, and pulled them into the house.

He waited until he had them at the back of the house in the kitchen before he said anything else. "It's good to see you both."

Robert's mother made no attempt to brush away the tears watering her laughter. "How? Where did you come from?" She reached up to pat his cheek. "It's really you?"

Aunt Pearl gripped his hand tightly and wouldn't let go.

Robert settled them both in chairs around the table. "I can't stay long," he said quietly. "I have to get back. It won't be safe for you if anyone finds me here, but I couldn't leave without seeing you."

"They were going to burn Oak Meadows," his mother gasped. "Then a friend of yours..."

"Matthew Justin," Robert said. "I saw the whole thing."

"What?"

"I was hiding up on the knoll. I got here just as the soldiers did, but there was nothing I could have done," he admitted. "Matthew saved Oak Meadows."

"He is a good friend," his mother said. "Though from what he said, you've given him every reason to be." She told him about Matthew's description of the prison escape, and about the captain's friend who had found his way to freedom.

"We go back a long way," Robert said. "We decided we wouldn't let the war destroy our friendship. He means a lot to me."

His mother settled back in her chair. "I can only hope there are more friendships like yours when this war is over."

Robert gripped her hand. "How are you? I found your note a few weeks ago, so I thought you were in Winchester."

"I saw the letter was gone when I got back. I so hoped it had been you."

"Winchester didn't seem like a wise place to stay once the North won that last battle," Aunt Pearl snapped, her eyes angry but sad. "They commandeered my home as a hospital and suggested we find somewhere else to live. Like we had another place around the corner," she snorted.

"Thank God we have Oak Meadows," his mother murmured. She turned to him with a deeply troubled look. "They're all gone, son."

"Who is?" Robert asked, though he was certain he knew.

"Our slaves. They are all gone."

"Yes."

His mother peered at him. "Yes? That's all you have to say?"

Robert could tell his mother was confused. "I don't have time to tell you the whole wonderful story, Mother, but I have changed. I would have given all the slaves their freedom anyway. I'm glad they got an early start on it."

Silence was thick in the kitchen as his mother stared at him.

Robert squeezed her hand. "You once told me I had become like Father. You were right. Anger and hatred were eating my soul, but a wonderful black family saved my life after I was wounded in battle. Being in their home for six months completely changed me."

His mother finally found her voice. "I'm glad," she said, tears once more streaming down her face. "I so look forward to hearing your story. Oh, Robert! Knowing your heart is free means the world to me." She reached forward to stroke his cheek.

Relishing her touch, Robert closed his eyes for a moment. For too long, the anger in his heart had built a barrier between him and his mother. The gentle gesture coming to him now as a war-weary soldier was more welcome than he could have imagined.

"I love you, son," she whispered.

Robert opened his eyes, not ashamed of the tears that made them bright. "And I love you, too," he told her, gazing into her strong eyes that suddenly blurred with tears again. "Mother? What's wrong?"

"Your brother..." she whispered.

"What happened to Daniel?" he asked, dreading the answer that was sure to come.

"I received word a few weeks ago that he was killed in Atlanta," she said thickly. "He didn't want to fight—" Her voice broke.

"But they're calling up everyone of fighting age, and he didn't have a choice," Robert finished, a deep ache swallowing his heart and welling in his soul. Vivid memories swirled through his mind. He could see his brother laughing as they explored the mountains for days on end, camping around glowing fires and eating game they killed and cooked.

His mother stroked his cheek again. "I'm lucky to still have you. So many have lost their sons and their husbands. I pray this war ends soon so it doesn't take you."

Silence gripped the room as sadness swirled through like a thick, relentless fog. Robert shook off the sadness, knowing his brother's spirit would ride with him all the way back to camp. Robert would let the loss penetrate his heart then, when the memories surrounding him at every curve would help him deal with it.

"You have a new wife, too, don't you?" his Aunt Pearl asked.

Robert let her change the subject from death to life. "The most beautiful, wonderful woman in the world," he said. "I still can't believe how lucky I got. Both of you will love her."

A sound in the distance had him snapping to attention and springing to the window. He held up his hand to the women to keep them quiet as he listened carefully. He finally breathed a sigh of relief and turned back to them. "I've got to go," he said reluctantly. "Will you be okay here?"

His mother nodded quickly. "This war has toughened all of us," she said. "I've learned to do things I never thought I could, and I find I enjoy taking care of myself. We have enough food in the cellar to take us through the winter. Thanks to Matthew, we still have a home. We'll be fine."

"Then I must—"

His mother interrupted him. "Robert! I almost forgot about Lily."

"Lily Champion?" She had been a grand friend when they were growing up. He could hardly wait for Carrie to meet her. "What about her?"

"Matthew told me their place was burned today. Her husband, Crandall, was killed at Manassas. She's been raising those four children on her own ever since. They had only two slaves, and both of them are gone. They stayed until a few months ago because they love her so much, but those Union soldiers convinced them they were making it harder for the North to win if they stayed."

Robert tightened his lips and nodded. "I'll go get them," he said. "It'll take me a while because I have to stay in the woods, but I will bring them back." He turned and strode out the door.

Frost lay heavy on the ground when Robert finally broke out of the woods into the clearing around his mother's house. Lily carried her youngest daughter, Matilda. Robert cradled six-year-old Luke in his arms. The two older children were exhausted, but the excitement of riding Granite through the woods had kept them awake enough to cling to the saddle as Robert led him through the darkness.

Robert's mother and aunt had been watching for them. As soon as they walked onto the porch, the door swung open, and the exhausted family was ushered into the parlor. The children stood numbly in front of the flickering flames, their faces reflecting their confusion and loss.

"You poor babies," Robert's mother murmured. She turned to Lily. "Your rooms are ready," she said. "There are plates of cornbread and glasses of milk for all of you. You'll have a real breakfast in the morning."

Tears shone in Lily's eyes. "Thank you. I don't know what—"

Mrs. Borden stopped her. "Hush now. That's what neighbors are for. You get some rest. We'll talk in the morning."

Aunt Pearl led them to their rooms. When they had disappeared, Robert turned to his mother. "She and the kids were huddled under the big oak tree, shivering and almost in shock when I got there. Matthew didn't only save our plantation, he probably saved Lily and those four children." He shook his head and yawned. "I have to go now."

"You should get some sleep," his mother protested. "You must be exhausted."

"I've got to get back."

"What's going to happen, Robert?"

He didn't pretend to misunderstand what she was asking. "We will lose the war," he said. "It's just a matter of time."

"How much time?" his mother asked, the small catch in her voice was the only thing that revealed her deep emotion.

"I don't know," he answered honestly. "I know Lee can stretch it out longer than anyone else, but quite frankly, all that means is that more people will die and more property will be destroyed. The South simply doesn't have the ability to win this war."

"I'm so glad my boy is still alive," his mother said fervently, her eyes glistening with tears.

Robert caught his mother in a warm embrace. "I'm so grateful I was able to see you, and that you and Aunt Pearl still have a home."

"It's because of you," his mother whispered.

Robert shook his head. "Matthew saved it."

"Yes, but your kindness set all that in motion," she said softly, touching his face again. "Each day, I learn that every single action we take has its own consequence, for either good or bad. Your decision to help Matthew and his friend escape, and Matthew's decision to let others escape through the tunnel, put a kindness into action that has found its way to Oak Meadows."

His mother turned around and stared at the columned house and then swung her gaze out to the barns. "Your friend Matthew has quite a way with words. He said something to the captain that I've been thinking about all night."

"What was that?"

"He said, 'When this war is over, our country will need acts of compassion to balance the acts of vengeance and destruction. You have a chance to be responsible for one of those acts of compassion, Captain. I predict the ramifications will reverberate down through our nation's history much longer than an act of destruction.' He was so right."

Robert stared at her, the truth of Matthew's words sinking into his heart. "Thank you," he whispered. Then he hugged her again and strode out into the cold night.

Granite looked up from the bucket of oats Robert's mother had left out for him, and snorted as if to say he was ready for what came next. Not wanting to delay, Robert swung up into the saddle and headed into the woods.

Chapter Twenty

Carrie had already heard the news when her father stomped up the front steps, strode into the foyer, and scowled at her. "Lincoln was reelected," she said softly, knowing the news had crushed any hopes her father still had left.

Thomas nodded morosely, looked around at all the sober faces in the parlor, and sank down in his chair next to the roaring fire. "Yes. Lincoln was reelected."

"What does it really mean?" Georgia asked, dressed completely as a man since all the boarders were there.

"It means we're done," Thomas growled. "Any hope of a government led by McClellan that would have let the South go in peace is now over."

"And Davis will not concede defeat," Jeremy said.

Carrie saw her father's eyes brighten when Jeremy stepped into the room. The bond between the two had deepened since Jeremy moved in several weeks earlier. They would sit long into the night talking, debating, and laughing. Biologically, they were half-brothers, but she knew her father saw Jeremy as the son he'd never had, and Jeremy looked to Thomas as a father figure now that Pastor Anthony was gone. She was happy for both of them.

"Are you sure Davis won't surrender?" another boarder asked.

In response, Jeremy picked up a paper. "This is what Davis had to say yesterday to the Congress.

"'There are no vital points on the preservation of which the continued existence of the Confederacy depends. There is no military success of the enemy which can accomplish its destruction. Not the fall of Richmond, nor Wilmington, nor Savannah, nor Mobile, nor all combined can save the enemy from the constant and exhaustive drain of blood and treasure which must continue until he shall discover that no peace is attainable, unless based on the recognition of our indefeasible rights.'"

Jeremy finished reading and set down the paper.

"Those are some mighty fancy words," Georgia said.

"Yes, they are," Thomas agreed. "They're also very dangerous."

"Dangerous?" Georgia echoed, her face saying she still wasn't sure what had been said in the first place.

Carrie had talked with her father at length the night before. "What President Davis is really saying is that the Confederacy will continue, even if we have to abandon every one of our cities and not rely on any fixed bases."

Georgia stared at her and slowly said, "So the war would become like guerilla warfare, with everything hidden away?"

Jeremy nodded. "Yes. Davis is holding on to a desperate hope that if the North wins, they will eventually be poisoned by hatred and terror and will want to leave us alone."

"That doesn't sound like the Confederacy that was created in the beginning of all this," Georgia said quietly. "Why would he do that?"

"He's under tremendous stress and tension," Thomas explained. "It's not what Davis wants, but he doesn't see any other way."

"He reckons we're going to lose?" Georgia asked.

"It does not look good," Thomas admitted. "Optimism was running pretty high in Richmond, until word came through about Lincoln's reelection. There is no longer any hope for a peace administration in Washington, and Lee is getting weaker."

"The Federals haven't been able to bust through our lines," Georgia protested.

"No, but there have been tremendous losses, and Grant is still there. He has all the advantage in this game," Thomas added solemnly.

"Why?"

"Because," Jeremy said, "Lee doesn't have enough resources. He's told Davis we have no troops disposable to meet movements of the enemy or to strike when opportunity presents itself, because to do so would take men from the trenches and expose some important point that would leave Richmond vulnerable."

"So we just have to sit here and wait?" Georgia asked with a frown. "Do nothing?"

Jeremy shrugged. "The general has more and more ground to hold, and fewer and fewer soldiers to hold it with. Lee has suggested that all the soldiers serving as cooks, mechanics, teamsters and laborers should return to fight and let slaves do those jobs."

"That's not all he's suggesting!" one of the boarders said with a scowl. "He thinks we ought to arm the slaves and turn them into soldiers. That's the craziest thing I ever heard."

"There is talk about that," Thomas said, "but no one is seriously considering it. Lee is simply looking for answers. More and more soldiers are deserting, or not showing up to fight in the first place. State governors are granting pardons and exemptions to many who could fight."

"But why?" Georgia asked.

Carrie listened carefully, seeing something in Georgia's eyes that hadn't been there the day before.

"The states are adamant about states' rights," Thomas replied. "Especially in Georgia. There is great fear that actions from the Confederate government could destroy any state government at any time. The governors believe it would make the cherished principles of states' rights a nullity."

Georgia absorbed that for a few minutes as silence filled the room. "As far as I can figure, the most immediate threat to Georgia's rights ain't coming from the government—it's coming from General Sherman."

Jeremy chuckled. "I wish everyone could see it as clearly as you do." He sobered. "People will always respond from fear first. It doesn't have to make sense. It's just what they do."

"So what happens now?"

A long silence filled the room.

Thomas was the first to break it. "That is the question of the day, George. Right now, we have a major army trying to break through our lines in Richmond. The Shenandoah has been lost. Sherman is sitting in Atlanta right now, but we don't know how long that will last."

He stopped and stared at the flames for a long moment. "I think everyone had been waiting for this election. Now that it's over, I believe the North will move to gain total victory. This winter is not going to be fun," he said tensely.

Carrie watched the emotions play over Georgia's face until May called them into dinner.

Georgia ate quickly and left the table just as quickly.

Carrie followed her and watched from the doorway as she threw some belongings into a bag. "You're leaving?"

Georgia glanced up. "Yes. It's time. I've gotten real comfortable being here in this house in a nice, warm bed, but we still got a war going on. My arm is as good as it's going to be," she said, flexing it to almost full extension. "It's my place to fight."

"Is it?" Carrie asked, knowing she couldn't stop her, but hating the idea of Georgia going back into battle.

"Yes," Georgia said. "I made a commitment, and I aim to keep it. I don't know what I'll do when this war is over—whether I'll choose to live as a man or a woman—but I know what I have to do right now."

Carrie blinked back the tears in her eyes. "I'm going to miss you."

Georgia scowled for a moment as if she wanted to ignore the deep emotion, and then sighed heavily and sat on her bed. "I'm going to miss you, too," she admitted. "You. Janie. May." She had to blink back her own tears. "I will miss your father, too. I lost mine so young. We've had some good talks in the last few weeks."

"You always have a family here," Carrie said. "We'll pray for you every day." She reached over and took Georgia's hand. "If they give you any leave, you come back here."

Georgia took several deep breaths, obviously trying to control her emotions, and met Carrie's eyes squarely. "You have changed my life, Carrie Borden. Thank you. I can't even imagine what things would be like right now if you hadn't been the one in that hospital ward."

"You've changed mine, too," Carrie said softly. "You've made me understand how truly hard it is to be a woman in the South, but you've also made me more open-minded when it comes to the choices people make about their lives."

"What difference does all that make to you?" Georgia asked, watching her closely.

"This war will end," Carrie answered. "When it does, I know I'm going to have to fight to become a doctor, but I'm also more determined than ever to fight for women's rights. I have a good friend up north who is already very involved. It's time Southern women stepped into the battle. I intend to be right at the front." She squeezed Georgia's hand. "Whether you decide to live as a man or a woman, I don't want the choice to have to be made because you have so few options as a woman."

Georgia nodded thoughtfully. "Thank you for teaching me how to read."

Carrie laughed. "You've been devouring Father's library."

"I knew I didn't have very long. I wanted to absorb as much as I could while I was here." Georgia reached over and picked up the book on her nightstand. "Please put this back in the library. I reckon everything I've soaked up will stay with me."

"And you'll have the rest of your life to learn more," Carrie said firmly, refusing to even consider that Georgia might not make it through the war.

"I ain't saying goodbye to everyone," Georgia said suddenly.

"But..."

"I can't," she whispered brokenly, dashing at the tears pooling in her eyes as she looked at Carrie beseechingly. "I'm going to slip out tonight when everyone is asleep. Please let me do it my way. You can tell them goodbye and thank them for me."

"May will be very sad."

Georgia smiled through her tears. "Who would have thought you could become so close to a slave?" she said with wonder. "I swear that woman has become like a mother to me. We've had such good times reading books and talking about them."

"You opened up a whole new world for May," Carrie said tenderly. "I'm so proud of you."

Georgia flushed a bright red, but the pleased look in her eyes spoke volumes.

Carrie stepped forward to wrap her friend in a warm embrace. "Please be safe and come back to us," she said.

Georgia nodded and turned back to her packing. Carrie slipped back down the stairs to be with her father.

Louisa stepped out onto the porch and breathed in deeply, delighted when her baby kicked. She grinned as Perry came out to join her. "I feel certain this baby of ours is a boy. I can't imagine a girl kicking this hard."

"It could be a girl if she has the same spirit as her mama," Perry said, answering her grin with one just as big. "It's a beautiful day. I'll do some work on the cotton gin today and start on a bigger storage building. This war has to end at some point. When it does, I want to be ready to handle the cotton our neighbors will grow."

He let his gaze sweep over the fields that spread out as far as the eye could see on either side of their house. "I aim to become one of the largest cotton processors in this area. I may not have the most land, but I know how to gin the cotton better than almost anyone around here, and having one leg won't slow me down."

Thrilled by the happy look on his face, Louisa gazed up at her handsome husband. They'd been home for over two months. Those two months had worked miracles. Perry's battlefield nightmares had almost subsided entirely. The phantom pain from his missing leg was practically gone, and he had learned how to do every chore with his wooden stump. During the mild fall months, her sweet husband had winterized their home and built a crib for their first baby. If she had less confidence than he did about his plans to dominate the cotton market, Louisa certainly did not intend to express them.

"What are you thinking, Mrs. Appleton?" Perry asked, watching her with narrowed eyes.

Louisa should have known she couldn't hide her thoughts from Perry's knowing eyes. In the last two months, without the pressure of her mother requiring constant care, they had become closer and closer. "Oh, I'm thinking about what a wonderful fall this has been," she said lightly.

"Yes, it has," Perry agreed, "but you're thinking something else. How long will you make me pry?"

Louisa sighed. "I know you can gin cotton better than anyone, but how are our neighbors going to grow cotton without slaves? It's quite labor intensive."

"Your father would be proud of you for knowing about growing cotton," Perry observed.

That got a laugh out of Louisa. "He certainly would. I couldn't have cared less about what it took to grow tobacco when I was growing up. I really didn't care about anything but dances, parties and shopping," she admitted as she tried to conjure solid memories of those years. After more than three years of war, her recollections seemed nothing but a vague mist. "Those years were like living a different life."

"They were," Perry said, bitterness tingeing his voice. Then he took her hand and gazed down into her eyes. "That life will never return," he said matter-of-factly, the bitterness swallowed by practicality, "but cotton will always be a staple of the South. Plantations will be smaller, and less cotton will be grown, but that will only make it more valuable. It will take a long time for the South to come back from this war, but we'll come back. I intend to be a major part of it," he said, his gaze sweeping across the land.

Louisa's eyes followed his. While fields stretched out on either side, the back of their home was sheltered by a grove of woods. More leaves had fallen during the night and created a deeper carpet of red and gold that she dreamed of her baby playing in soon, joined by siblings in the future. In her dreams, delightful laughter rolled through the air, and everyone felt safe.

"When will it end?" Louisa asked, knowing Perry could not answer her question.

"Sherman still occupies Atlanta the last I heard. He'll have to go back up through Tennessee to have a way to move his troops. He may send some of his men through

Georgia, but he has to have a steady supply of food and forage to move his large army. He'll have to stay close to the railroad."

"And far away from our little farm," Louisa said contentedly. "You and I will stay right here and be happy together until our baby is born. And then there will be one more of us, which will make us even happier." She reached down and patted her swollen belly.

Perry smiled tenderly and wrapped her in his arms to protect her and his baby from the morning chill.

The last two months had been busy, but rows of stored food in the cellar would carry them through the winter. Their garden had still been producing when they returned from Atlanta, and a mild fall had kept the crops coming. A hard frost the week before had ended the growing season, with the exception of pumpkins dotting the field and apples gleaming in the trees. The smell of apple and pumpkin pies would soon fill the house with their delicious aromas.

"On a day like today, it's easy to believe the war isn't going on."

"What's that?" Perry asked suddenly, shading his eyes as he peered at a cloud of dust in the distance.

They both waited, Louisa trying to shake off her feeling of alarm as the dust turned into a lone horseman riding at full speed. He rode right up to the porch and pushed his hat back from his eyes, as dust and sweat traced rivulets down his cheeks. His horse's sweaty flanks were heaving.

"Sherman is headed this way!"

"What are you talking about, man?" Perry asked.

"Just what I said. Sherman's entire army—looks like over sixty thousand men—is making its way across Georgia."

Louisa stared at the messenger. "That's not possible," she protested. "How can an army survive without supplies?" Her mind spun as she tried to grasp the implications of what she was hearing. She wanted to deny the possibility, but her intuition told her he spoke the truth. She gazed hard at the horizon, but all she could see were the same blue sky and puffy white clouds.

"Word leaked out after he burned Atlanta..."

Perry stepped forward and grasped the porch railing so tightly his knuckles whitened. "Sherman burned Atlanta? The whole city?"

"Might as well have. He had his men set fire to all public buildings, the machine shops, the depots and the arsenals." The messenger's voice faltered. "The city is ruined."

"And now?" Louisa asked, trying to calm her shaking hands as she touched her stomach.

"I hear the army will be living off the land. A spy in the city got out some of Sherman's plans."

"Which are?" Perry asked, taking a deep breath.

"They're heading for Savannah."

"They're crossing the whole state?" Louisa asked in disbelief.

"Yes. They're planning on living off all our crops and livestock. They aim to take whatever they want and..."

Perry leaned forward when the messenger faltered. "Go on. Tell us everything." His voice was as hard and flat as his eyes.

"They aim to destroy all our cotton gins and mills and anything else that supports food-making."

"Like our barns and crops," Perry finished, a quiet anger ringing in his voice. "They're going to burn Georgia like they did the Shenandoah Valley."

"Yes," the messenger agreed, regret and anger reverberating in his tired voice.

"Are they killing people and burning homes, too?" Louisa asked, panic making her voice wobble.

"Not unless you put up a fight," the messenger said earnestly. "That's why a bunch of us are trying to spread the news. We knew about your cotton gin, Perry." He glanced at Louisa. "We also know you done gave a leg for the war and that you got a new baby on the way. We made sure your house would be one of our stops."

Perry nodded, gratitude glimmering through the anger. "How long do we have?"

"I reckon they're about four hours behind me," the messenger responded. He spun his horse around. "I got more stops to make. I wish you the best."

"Wait!" Louisa ordered. She dashed to the well to pull up a bucket of water. "For your horse," she said as she came striding back, dipped a cup and handed it to the rider.

Both drank thirstily for several minutes. "Thank you, ma'am," the rider said gratefully.

Within moments, the only evidence of his being there was a plume of dust in the distance.

Louisa grasped Perry's hand and tried to take even breaths. "What are we going to do?"

"I'm not letting them destroy the cotton gin," Perry said, his burning eyes flying to the sturdily built barn about a hundred feet from the house. Housed inside were all his hopes and dreams.

"What?" Louisa cried. "You heard the man. They're not hurting anyone or burning houses unless people fight back." She planted her hands on her hips and tried to force back panic. "How do you plan on defeating a whole band of soldiers? Even with both of us shooting, there's no way we'll do anything but make them angry and insure they'll destroy everything we own." She didn't mention she could hardly shoot a target, though Perry had insisted on giving her shooting lessons.

She watched as the truth sank into Perry's mind and took all his earlier hope with it. "So we're not safe from the war even here," he said bitterly.

"There are still things we can do," Louisa replied, knowing she had to be the voice of reason right now. Perry had lost too much to see beyond more loss right now. "We've got to save the horses and the cow. The pigs and chickens, too, if we can."

"And how do you plan on doing that?" Perry asked, his eyes dark with defeat.

Louisa gripped his hands. "We have to try," she said. "I remember you telling me about the cave you found in the hills a few miles from here."

Perry stared at her and then nodded his head slowly, his eyes telling her he was trying to latch on to her hope.

"That could work. We could all go there and wait for the army to leave. If Sherman is headed for Atlanta, he's got a lot of ground to cover. He won't stay in any one area for long."

Louisa thought quickly. "We'll load as much food and hay as we can into the wagon. I know you can't pull it into the cave, but if it's way back in the woods, perhaps no one will find it." She saw the protest in Perry's eyes. "We have to at least try."

Perry took a deep breath and reached for her hands. "You're right, Mrs. Appleton. We'll move fast and be out of here within the hour."

Louisa shook her head. "Just you," she said simply. "I'm staying."

"You're out of your mind," Perry growled. "I will not leave you alone here," he snapped. "Don't even bother trying to change my mind."

Louisa understood his fear and anger, but she knew she was right even if the idea of it terrified her. "Think about it, Perry. If the soldiers get here and they find an empty house, they may decide to go ahead and burn it. You heard the messenger. They're not hurting people or destroying homes if no one resists." She fought to think clearly. "They're certainly not going to hurt a pregnant woman who can't put up a fight."

"But what if they burn the barn and it catches the house on fire?" Perry asked. "No! I can't take that chance. You're coming with me. I can handle losing the house, but I can't handle losing you."

"You won't lose me," Louisa insisted. She softened her voice and laid her head on his chest. "Please. Let me do this for our family. Our baby is due in two months. If they burn our home, we'll have nowhere to go."

"But if they destroy all our food, we can't stay here."

"Which is why you have to take the animals and the wagon to the cave," Louisa said calmly, certain her plan would work.

"The gin," Perry said thickly. "What about the future?"

Louisa thought about all their bright hope just minutes before. "Our future is each other," she said. "You and me. Our baby." She prayed her words would penetrate his defiance. "Everything else can be replaced as long as we have each other."

She saw Perry's eyes accept the truth. "We've got to move fast," she said.

Five hours later, Louisa watched from behind her curtains, her heart beating in terror as a cluster of soldiers, their guns drawn, approached the farmhouse. Immediately, she very much regretted sending Perry away. The idea of facing these men on her own was more than she could bear. A swift kick from her unborn baby reinforced her earlier courage.

"Anyone home?" An officer broke free from the group and rode to the porch. "If anyone is in there, you need to come out," he called authoritatively.

Louisa took a deep breath and stepped out onto the porch. "What can I do for you, gentlemen?" she asked calmly. Now that the moment had arrived, she must implement her carefully thought-out plan.

"We are soldiers of the Union Army," the man said. "My name is Lieutenant Hansen."

"Why, hello, Lieutenant," Louisa said sweetly. "It's a lovely day, isn't it?"

The lieutenant's eyes narrowed. "That it is, ma'am." His eyes settled on the open door. "Your husband home, ma'am?"

"I'm sorry to say he's not," Louisa said, letting tears fill her eyes. "He was killed two months ago when you took Atlanta." She let her voice drift off. "I'm afraid it's just me and the baby," she replied, laying her hand on her belly, knowing from the look on the lieutenant's face that her blue eyes still had their magical effect on men.

While Louisa and the officer talked, his men had spread out to poke into the surrounding outbuildings. "Hey, Lieutenant! We've got a real nice cotton gin over here!"

"Your husband worked in cotton?"

Louisa nodded sadly. "Yes, but now that is over. You boys are welcome to that old gin if you want it. It won't do me any good now." She already knew they would destroy it, so it made sense not to fight it.

"Ask the woman where her livestock is!" another soldier yelled.

Louisa answered the question before it came. "I'm afraid things have been rather difficult since my husband's death, Lieutenant. I've had to sell both our horses and the one cow I had left to keep food on the table."

The lieutenant looked sympathetic but then gazed over at the garden. "Looks like you had a garden this summer. What happened to all the food?" he asked.

Louisa hid her chuckle as she opened her eyes wide and blinked back big tears. "Oh, Lieutenant, I've had such a difficult pregnancy since the death of my husband. It seems like the sorrow sucked right into my baby, too. I've hardly been out of bed at all since returning from Atlanta." She shook her head. "My neighbors tried to help, but no one had the time to put up my garden. They bring me food when they can, but I'm having to make do the best I can."

"I'm sorry, ma'am."

Louisa gazed up at him again, almost wishing Perry was here to see her act. What fun she would have telling him! A sudden vision of what would happen if he was found hiding in the cave caused the fear on her face to become very real. "Winter is on the way, Lieutenant. Selling off our livestock was the only thing I could think to do. Most of the hay went with the animals," she added, thinking quickly as she saw his men head toward the hay barn.

"Hey, Lieutenant! What if the animals are in the woods?"

Louisa straightened. "Your men are welcome to search the woods," she said with quiet dignity. "I assure you they will find nothing."

The lieutenant smiled apologetically but waved for his men to go search behind the house.

Louisa gasped and doubled over. "Oh my," she cried.

"Ma'am?" The lieutenant's voice was full of alarm.

Louisa slowly straightened. "I'm so sorry, Lieutenant. Seems all the ruckus is making my baby a little anxious." She tried to smile, only this time it wasn't acting. Fear filled her heart as she tried to think what she would do if she went into labor right here on the porch. Her face twisted when another spasm stole her breath.

"Sit down, ma'am," the lieutenant ordered and then turned to his men. "Destroy the cotton gin and take whatever hay and feed are left," he ordered. "Then torch the barns and outbuildings."

"There's a bunch of pumpkins and apples our men will sure enjoy!" one yelled.

"Take them."

Louisa didn't have to fake the tears that rolled down her face as the men sprang to do the officer's bidding. All she could do was sink down into the rocking chair on the porch and watch as the buildings begin to curl with smoke and flames.

"I'm sorry, ma'am, but I have my orders."

Louisa gazed at the lieutenant for a long moment. "I do believe you are sorry, sir. I thank you for that. I also thank you for leaving my home standing. At least my baby and I will have a home."

"We're under orders not to destroy any homes or harm anyone as long as they don't resist," the officer informed her. "Your baby should be glad it has such a smart mother."

"Smart enough to know one very expecting woman wouldn't stand much of a chance against twenty men with guns? I'm not sure that's intelligence, Lieutenant." Louisa tried to smile through her tears as smoke and flames created a roaring noise. She prayed the wind wouldn't shift and blow sparks onto the house.

The lieutenant read her mind. "We'll stay until the fire dies down to make sure your house is safe," he said.

"What about food?" one of the men yelled. "We need to find out what she's got down in her cellar."

"Not here," the lieutenant barked. "I hardly think we need to take food from a woman all alone and about to have a baby. The apples and pumpkins are enough."

The charred buildings disappearing before her eyes tempered Louisa's gratitude. However, she could be grateful Perry was not here. She was not at all sure he could have held his temper when the buildings were set on fire. She was *quite* sure how the soldiers would have handled his anger.

Louisa sat until the flames had subsided enough to ensure the house was safe. All the while she struggled to take deep even breaths, grateful the spasms had passed.

When the soldiers had the rest of the hay and feed loaded into their army wagon, the lieutenant turned to her. He exchanged a long look with Louisa. Neither said a word. They simply looked at each other before the officer touched the brim of his hat, turned, and cantered off to catch his men.

⁓⁓⊰⦁⊱⁓⁓

The sun had set, but Louisa refused to leave the porch. Her one concession had been to walk inside and pick up a thick quilt along with a pitcher of water. She had done nothing but rock and croon to her baby since the soldiers had left, letting the tears that streamed down her face wash away the bitterness as she stared at the burned-out remnants of their farm. It took every bit of energy to focus on gratitude that their house was standing and the baby was unharmed.

Every sound had her straining forward in her chair as she prayed Perry would come home. She had tried with very little success to block out images of him hurt and wounded in the woods, attacked before he ever reached the safety of the cave. She'd also had very little success blocking out images of what her life would be like without him.

All she could do was rock and croon, her hand involuntarily stroking her stomach with maternal instinct, trying to give as much comfort to the baby as the baby was giving to her. Louisa wrapped the blanket more tightly around her swollen body and tried to breathe evenly.

"Perry," she whispered for what must have been the hundredth time.

A sudden rustle in the woods had her jerking forward, holding her breath as the baby kicked in protest. Perry materialized next to the porch. "Louisa?" he asked softly.

"They're gone," she cried, jumping up and hurrying down the steps to throw herself into her husband's arms. "They're gone!" The tears flowed freely again. "You're safe. Thank God, you're safe!"

Perry gathered her close and stroked her hair until her breathing became more even and the tears stopped flowing. "It's okay," he murmured over and over. "Everything is okay."

Louisa took a deep breath and pulled back in his arms to look up at him. "The livestock? The wagon?"

"Everything is safe," he assured her. "I left them there so I could come back to check on the farm. I'll get them tomorrow." His jaw clenched with fury as he looked past her at the burned-out hulks of their farm buildings.

Louisa gripped his face in her hands and forced him to look at her. "We still have each other. We still have our home. We can rebuild everything else in time."

"Our food?" Perry asked.

Louisa's laugh rang out through the night until she doubled over. She glanced up at Perry's concerned face and started laughing all over again. "Oh, Perry," she gasped, "you should have seen me. I do believe I may take up acting."

She relayed her conversation with the lieutenant until both of them were holding their sides in laughter. "So, yes, Mr. Appleton," she said demurely, batting her lashes at him, "our food is fine. The lieutenant didn't want to take the only food supply from the poor fragile widow with child."

"The poor man," Perry said once his laughter had died down. "He didn't stand a chance against you."

"That would be correct," Louisa said primly.

Perry wrapped her in his arms as he stared out over the ruins of their farm, and then led her inside and closed the door. "I will start to rebuild tomorrow," he said. "Right now, I'm grateful we still have the most important things." He looked at her tenderly. "And you, my love, are the most important thing."

"Well, that and my apple pie."

Perry frowned. "I came through the field and saw all the pumpkins are gone. I'm afraid they took the apples, too."

Louisa smiled. "I had to do *something* while I waited for the soldiers to get here. Did you really think I would let you go all winter without pie? Everything was ripe enough to pick, though I admit, holding the pumpkins on top of my belly was quite a balancing act. I didn't get everything, but you'll have your pies this winter."

Perry merely stared down at her, tears gleaming in his eyes. "You are a remarkable woman," he finally murmured, turning to lead her into the house.

Louisa smiled up at him brilliantly and let him take her inside.

Chapter Twenty-One

Carrie opened her eyes slowly and gazed over at Georgia's empty bed. She'd heard nothing since Georgia had rejoined Lee's troops protecting Petersburg, but she'd also not found Georgia's name on any of the killed or wounded lists, so she remained hopeful.

The heaviness in her heart this morning was nothing but loneliness. Even after Janie had married and moved into the other wing of the house with Clifford, Carrie had shared her room with Georgia. Having someone there protected her from the dark dreams about Robert and his safety.

Since she had been sleeping in her room alone, Carrie's constant dreams of Robert wounded or dying kept her drained and tired. In the bright light of day, she was capable of choosing joy, but she had yet to figure out how to handle the dark terrors of night.

Carrie frowned as she stuck her head above the covers and felt the frigid cold in the room. December's winter freeze had blown in, and now the parlor was the only room they had enough wood to heat.

"Do you think maybe I could wipe that frown off your face, Mrs. Borden?"

Carrie jerked upward and searched the early morning darkness of the room. "Robert?" she whispered, stunned to see him sitting in the corner. "Robert, is it really you, or am I still dreaming?" she asked, praying he was real as she reached out a hand, tears springing to her eyes.

Robert moved to her side and reached down to enfold her in his arms. "I didn't want to wake you," he said tenderly. "I enjoyed watching you sleep."

"How long have you been here?" she asked, reaching up to stroke his face.

"Not long," he assured her. "May let me in. Your father left early for the Capitol."

"You're here," she murmured, holding his face. "You're really here." She tensed. "For how long?" She prayed this time it could be more than a few hours.

"Lee has given me five days," he replied, his eyes devouring her. "I report back the morning after Christmas."

Carrie laughed joyfully and threw back the quilts. "Are you really going to stay out there in this cold room? It's much better under here, sir."

Robert took only moments to undress and slip in beside her.

Wanting to imprint him into her mind and heart, Carrie burrowed into his arms and took deep breaths. She kissed him eagerly when his lips reached down to claim her mouth. "I love you," she whispered. "Oh, how I love you."

Robert kissed her until she was breathless, and then he lifted himself to gaze into her eyes. "And how I love you," he said gruffly.

Those were the last words spoken until sunlight streamed into the room.

Trying to ignore the pitching seas and white-capped waves, Matthew scrambled up the ladder to the USS *Pawnee*. A winter storm off the coast of Georgia had made even reaching the sloop of war a challenge, but his editor was determined he be there to cover the capture of Savannah.

"About time you got here for the party!" a familiar voice shouted from above.

Matthew looked up and laughed at Peter, grinning and peering over the side of the boat. He hadn't seen his friend since they had parted in the Shenandoah. "Guess they'll let anybody come to one of these shindigs," Matthew yelled back.

With hope that a giant wave wouldn't sweep him right over the side, he grabbed Peter's hand gratefully and crawled over the side of the ship.

"The ocean doesn't seem real happy to see you," Peter said cheerfully, laughing harder when he looked at Matthew's green face. "I take it your stomach is not thrilled with this assignment."

"Give me a little time," Matthew muttered, forcing himself to take deep breaths as he gazed around the ship to keep his mind off the pitching seas.

"Quite a boat, isn't it?" Peter asked as he settled down next to Matthew.

Matthew shook his head in amazement. "I sometimes can't believe how far the Union Navy has come in four years of war. We couldn't have even dreamed of boats like this one before then."

"Or that a navy with forty-three vessels would expand to over six hundred fifty-five," Peter commented. "I believe this is a perfect example of the old adage *'necessity is the mother of invention.'* "

Matthew continued to look around as he prayed for his stomach to settle. "Are those the Dahlgren rifles I've heard so much about?"

Peter chuckled and nodded. "If you can call a fifty-pound gun that shoots cannon balls with incredible accuracy a rifle, I reckon it is."

Matthew focused his attention on the gun to keep his mind off the heaving ship. It had taken him two days to get here on a smaller vessel. It wasn't until today, when the storm churned up the waves, that he'd had trouble.

"Admiral Dahlgren, the commander of the *Pawnee*, headed the navy's ordnance department."

"With good reason," Peter agreed. "The man is a genius. The guns and cannons he has designed are a big reason we're winning this war. Besides creating the designs, he also directed the navy in establishing its own foundry to manufacture new equipment."

"Impressive."

"Definitely. About a year and a half ago, he was promoted to rear admiral and took command of the South Atlantic Blockading Squadron. He's not one to mess around." Peter paused. "He's also representative of what makes this whole war so crazy."

Matthew cocked an eyebrow, still too ill to really care what Peter alluded to.

Peter grinned. "Need more time to recover?"

Matthew nodded, his attempt at a smile failing.

"When the war started," Peter continued, "his superior in the navy yard resigned to join the Confederate Navy, so Dahlgren was promoted to captain and took over. It was his son..."

Suddenly, Matthew remembered, and his eyes widened. "His son was the colonel who led the cavalry raid into Richmond. Dahlgren's son was to assassinate Jefferson Davis and get us out of Libby Prison." Matthew frowned. "But Colonel Dahlgren was killed."

"Yes. The papers found on Dahlgren's body indicated plans for the assassination and were widely circulated throughout Europe as an example of Union barbarism. Assassination plans created quite the uproar in the South, as well as in Europe."

"Must have been tough on Admiral Dahlgren," Matthew said sympathetically.

"Yes. Then there's his other son," Peter continued cryptically.

"I didn't realize he had another son," Matthew replied. "Does he serve?"

"Oh, yes," Peter said quietly, "but not on the same side."

"He's a Confederate?" Matthew asked with surprise.

"A Confederate brigadier general and a strong proponent of slave ownership. He's the commander of the Third Brigade, Army of Mississippi. He happened to fund it himself."

Matthew looked out over the pitching waves, his stomach forgotten for the moment. "I can't imagine what it will be like for Dahlgren's family when this war is over," he murmured. "How do you overcome such disparate beliefs and actions?"

"It'll happen in far too many families," Peter agreed, and then he narrowed his eyes as he examined Matthew. "You look like you're feeling better. Are you ready for the real news?"

Matthew was surprised to find he was indeed feeling better. A glance over the side of the boat revealed the waves had diminished, and the talking had taken his mind off his stomach, giving it time to settle. "Let's have it," he answered, managing to give what passed as a real smile. "My editor seems quite sure Savannah is about to fall."

"There's no way around it," Peter replied. "But first, I expected you to be assigned to Sherman's march across Georgia. What happened?"

Matthew shrugged. "I was assigned. I refused."

"Refused?"

"I told my editor I had watched plenty of burning in the Shenandoah Valley and that I would not spend weeks watching more of the same." Matthew's eyes darkened with the memories of what he had seen during those weeks.

"His reaction?"

Matthew shrugged. "He wasn't pleased. I told him he could have my resignation or send me somewhere else. He'd never had me refuse anything before, so he sent me down to Washington to cover Lincoln's election. I've been hanging around in DC and Philadelphia for almost six weeks." He looked at Peter. "What about you?"

"I was with Sherman," Peter said quietly.

"You were?" Matthew gazed around him. "How did you end up on this boat then?"

"I was with the troops that took Fort McAllister on the thirteenth. It opened up the supply link between the Union Navy and Sherman's troops. My editor assigned me to the *Pawnee* in case there is a bombardment of Savannah."

Matthew gazed at him and recognized the look in his friend's eyes. "What was it like?" he asked. "Being with Sherman's army?"

Peter sighed. "It was bad," he said. "I truly believe General Sherman is confident he took the course necessary to end the war, but the hatred and seeds of bitterness his actions took will be felt for a very long time."

Matthew understood the shadow that fell over his friend's eyes and the tightness that turned his face to stone.

"The army pretty much destroyed every part of Georgia they touched. They burned farms and plantations, took crops and livestock, killed people who resisted..." Peter's voice thickened. "Sherman's men destroyed every manufacturing facility they found and totally demolished hundreds of miles of railroad tracks."

"His goal was to inflict maximum psychological, economic and tactical damage to the Confederacy," Matthew observed, understanding the agony Peter had endured for the last weeks.

"Sherman accomplished it," Peter said shortly, then gazed out over the water, his eyes betraying his confusion. "It's so hard to know what is right."

"You can't possibly think all that destruction was right," Matthew protested.

"No, but what is?" Peter's face twisted. "That's the question that keeps me awake at night. I don't agree with what happened, but I don't know what could have been done differently that would have had the same impact."

"Do you think it was worth it?"

Peter stared out at the waves for long moments, and then he finally shook his head. "I can't possibly answer that question. I don't think anyone can right now because we don't know the ramifications of Sherman's actions. The immediate results may indicate it was worth it, but what about when the war is over? What about fifty years from now when bitterness still mandates how people think?" His voice trailed off. "I don't know."

"So, what now? I understand Savannah is well protected behind solid entrenchments."

"It is," Peter replied. "When Sherman got here on the tenth, he discovered Hardee with ten thousand men in good positions. In addition, Hardee had flooded all the surrounding rice fields, leaving only narrow causeways available to approach the city. Sherman was blocked from hooking up with the Union Navy, and he was running out of supplies."

"Until he attacked Fort McAllister."

"Right. The battle only lasted fifteen minutes, but it opened up the supply lines."

Matthew stared toward the spires of Savannah he could see in the distance. He'd spent time there before the war and loved the elegant city with its carefully laid out city blocks. "What now?"

Peter shrugged. "It's up to them." He pulled a sheet of paper out of his pocket. "Sherman sent a letter to Hardee three days ago."

I have already received guns that can cast heavy and destructive shots as far as the heart of your city; also I have for some days held and controlled every avenue by which the people and garrison of Savannah can be supplied, and I am therefore justified in demanding the surrender of the city of Savannah, and its dependent forts, and shall wait a reasonable time for your answer, before opening with heavy ordnance. Should you entertain the proposition, I am prepared to grant liberal terms to the inhabitants and garrison; but should I be forced to resort to assault, or the slower and surer process of starvation, I shall then feel justified in resorting to the harshest measures, and shall make little effort to restrain my army—burning to avenge the national wrong which they attach to Savannah and other large cities which have been so prominent in dragging our country into civil war.

Matthew pondered the words for a minute. "That's pretty clear. The people of Savannah have to have a fairly clear picture of what could happen to their town if they don't surrender."

"I'm sure the people of Savannah do," Peter agreed quickly, "but Hardee may not feel the same way. If he tries to hold it, I fear it will be another Atlanta."

"Do you think he will try?"

"My understanding is that he wrote a letter back saying Sherman was overstating his position and that he has no intention of surrendering the city."

Matthew winced. "There may be no cities left in the South if this continues."

A sudden holler from the water caught their attention. They watched as a smaller boat pulled to the side, the men in the boat waving their arms wildly.

Peter ran forward. "Those are journalists from New York City. They snuck into town this morning to see what they could discover. I've been watching for them all day, wondering if they would make it back."

He and Matthew, along with a couple more men, helped the journalists onto the *Pawnee* and waited for them to speak.

"They're gone," one man said excitedly.

"Who?" Peter asked.

"Hardee. And his entire army."

"How?" Matthew sputtered, turning to stare at the shore. "How did he move ten thousand men?"

The man who had spoken looked at Matthew for a moment. "You the journalist from Philadelphia who escaped Libby Prison?"

Matthew nodded.

"Then you'll appreciate what Hardee did," he said with a grin, stepping forward to shake his hand. "I'm Frank McCanna. I've been an admirer of yours for a long time."

Matthew flushed, but shook the man's hand firmly. "Tell me how Hardee pulled it off."

"In spite of his earlier reply to Sherman, Hardee realized if he didn't want to lose his entire army, the only course he really had was to retreat." Frank looked around at the listening men. "Anyone know what a rice field flat is?"

Matthew nodded. "It's a shallow skiff about eighty feet long. They use them to harvest the rice. But what…"

"Hardee linked them as floats for a bridge from the foot of West Broad Street in the city to Hutchinson's Island, to Pennyworth Island, and then onto the South Carolina shore."

All the men listening whistled in amazement.

"Railroad car wheels were used to anchor the flats in the river, and planks from waterfront buildings served as the bridging material," Frank continued. "They even covered the whole thing with rice straw to muffle the noise."

Matthew shook his head in amazement. "Ten thousand men?"

"And forty-nine field guns," Frank confirmed. "They're gone."

All the men sat silently as they absorbed the news. "Have to admire that kind of ingenuity," Peter observed. "It's another army we have to finish off before the war will end, but I can't feel anything but admiration for Hardee."

"What now?" Matthew asked the obvious question.

"Richard Arnold, the mayor of Savannah, rode out this morning and surrendered the city." Frank grinned. "How do you think we got so much information? Federal troops reached the City Exchange early this morning and raised our flag."

Matthew and Peter cheered with the rest of the men. Matthew wasn't sure whether he was more excited about the victory the North had won, or about the fact he might find a bed on solid ground that night.

Carrie was used to the sound of her father's heavy footsteps. Nothing but bad news was coming from every direction as Christmas approached. Her heart ached for him as he stepped in the door, his face creased with heavy lines.

"Not much good news, I'm afraid," Robert said when Thomas walked through the door.

The frown lines disappeared in a warm smile. "Robert!" Thomas exclaimed, striding forward to grasp his hand and pull him into a hug. "When did you get home?"

"This morning. You had already left for the Capitol."

Thomas looked over at Carrie. "Obviously the two of you have had a wonderful day. I haven't seen my daughter this happy for quite some time. She has her glow back," he said approvingly.

Carrie threw another couple logs on the fire and answered her father's question before he asked it. "Micah is helping May in the kitchen. She insisted on a special dinner tonight since Robert is home again. She's pulling some vegetables out of the cellar. I don't know what she's doing in there, but it smells heavenly. I told Micah I would keep the fire going."

Thomas nodded and sat down in his chair, the frown settling on his face again.

Robert settled down in the chair beside him. "It's no good to pretend our situation isn't dire, Thomas. Is there more news?"

Thomas stared into the flames for a long moment. "Savannah has fallen."

Robert frowned. "So quickly? Sherman got there less than two weeks ago. I wasn't aware there was a battle."

"There wasn't," Thomas said. "Hardee took all his men and escaped."

"All of them?" Carrie asked. "How?"

Thomas explained Hardee's escape. "Word came through today. It was a brilliant escape, but we have lost another city."

"Hardee didn't stand a chance against Sherman's army. They had four times as many men," Robert observed. "If he had stayed and fought, Savannah would have been destroyed the same way Atlanta was."

Thomas flushed with anger. "Ah yes, Atlanta..."

Carrie gazed at him with sympathy. She knew how much he had loved the Georgia city. It had almost broken his heart when he heard it had been burned.

"Is the news from Georgia as bad as I've heard?" Robert asked. "We got some news up in the Valley, but I'm sure we didn't get the whole story."

"If you received enough news to know the Union Army destroyed Georgia, you got the gist of it," Thomas said, bitterness edging into his voice.

Robert nodded heavily while Carrie's thoughts flew to Louisa and Perry again.

"Sherman set out to destroy not only a state, but also the morale and determination of a nation," Thomas said.

"And did he succeed?" Robert asked.

Thomas looked up sharply. "You sound as if you hope he did, Robert."

Robert gazed at him evenly for long moments, the crackle of the fire the only sound in the room. "You know as well as I do that we cannot win this war, Thomas. Any hope of their letting us go died with Lincoln's reelection. Now the North will continue to wear us down and burn us out. For how long?" He stared into the flames. "How much more destruction? How much more death?"

Carrie knew the sorrow he carried from what he had witnessed in the Shenandoah Valley. She had lain beside him while he napped, holding him close when his body jerked with nightmares and his breathing turned to gasps. She longed to soothe all the pain from his tortured eyes, but she knew only time and love could do that. She had prayed all day that even that would work. But first the war had to end...

Thomas locked eyes with him. "I don't know how to do anything but fight," he finally murmured. "What will happen when the war is over?" His shoulders slouched under the weight of his thoughts.

He looked up at Robert. "Will you continue to fight?"

Robert nodded. "I will. Everything will soon center on Richmond. Sherman has taken Savannah, but I'm sure he will move north at some point to join Grant's army. I don't know that I really have a choice, but I will fight to protect the ones I love. Carrie... You..."

Carrie blinked back the tears as she watched the tortured expression play over Robert's face in the firelight. A cold wind whistled down the chimney as the lanterns around the room flickered into the shadows. Her heart was breaking as she stared at the two men she loved most, both dealing with so much pain and loss.

She was so happy Robert was home, but she knew it was only temporary. And then she would go back to the worry and agony of separation.

Suddenly, an image of the rainbow sprang to mind. *Choose joy for just this moment, Carrie,* she reminded herself. *For just this moment.* She took a deep breath and forced a smile to her face.

"What will come, will come," she said, "but for tonight, we have each other. We have a warm home and an amazing meal that May will soon serve. We can't change what is happening, but we can change how we live tonight."

Both Robert and Thomas gazed at her, obviously trying to break free from their feelings, if only for her sake.

Thomas was the first to speak. "She won't let me wallow in my self-pity," he said, managing a weak smile. "She keeps telling me I have so much to be grateful for."

Robert walked over and wrapped his arm around Carrie. "And, as usual, she is right. Savannah is gone. Grant is here, and Sherman is coming. But not tonight," he said. "Tonight, we have each other."

The door opened, with the wind catching it and banging it against the wall, the chandelier swaying and tinkling. Janie and Clifford walked in laughing, Jeremy on their heels.

Jeremy was the first to notice Robert. "So you're the famous husband," he said, smiling as he came forward to give him a strong handshake.

"And you're the uncle who will help me keep my willful wife in line," Robert quipped, laughing with everyone else as Carrie merely raised her eyebrows in disdain.

Janie was next as she pushed forward and wrapped Robert in a warm hug. "I'm so glad you're home," she said. Then she pulled Clifford forward. "Meet my husband."

Soon laughter and talking filled the room. Everyone moved into the dining room when Micah and May, wide smiles on their faces, carried out platters of food. The light of love and friendship forced horror, loss and pain into the shadows of the background.

At least for the night...

Chapter Twenty-Two

"Miss Rose! Miss Rose!" Carla came running down the road, her eyes bright from the cold, but her body snuggly warm from the coat Aunt Abby had sent down in one of her barrels the week before.

Rose stopped, waited for Carla to catch her, and thought how Aunt Abby had become a heroine to everyone in the camps for the constant stream of supplies that came in what everyone called her *'magic barrels.'* Other groups sent barrels, but when Aunt Abby's arrived, everyone crowded around eagerly, knowing the barrels would be full of the things they needed and wanted most.

Rose was quite sure she had the best equipped school of all the contraband camps. She didn't know how Aunt Abby kept the supply of paper, pencils and books coming, but all the students had everything they needed.

Finally, Carla ran up and slid to a stop, her breath coming in huge gasps, her eyes wide with excitement.

"Is there a fire somewhere?" Rose teased. She could tell by Carla's shining eyes that there was no reason for her to feel alarm.

"No, Miss Rose, there ain't no fire."

"No, Miss Rose, there isn't a fire," Rose corrected.

"That's what I said," Carla insisted, smiling slyly.

Rose merely looked at her until Carla squirmed.

"Sorry," the little girl finally mumbled. "No, Miss Rose, there isn't a fire."

Rose laughed. "That's not so hard, is it?" she asked. "It didn't hurt much to say it correctly, did it?"

Carla caught her breath and stared up at her. "Why is it so important to you, Miss Rose, that we always say things right? It gets awful tiresome at times."

Rose leaned down to give the girl a warm hug. "I know it does, honey, but when this war is over and you leave the contraband camp, you're going to be living in a brand new world." She smiled as she thought about it. "It will be a world where you can be anything you want to be. A teacher. Or a doctor. Or anything else." Her voice grew serious. "But it will be hard, Carla."

"If it will be hard anyway, what does it matter so much?"

"Because it will be *easier* if you speak correctly, and if you can read and write." Rose lifted Carla's chin until her eyes met the child's. "I love you, Carla. I want you to have everything you dream of. It's my job as a teacher to prepare you to be able to do that."

"You're sure good at it," Carla said. "I hope one day I'm gonna...*going to* be like you. That's what I want, you know. I'm going to be a teacher like you."

"And you'll be a great one," Rose said, tears misting her eyes. "When it's time, I would love for you to teach with me."

Carla gasped. "Really, Miss Rose? Me?"

"Absolutely," Rose said. "I can hardly wait until that day comes. I've watched you help the younger students. You're a natural teacher." She took a deep breath as she thought of all the things she could hardly wait to have happen. Then she forced them from her mind. She was learning to live one day at a time. Wishing for things she couldn't have, only sapped her energy. "Now, why did you come to find me?"

"Oh, I almost forgot!" Carla cried. "It's real important!"

"Then why don't you tell me what it is," she said.

"My mama wants you to come for dinner tonight," Carla said. "I'm to bring you right now."

Rose frowned. "Carla, I'm sorry, but I can't do that. I promised June I would be home in a few minutes. She's taking care of John and Simon."

"June is already there," Carla insisted. "She and the boys came a little while ago."

Rose stared down the road toward their house. She appreciated the kind offer, and rarely a day went by that one of her students' families didn't have her for a meal or drop food by for her and June, but she had to admit she was looking forward to a quiet evening. As much as she loved Carla's family, Rose longed to sit by her fire and play with John.

"Come on, Miss Rose," Carla insisted, tugging her hand. "Mama said to bring you right back and that's what I'm going to do." She seemed to sense Rose's hesitation as her face screwed up in thought. "I ain't supposed to say nothing..." She stopped in mid-sentence when Rose lifted her eyebrows. "I mean, I'm not supposed to say anything, but there's a surprise for you."

Rose's heart melted when she saw the burning excitement in Carla's eyes. She knew what it was taking for the girl to keep her secret. She grabbed Carla's hand and started back down the road, pushing away her desire for a quiet evening. "Then I suppose we best go find out what it is. We ain't wantin' to be late for no surprise."

Carla gasped and looked at her wide eyed. "Miss Rose, you didn't say that right!"

Rose laughed and kept walking. "How *should* I have said it?" She let Carla teach her the rest of the way.

~~~

The cold wind whipping through the camp kept most people inside, so Rose was curious why so many of Wally and Deidre's neighbors were out on their porches in the waning sunlight. Surely they would rather be inside around their fires.

Rose nodded, smiled and spoke to everyone as she and Carla hurried up to the house. As soon as her foot reached the first step of the porch, the door was flung open and a well-dressed lady, her face wreathed in smiles, stepped out.

"It's about time you got here, young lady. I thought I'd have to go get you myself."

"Aunt Abby!" Rose cried, leaping up the final step and throwing herself into the woman's arms. "I can't believe you're here!" She laughed with delight while tears of joy coursed down her face.

"Surprise!" Carla yelled, dancing around and waving her arms. "I told you there was a surprise!"

Aunt Abby wiped away her own tears and waved to all the neighbors who were laughing and applauding. "We've all been waiting the last hour for you to get here."

"I had a student who needed some more help..." Rose started to explain.

"Say no more." Aunt Abby laughed, waving her hand. "I already suspected that was holding you up. I'm glad you're here, though, because I don't think I could have waited one more minute to see you!"

Rose turned to see Wally and Deidre standing in the doorway, their faces glowing with the fun of their surprise. Wally, needed for supply work at Fort Monroe, had gotten home a few weeks earlier. Deidre had been glowing ever since. "How long have you known?" Rose asked.

"We got a letter two weeks back," Wally admitted.

Rose stared at Deidre. "You kept a secret for *two weeks*?"

"I can keep a secret if it's real important," Deidre said primly, her eyes dancing with fun.

Wally snorted. "I told her if she let the secret spill, I wouldn't dance with her at the Christmas dance tomorrow."

"My man does know how I love to dance," Deidre said, smiling prettily. "Of course, since he's about the only man around the camp, I know I'll have to share him."

Rose laughed and pulled Aunt Abby into the warm house.

June sat with the boys by the fire. "I told Carla to hint at a surprise if you resisted. I know you can't stand not knowing about a surprise."

Rose gazed around the room, so grateful for all these people who loved her and knew her so well. Sudden tears filled her eyes again, but she blinked them away. She refused to feel sorry for herself that Moses wouldn't be with her for Christmas when she was surrounded by so much love.

"You're looking nervous," Moses observed, ducking his head against the cold wind, his heart singing with excitement.

Simon nodded slowly, his body hunched forward in his saddle. "The first thing I'm nervous about is that this here horse is gonna throw me right off." He shifted in his saddle and gripped tightly to the saddle horn. "How much farther we going to be riding these horses?"

Moses laughed loudly as he glanced around at the small band of men riding with him. All of them looked equally uncomfortable on their horses. "Would you rather *walk* to Fort Monroe?"

"Right about now I would say yes," Simon retorted. "Of course, the way my legs are feeling, I might never walk again." His grin shone through. "I reckon it's for a good cause, though." His eyes glittered brightly above his tightly buttoned coat. "I can't hardly wait to get my woman back in my arms." His grin grew bigger. "And to see my baby boy."

"And I can't wait to see Rose and June's faces when we surprise them at the dance tomorrow night," Moses replied.

"Don't know how I'm supposed to dance when I can't even walk," Simon muttered.

"That's what I been thinking," another of his men complained. "Can't we get off and walk for a while?"

Moses took pity on them and reined his horse to a stop, but he knew they would all be clamoring to get back on their horses soon. He smiled when all of them groaned in relief as soon as their feet hit solid ground.

"Now this is more like it," Simon said.

Moses looped his reins over his arm and picked his way carefully through the muddy ruts running as far as the eye could see. He thought about the last few days to keep his mind off his misery. He knew it wouldn't be long before his men begged to be back in the saddle.

He had been reading a letter from Rose when the summons to Captain Jones' tent had come. Ten minutes after striding into the tent, he strode back out, his face bursting with a smile, and went in search of the five men who were now riding with him.

Captain Jones, who was now as much mentor and friend as he was his commanding officer, had told him his men were being rewarded for their role in the Darbytown battle. All of his unit would receive extra rations for Christmas, but he also gave Moses special permission to spend five days at Fort Monroe and to take five of his men with him. All the men he chose had wives living at the contraband camp. Moses grinned when he thought of the ruckus they would cause when he and his men walked into the Christmas dance. Not even the raw, cold wind biting at him as he stumbled in the deep ruts could diminish his excitement.

"Uh, Moses?"

"Yes?" It had taken less time than he hoped for the men to get tired of battling the muddy trenches.

"Me and the fellas think we could ride again now," Simon said.

Moses bit back his laugh and nodded, remembering his first long haul after he had learned to ride. "Sounds like a fine idea."

"You ain't even going to laugh at us?" one of his men demanded.

Moses shook his head, but he couldn't hide the glimmer in his eyes or the quirk of his lips. He turned and swung into his saddle. When he turned to watch his men pull themselves heavily on top of their horses, Moses lost control and burst out laughing. Soon the afternoon rang with laughter.

"I know it will all be worth it when we get there," Simon admitted, "but I ain't never hurt like this in my life."

"And you're riding along like this ain't nothing, Moses," another of his men groaned. "I can't believe this can actually get easier. I would rather be heading out on a twenty-mile march in the burning sun!"

"Down these rutted roads?" Moses asked, still smiling.

"No. That be the only reason we're back in these saddles," Simon retorted. "Of course, if we had to, I would crawl there on my hands and knees," he admitted as he stood slightly in the saddle to take some pressure off his rear end.

Moses knew they still had hours of riding before they could stop for the night. He knew of one sure way to help keep their minds off their pain. He opened his mouth and began to sing, his deep bass rising into the cold air.

Swing low, sweet chariot
Coming for to carry me home,
Swing low, sweet chariot,
Coming for to carry me home.

I looked over Jordan, and what did I see
Coming for to carry me home?
A band of angels coming after me,
Coming for to carry me home.

Swing low, sweet chariot
Coming for to carry me home,
Swing low, sweet chariot,
Coming for to carry me home.

Sometimes I'm up, and sometimes I'm down,
Coming for to carry me home,
But still my soul feels heavenly bound.
Coming for to carry me home.

Swing low, sweet chariot
Coming for to carry me home,
Swing low, sweet chariot,
Coming for to carry me home.

The brightest day that I can say,
Coming for to carry me home,
When Jesus washed my sins away.
Coming for to carry me home.

Swing low, sweet chariot
Coming for to carry me home,
Swing low, sweet chariot,
Coming for to carry me home.

If I get there before you do,
Coming for to carry me home,
I'll cut a hole and pull you through,
Coming for to carry me home.

Swing low, sweet chariot
Coming for to carry me home,
Swing low, sweet chariot,
Coming for to carry me home.

If you get there before I do,
Coming for to carry me home,
Tell all my friends I'm coming too,
Coming for to carry me home.

Moses was glad the cold winter day was sure to drive any Confederate scouts around a warm fire. The combined voices of all his men rang for quite a distance, but they were smiling again. It was worth the risk.

When their voices faded away, another would start a new song. The miles faded away beneath their horses' hooves, the sky growing dark as the icy wind continued to blow.

›‹⊂⋅⋅⊃⋅‹

Rose smiled brightly as the large barrack filled with people from the camp. She was so grateful the army made this building available to them for their annual Christmas dance. The mass of food spread out on the tables continued to swell as families arrived, dressed in their finest clothes, their faces wreathed with smiles. Children squealed with laughter as they pulled free from their mamas' hands and ran to join in games with their friends.

The Christmas dance would be mostly women and children, since all the men were off fighting or serving the army, but the women had learned not to let the absence of men diminish their dancing.

Rose nodded and spoke with all who stopped to talk to her, which was almost everyone. John babbled on her shoulder, waving his hands in demand to get down, but the room was so crowded she was afraid he would get swept under someone's feet. He was walking, but he was still unsteady at times. She wanted him where she could keep an eye on him.

"Will you look at all that food!" Aunt Abby exclaimed. "What a difference from two years ago."

Rose nodded happily. "Everyone has a big garden, and the number of livestock has exploded. Almost every family has chickens and pigs, and we've got enough cows to supply milk for all the children. Not to mention the army always provides us with ham and turkey for the Christmas dance."

"People seem healthier this year," Aunt Abby observed, gazing around.

"They are. More medical people have been sent down, but it's mostly because everyone is eating so much better, and everyone has enough clothes to keep warm. It's made such a difference."

"They're learning to take care of themselves," Aunt Abby said with satisfaction. "And they have you to thank for it."

"Me?" Rose protested. "I'm just their teacher. You're the one who has made it possible to get medical help and supplies, and your mountain of barrels keeps everyone in clothes."

"Perhaps, but it's the fact they are learning that has given all these people the hunger to take care of themselves and make something of their lives. The very spirit of this place has changed in the last two years. I see pride and self-respect on every face."

Rose nodded, her gaze sweeping the room. "I know this is a small group compared to the millions of my people who will have to learn to direct their own lives when the war is over, but I believe it's proof that education will work."

"I'm already pulling together women who will help establish black schools when the war is over," Aunt Abby revealed, her eyes shining with excitement. "When I told them about what you and the other teachers are doing down here they were all eager to help."

Rose clapped her hands together with delight. "Oh, Aunt Abby! What would I do without you?" She grabbed her in a big hug. "Thank you so much."

Aunt Abby hugged her back. "We'll be helping each other make a difference for a very long time, my dear. This is only the beginning."

Rose felt a wave of sadness sweep over her. "Carrie would love this," she murmured. She closed her eyes as memories assailed her.

Aunt Abby squeezed her hand tightly. "We will celebrate Christmases with Carrie," she said. "Surely you realize the war will end soon?"

Rose nodded. "Yes. I realize the South has to be close to losing this war, but what if—"

Aunt Abby held a finger to her lips. "Not another word. It will do nothing but suck life from your spirit. I predict all of us will be celebrating Christmas together next year. Can't you see it?"

Rose smiled as new images flowed into her mind.

A sudden scream from the doorway jolted her out of her dreams. "What was that?" The wild screaming continued, and then cheering and applause broke out. Rose shifted John to sit more squarely on her hip, and began to work her way through the crowd to find out what was happening.

Another scream from a different direction had her whirling around, her mind spinning with confusion. Was something wrong? She knew there were soldiers watching the building. How could anyone have gotten through?

A scream she recognized split through the bustling room. "June!" Rose cried, turning quickly and heading toward the sound. "Aunt Abby, we have to help June," she gasped.

"I don't think she's needing any help," Aunt Abby said merrily as she stretched to her full height. "The advantage of being tall is that you can see over crowds. June looks happy to me."

"But the screaming..." Rose muttered and continued to push her way forward. When she broke out of the crowd, she finally understood the reason for all the excitement, and a wide smile lit her face.

June was laughing and crying as she gazed up into the face of a tall, handsome man who had her wrapped tightly with one arm. His other arm was holding Simon. The baby laughed with delight even as he looked at the strange man with bewilderment.

"Simon!" Rose gasped. "It has to be Simon!" Suddenly, she realized everyone had turned away from the drama unfolding before them and was now staring at her. She gazed back at them in confusion, until she realized they weren't looking *at* her but *past* her. Her heart began pounding with anticipation even while her mind told her it wasn't possible.

Moses' arms swept around her as she was turning. "Merry Christmas, Mrs. Samuels," he said tenderly, pulling John into one arm while he lowered his lips to hers.

Not caring that the entire room was watching, Rose kissed him back fervently, her arms reaching up to encircle his neck. "Moses. Oh, Moses!" Tears blurred her eyes, but she knew those tears didn't diminish her smile. "It's really you."

"Yes, ma'am, it's really me." Moses grinned like a little boy. "And I have five of my men with me. All of them have wives here in the camp." Another scream rent the building. "That would be another one finding his woman," he said, delight filling his face as he pulled Rose close again.

When he raised his head, his eyes moved beyond her and grew wide. "Aunt Abby!" he cried. He released Rose long enough to crush the older woman in a hug and then laughed delightedly. "Now this is what I call a Christmas dance."

Rose laughed and spun in a circle. "You do realize every woman here will want to dance with you, don't you?"

"I warned all the men we would be a rare commodity. They have four days with their wives—their mission for tonight is to dance with as many women as they can."

Rose focused on only two of the words he said. "Four days? John and I really have you for four days?" she gasped.

"Rose! Rose!"

Rose turned as June hurtled across the room, pulling a man almost as big as Moses. He still held little Simon, grinning as he followed June.

"This is my Simon, Rose! This is my Simon!" June cried. She saw Moses and threw herself on him. "Thank you," she cried. "Thank you for bringing my Simon to me."

Moses brushed at the tears in his eyes. People all around them were crying with the joy of the reunions throughout the room.

"You're welcome, little sister," he said. He looked over at Simon. "That's a mighty fine son you have there."

Simon grinned so big he looked as if his face would split. "That he is," he said proudly. "That he is." He reached out to tickle John under his chin. "You got a right handsome boy yourself. I'm right proud to be his uncle." He pulled June close to his side again and gazed down at her. "It's been more than three years," he murmured. "You're more beautiful than ever."

Rose felt her heart would burst with happiness. She also understood the yearning in June's eyes. She leaned closer to her and whispered. "Go back to the house. I'll keep Simon here with John so they can play. You'll have the place to yourself for a few hours." She glanced at Moses. "I think the women can do without one dance partner," she said quietly. "In fact..." She let her voice trail off meaningfully.

Moses nodded easily. "I reckon they can." He raised his voice so that everyone in the room could hear him. "Hello, everyone. I know every woman in this room understands how they would feel if their husband, who they haven't seen in several years, suddenly appeared in the room. I had told the men they would have dance duty tonight, but I believe all of you will agree with me that they should spend time with their wives. I promise you we're all fighting as hard as we can to make sure *your* men come home soon."

Applause and cheers broke out as Moses' men grabbed their wives and pulled them from the building.

"I have to stay here until the dance is over," Rose said when Moses turned to her, responsibility and desire warring in her heart.

"Of course you do," Moses said, holding her with his eyes and reaching for her when the dancing started. "I've been dreaming of dancing with you. Let's show these people how it's done."

"Go!" Aunt Abby urged. "I'll watch little Simon and John while you two dance. Nothing would give me more pleasure."

"Thank you, Aunt Abby. I'll be back for you in a little while," Moses promised.

Rose laughed happily and allowed her husband to pull her out onto the floor. Everyone else in the room melted away as she gazed up into his intense eyes. The music flowed around them and created a swirl of magic that wrapped her up and made anything seem possible.

When the music faded, Rose stayed wrapped in Moses' arms. "Aunt Abby believes we'll be with Carrie next Christmas. Tonight, it feels like anything is possible."

"The war will be over," Moses said with absolute certainty. "The South is done. They haven't given up yet, and we're probably going to have to finish things at Richmond, but I don't think it will be much longer."

Rose stiffened when he spoke of Richmond.

Moses pulled her closer. "We're going to think good thoughts about Carrie," he whispered. "This war will end, and we'll find a way to be with her again."

Rose nodded, praying his words were true. "Aunt Abby has already opened doors for her to go to medical school. I wonder if she'll still want to..."

"Carrie wants to be a doctor the way you want to be a teacher. I don't believe war will change that. In fact, from what Matthew tells me, she wants it more strongly than ever."

Rose nodded. "He told me the same thing when he came through here after his escape." She turned her eyes toward Richmond. "Christmas with Carrie. I pray it will happen soon."

The music started again, and Moses pulled her into a wild dance. Rose cast aside her fears and worries and lost herself in the joy she felt with Moses. She knew the four days would fly by, but she, June and the other women would create enough loving memories to carry them through.

"You reckon there will be enough food here?" Hobbs asked, his eyes dancing with laughter.

Carrie looked up from the box she was packing. "There's no use in pretending all the soldiers will get anything even similar to what they've known for Christmas in the past, but I do hope all of them get something."

She allowed herself to gaze toward Petersburg and held close the memory of Robert being home for five glorious days. Christmas dinner had been very simple, with none of the splendor of Christmases past and much less than even the three years before, but she'd had all she needed and wanted because she'd been surrounded by the people she loved most. The only gift she needed was waking up each morning warm and snug beside Robert.

With Robert back in the trenches in front of Petersburg, she was doing all she could to support him. A group of women had descended on the Ballard House to cook for hours on end. The aroma from all the food filled the neighborhood. Every person who passed the house regarded it hungrily, but no one attempted to steal any of it.

"Where did all these hams, chickens and turkeys come from?" Hobbs asked in wonder.

"The same place as the beef, mutton and sausage," Carrie said, filling her box to the brim with savory cooked meats. "People have been hiding them all through the war." She closed the box with a snap and looked up with flaming eyes. "Those men out there are starving. They're standing in those awful trenches without overcoats and shoes in an effort to protect us. The least we can do is give them a special Christmas meal."

"Even though it's January second?" Hobbs asked.

"They'll appreciate food no matter when it comes to them," Carrie said firmly. "Our soldiers are suffering horribly. I feel bad for the ones in the hospital, but at least they're warm and have some kind of food. That's more than I can say about our soldiers in the field."

Hobbs gazed at her for a long moment. "Robert told me that in most regiments only about fifty men even have shoes."

Carrie shuddered, so thankful Robert at least had warm clothes. Her father had spent some of his rapidly dwindling fortune to make sure of it. While she had been thankful to have Robert with her, she hated that his men were suffering, and now she was fearful of what would happen to her husband when the fighting started again.

"Lee is calling up every single man who can do *anything*," Hobbs said quietly.

Carrie's heart clenched, but she met his eyes squarely. "You're going to join them?"

Hobbs' eyes begged her to understand. "I can still hold a gun. I can still cook or clean dishes or do whatever else is needed."

"You know Sherman's entire army will head this way to join Grant's?"

"I reckon they will."

"And you want to fight again?"

Hobbs frowned as his gaze shifted away. "*Want* to fight? I don't reckon there's a soldier left on either side that *wants* to fight." He stared at her, his eyes intense. "But there are people here I care about. You're one of them, Miss Carrie. I'll do whatever I can to keep the Yankees from taking Richmond."

Carrie stared at him, knowing it was useless to argue. But still... "You know the South will lose, don't you?"

Hobbs' eyes flamed, and he opened his mouth to protest, but then closed it without a word. Long moments passed before he slowly nodded. "Me and Robert talked about it."

"But still you feel you have no choice?"

"Choice? You done taught me I always have a choice, Miss Carrie. I've decided going back to join Lee is the only choice I can live with. Once I decided that, I was able to accept that I can live with whatever consequences come with it."

Carrie took a deep breath and walked over to give him a warm hug. "I'll miss you."

"You reckon you'll be all right?" Hobbs asked anxiously. "Me and Robert talked about how you would stay safe going down to the black hospital if I'm not with you."

"I'll be fine," Carrie said. "I have my gun, which I've become quite good at using. Plus, Janie and I can always get Jeremy or Clifford to join us. There have been no threats in many months. It's so cold now that I doubt anyone will venture out to bother us."

Hobbs heaved a sigh of relief. "That's what me and Robert figured."

Carrie smiled tenderly, thankful for the concern, even though every man in her life knew she would go ahead and do whatever she felt needed doing when the time arose. She appreciated their effort to care for her in a way that wouldn't challenge her independence. "Hobbs, I'm much more concerned for you than for me."

"Aw shucks, ain't nothing going to happen to me," he insisted, his brown eyes gazing at her from under his long rusty hair.

Carrie said nothing. Both of them knew anything could happen. He already had one wounded leg that would never be the same. She couldn't stand the idea of anything else happening to him, but she knew she had no ability to change the situation. "Will you be in Robert's unit?" she asked.

"Yes, ma'am," he said with a wide grin. "Me and the captain will be fighting together again. I figure that's a good sign."

"I thought you said you were going back to do anything, even cooking," Carrie said suspiciously. She narrowed her eyes when Hobbs flushed and looked down. "You're going back to fight, but you were trying to protect me from knowing," she said.

Hobbs flushed brightly but looked up and met her eyes. "You've had a powerful lot of worrying to do," he admitted. "I didn't want to add to it."

"Oh, Hobbs," Carrie cried. "I'll worry the same whether you're fighting or cooking. You forget that I care for soldiers every day who have lost limbs because a shell landed on their cooking tent. You're not safe anywhere!" Her voice softened. "I know you believe you have to do this. I'll continue to pray for you every day."

She decided to change the subject. "What will you do when the war is over?"

Hobbs relaxed as his eyes took on a shine. "I'm going home, Miss Carrie. I'm hoping my Coonhound, Bridger, is still alive. I dream of heading up into the mountains on hunting trips. Just me and Bridger."

Carrie watched his eyes come to life and hoped with all her heart Hobbs would get his wish. After almost four years of war, he was still not quite twenty years old. He could never reclaim his childhood, but perhaps he could heal from all he had experienced and create a new life. "That sounds wonderful," she said.

They both looked up as wagons rolled up to the house where they were working. Each grabbed the boxes of food they had packed and carried them out into the cold morning and then came back for more.

When the wagons were full, Carrie watched as they rolled into the distance, hoping every soldier would receive something so that they knew the people of Richmond appreciated what they were doing and how much they were suffering.

Hobbs read her mind. "The fellas will be right thankful," he said.

"It's so little," Carrie replied, "but I know we did the best we could." She looked over at Hobbs. "When are you leaving?"

"Tomorrow," he said. "I decided to stay to help with the food, but I'll be reporting tomorrow."

Carrie nodded heavily and reached over to squeeze his hand. "You and Robert take care of each other."

Carrie stood silently for long minutes after Hobbs went to get their carriage. Her breath created white clouds, but she felt quite warm in her snug coat and scarf. She wanted to cry when she gazed at the hungry, pinch-faced children plodding through the icy winds, gripping small pieces of wood to try to help warm their homes.

1865 had blown in with frigid air, bringing even more misery to the besieged residents of Richmond. People were starving and freezing everywhere—not only in Richmond, but also in Georgia, in the Shenandoah Valley, in the Carolinas and in every place the war had touched. But Richmond had seen the majority of the relentless attempts to break the South. Somehow the city's citizens had managed to hang on, but expressions on every face said they didn't believe they could hold out much longer.

Chapter Twenty-Three

Louisa hummed quietly as she mixed oatmeal in her big, black kettle over the simmering fire. Snow was piling up outside, but the cabin was toasty and warm. Perry was outside tending to the livestock he had hidden from the Union Army. A large swath of Georgia was a burned wasteland, but Louisa and her husband were still alive, and somehow they would carry on.

She looked outside, glad to see the burned foundation of their cotton gin building completely obscured by mounds of deep snow. She hoped the snow's blanket would help erase the pain from Perry's mind. He had cut numerous trees to begin to rebuild the barn in the spring, but there was no way to know when he might be able to replace the cotton gin.

He had already built another barn for their animals, working quickly with the help of neighbors who arrived the day after the destruction. It was not as grand as the one that had burned, but it sheltered their cows and horses, and the chicken coop he rebuilt was filling up again with fowl that produced plenty of eggs.

Louisa sighed with contentment and smiled when her baby kicked her forcefully. "Eager to get out of there, aren't you, little one?" she murmured, patting her extended belly. She knew the baby should come any day now. The crib was ready. Polly, their midwife neighbor, had prepared them well.

Louisa yearned to hold her child close, to feel the evidence that life was indeed continuing on, no matter how many terrible things had happened. She watched as Perry emerged from the barn, his breath coming in puffy white mists. He struggled to get through the snow with his peg leg, but he insisted on doing it himself, and he was learning how to manage.

"Oh my!" Louisa gasped as she doubled over with a sudden, sharp pain. Her eyes widened as warm liquid pooled between her legs. As the pain eased, a smile exploded onto her face. She made her way quickly to the cabin door and pulled it open. "Perry!"

He appeared at the foot of the porch almost instantly, took one look at her face, and knew. "It's time?"

Louisa nodded. "It's time," she agreed. "You'd better go get Polly."

"And leave you here alone?"

Louisa smiled at his alarmed face. "We talked about this. There should be plenty of time for you to get Polly and come back," she said calmly as she reached out to grab his hand. "I'd appreciate it, though, if you did it quickly. I'd rather have you with me."

"I'll have her here fast!" Perry climbed onto the porch, gave her a quick kiss, and fought his way back to the barn through the snow.

Louisa watched from the window until the horses took off down the snowy road at a rapid trot, and then she turned back into the kitchen. She doubled over when another spasm tore through her body, and decided sitting would be a better option. After the pain passed, she carefully pulled the kettle off the fire, stoked the flames with pieces of split wood to keep the house warm, and settled down into her rocker, pulling her quilt tightly and singing softly to herself.

Louisa was determined not to be afraid. They had been through so much already. The birth of a new baby was not something to panic over. Mothers birthed new life every day. She had calm confidence that, after all they had been through, their baby's birth was going to be easy and smooth.

The fire sputtered and crackled as she allowed her thoughts to travel back to Blackwell Plantation. She imagined giving birth in the sumptuous room she had grown up in, surrounded by slaves eager to do her bidding. As she stared around the simple cabin and felt its quiet solitude, she discovered she would much rather have it this way.

She smiled happily as she continued to stroke her belly. "Baby, you're about to enter into a world of love." Louisa frowned as she thought of the war raging through the country. "Oh, the country does not feel a lot of love right now, but your mama and daddy will love you with all their hearts. This crazy war will end, and you will have this home with your daddy and me, little one."

Praying she was speaking the truth, she stared out at the deepening snow and fought to remain calm as another spasm, stronger than all the others, stole her breath. "One of these days I'll tell you how you were born in a fierce Georgia snowstorm that kept your daddy from coming right back with the midwife. I'll tell you how it was just you and me. How I knew I would go through anything to hold you in my arms."

Louisa fought harder to remain calm as the spasms came faster and stronger, just like the snow creating a white curtain outside the window. She could imagine Perry's panic about leaving her alone for so long. She had to face the possibility snow might have made roads impassable and that she was on her own.

"Well, little one, what will we do if your daddy doesn't make it back in time?" She managed to keep her voice calm, and reasoned that if she didn't impart fear to her baby, everything would be easier. She didn't know if it mattered, but fighting to remain calm was better than giving in to absolute panic, which was exactly what her mind was screaming to do.

Louisa stood unsteadily, realizing that if Perry didn't make it back in time, she would be much better off in bed. She staggered across the room, gripping the wall, and then collapsed onto their bed, realizing too late she should have put strips of cloth on to boil—though what she would do with them, even if she could reach them, she had no idea.

"Oh!" This time she couldn't hold back her scream of pain as a spasm ripped through her. "Perry..." she whispered as the door burst open.

"Louisa!" Perry cried, rushing to her side. "A tree was down over the road—"

"You can tell her the story later," Polly said, her voice a study of calm and competence. "I told you what I would need. I suggest you get it."

Perry sprang to follow the midwife's instructions. He stoked the fire into roaring flames and poured water into a kettle that he hung over the fire.

Louisa turned her face to the warmth radiating through the cabin and felt her fear ebb away. Everything would be okay now.

Polly smiled down gently at Louisa. "Sorry you had to be on your own for so long," she said easily. "Let's take a look."

Relieved beyond description that she wouldn't have to have their baby on her own, Louisa took several deep breaths. "I do believe this little one is about ready."

Polly looked up moments later. "I do believe you're right," she said, only her eyes showing anxiety. "I reckon we got here in time."

"Polly? What can I do?"

Polly turned to Perry. "Give me those rags and blankets, and go settle down in the corner. Usually I would send you outside, but I believe you've had enough time out in that snow."

Polly kept up a steady stream of soothing conversation, her hands moving as she positioned Louisa.

Louisa had no idea what Polly was saying because she was lost in a haze of unrelenting pain, but the sound of her voice gave Louisa something to anchor herself with.

"Oh!" She gasped as a contraction harder than any yet seemed to almost rip her in half.

"It's time," Polly said. "When I tell you, I want you to push harder than you ever have in your life, Louisa." She waited a few seconds. "Now!"

Louisa screamed and pushed until she was sure she would pass out. She fell back against the pillows, limp with exhaustion and vaguely aware of Perry's horrified face. She was also aware of an immediate relief.

Moments later, a strident cry filled the cabin. Wonder filled Louisa as she looked at Polly and then at the newborn she held. She watched in silence as Polly cut the umbilical cord and gently washed her baby with warm water.

Polly finally turned to them. "Mr. and Mrs. Appleton, I would like to introduce you to your little boy."

Louisa stared with awe. "Nathan Perry Appleton," she said softly, her eyes filling with tears as she reached for the tiny bundle Polly had swaddled in soft cloths. "He's named after my brother."

Perry stood to the side. "Can I come over?" he asked nervously.

Polly nodded. "Come meet your son and kiss your wife for being such a brave woman." She stared hard at Louisa. "You almost had that baby on your own. From what I heard, you come from a fancy plantation up north in Virginia. I figured you would be soft and spoiled, and that you would be a screaming, nervous wreck when we got here. I reckon I was wrong."

Louisa laughed softly. "I was all those things back then," she admitted, "and if I'd thought being a screaming, nervous wreck would have helped, I might have been tempted. Thankfully I knew it wouldn't." She looked over at Perry with a warm smile. "The war changed me."

"It's changed us all," Polly agreed. She smiled down at Nathan. "But I figure as long as babies keep coming, that's God's message to us that he hasn't given up on the world yet."

Louisa looked up at her and then gazed tenderly at Nathan. "That's what I think, too. It gives me hope for all of us."

~⚜~

Abby brushed the snow off her coat and hat before she opened the door to her home and moved into the warmth, thankful she'd had someone come in and stoke the furnace during these frigid days. She'd stayed an extra week in Virginia at Fort Monroe with Rose. It had been unusually cold in Virginia, but not this bone-aching freeze that had wrapped its tentacles around Philadelphia. Three weeks back at home had her longing to be somewhere warm.

"Maybe I'm getting too old for these winters," she muttered, thinking of the trip she had taken to St. Simons Island, Georgia several years earlier. She rubbed her hands in front of the fireplace as she visualized the sunny beaches and moss-draped live oaks that lined the winding roads. She frowned when she realized that whole area was part of Sherman's devastating march. It made her sick to think of the glorious plantations destroyed and burned.

She sank down into her rose-colored wingback chair and turned up the oil lantern, shuddering as warmth seeped back into her body. She could feel the wind slapping against the windows, icy pellets hammering for entrance. Needing time to relax before she prepared dinner, Abby closed her eyes for a moment. Sometimes, she thought herself silly not to hire a house servant, but she valued her independence and self-reliance too much. Still, after a long day of work, it would have been nice to come home to a hot meal.

"Quit feeling sorry for yourself," she scolded. She thought of the many women she had hired lately who were going home to dark hovels they couldn't afford to heat. With thoughts like that, it didn't take long for Abby to put things back in perspective.

A loud knock brought a tired scowl to her face. She briefly considered not answering, but couldn't imagine leaving someone outside on a night like this. She got to her feet and moved to the door, fixing a smile on her face as she opened it, only to have it burst back as a small group of people pushed past her and slammed the door closed again.

"We did it, Abby!" John Stone crowed as soon as the howling wind was shut off.

Forcing numb fatigue from her mind, Abby blinked her eyes at the ten friends who had descended on her house.

"Surely you know what today is?" a portly woman cried, removing her own coat and hat.

Abby shook her head. "I'm sorry, Catherine," she said contritely. "It's been an extremely long day." Then slowly the fog lifted. She realized only one thing could put the look of absolute delight on these people's faces. She struggled to bring the calendar to the front of her mind and then gasped. "It's January thirty-first!"

"More importantly," John said solemnly, drawing himself to his full height as he deepened his voice dramatically, "this is the day the amendment to abolish slavery passed."

Fatigue fled as Abby stared at him, and then a wide smile split her face. "It passed? It really passed? Slavery has been abolished in the United States?" Joy pulsed through her, sparking energy where there had been nothing but exhaustion.

Suddenly, everyone in the room was laughing and talking at once.

Abby absorbed it all and threw back her head with a hearty laugh. "We must celebrate!" Then she sank down in her chair. "But first, you must tell me everything. I can't believe I forgot what today was."

"Especially after you have worked so long and hard for it," Catherine commented.

"As we all did," Abby responded.

"You're forgiven for forgetting," John replied, "since you are solely responsible for putting more women and blacks to work in this city than any other employer." He moved over and sat down next to her. "You must be exhausted."

"Not anymore," Abby assured him with a brilliant smile. The dream she had worked so hard and so long for was finally a reality. Lincoln had been moving toward it all along, though she was quite sure he hadn't known it. When the war began, he endorsed a statement of war aims saying slavery was not to be touched. When he created the Emancipation Proclamation, he did it hesitantly—more for political reasons than anything else—but each step had taken him closer to an understanding of the real issue.

After his reelection, Lincoln believed the time to strike off all the chains had come, and he knew an amendment was the only way to do it.

Abby shook her head in amazement. "Only four years ago, President Lincoln accepted a proposed amendment specifying that the Constitution could never, in all time, be changed in such a way as to permit interference with the institution of slavery."

"Thank God it never went through," Catherine said fervently.

Abby nodded and looked at John. "Tell me everything about it."

"You know there has been so much argument in the House about this issue. Getting it through the Senate was easy, but getting it through the House was always the issue."

Abby nodded. "Wasn't Fernando Wood, the Democrat from New York, going to speak?"

"Oh, he spoke," John said with a scowl. "In fact, I wrote it all down because I fear what it will mean for the future."

Abby watched him while he dug in his pocket for the piece of paper and smoothed it out enough to read.

"*We may amend the Constitution; we may by superior military force overrun and conquer the South; we may lay waste to their lands and destroy their property; we may free their slaves. But there is one thing we cannot do: we cannot violate with impunity or alter the laws of God. The Almighty has fixed the distinction of the races; the Almighty has made the black man inferior, and sir, by no legislation, no partisan success, by no revolution, by no military power, can you wipe out this distinction. You may make the black man free, but when you have done that, what have you done?*'"

Silence gripped the room as the icy pellets increased their pounding noise.

"When all was said and done," John continued, "the amendment passed the House by one hundred nineteen votes to fifty-six. Pandemonium broke out."

Abby nodded. "Yes, of course it would," she murmured, still gripped by the words spoken by Fernando Wood.

John read her mind. "It feels like the ending of a huge fight, and in some respects it is, but it is the beginning of a much larger struggle."

Abby nodded, appreciating that he shared her thoughts. "One, I fear, that will go on for generations," she said in a troubled voice. "So many people feel the way Wood does, both North and South." She carried vivid memories of the spirited intelligence shining in the eyes of her friends in the contraband camp. Snatches of in-depth conversations she'd had with Rose about educational opportunities for blacks filled her mind. "What will it take to show people that slaves are just like us? They will rise to the occasion and will become so much more than they'd envisioned for themselves when given the opportunity."

"I agree we still have a huge battle ahead of us," Catherine said, "but I also recognize we have won a huge victory that many people have worked hard for. I, for one, would love to celebrate that. Tomorrow, along with the battles it brings, will come soon enough."

Abby shook off her thoughts and jumped up. "Of course, you're right!" she exclaimed. "I had a friend bring by two cakes yesterday. I had no idea what I would do with them. Now I know." She moved toward the kitchen. "I'll fix some coffee, and we'll have a victory party!"

～･✦･～

Moses looked up from his huddled position next to the fire when a messenger stopped beside him. "Captain Jones wants you in his tent," the man snapped before he moved on, obviously eager to find his own source of warmth.

Moses wrapped his coat more tightly and stepped away from the fire. He glanced over at the Rebel trenches and realized that, as miserable as he was, the Southern boys had it much worse. At least Moses and his men had log structures in the trenches to build fires in. They also had food and clothing. He could hear the hacking coughs coming from the other side that told him how sick those men must be. Watching them during the day and seeing them in battle, Moses knew most of the Rebel soldiers had hardly any clothes, and he knew their food supplies must be scarce. He could want to win the war but still feel sorry for the ones about to lose.

"You sent for me, Captain?"

Bundled against the cold, Captain Jones looked up from the table he was seated behind. "Yes. Have a seat, Moses. I'll only be a minute."

Moses settled into a chair and relaxed in the relative warmth of the tent—not that any place could be warm when it was this frigid. He watched as the captain finished reviewing some papers, pushed them aside, and looked up with a smile.

"You and your men have some celebrating to do tonight," he said lightly.

"What are we celebrating?"

"Well..."

Moses watched as the captain drew out his words, obviously wanting to play up the moment. Moses had no idea... Suddenly, his eyes grew wide, and he leaned forward in his chair with anticipation. Cold misery had almost made him forget what day it was.

Captain Jones chuckled and nodded his head. "Yes. The amendment to abolish slavery passed."

Moses took a deep breath and settled back, letting the import of the words sink into his heart and mind.

"It's men like you and your soldiers that helped make this happen," Captain Jones said. "The argument for slavery that said blacks couldn't take care of themselves, and were less intelligent than white men was shot down in flames when your people became great soldiers."

Moses gazed at him. "I hoped it would be," he murmured, almost overwhelmed with the emotion sweeping through him.

"Lincoln figures the amendment will help us win the war sooner," Captain Jones said, "because abolishing slavery will make the South realize it is useless to prolong a losing fight in the hope of winning some slavery-saving concession. Although, I suppose we've made too many military gains for that to matter much now."

"It's a matter of time until the war ends," Moses agreed. "I believe the passage of the amendment was more about the future," he added.

"How do you figure that?"

"We're winning the war anyway," Moses answered. "The amendment is more a *consequence* of our victory than a probable cause of it." He chose his words carefully. He had thought of little else for the last few weeks. "To kill slavery now is to prepare to step out of the war and enter the future. I don't figure the amendment will exactly define the future, but it for sure is saying the future for my people will be totally unlike the past."

Captain Jones nodded solemnly. "It's past time for this to have happened. The question for our country will soon be, having won this victory what will we do with it?"

"It's a big question," Moses said. "The answer won't be much easier than the fight to have the *right* to answer it."

"You don't sound too disturbed by that." Captain Jones stared at him intensely.

Moses shrugged. "Being disturbed isn't productive. Oh, I certainly have my feelings about everything that has happened to my people, and I'll do everything I can to help change things, but I already know it will take time. Knowing that, I can deal with frustration when things don't happen overnight."

Captain Jones settled back in his chair. "You're a natural leader, Moses."

Moses nodded. "I believe I am. Sometimes I'm glad about that, and sometimes it's nothing but a burden, but the way I feel about it doesn't change what is. I hope I can be the kind of leader required, not only for my people, but for white people, too. How they see me will influence how white people see everyone with black skin."

"That's rather a heavy burden."

"Not any heavier than the one you've carried through this war," Moses observed. "Especially when you asked to lead black regiments, Captain. I know plenty of soldiers have given you a hard time about that." They had never talked about this, but the intimacy of the tent enclosed by howling winter winds offered the opportunity.

Captain Jones exchanged a long look with Moses. "Change never happens unless people are willing to stand up to the pressures of making it happen. It's been an honor to lead the black troops, and it's something I'll be proud of for the rest of my life." Obviously uncomfortable with the emotion shining in his eyes, Captain Jones stood. "I think you've got some men who will be really excited to hear this news. You'd best go share it with them."

Moses rose and extended his hand. He gripped the captain's for a long moment and then strode from the tent, his grin growing wider with each step he took. He no longer felt the misery of the cold wind or the hard, frozen ground.

Simon looked up from the fire as Moses drew close. "That's a mighty big grin. I'm hoping you got some good news that will warm these men up."

Moses raised his voice until he almost bellowed, wanting his words to carry over the wind to his men. "The amendment to abolish slavery passed today!" He raised his fist in triumph and shouted. "Slavery is dead!"

Shocked silence fell on his men for several moments. Then their victory yell rose and soared through the cold air—the sound, no doubt, carried by the spirits of dead slaves who had hoped and prayed for a moment such as this.

The cold forgotten, his men jumped, danced and sang. Smiling hugely, Moses watched them. From slaves to soldiers, these men had given their lives—first because others believed they could own and oppress humans, and last because they willingly fought, sometimes suffering great loss, to earn freedom. The cold would settle back into their bones, but the news had lit a fire in their hearts that no bitter wind could diminish.

Carrie had already heard the news before she got home. She and Janie celebrated on their way down the hill from the hospital, but she was prepared for whatever reaction her father might have. She knew how far he had come in regard to his feelings about slavery, but certainly he realized this was one more step toward the complete demise of the Confederacy.

Janie, as usual, read her mind. "How will your father take this?"

Carrie shook her head. "I don't know, but personal feelings don't really matter at this point. The war will end, and when it does, every black person in this country will be free." The smile on her face widened as she imagined Rose and Moses' reactions to the news. Her smile split into a grin when she thought of Aunt Abby and all she had done to make it possible. "I can be nothing but happy about it."

"What do you think things will be like?" Janie asked. "When the war is over?" She gazed out over the snow-covered city. "I know we're going to lose. What will life be like then?"

Carrie sobered at the question. She had wondered the same thing many times. After almost four years of giving everything for the effort, what would the people of the South do? How would President Lincoln and the North handle things? "President Lincoln seems to be a reasonable man."

Janie stared at her, bemused. "And you would know this how?"

Carrie shrugged, realizing she really didn't have much of a basis for her opinion. Communication had been so limited during the war. "I don't," she admitted. "I guess I'm hoping. The North is focused one hundred percent on winning the war. I can only hope they have a plan equally as powerful for how they're going to put the country back together again."

They walked the rest of the way in silence, both lost in their thoughts.

Thomas and Jeremy were standing by the fire when they walked in. One look at her father told Carrie he was not handling the news well. She exchanged a long look with Jeremy and walked over to put a hand on her father's arm, but she said nothing.

"You've heard the news," Thomas said.

"Yes."

"And you're happy, of course."

Carrie saw no reason to lie. "Yes. It's time," she said.

Her father jerked his head to stare at her and nodded abruptly. "I don't know why it's bothering me so much. I know I've already lost everything."

Carrie's heart ached at the bewildered look on his lined face. He had lost so much already. "It's just one more thing."

"Yes. It's just one more thing," he agreed absently. He turned to stare into the flames. "It's funny, though... I feel sad, but I don't feel bitter. I suppose resigned is the best word for it."

Carrie felt relief flow into her heart.

"I don't know what the future holds, but I do know that living life as it comes will reveal that." Thomas looked up from the flames, his eyes grim. "Richmond won't survive, you know," he said sadly.

Carrie stared at him, alarmed by what she saw in his eyes. "What do you mean? The Union troops didn't destroy Savannah when they took it."

"No, but neither did Savannah defy their efforts for almost four years. The mayor rode out and gave the city to them," Thomas said. "But that's not what I'm referring to." He paused, obviously trying to choose his words carefully. "I was in a meeting today about what will happen if the city falls."

"And?" Carrie asked, breathing deeply against the dread trying to infiltrate her earlier happiness.

"Government officials will destroy sections of the city," he said. "All the arsenals. Tredegar Iron Works. All the warehouses down by the river. Some of the bridges."

Carrie gasped, her reaction echoed by Janie and Jeremy. "The entire city will burn," she whispered, her mind spinning. "Why have we fought so long to keep it if we're going to destroy it ourselves?" She tried to make sense of it.

Thomas turned to stare at the flames again. "The Confederate government will evacuate the city and move to a place they can continue to operate from. The officials feel they can't just hand over everything here in Richmond."

"Continue to operate so more men can die?" Carrie asked angrily, suddenly more sick of the war than she had ever been. She almost looked forward to the fall of Richmond and was hopeful it would mean the end to the suffering.

"You think we should give up?" Thomas asked.

Carrie took a deep breath and fought to speak calmly. "It's over, Father. We may hold on for a while longer, but it's over." She was tired of holding her thoughts inside. "The only thing that will happen now is that more people will die trying to stop the inevitable. For what purpose?" She turned to gaze in the direction of Petersburg. "Thousands of our men are out there right now. Robert. Hobbs. Georgia." Her mind filled with memories of all the soldiers she had treated who returned to battle. "They're freezing and starving, and many more will die this winter as we make a futile attempt to stop an avalanche."

Thomas stared at her. Carrie met his gaze levelly. She was no longer a girl. She was a woman who had grown from hardship. A woman who sacrificed and matured through suffering and supported the efforts of a war she didn't believe in. She was done being quiet.

The only sound in the room was the explosion of sparks from the logs. Thomas finally walked over and sank down into his chair, his hands hanging between his knees as his shoulders slumped.

Carrie's heart swelled with tenderness, but she waited for him to speak.

"What I believe, or don't believe, doesn't matter," he finally said hoarsely. "Richmond will not survive if it falls. The only thing standing between us and certain destruction is those men in the trenches. When they can no longer hold it, the government will leave." He took a deep breath. "I have been ordered to evacuate with them." He ignored Carrie's gasp and continued. "I want you and Jeremy to join me." He looked over at Janie. "I hope you and Clifford will come, too, but that will be your choice."

Carrie let the sound of snapping logs fill the air for a long moment before she walked over to take her father's hand. "And it is my choice to stay here in Richmond and wait for Robert. No matter what happens, I will be here caring for the soldiers who will surely continue to come."

Thomas stared up at her, agony swelling in his tortured eyes. "I knew you would say that." His eyes sank to his hands again, and then he looked up at Jeremy.

Jeremy shook his head. "For now, I believe it's my place to stay in Richmond. At some point, Thomas, Richmond will have to rebuild. The city will need both of us. I believe you'll return. When you do, I'll be here."

Carrie knelt down in front of her father and gazed up into his eyes with love swelling in her heart. "I love you so much. The immediate future will not be much easier than the present, but somehow we will survive it."

Thomas stared at her silently, his tortured look saying he couldn't find the truth in what she said.

Chapter Twenty-Four

Carrie snapped her head up as she heard the rumble of wagon wheels coming up the hill to the hospital. She'd not heard the guns of battle, so it could only mean more soldiers falling victim to the horrible conditions in the trenches. She took deep, calming breaths as she looked up and locked eyes with Dr. Wild. He reached the door at the same time she did. They stepped out together, closing the door quickly to preserve the precious heat.

Carrie wrapped her coat around her body, turning slightly to allow the hospital barrack to shelter her from the worst of the punishing wind. Frozen tree branches clattered like a symphony of drumbeats as thick clouds pressed down heavily on everything, like the somber sound of a bass tuba. Deep banks of snow pressed against all the wards, narrow paths fingering out like the strands of a spider web.

"Will this winter never end?" she asked. "More snow is coming, and the temperatures keep dropping." She scowled as she watched the line of wagons making their way up the hill slick with ice. "I dread what's coming in those wagons," she admitted, only acknowledging to herself how much she feared finding Robert in one of them.

Dr. Wild nodded, even his cheerful eyes now dull with the weight of the constant, unending suffering. "It's going to be bad, Carrie."

Carrie whipped her head around to stare at him. "What is it?" She reached out to grab his arm when he looked away. "How can it be worse than what we've already dealt with?" Vivid images of amputated limbs and hideous wounds filled her mind.

"This is different," Dr. Wild muttered, angry disgust twisting his face. "This is our fault. We can't blame the Union Army for having our men in conditions no human being should live in."

Carrie watched him, knowing he had made a trip out to the Petersburg trenches the week before. Although he had not said a word about it when he returned, anger had simmered in him ever since.

"I shouldn't have to amputate because we can't put warm shoes and clothes on our soldiers."

Carrie didn't have time to respond as the first wagon stopped in front of their door. She stepped back as men hurried forward to carry the soldiers into the ward. She caught a vision of white, wooden faces but had to wait until the last soldier lay in a bed before she began her examinations.

Her first patient was a middle-aged man with stringy brown hair and dull brown eyes almost crusted shut. He was barely breathing, his face white and hard looking. She reached out gently to touch it, and almost jerked her hand back at the wooden feeling of his skin. He opened his eyes a mere slit and moaned.

"You're in the hospital," Carrie said gently. "You will be taken care of."

"Too late," he muttered as he closed his eyes and sank into unconsciousness.

Dr. Wild appeared at her side and motioned for her to pull the blankets away from her patient's feet. Carrie barely bit back her cry of dismay as she stared down at his solidly frozen feet. They looked like wood that had taken on a bluish-gray discoloration. She looked up in horror at Dr. Wild and then down the row of twenty-five soldiers who had been deposited in their ward. She knew at least two hundred men had been in the wagons. "All of them?" she whispered, her voice shaking.

Dr. Wild gazed back at her grimly. "All of them." He kept his voice low so that no one else could hear. "I told them last week that these men needed to be in the hospital. If the army had listened to me when these men had superficial frostbite, we might have saved some limbs. Instead, they waited until the soldiers were incapable of walking."

"We can't save his feet?" Carrie thought she would be sick. She suddenly understood Dr. Wild's anger.

"No. In cases of deep frostbite, it's not only the skin and subcutaneous tissue that are frozen. Nerves, large blood vessels, tendons and bones are also frozen solid. There is nothing we can do to save them. If we do nothing, his feet will turn black with gangrene, infect his entire body, and kill him."

"But *both* his feet?" Carrie asked breathlessly. "What kind of life will he have?"

"That is always the question in situations like this," Dr. Wild admitted. "Our only other choice is to let him die." He brushed a hand over his eyes. "It might be the kindest thing, but it's not our decision to make. The odds are," he added, "that he won't make it anyway. But we have to try."

Carrie gazed down the row of soldiers and straightened her shoulders. "Let's get started." She had learned that endless activity was preferable to imagining the lives these soldiers would live—*if* they lived.

The day passed in a haze of endless surgeries. Carrie let her mind drift into numbness as the pile of amputated feet, toes, hands and lower arms grew outside the tent. She tried to be thankful the cold and ice would keep them from attracting swarms of flies, but she could feel nothing except befuddled disbelief.

The first man had indeed lost both his feet as well as the fingers on his left hand. Everyone who had been brought in lost at least one foot, with a few amputations up to the knee. If these patients lived, they would probably lose more limbs to infection and gangrene, but doctors and staff would at least try to save some of them by doing a slow defrost. Orderlies moved up and down the rows with buckets of cool water in an effort to bring frozen limbs back to life.

Carrie was shaking with fatigue and anger by the end of the day. She stepped outside after they finished with the last patient, grateful for the harsh, roaring wind that swept air into her depleted lungs and mind. She stood silently, trying to close out the horrific memories. Dr. Wild was right. This was worse.

Her anger burned hotter as she thought of the thousands of men likely to experience the same fate as the men now lying in the ward, only because they had no shoes and warm socks to wear while they huddled in those frozen trenches hour after hour, day after day.

"Mrs. Borden!"

Carrie spun around and ducked back inside the barracks when she heard the orderly call her name. "I'm here."

"The patient down in bed four is asking for you," the orderly said gravely.

Carrie nodded and made her way down the aisle, grateful most of the men were still unconscious. The patient in bed number four was barely out of his teens. Filthy blond hair was plastered to his dirty scalp. His starved body looked very much like a skeleton. "Hello, soldier," she said gently, pushing back her anger in order to give him all her compassion.

"Howdy, ma'am," he gasped. He reached out and grabbed her hand. "How bad is it?"

Carrie stroked his hair back and motioned for the orderly to bring her some warm water so she could clean his face. "You focus on getting better," she urged. She held a cup of water to his lips. "Here, drink this."

The soldier drank thirstily but didn't take his burning eyes off her. "Please, I need to know. How bad is it?"

Carrie frowned, searching for words.

"I can take it," he insisted. "I need to know."

"We had to take off your right foot, all the toes but your little one on the left foot, and three of the fingers on your left hand," she finally said, stunned when she saw a look of relief flood into his eyes.

He closed his eyes for a long moment and then opened them again to stare at her. "Is it crazy that I'm glad?" he whispered.

Understanding flooded her mind, and Carrie stared back at him. "It must be horrible out there," she murmured, her stomach twisting.

"Yes, ma'am, I reckon it is," he said as a shudder convulsed his body. "If I had to lose a foot, some toes and some fingers to get out of there, I guess I see it as an even trade." His eyes sharpened. "You ain't gonna send me back out there, are you?"

"Absolutely not," Carrie said. "What's your name, soldier?"

"Jasper. Jasper Appleton."

Carrie looked at him more closely. Even through his starvation and filth, she could see a resemblance. "Appleton? Do you know Perry Appleton?"

A smile flitted across his face. "Perry is my big brother. I ain't seen him for the last year. I heard he lost a leg and got to go home," he said enviously.

Carrie was amazed anyone could be envious of someone losing a leg, but she understood in a way she never had before, how horrible this war was for these men.

"Perry was my patient," she told him. "He's married now to my friend Louisa. I was matron of honor at their wedding, right here in this hospital ward."

That was enough to evoke a real smile, however weak. "Right here? Me and Perry ended up in the same place?" Jasper gazed around the ward. "Did Perry go back home?"

"I know that was the plan," Carrie said. "I'm afraid the lack of communication has kept me from getting any news."

"Perry had himself a right nice little farm down in Georgia. He bought the land close to our parents' before our mama and daddy died a couple years before the war started. He had some big plans for that place."

"And how about you, Jasper?"

"I always figured I would be a farmer," he admitted, locking his eyes on her face. "I aimed on going back home and taking over my parents' place. You reckon I can do that now?"

Carrie stared into his eyes and spoke with all the confidence she could muster. "I think people can do almost anything they put their minds to. It won't be easy, but you'll learn how to compensate for what you've lost, and figure out how to do things a different way."

Obviously trying to draw strength from her confidence, Jasper stared back into her eyes. Finally he nodded. "I reckon that's the truth," he said, tiredness weakening his voice and causing his eyes to flutter. "I aim to be a farmer when I get back home." He managed a weak grin before he closed his eyes and fell asleep.

Carrie stayed where she was, bathing his face and washing his hair. When he woke, he would be clean and warm probably for the first time in months. As she cleaned him, she prayed Jasper would find the courage and determination to create a new life.

5 ~·€.·ı .·≈~ ₹

It was already dark before Carrie finished with her last patient and prepared to go home. Dr. Wild had promised to wait for her and walk her down the hill to her father's house. She reached for her coat and scarf when she heard someone call her name. She looked up wearily, ready to pass off whatever it was to an orderly.

One of the ward assistants moved quickly down the row of patients. "It's Jasper Appleton," she said. "I know you took a special interest in him."

"What's wrong?" Carrie asked, already moving in that direction.

"He started running a fever about an hour ago. Now it's spiked really high, and we can't get it down."

"We'll check him together," Dr. Wild said as he reached her side.

Carrie smiled at him gratefully but groaned when she saw Jasper's flushed face and heard his rapid, shallow breathing. She reached down, gently unwrapped the bandages from his amputated foot, and stared at the angry red lines shooting up from the badly swollen stump.

Dr. Wild removed the other bandage, revealing the same angry infection spreading out from the amputated toes.

Carrie took a deep breath and moved quickly to take her coat off. "Bring me some goldenseal salve," she said crisply, willing energy to replace her fatigue.

"Do you know this one?" Dr. Wild asked.

"Remember Perry Appleton from last year?"

"The one who married your friend Louisa?"

"Yes. Jasper is Perry's brother. He's actually happy we amputated everything because now he won't have to go back to the trenches. He wants to be a farmer," Carrie finished, fighting back tears of sorrow and fatigue.

Dr. Wild nodded grimly. "Let's see if we can send him home to do that."

Long past midnight, Carrie arrived home from the hospital and said goodnight to Dr. Wild, who hurried on to his lodging for a few hours of sleep. She was dismayed to find Thomas and Jeremy waiting up for her. In no mood for conversation, she managed a weak smile as she turned for the stairs.

"Carrie, wait," her father said.

Carrie took a deep breath and turned. "I'm exhausted, Father. Can we talk in the morning?"

"Yes, of course, but why are you home so late?"

Carrie bit back the burning words that yearned to spew out of her mouth. "We had many patients today." She didn't trust herself to say more.

"But there were no battles today," Thomas protested.

"No, there weren't," Carrie said, refusing to look at Jeremy because she knew he would see past her control. The fact that her father didn't, told her he also had an upsetting day, but she couldn't take anything else tonight.

"There wouldn't be any more battles if Lincoln wasn't such a hard-headed and unreasonable man," Thomas said bitterly.

Carrie sighed. What had made her think she could slip up to her room and fall across her bed? She waited for her father to expound on whatever had happened in the Capitol.

Thomas took her silence as a desire to listen. "President Davis had a visit from Montgomery Blair. He came with a pass from President Lincoln, so our own president, of course, assumed it meant Lincoln had some desire to talk peace."

He paused, waiting for Carrie to say something. When she said nothing, he continued. "President Davis named Vice President Stephens, Assistant Secretary of War Campbell, and Senator Hunter as the three men who would confer with Lincoln. He sent them over the lines to Grant's headquarters two days ago."

Carrie knew better than to think the story could end well when her father was so upset, but the word *peace* had her hoping for the impossible. "And?"

"Grant sent a telegram to Washington urging the president to meet with them. They met yesterday at Fort Monroe."

Carrie was too tired for details. "What happened, Father? Is there going to be peace?"

Thomas snorted. "Lincoln made it very clear to them there would be no peace without complete reunion and the abolition of slavery. When Vice-President Stephens proposed some kind of armistice that would allow us to exist as separate countries, Lincoln told him, *'The only basis on which I would entertain a proposition for a settlement is the recognition and re-establishment of the national authority through the land.'* " Thomas stopped and waited for Carrie's reaction.

She merely looked at him, the fatigue from the long day swamping through her like a tidal wave. Her eyes blurred as she thought longingly of turning, walking upstairs, and falling into bed.

"Don't you find that appalling?" Thomas demanded.

"I find it rather expected," she said bluntly, somehow forcing her brain cells back to life.

"Expected?"

"Yes." Carrie no longer cared what impact her words would have. "Our representatives seemed to have gone in with the thought of negotiating on equal terms. I'd say the South has no negotiating strength since we're on the brink of extinction, and the North is obviously winning the war."

Thomas stared at her, disappointment shining in his eyes.

The disappointment shredded Carrie's last bit of self-control. "I'm sick of all of it!" she cried. "I don't care about stupid men trying to play politics while they gamble with our lives."

"*Stupid men?*" her father asked, anger sparking in his eyes. "You are talking about very important men."

"I'm talking about men who couldn't see past their noses four years ago, or we wouldn't be in this war," Carrie snapped, his anger fueling her own. "Not one person thought past his own agenda, and they're still not thinking past their own agendas, or I wouldn't have spent all day amputating frozen feet and hands off the soldiers these *important men* make fight in a war they have no hope of winning!"

She saw alarm on her father's face, but now that the words were flowing, she could not turn them off. "This morning I helped amputate the right foot, all the toes, and three fingers from the left hand of Jasper Appleton, Louisa's brother-in-law, who she will never have the pleasure to meet because of this war. I held him an hour ago while he died from a massive infection that set in because *important men* sent him and hundreds of other men to entrenchments in this freezing weather without socks, shoes, gloves or warm clothing. Many of those men arrived at the hospital today to have limbs amputated because *important men* recklessly sacrifice *other* men."

She spun around and stared at the room. "We stand here in this warm house beside a hot fire and pretend we have some idea of how these men are suffering, but we know nothing, and we continue to think it's important for them to suffer and die in those horrible trenches because we're afraid of losing what we value."

Thomas cleared his throat and stepped toward her, his anger turned to alarm as he reached out to take her hand. "I know it's difficult, Carrie—"

"*Difficult?*" Carrie cried, moving out of reach, anger surging through her like a burning fire. "Do you know Jasper was happy for us to cut off his foot because it meant he would never have to go back to the trenches? Do you know our men hardly ever sleep because the Union sends over artillery every few minutes to keep them awake? Do you know they go days with no food at all, or just a few bites? Do you know how many of those soldiers defending what *important men* believe needs to be defended aren't wearing shoes?" She gasped for air as anger and sorrow threatened to strangle her. "How many of those *important men* would leave their nice warm homes to go spend time in the trenches?"

"Now wait a minute," Thomas replied. "Everyone knows the price those men are paying."

"Oh, really?" Carrie was far beyond caring what anyone thought. She stormed out onto the porch, picked up a large crate, and walked back inside, dropping it on the floor. "There's your price, Father!"

Complete silence wrapped the room as Thomas and Jeremy stared in horror at the crate full of amputated feet, hands, toes and fingers.

Carrie was vaguely aware of Janie entering the room. She leaned into her friend when Janie walked up close beside her and wrapped an arm around her waist. The touch drained all the anger from her and left her a hollow shell. She stared down at the box of carnage as tears poured down her face, sobs wracking her body. Janie pulled her into her arms and held her as the tears flowed.

Thomas was the first to speak. "What can we do?" he asked quietly.

Carrie looked at him sharply, relaxing a little when she realized he was serious. The box on the floor had brought the truth home to him. At that moment, she loved her father more than she ever had. In spite of his own burdens, he was putting aside his anxiety to offer help now that he could see how devastated she was.

Jeremy walked over and put a hand on her shoulder. "We have to do something," he murmured, his eyes burning with the fire of anger and sorrow.

"Yes," Carrie whispered. "I have a plan."

The next morning, after Janie's strict orders had her sleeping until long after the sun was up, Carrie gathered in the kitchen with Janie, Clifford, Thomas and Jeremy.

A good night's sleep had restored her energy but done nothing to alleviate her disgust and determination to do something. More snow had fallen during the night, but now a weak sun glistened on the heavily laden limbs.

Carrie carefully outlined her plan, grateful her father and Jeremy had taken the day off.

"It will certainly shock people," Janie murmured.

"As well it should," Jeremy agreed. "Sometimes it takes the shock effect to get people to take action."

Now that the plan was in place, Carrie was having second thoughts. "We won't get enough for everyone," she muttered.

"No," Thomas agreed, "but we will help many of them." He paused and gripped her hand. "If we can keep some from having their feet amputated, it will be a great thing."

Carrie caught herself before she said that a *great thing* would be if the Confederacy gave up and let all the soldiers go home. She knew, however right it would be, that it was also completely unrealistic. The best thing any of them could do was focus on what *could* be done.

She gazed around the room. "Are we ready?" As everyone nodded gravely, she went out onto the porch, picked up the box she had brought home the night before, and deposited it into the carriage Spencer had waiting for them. His face tightened when he looked down at the contents, but he didn't say anything.

It took minutes to get downtown. The roads were mostly empty of carriages, but even on a frigid day people were roaming the streets looking for human connection in the midst of war.

Carrie placed the crate on its side so that the frozen limbs spilled out onto the street. All of them took their posts and waited for people to take notice.

In less than one minute, the first small group had gathered, staring in disgust at the contents of the box. Carrie had to agree the bloody stumps made a strong impression. She was counting on it.

"What's this all about?" a warmly dressed woman demanded. "You can't have this kind of thing out here." Her lips tightened with disgust.

Carrie stepped forward. "I agree it's disgusting," she said, making sure her voice was loud enough to carry. "I'm afraid what is even more disgusting is that these feet, fingers, toes and hands were amputated from our own soldiers yesterday." She gazed around as more people stopped, drawn by the growing crowd. "They were not amputated because of battle..." She let her voice draw out dramatically. "They were amputated because our soldiers are in those trenches without shoes, socks, gloves or warm coats. They were amputated because their feet froze, and our only recourse was to amputate them."

"How did you get them?" one of the bystanders asked suspiciously, eyeing her as if she were dangerous.

Carrie kept her voice even. "I assist one of the surgeons at Chimborazo Hospital. Over two hundred men were brought into the hospital yesterday. Every single one of them had something amputated—had their lives destroyed—all because they are freezing to death." Her voice choked on the words.

Thomas stepped forward. "I serve in the Virginia government," he said loudly. "I was oblivious to how terrible the suffering was until my daughter brought home this box last night." His voice grew louder. "We can all do something about it. I'm willing to bet most of you have an extra pair of shoes, a coat, wool socks, or something the men can wear as gloves." He gazed around the crowd. "I know everyone in this city is suffering, but thousands of men are risking their lives for us right this minute as they fight in the trenches around Petersburg. The least we can do is make sure they don't die or become dismembered because they don't have clothes."

"We can't help them all," one woman muttered.

Jeremy stepped forward then. "No, we can't help them all, but we can help a lot of them if everyone in this crowd brings something back. We can help more if you share this with your neighbors and ask them to help."

The crowd had grown to several dozen people. Jeremy picked up the box and held it where everyone could see. "This could have been your husband, your brother, or your son. This didn't have to happen," he called out. "We *let* this happen because we haven't provided enough clothing or food for our soldiers." He anticipated the argument in people's minds. "Yes, our government is responsible for supplying our troops, but I would like to suggest that responsibility is not the issue here. It's a matter of compassion. Can you really look at this and not do something to help?"

"How do we even know it will get to them?" another called.

Thomas stepped forward again. "I know there is reason to distrust the people supplying our troops. It hurts me to admit it, but I know it's true." He waited while silence fell on the crowd. They listened attentively. "The five of us will be taking everything down ourselves. We'll make sure it gets straight into the hands of our brave men."

Janie stepped forward. "We're counting on all of you to help. Please go home and gather what you can. Anything will help. Even warm cloth can be used to wrap feet that would freeze. I promise you it will all be put to good use."

Carrie held her breath as she watched the faces of those in the crowd. One by one, onlookers drifted away, talking amongst themselves. "What do you think they'll do?" she asked Janie.

"That's not up to us," Janie said. "We've given them an opportunity to help. That's all we can do."

Another crowd began to gather. Carrie stepped forward to repeat what she had said earlier. All morning long crowds gathered, growing bigger every time as the word spread. At one point, she saw her father talking to several Richmond policemen who looked as if they had come to put an end to things. After her father spoke to them for several minutes, they smiled, nodded their encouragement to Carrie, and moved on.

But the crowds didn't listen and drift away. They left and came back with items they placed on the ground next to the box of body parts.

"Look at all of it," Janie whispered excitedly, her eyes glowing.

Carrie wiped away tears and stepped up to deliver her speech again.

Early the next morning, as the sun was cresting the horizon, the five of them met again around the table. May ladled up steaming bowls of oatmeal as they waited for the four wagons the army had agreed to provide to carry everything that had been gathered.

Carrie was exhausted but excited. She and the others had stayed on the streets until dark drove everyone inside to the warmth of their homes. The pile had grown throughout the day. "I wasn't sure the army would let us deliver it," she said, trying to push aside the hope that she would see Robert. With over ten thousand men in the trenches, it was unlikely they would meet.

"The *army* wouldn't," her father stated. "It took a personal visit from Governor Smith to convince them otherwise." He looked around the table. "I want to make sure everyone here understands what a risk we are taking. Fighting could break out at any time, or a shell could land on us. We're going into a war zone."

"We promised," Carrie responded. "More news has come out about how little of the food we prepared for the Christmas dinner actually reached our troops. It seems corrupt speculation isn't limited to business owners." Her voice thickened with disgust. "I still can't believe the people responsible for taking that food sold some of it for profit."

Janie laid her hand over Carrie's. "It won't happen with these clothes," she said firmly.

Clifford nodded. "The army is providing an armed guard along with the wagons. They realize we are accepting the risk. They're so grateful to be getting the clothes, they're willing to let us do it our way."

Carrie looked up as she heard the wagons rumble to a stop in front of the house. She walked outside and smiled at Jeremy, who was perched on one of the seats. He insisted on staying with everything they had gathered last night to make sure speculators didn't take off with it. His eyes were glazed with exhaustion, but his triumphant smile said it had been worth it.

It would take about an hour for the wagons to jolt their way down rutted roads to the front. Snow was still deep on the roads and piled high on the sides. Unable to comprehend being out in this frigid weather without warm clothing, Carrie rode in the lead wagon and shivered into her coat. Her mind raced through everything they had in the back of the wagons. How would it get to the men who needed it the most? Suddenly, she knew what needed to be done.

She leaned forward and tapped the driver on his shoulder. "I want all of these items to be taken to Captain Robert Borden's battalion," she said.

The soldier opened his mouth to protest and then closed it again, his eyes betraying his belief that it would indeed be the best way to distribute everything.

"Yes, ma'am."

"Are many of your friends without shoes?" Carrie asked.

"Too many." The soldier looked over at her. "What you did yesterday has gotten around. It was a wonderful thing."

Carrie shook her head sadly. "It's too late and much too small, but it's something." Her eyes filled with tears. "I wish we could help you all."

"The ones who don't have freezing feet tonight will be real grateful to you," the soldier said. "I had one of my buddies go off in the hospital wagon two days ago. I already know he won't be back." His eyes sparked with anger and grief.

"No," Carrie agreed. "He won't be back."

They said no more as the horses fought to pull the wagons through the snow. She could be nothing but grateful that Granite was snug in the stall behind their house. He was thinner because of inadequate food, but at least she didn't have to worry about his being shot or maimed by a shell, and what he was eating was certainly more than these emaciated animals had. This one time, Carrie had refused to let Granite go. He wasn't needed for battle in the trenches, and she saw no reason for him to stand in the cold as a target. When Robert had returned from the Shenandoah Valley, Granite was retired as an army horse.

As they rode along, she dreamed of the day Granite would once again run freely through the fields of Cromwell Plantation, not sure whether it was a dream or a ridiculous fantasy. For all she knew, Cromwell had been destroyed. The odds said it had met the same fate as many of its neighboring plantations. Carrie shook her head and pushed the vision from her mind. There was no sense in trying to answer questions that couldn't be answered.

She waited quietly while the wagon driver approached the lines and leaned over to speak to several of the soldiers. One disappeared, conferred with two men in a tent, then came back out and pointed. The driver nodded, picked up the reins, and started moving south.

Carrie gripped the sides of the wagon and stared in horror at the hollow-eyed, emaciated men staring back at them as they made their way through the camp. For every decently clothed man, far more wandered around in tatters or huddled as closely to a feeble fire as they could. Bile rose in her throat. Carrie wanted to scream out her protest, but knew it would do no good. All she could do was what she had come to do—ease the suffering of as many as possible.

She jumped when a shell landed about a hundred feet from one of their wagons, but she gripped the wagon sides harder and scanned the faces for the one she cared about the most.

Finally, the driver pulled to a halt. The remaining three wagons pulled up behind them. Several men looked up numbly from their positions on the ground. Carrie knew most of them were hunkered down in the trenches while waiting for an attack from the Federals.

"Where is Captain Borden?" the driver called out.

A nearby soldier shrugged wearily. The rest stared up at them.

Carrie scanned the area and looked for Robert. Finally, she stood up in the wagon and faced the men.

"My name is Carrie Borden. I'm looking for my husband. We have something for all of you."

The soldiers came to life immediately. "Why didn't you say so in the first place, ma'am?" a young boy asked. His hands and feet were bare, his face gaunt beneath filthy black hair, but his bearing was proud. "The captain has told us about you, and Hobbs makes you sound like an angel."

Carrie blushed as she smiled at him. "I'm hardly an angel, but you'll be happy we showed up today if you'll help me find my husband."

"I'll get him for you," the same soldier offered. "He's over in the trenches with some of the fellas. Most officers let us do all the hard work. Captain Borden suffers right with us."

Carrie shuddered to think of what Robert was going through, but recognized the loyalty his actions inspired. Her heart warmed with pride. She waited while the soldier hobbled off, aware she had become the center of attention for every one of Robert's men.

A sudden commotion had her eyes turning toward the trenches. She wanted to weep when she saw Robert's filthy, tired face, already thin after five weeks away, but she kept her smile steady as her heart sang with joy that he was still alive.

Robert rushed up to the wagon and swung her down to the ground, his eyes bright with delight, his face creased with worry. He crushed her to him and then held her back. "What are you doing here?" he asked sharply. "It's too dangerous."

"We came to bring you something," Carrie said, pressing a kiss to his lips that brought cheers from his men.

"We?" Robert asked, confusion filling his face as he looked around.

Thomas, Jeremy, Janie and Clifford waved from their wagon seats.

"What…"

"I know many men are suffering," Carrie explained. "We did what we could about it." She motioned to her driver, who stepped forward with a box of shoes and socks. She watched Robert's jaw drop in shock. "We thought these would help." Then she waved her hands toward the wagons. "They're full," she said.

Robert stared at the wagons and then stared back at her as his face exploded in a huge smile. "You're amazing," he whispered, enfolding her in a hug.

Carrie laughed and pulled away. She quickly explained what had happened. "The citizens of Richmond care about what's happening out here," she finished.

"I made them bring me to your camp for two reasons," Carrie continued. "I want every one of your men to be warm. Secondly, I want you to pick the ones you know you can trust to distribute these items to the men most in need. We can't help everyone, but we have quite a lot."

Robert stared at the mounds of crates and barrels in the wagon. "There's enough for more than a thousand men—more if they share." He made no attempt to wipe away his tears as he turned to his men. "Remember that miracle some of you have been praying for? It rolled up."

Within minutes, he had his men organized. There was quiet jubilation as his barefooted men found shoes, and shivering men found coats. Frozen hands slipped gratefully into gloves, but the looks of humble gratitude warmed Carrie's heart the most. These men needed to know people cared about them and appreciated their sacrifice.

Barely a dent was made in the mountain of supplies in the wagons. Robert called fifty of his men and quietly gave them orders. "I'm entrusting these supplies to you because I believe in your integrity," he said, gazing around at their intense faces. The soldiers stared back at him without wavering. "You are to go through the camps and find the men who truly need what we have. Pull them to the side and give it to them. It may take a day or two to distribute all these supplies, but I want to be sure they only go to the men who need it." He let silence fill the air for a moment. "Can I trust you?"

"Yes, sir!" the selected soldiers responded, their eyes bright with pride.

Carrie felt a catch in her throat when she saw the obvious respect and love they had for Robert. When he turned back to her, she gave him a warm kiss.

Another shell exploding nearby had Robert muttering under his breath as he released her. "You have to get out of here, Carrie."

"I know," she agreed. "We promised we would leave as soon as we made our delivery. Another driver is waiting to take us back to Richmond." But before she went, she had to ask. "George? Have you seen him?" She would say nothing to betray Georgia's secret.

Robert smiled tenderly. "I found him two weeks ago and had him transferred to my unit. He's in the trenches now. George is miserable like the rest of us, but he's okay. The clothes you provided for him have made that possible."

Carrie breathed a sigh of relief. "Thank you," she whispered.

Robert wrapped her and Thomas in strong embraces. "You may never know how much this means," he said, stopping when emotion choked his voice.

Thomas grabbed his hand and pulled him into another hug. "Thank you for what you're doing," he said hoarsely. "I pray this war will end soon so the suffering will stop."

Carrie gazed at her father and knew his brief time in the camp had given him a different perspective that nothing else could have. She wished that every Confederate official, as well as every Union official, had to spend a day in camps and in field hospitals. Surely they would work harder to come up with a way to end the war if they truly understood what it meant.

Robert pulled Carrie to him for another deep kiss before he released her. "I hope I'm cleaner the next time you see me," he joked.

"Just stay alive," Carrie whispered. "Just stay alive."

Unable to free her mind of images of frozen men with barely any clothes huddling next to an inadequate fire shared by twenty or more, Carrie burrowed under her thick mound of quilts that night and couldn't sleep.

Robert's men had cheered her group when they left the front with the army driver, but Carrie couldn't help feeling they had done too little. As full as the wagons had been, she knew it hadn't been enough to take care of every soldier who needed warm clothes.

You did all you can do.

The whisper floated into her mind as she listened to sleet pelt the windows once more. She wished it brought her comfort, but frustration wouldn't release its hold on her soul. The hollow-eyed, gaunt faces of the men protecting Richmond haunted her every time she closed her eyes.

Wanting to close out the memories of the day, she squeezed her eyes shut once again and began to pray. Instead of suffering men, a glowing rainbow appeared. Carrie gasped and held in her mind the vibrant colors that radiated warmth. Memories of the rainbow she and Janie had seen when they walked down the hill last summer swallowed the frustration and fear.

The night always ends. God always shines light into the darkness. Always.

Her hope took wing and soared as she remembered the words that had sustained her during the last year.

This year will be an awful last, long night, but it will end. We have to hold on to that!

Chapter Twenty-Five

Robert shifted to find a comfortable position in the muddy trench but knew it was impossible. He was grateful for the break in the weather that had freed the soldiers from frostbite and freezing nights, but he knew the relentless rain had created almost as much misery.

Thoughts raced through his mind as he stared into the night sky, finally shimmering with stars since the rainclouds had parted. The whistling wind didn't touch him or his men in the trenches.

"Somethin's about to happen, ain't it, Captain?" Hobbs asked.

Glad that Hobbs was with him again, Robert looked over at the young soldier. If it had seemed odd early in the war to count on someone so young, it no longer did. Years of war had erased age barriers. Hobbs was his friend.

"Yes," he replied quietly.

"Can you tell me about it?"

Robert looked around to make sure no one else was listening and realized the wind would cover his voice. "Things look worse than they ever have," he said grimly.

"They been pretty bad for a long time," Hobbs replied.

Robert nodded. "You're right, but I met with some officers last night and got caught up on everything." He took a deep breath. "Wilmington has fallen. Sherman marched out of Savannah and went up through South Carolina. He took Columbia a little over a month ago. The city almost completely burned, though no one seems sure who started the fires. Sherman is marching through North Carolina now."

Hobbs gasped and clenched his fists.

"It gets worse," Robert said heavily. "Charleston has fallen, and Sherman has left much of South Carolina in the same devastated condition his troops left Georgia in last year." He took a deep breath. "We're outnumbered more than two to one, and that will get worse when

Sherman arrives. And Sheridan is on his way down from the Shenandoah, which will stack the odds even more in their favor."

"We won't be able to stop them," Hobbs said bluntly.

"No," Robert agreed, "we won't be able to stop them. Even if we were healthy and had plenty of supplies, those odds are almost impossible to beat. Add in the fact that hardly one man in Lee's fifty thousand-man army is well, and we simply aren't left with a good scenario." Robert smothered a cough as he spoke, glad Carrie couldn't see how gaunt he had gotten in the six weeks since she'd been to the front.

"You're not sounding so good, Captain," Hobbs said in a worried voice.

"So says the man stomping around in this despicable mud with an elevated shoe and crutches," Robert said, forcing a smile to his lips as he fought to control his cough. He'd thought Hobbs was crazy to come back to fight, but he had to admire his spirit and loyalty.

Hobbs shrugged. "At least I don't sound like I'll hack up my lungs."

"No, you don't. Obviously they make men tougher in western Virginia than they do down in the lowlands."

"You just figuring that out?" Hobbs asked, his eyes glistening with laughter. "I've been knowing that for a right long time."

Robert grinned and then sobered. "You'll have to be tough for what will happen tomorrow."

Hobbs stiffened to attention. "What's that, Captain?"

"Lee has decided to launch an attack." Robert saw Hobbs jerk his head around, but he stayed silent, waiting for details. "I don't know everything. I do know Lee is not going to sit here and wait for more than one hundred thousand men to join Grant. Lee's plan is to launch an attack that will force Grant to shorten or weaken his lines so we can get out of here. Part of the plan is to capture a Union supply depot about a mile from here."

"Where we going?" Hobbs asked, his eyes dancing with excitement.

"That's a good question," Robert replied. "One I don't know the answer to. Perhaps we'll join up with our forces in North Carolina. I don't know."

When Robert saw Hobbs frown, he knew he had seen the bigger picture.

"What about Richmond?" Hobbs asked hesitantly.

Robert remained silent, not willing to give voice to his thoughts. Both of them knew if Lee abandoned the trenches, Grant would send enough of his army in to take Richmond. Robert couldn't bear the images of Carrie and Thomas in Richmond surrounded by burning buildings.

"We going to be in on the action?" Hobbs finally asked, his somber voice revealing similar thoughts.

"Yes," Robert replied. "But you will not be in on it. Sitting in the trenches and firing a gun with a bad leg is one thing. Tromping through this mud in an attack is another. Speed and surprise will be the key to success." He saw disappointment flash through Hobbs' eyes, followed almost immediately by a spark of relief he could totally understand. "If we break through, you'll have transportation to come with us."

"I reckon I wouldn't be able to help very much," Hobbs agreed gravely, "but I'll be back here waiting. When will the attack happen?"

"Four o'clock tomorrow morning," Robert replied grimly. "We have six hours. I'm going to try to get some rest." He knew when he said the words he would have no sleep that night. His thoughts were back in Richmond with his beautiful wife. How could he break through the Union lines and run, leaving her behind?

Silence fell on the trench as both men lapsed into their own private thoughts.

Moses glanced over at Simon hard at work on a letter to June. Moses had finished one to Rose and already sent it on its way. Three months had passed since he surprised her at the Christmas dance. Memories still flooded his mind, but they weren't enough to ease the ache of missing her that battered his heart daily.

"Got something on your mind, Moses?" Simon asked, looking up from the paper he carefully wrote on.

"Captain Jones called me to his tent today."

"I saw that. I figured you would tell me about it when you was ready."

"He doesn't think Grant will wait much longer to attack. Sheridan is almost here with his men from the Shenandoah, and Sherman is almost here, too."

Simon nodded. "I'd say we have a pretty good chance of breaking through those lines and taking Richmond with that kind of strength," he said confidently.

Moses nodded. "Grant is about ready to make his move. Captain Jones thinks it will happen in five days."

Simon gazed at him. "How do you feel about taking Richmond?"

Moses swallowed hard. "I have mixed feelings. I know we have to take it for the war to end, but I'm scared of what will happen to Carrie."

"From what you tell me, she'll probably be up in the hospital away from the fighting."

"Yes," Moses agreed, "but I've heard too many stories of what happened in Atlanta and Columbia to feel very relaxed about it."

Simon frowned. "I hear tell that Sherman says he didn't start that fire in Columbia."

"It did the same kind of damage no matter who started it," Moses said. "The only thing that gives me any kind of peace is knowing I'll be there. My goal is to find Carrie and make sure she stays safe."

"She's lucky to have you for a friend."

"I owe my life and freedom to her," Moses said quietly. "And she's Rose's best friend. I would do anything for her."

Simon nodded but added with a scowl, "I hate being stuck away in Fort Stedman like this. Not much is likely to happen here."

Moses gazed over the top of the trench at the earthen walls of moated Fort Stedman less than fifty feet away. "About the only thing that can be said for this position, is that we're the closest to the Confederate lines." He smiled tightly. "Did you know some of their men came over a few weeks ago to do some trading?"

He smiled at Simon's astonished look. "They didn't have much to trade with, but I hear they went back with some much desired tobacco and coffee." He shook his head. "I heard our boys were laughing it up with them, and then about thirty minutes later, they went back to their trenches and we were exchanging fire again."

"You reckon that's true?" Simon asked.

"It's true," Moses confirmed. "There is nothing normal about this war. I've known it since the beginning, but as it draws to a close, it seems to get more bizarre." He stared over at the Confederate lines. "I can't help pitying those men."

Simon nodded. "You can hear their coughing and hacking all night long. Don't sound to me like *any* of them are well. We may be miserable, but at least we have warm clothes and food."

"I've seen a bunch of them changing places in the trenches. They don't look like much more than skeletons," Moses said sympathetically. "It's pathetic."

Simon gazed toward the rebel fortifications. "I wonder what keeps them fighting."

"Same thing that keeps us fighting," Moses said. "They're being told to fight, and they have loved ones to protect." He grew pensive. "I wonder if they realize it's almost over. There's no way they can stop what is about to hit them."

Simon nodded. "What will you do after the war, Moses?"

Moses smiled. They'd had this discussion what seemed like a thousand times, but he knew thinking of the future made living the present more bearable.

"I'll spend every moment glad I can be with Rose and John, and then we'll have many more children who will grow up free." His smile grew broader. "I'll find a farm somewhere and help Rose become a teacher. My goal is to have one of the biggest tobacco farms in the South one day."

The misery of the muddy trenches dissolved into the glory of a shining future alive in his mind. He turned to Simon. "What about you?"

"I'm headed north," he said, swinging his gaze in that direction. "Me and June talked about it over Christmas. We had enough of the South. We might come back someday, but we don't reckon things will change very fast even though we're free. We figure we have better opportunities in the North."

Moses nodded thoughtfully, wondering, as he had for weeks now, whether he should tell Simon he had discovered that racism was rampant in the North, too. So far, Moses had remained silent, knowing it wasn't *worse* than in the South, but pondering whether he should prepare Simon for that reality. For the moment, Moses decided to let Simon's fantasies make his days easier.

Simon went back to writing his letter to June. "I'm telling her we're sitting around until Grant is ready to take action."

Robert gripped his gun more tightly as he waited for the word that would send him surging forward with the eleven thousand men Lee had given to General Gordon. He was quite sure the pre-dawn attack would be a total surprise. No one expected the Confederates to be bold enough to launch an attack, which was probably the only reason it might work. Robert wished he could quell the uneasy feeling spiraling through his gut, but also realized he felt that way before every battle. Lee's audacity had paid off in the past. The general might pull off another miracle.

The nine-foot-tall earthen walls of Fort Stedman stood in dark shadows in the frosty distance. Robert knew from his briefing what would happen soon. General Gordon had selected lead parties of sharpshooters and engineers masquerading as deserting soldiers to go out first to overwhelm Union pickets and remove wooden obstructions that would delay the infantry advance.

The rest of the attacking infantry would wait for the signal to advance. Robert worried about the early morning air, clear and calm, which would carry voices and other sounds clearly. Anything that gave away the surprise attack would be disastrous.

Robert watched with suspended breath as the lead brigade moved into the tall cornfield across from Fort Stedman. White strips of cloth pulled diagonally over the men's shoulders and tied around their waists stood out clearly. The precaution was to make sure Rebel soldiers could recognize each other in the darkness.

Robert stiffened as the voice of a Union sentry rang through the frosty air. "I say, Johnny, what are you doing in that corn?"

The answer came quickly. "All right, Yank, I'm just gathering me a little corn to parch."

The brief silence resonated more loudly than the spoken words as Robert tensed, ready to rush forward if the game was up. While sharpshooters might rule in daylight, one oddity of war was that, at night, the opposing guards, separated by less than five hundred feet, often became quite chummy. This plan of attack depended on that.

"All right, Johnny, I won't shoot."

Robert sagged with relief and sensed his men up and down the line doing the same thing. He fought to control the cough struggling to escape.

Long minutes stretched out until another call came from the Union picket. "I say, Johnny, isn't it almost daylight? I think it's time they were relieving us."

Robert grinned as the answer rang back clearly. "Keep cool, Yank. You'll be relieved in a few minutes."

Robert knew the relief his fellow soldier had in mind would not be what the Union private was anticipating. The rustling noises in the corn had been lead soldiers carefully dragging aside sections of *chevaux-de-frise*—spiked wooden barriers chained end to end—to create an opening through which Rebel infantrymen could attack the Federal lines.

Robert also knew a line of sharpshooters had crept as closely to the Union picket line as possible and lay waiting. From his place at the front of the long columns, Robert had a clear view of what was happening, though early morning fog was starting to gather in the hollows.

The drama continued to unfold as a small group of sharpshooters, pretending to desert, moved toward the Federal picket lines. The irony of the scene struck Robert because enough men had actually deserted to make this charade seem real.

Robert held his breath as the sharpshooters' commander jumped up and, in an effort to make it more realistic, shouted, "Boys, come back! Don't go!"

"Come on, Johnnies," a Union picket yelled, but quickly fell silent as the masquerading deserters overpowered him and knocked him out.

Robert could see scuffling black shadows until one Union picket escaped, fired off his gun, and shouted, "The Rebels are coming! The Rebels are coming!"

Moments later, three quick shots from the Confederate side signaled the attack. Robert rose with the rest of his men and surged forward. Their job at the front of the columns was to remove obstructions so that the men could pass through quickly.

***

Moses bolted upward as the sharp Union cry and the crack of rifle fire jolted him from sleep.

Simon sat up staring at him. "What was that, Moses? I heard someone yell!"

Once more the cry rent the air. "The Rebels are coming!"

Moses jumped up, grabbed his rifle, and called for his men. He listened urgently for the order telling him what to do.

***

Robert continued to move, pulling aside obstructions until he was almost to the walls of Fort Stedman. So far, no counterattack had begun. The element of surprise, however, vanished when a unit of sharpshooters ran forward, yelling crazily.

Robert groaned and sprinted forward as the fort's cannons opened up. He led his men at top speed, gasping with relief when he realized they had all gotten under the line of fire without being hit. He refused to allow himself to think about men further back. When they reached the spiked logs protecting the fort parapet, they worked quickly to tear them apart, hacking and dragging them out of the way.

With the logs demolished, Robert saw his men look to him for direction. He realized they couldn't climb the slippery parapet with increasing fire coming down from Union infantrymen above. He took a deep breath, raised his rifle to his shoulder, and commanded, "Shoot every Yankee that shows himself!"

His men cried out their Rebel yell and surged forward. Robert spied a low spot in the parapet and led the way by scaling it. He waited until his men had followed, then his troops formed a line, and they moved forward.

"We got 'em, Captain," one yelled. "Look, they're taking prisoners!"

Robert nodded grimly and knew much fiercer resistance would occur when word of the attack reached Union command. He watched for a moment as individuals and then groups of Federal soldiers threw up their hands and surrendered. "Keep moving, men!" he hollered as he gripped his rifle and sprinted forward, his eyes sweeping the darkness for more enemy combatants.

⟩⟨

"Take your men and get up on the walls," an officer yelled to Moses.

Relieved to have an order, Moses turned immediately and called for his men. They all leapt from the trench, climbed to the top of the fort, and began firing down at the mass of men moving toward them in the darkness, while the sun brightened the eastern horizon a deep blue. "Stop them!"

It took only a few minutes to realize that wasn't going to happen. The Confederate attack had been well thought out, focused on what was possibly the weakest point in the entire Union line. Once again, Lee's determination to take the offensive had been underestimated.

Suddenly, Captain Jones appeared behind Moses. "Take your men and retreat," he yelled. "We won't stop them here."

Moses stared down at the endless shadows of men streaming toward them. "We can stop some," he yelled back.

Captain Jones shook his head. "Fall back and wait for orders." He stepped closer and shouted into Moses' ear. "You don't want your men captured!"

Moses stiffened, knowing Captain Jones was referring to the massacre at Fort Pillow. He whipped around, raised his arm, and yelled. "Retreat, men! Fall back!" He prayed the darkness and chaos would allow his men to escape.

As Moses gathered with his troops outside the fort walls, he heard the Rebels cheering in victory. Fort Stedman now belonged to the South. Moses retreated with his men back into the woods' dark shadows as he looked for a commanding officer to put them to use.

"Keep moving, Captain Borden! We take Fort Haskell next!"

Robert allowed himself a moment of exhilaration that Fort Stedman was now in Confederate hands, but he knew the day had only just started. He yelled for his men and continued to press forward in the dark, firing at anything they saw moving in front of them, knowing they had found a target when they heard screams. He could see the shadows of Fort Haskell in the distance, but he tensed when absolutely no response came from within.

He stared with confusion at the hulking fort. There was no way the alarm had not been raised. His understanding was that his men were coming at the fort from the rear, a possible explanation for why their approach was so easy, but his gut was screaming something was terribly wrong as they drew closer. He felt certain the Rebel forces were moving into a trap, but all they could do was press forward.

Moments later, the guns of Fort Haskell exploded in horrific roars that split the night and his men's charge. He groaned as man after man fell around him, but Robert continued to run forward, knowing his orders were to take the fort.

As more and more men fell, and the guns—with accurate aim now that daylight was coming—continued their relentless thundering, he knew it was hopeless and called for his men to retreat. Robert was done with sending his men into senseless slaughter.

As his men moved back and waited for new orders, it struck him that there was little panic on the Federal side. General Gordon had hoped for disintegration of the Union lines under the fury of their surprise attack.

He wasn't getting what he had hoped for.

Moses watched the wild chaos, uncertain what to do next as he pulled his men into the woods. The sun had lightened the sky enough to make hiding a poor option, and the Rebels had given up any pretense of stealth as they began shelling from Fort Stedman.

"I reckon we best keep moving," Simon observed.

Moses nodded and waved his men forward through the woods, farther into the Union lines while he looked for a unit they could join. Moses knew it was a matter of time before the tide turned. The Federal response would overwhelm the weaker Rebels.

Just as Robert thought, there was no hope of taking Fort Haskell. He realized other Union forts had begun to fire on the fort themselves, not realizing it had not yet fallen. Robert stopped his retreat, turned, and waved his men forward. "Let's get them!" His men turned with a roar and joined the new divisions surging toward the fort.

It wasn't long, though, before he saw a detachment of Union soldiers break free and wave their colors to other Union troops as a signal that the fort had not fallen. Three of the Union men were shot down before the rest slipped back inside, but their mission was fulfilled. As the roar of cannon stopped from the other forts, Confederate sharpshooters, determined to take the fort, rose from their hiding places and raced forward.

Blistering fire from Fort Haskell obliterated their advance.

As Robert dropped to the ground with his men, the sun had come up enough to reveal how desperate their position was. Fort Stedman lay at the apex of an arc, with Fort Haskell and Fort McGilvery at the ends. Union artillery commanded the ground behind Fort Stedman, making any Rebel withdrawal risky.

Alex slithered up next to him through the brush. "Ain't looking so good, Captain," he said breathlessly. "What do you want us to do?"

Robert shook his head and sank lower when Union gunners on the high ground east of Fort Stedman opened fire with a hurricane of shells.

When he heard the order to retreat, Robert knew it would be even more dangerous than the advance. Nothing was there to protect them from the sights of massive artillery batteries.

"What do I want you to do?" Robert shouted, as he raised his arm and sprang to his feet to sprint forward. "Retreat! And stay alive!"

The Union assault grew even more brutal when they saw the Confederates waver. Wave after wave of infantry attacked, the barrage of blistering shells relentless. Robert groaned as he and his men ran through no-man's-land and leapt over fallen bodies in the field of slaughter. He knew some men would choose to be captured, but he would give his all to get back behind the lines of protection. Robert had seen what prison did to Matthew. He had no desire to experience that for himself. That and the agony Carrie would go through if he was taken prisoner kept him running.

He ran, expecting a bullet to penetrate his body at any time. When he reached the other side and dove into a trench, only then did he risk looking back at the battlefield. He gasped, groaning at the sight of the spreading carnage.

Moses heaved a sigh of relief when he ran into an officer advancing on the Rebels.

"What are you doing, soldier?" he asked Moses curtly.

"Looking for someone to fight with, sir!" Moses replied.

"You've found someone," he snapped. "Join with my men to drive the Rebels all the way back!"

Moses' unit turned with a roar and pressed forward, determined to take back what had been taken from them. They pressed forward into sight of Fort Stedman and continued to fire steadily, cheering when the Confederate retreat turned into a panicked rout.

Moses grinned at his men and waved them toward the fort. "Let's take our fort back!" he yelled, before he saw the guns of the fort swing in their direction.

As he raced forward, he felt a heavy force slam into his chest and propel him backwards. He slammed into the ground and struggled to stand again to continue forward. Confusion overtook him when he couldn't move.

His eyes wide with alarm, Simon knelt beside him. "Don't move, Moses. You been shot."

"You have to keep moving," Moses gasped. "Stay with the men..."

Simon shook his head. "You my best friend, Moses. The Rebels is on the run. It's over. I'm right here with you."

Still not feeling any pain from getting shot, Moses stared up at him. "Is it bad?" he asked, the look on Simon's face saying it must be.

Simon hesitated, his eyes wide as he took Moses' hand. "It's bad."

Union men continued forward, racing around Moses and Simon, as they pursued the Rebels. Cannon fire and gunshots blasted a constant cacophony. All the while, the sun warmed the ground and a soft breeze sprang up.

Moses gritted his teeth against the pain that suddenly hit and thought about Rose. If he had to die, at least it was going to be on a pretty spring morning. He closed his eyes and saw the green sprigs of tobacco plants penetrating the soil, reaching for the light, Rose's shining eyes and brilliant smile gazing down at all of it.

He forced his eyes open, everything fuzzy as he looked up and saw Simon's scared eyes. "You tell Rose I love her," he whispered. "Her and little John."

Simon wiped at the tears on his face as he grasped Moses' hand. "I'll tell her," he promised, "but you ain't dead yet, Moses." He moved his face into Moses' range of vision and stared down at him. "You got to hold on, Moses. You got to hold on!"

Moses squeezed his hand tightly. "When you get to Richmond," he gasped, "you find Carrie... Help her..." His eyes closed as his body went slack.

꒛ᬄᬊ꒛ᬘ

Four hours after the battle began, it was all over. Lee's attempt to break out of Grant's siege had failed miserably. The Confederate Army was weaker than ever. Federal morale skyrocketed as the Union force waited for reinforcements.

Chapter Twenty-Six

Carrie scowled as Spencer drove her past the three old red-brick tobacco warehouses on Cary Street in Shockoe Bottom that comprised Castle Thunder Prison. A wooden fence created a small prison yard with guards lining the top of the wall. She knew prisoners were separated among the three buildings. Confederate deserters and political prisoners in one warehouse; black and female prisoners in another one; and Union deserters and prisoners of war in the last warehouse. The prison was bulging.

Every time she thought of Opal's cousin Eddie incarcerated there, Carrie felt sick. She had tried many times to get word about him, but not even her father's attempts created any results. The only thing she'd been told through the years was that Eddie was still a prisoner.

She supposed she should be grateful for that—if it was true. Carrie knew the execution rate was high.

Spencer glanced down, saw her scowl, and interpreted her thoughts. "Any word on Eddie, Miss Carrie?"

Carrie sighed heavily. "No. It's as if he doesn't exist."

"That might be a right good thing."

"Why?"

Spencer shrugged. "That Castle Thunder be a bad place, Miss Carrie. I got friends telling me about the screams that come from there right often," he said. "Theys don't have no trouble putting the lash to peoples that don't behave like theys want them to. And they's the lucky ones. Lots of gunshots coming from that place."

Carrie blanched, knowing he was referring to prisoners being executed. Shortly after Eddie had been arrested, the commander of the prison, Captain George Alexander, was brought up before the Confederate Congress for investigation because of reports of inhumane and cruel treatment that poured from those brick walls. Carrie had so hoped something would be done, but the final determination supported his punishment methods because of the prisoners' behavior. His reign of terror was allowed to continue.

"What you reckon gonna happen with them prisoners when the Yankees break through our lines?" Spencer asked.

Carrie scowled again. "I wish I could say they will all be free, but my father says there are plans to move them soon."

"Where to?"

"He said they are emptying Castle Thunder and Libby Prison and taking the prisoners up to Danville."

<hr />

Eddie lifted his head wearily, listening once again for muted sounds of battle at the Petersburg lines. As long as fighting continued, he could hope he would eventually get out of prison. Already skinny when captured and tried for espionage, Eddie now resembled little more than a skeleton. Skin hung loosely from his emaciated frame, and his eyes were sunk deep into his head.

Three years in Castle Thunder had come close to breaking him, but visions of Fannie and the kids, their eyes shining with love for him, kept him hanging on. He could only imagine how much his children had grown. Susie would be a woman now. Carl, Amber and Sadie would be much bigger. He lowered his head and stifled a groan as the old questions arose. Were his children alive? Was Fannie alive? Had the harsh winters that had almost done him in been more than they could handle without him there to help with food and shelter?

The questions drove him crazy because he had no way of getting any answers.

He felt someone watching him. The years had taught him to be aware when anyone focused attention on him. He looked up and recognized a man who had been brought in a few days earlier. He felt pity when he saw the raised welts on the man's arms and legs that said the white man had taken the lash to him, but Eddie had survived for three years by staying totally to himself. He hardly spoke to anyone, keeping his focus on his wife and children foremost in his mind. He was starved for human connection, but he had seen the price prisoners paid when someone they talked to got into trouble. Everyone around that person paid the price.

Eddie was determined to stay alive and get out to experience the freedom waiting for him. He kept to himself, but he listened. He knew the amendment to abolish slavery had passed, and he knew the Union was winning the war. He listened for sounds of battle every moment and longed for the day he would be free.

Eddie opened his mouth to protest when the prisoner staring at him moved over to sit beside him, but pity kept Eddie silent. He understood the horror and pain in the eyes watching him. He'd felt the lash himself when he first arrived, and would always carry the scars and memories from those first horrific weeks.

"Been here long?" the prisoner whispered.

"Three years."

The other man gasped. "Three years! You been in Castle Thunder for more than two years? And you still be alive?"

"It can be done," Eddie said grimly. If he was going to talk to him, he might as well know the man he was talking to. "What's your name?"

"Abraham."

"What you in here for?"

"They trying to get slaves to be soldiers. I wasn't interested, so they dumped me here."

Eddie peered at him sharply. "Soldiers? The Rebels plan on giving guns to slaves and making them fight?" This was a new one.

"It ain't working too good," Abraham said smugly. "As soon as the word spread, most of the slaves still in Richmond decide it for sho time to leave, so they's headed on up north. They ain't goin' about it too smart."

"What do you mean?" Eddie asked, starved for information.

"Oh, they passed the bill a couple weeks ago. Lots of talk 'bout how Johnny Reb was gonna get three hundred thousand slaves to put on the Rebel uniform and go off to fight."

Eddie stared in disbelief. "That be crazy."

"Specially how they go about it. Right after they started recruitin', a couple slaves got caught breakin' into a house. They hung 'em up. Another one got caught with his white mistress. They whupped him almost to death."

Eddie nodded grimly. "Don't surprise me none."

"Yeah, well, that Governor Smith decided he would let them house breakin' slaves stay alive. He put them in the army instead. All the boys I talked to said they's even less excited about fightin' in this crazy war, now they know fighting be a punishment. Most of them decided it wadn't no better than hanging, so they took off. I figures the same way they does."

"They making *free* blacks fight, too?" Would any of his friends in the black quarter be left when he got out, or would they all take off up north to keep from having to fight?

"Ain't been no talk of that. They sho 'nuff figures they can make slaves fight, though. Building them trenches be one thing. Joining up and being shot at be another. I didn't take kindly to the idea. I be on my way out of town when I gots caught. It be a heap easier than it used to be to escape, but I guess they's real desperate for soldiers."

"*That* desperate?" Eddie asked, hope sparking in his heart.

"Sho 'nuff is," Abraham replied. "I listen real close to eberthing out there. Things going bad for the South. Don't reckon it gonna be long before Grant busts through them lines down at Petersburg." He glanced around. "No, suh, I reckon I ain't gonna be here long."

Eddie glanced at the windows letting in bits of air and light. "Can't happen soon enough for me."

Abraham looked around to make sure no one was watching and lowered his voice even more, barely moving his lips. "Been a right lot of people lettin' theyselves out of Castle Thunder."

Eddie stared at him and was certain he didn't understand what Abraham was saying. Something pushed him to be sure. "You mean escaping?" He leaned closer, using his body to block Abraham's lips from anyone who might be watching.

"Like I said, I listen real good."

Eddie shook his head. "I didn't think it was possible," he murmured. He kept his head and voice low, his eyes scanning the area for guards as they talked. If a word of this was overheard, it would be grounds for execution, but he was desperate to hear more. He had given up any thought of escape when the guards told him that if he tried, his wife and children would be hauled in and lashed as he had been. But now... He didn't know whether his body could hold out much longer.

"It be possible," Abraham confirmed, his eyes steady. "Some men done climbed out a window. Some climbed down a pole onto one dem outbuildings and got away. I heard 'bout some more that dug holes right through the walls and got out." He paused. "Course, they didn't have nowheres to go, so a bunch of them got caught and brought back."

Eddie thought about the gunshots coming on a regular basis from the back of the prison. He already knew what an escapee's punishment would have been.

Abraham looked around and continued in a low voice. "I also done heard they be plannin' to take all the prisoners up to Danville on the train."

Eddie gasped. "So they really believe Grant will take the city?"

"Don't see nothing that can stop that from happening," Abraham replied. "I actually feels sorry for dem boys fighting down there to try to stop him. A bunch of them soldiers not looking much better than you, and you looks like death, sho 'nuff."

Eddie's mind began racing as he absorbed Abraham's information. Then he stood up and walked away before any guard entering the room saw them together. He'd begun to formulate his plan, and he wasn't about to take any chances now.

Eddie watched as a sliver of moon appeared in the tiny crack of the window, in the huge room he shared with more than one hundred black inmates. When it disappeared from sight, it would be time to make his move. He fought to keep his breathing steady as he worked the plan through in his mind over and over. He knew if he were caught they would probably kill him on the spot, but he'd decided he wasn't going to be taken to Danville. He wouldn't get any further from Fanny and his kids. This prison had stolen three years of his life. It was time to take it back.

Unusual activity in the prison all day had kept guards more tense than usual. After talking with Abraham, Eddie knew something was about to happen. If he didn't make his move now, his chance would probably be lost forever. He was ready to take the risk.

He lay quietly watching the moon. When it edged from sight, he stood and slipped from the room into the darkened hallway.

"What are you doing, boy?" a guard snapped.

"I gotta go, sir," Eddie said meekly, glad the darkness covered the anger on his face as he adopted a subservient tone.

"Be quick about it," the guard growled.

"Yessuh," Eddie replied, ducking into the room with the pot that was emptied daily. He breathed a sigh of relief when he heard another guard call to the one he had just spoken to. He listened carefully as he heard the first guard's footsteps disappear down the hall. He knew he didn't have much time.

Now that he had decided to do it, he was amazed how simple it was. He raced forward and soundlessly opened the only window. No guard had secured it, probably because no one thought a prisoner would jump from a window three stories high.

Eddie had roamed inside Castle Thunder all day, moving slowly so he didn't attract attention. He'd looked through other windows so that he could scout out the best one to crawl through. He knew he risked a nasty fall, but now that he had made up his mind, nothing could stop him.

He almost didn't have the strength to pull himself up to the edge because he was so weak. He gritted his teeth and silenced his grunt as he finally pulled his skinny body through the small window, glad for the first time in three years that his body had been starved down to almost nothing.

As his body slid through the opening, he groped for the pipe he knew was there from his earlier explorations, listening for any sound behind him that would indicate the guard had returned. His breath came in gasps as his heart pounded against his ribs.

As soon as he grasped the pipe, he swung out. He knew there was no time to do things carefully. He had to keep moving. He gripped the pipe tightly with both hands while his feet searched for the narrow ledge he had seen earlier that day. His heart lurched as his body dangled. He took a deep breath when his body stopped its free fall, and then he slid down the pole smoothly, bracing his feet against the brick wall to slow his descent and praying the pipe wouldn't rip away from the building.

It felt like hours, but he knew it really took him only seconds to reach the bottom. Knowing that any second, the upstairs guard would come back to check on him and then sound the alarm, he scrambled back into a shadow.

He peered out from his dark hiding place, his heart dropping when he saw two guards talking together at the edge of the yard. He estimated how far he could move forward in the shadows without being detected and started to creep toward the wooden fence, wondering whether he had enough strength to pull himself over it if he got close enough to make the attempt. Failure would mean certain death.

He was barely breathing as he drew within ten feet of where the guards stood talking.

"Sounds like we'll be out of here tomorrow," one said.

"That's what I hear. We're going to move all these prisoners up to Danville. Unless we kill some of them off first," he added with a harsh laugh. "Sure would make it easier if we didn't have so many to move."

"Maybe we could offer to take care of it," the other said roughly.

A sudden call exploded through the night air. "Prisoner escape! Prisoner escape!"

Eddie shrank back against the rough brick wall, his body shivering in the cool spring air, and looked up wildly to see the third floor guard yelling from the open window.

Both guards he had been listening to stared up at the window and then raced in that direction, their guns drawn.

Eddie quit thinking. He simply acted. It would take only seconds to find him in the shadows. He jumped out of his hidden position and leapt at the wooden fence, grabbed the top, and began hauling himself up. His arms screamed, but his mind screamed even louder, somehow giving him the strength to reach the top.

"Hey! Stop!"

The guard's angry voice bellowed behind him as he launched himself over the fence and slammed to the ground, the impact shooting pain through his emaciated body. The sharp crack of bullets slammed into the fence above where he lay. Eddie sobbed in fear, tightened his lips, and hurtled himself forward into the closest darkness he could find.

He heard pounding feet as he took off running, his weakened body weaving as he staggered down the road. He knew he had the advantage of knowing the area like the back of his hand. He had thought of nothing else all day as he made his plans.

He ran down Cary Street and turned onto Eighteenth Street, expecting a bullet to take him down. He kept running, slipped into a darkened alley he knew was just past the livery, and then pressed forward to another narrow alley behind the little pharmacy. When he had run for ten or fifteen minutes and was gasping to catch his breath, he finally collapsed onto the ground behind the black church, sure that he had eluded the guards.

He knew the black section of town would be the first place they came to look for him. Where else would a black man go who was an escaped prisoner? He figured he had until morning, and he had to let Fannie and the kids know he had escaped, so they could go somewhere safe until the war was truly over. Visions of their being lashed with the whip made him willing to do whatever it took to warn them. He waited a few minutes more to make sure he didn't hear the sound of pounding feet, and then slipped back into the shadows and headed for home.

He'd only gone a few hundred yards when he realized how he stood out in his prison garb. He breathed a sigh of relief when he saw wash on a line that someone had neglected to bring in for the night. He sorted through it quickly, finding a pair of pants that were much too short and a shirt that was much too large, but they would have to do. He didn't figure people were too particular about clothes right now. They were too focused on survival. He hoped whoever he snagged them from wouldn't feel the loss too much.

Now that he was dressed, he could relax enough to appreciate the feeling of freedom. He took deep breaths of the chilly March air and breathed in the scent of trees and dirt. After three years of being crammed in a sweaty room reeking of urine, or freezing through long nights on hard concrete, freedom felt as wonderful as he thought it would.

The sharp report of a gun jerked him back to the reality that he was a wanted prisoner. He took a deep breath and turned into another alley that would take him directly to his home. He walked quietly, listening for anything that would warn him of trouble.

The night was quiet as he stood in front of his house and stared up at the windows where his children slept, and then let his gaze linger on his and Fannie's room. He could hardly wait to see her face when she saw him. The thought of it gave him the courage to slip around the back and rap lightly on the door.

A minute or so later, he heard footsteps and a man's gruff voice. "Who be out there?"

Eddie blinked in surprise and tried to relax. Fannie must be renting some of the rooms out to make extra money. He was glad she had male protection. "My name is Eddie," he said softly, standing as close to the door as possible. "This is my house. I'm here to see my wife."

The door swung open, and a strong arm reached out to pull him in.

Eddie stared into the eyes of a man much shorter than he was, but with a stocky build that said he was strong.

"You're in Castle Thunder," the man growled, holding up a lantern to stare at his face. "How'd you get here?"

"I escaped," Eddie said quickly. "I don't got much time. It ain't safe for anybody for me to be here. I come to warn Fannie and the kids. They need to go somewhere safe till the war be over. The guards might come looking for them."

Silence filled the kitchen as the man stared back at him, his face filled with an emotion Eddie couldn't identify.

"Don't you hear me, man?" Eddie demanded impatiently. "I need to see my wife." He moved to pass him and head up the stairs. At that moment, a sleepy-looking woman walked into the kitchen, holding a small boy by the hand.

"What's going on?" she asked, fear radiating in her voice.

"I'm here to see my wife, Fannie, and my kids," Eddie said, fear beginning to churn in his stomach. Something wasn't right. He stared at the man and woman gazing at him with a look he had finally identified as pity. "Excuse me," he said firmly, moving to pass them.

The man put out his hand and grabbed hold of his arm. "They ain't up there," he said.

"Where are they?"

The man shifted his eyes away and shuffled his feet.

His wife stepped forward and took Eddie's hand. "Fannie's gone," she said softly.

"Gone where?" Eddie asked, fighting to deny the truth he saw in her eyes.

"I worked with Fannie at the armory," she began.

Eddie wanted to slap his hands over his ears, wanted to stop what he knew was coming, but he had to know. "What happened?" he whispered.

"There be an explosion. The same day you was caught and got took to prison." She wiped at the tears in her eyes. "Fannie didn't make it."

Eddie stared at her, pain ripping through his entire body. "My Fannie is dead?"

"I'm so sorry."

Eddie stood frozen in place, staring at the couple as numbness crept into his mind. He'd survived three years in prison to get home to Fannie and the kids. "The kids," he gasped, tears choking his voice. "Where my kids?"

The woman shook her head. "I don't know. I does know they be with Opal."

"Opal?" Hope moved in to replace some of the pain. "My kids is still alive?"

"They was the last we know," the man replied. "Eddie, I'm so sorry."

Eddie nodded impatiently, knowing he had to get out of there. "How do I find Opal? How do I find my kids?"

"All I knows is we been told if you ever come back, that we was to tell you to go find Miss Carrie. She has your answers."

Eddie stared at them, trying to digest the new information. "Carrie Cromwell knows where my kids are?"

"That's what we been told to tell you," the man repeated. "It be all we know. I'm sorry."

Eddie nodded woodenly and backed out of the kitchen into the cold night. "Thank you," he muttered. "If the police or guards come..."

"They'll never know you been here," the man promised.

"You could be in danger," Eddie whispered. "I'm sorry if I brung trouble on you."

"Them guards ain't gonna know you been here because they ain't gonna find nobody at home. I figures me and my family gonna go stay with other family for a while till them guards stop comin' round."

The sun had barely crested the horizon when Carrie swung out of the house to head up to the hospital. Wagons full of wounded soldiers had arrived the day before from the battle at Fort Stedman. She'd gotten home a few hours earlier, grabbed some sleep, and was headed back to her ward. The only thing she could find to be thankful for was that Hobbs had arrived at the hospital to serve as her assistant again. The army had decided he could be of more service in the hospital.

From him, she had learned Robert was still alive, so she was pouring all her energy and focus into helping the new rows of patients waiting for her.

"Miss Carrie!" a harsh whisper broke the morning stillness.

Carrie jolted to a stop and stared into the bushes next to the porch. "Who's there?" she demanded, startled but not afraid.

She gasped when a skeleton-thin man stepped forward hesitantly. "Eddie?" She blinked her eyes and stared again. "Is it really you, Eddie?"

"It's me, Miss Carrie," he said gruffly, shivering in the morning air. Spring had come, but the mornings were still chilly, and he was poorly dressed.

"Where? How?" Carrie stared at him, thinking of her conversation with Spencer the day before. Then she grabbed his arm and pulled him into the house. "You must be starving," she said softly as she pulled him back to the kitchen, glad the rest of the house hadn't stirred yet. She knew May would already be cooking.

May looked up when the kitchen door swung open. "Miss Carrie, what you..."

"Eddie needs food," Carrie replied. "Give him all he can eat."

May looked with sympathy at the man in front of her and began scooping up a huge bowl of porridge. "It won't be fancy, but it's got to be more than you been getting," she growled, tears glistening in her eyes as she stared at him with pity. "I be real sorry about your wife, Eddie," she said softly.

"You know me?" Eddie stood in the kitchen reveling in the first warmth he'd felt in months and stared at the huge bowl of porridge steaming on the table. A sharp pang of hunger stabbed him, as the warmth made him relax enough to sway with fatigue.

"We been praying for you and your family down at church ever since Fannie died and you got caught. How'd you get out?"

"I escaped."

Carrie gasped. "We have to find a safe place for you."

"I gots to know about my family," Eddie said, gripping the back of the chair in front of him to keep him steady. "I been told to come here," he said. "Where be my kids, Miss Carrie? Where is Opal?" he asked desperately. "Please say you can tell me."

Carrie smiled and motioned for him to sit down. "Eat," she commanded. "I'll tell you what you want to know."

The look she sent May said to keep filling the bowl for as long as Eddie could eat. She waited for him to begin spooning the hot food into his starving body before she began to speak. "The first thing I want you to know is that Fannie wasn't alone when she died. They got word to Opal after the explosion. She arrived right before Fannie died. Fannie asked her to tell you how much she loved you, and then she asked Opal to take care of the kids."

Eddie blinked back tears as the swell of emotion threatened to overwhelm him, but he went back to shoveling in food, knowing he would need strength for whatever was coming next.

"It wasn't safe here for Opal and the kids," Carrie continued. "She didn't have a way to take care of them."

"Where they go?" Eddie demanded.

"Cromwell Plantation," Carrie replied. "They're living with Sam in my father's house. They're healthy and as happy as possible after losing both parents. I haven't been there in more than a year, but I believe they're safe." She could only hope her words were true and that the plantation was still there.

"Cromwell ain't been burned?"

"I don't know," Carrie replied honestly, "but even if the Union destroyed it, I know they are taking former slaves and other blacks to the contraband camp. Opal is committed to your children, Eddie." She reached out and grasped his hand. "They're waiting for you to come back to them."

She waited for him to absorb the news. "Susie is waiting for you, too. She and her husband, Zeke," she finished with a smile.

Eddie sucked in a breath. "My Susie girl be married?"

"Yes, to a wonderful man. You'll like Zeke when you meet him. She met him on the plantation when Zeke escaped from North Carolina. He had to agree to stay on at Cromwell until you got out of prison, or she wouldn't marry him."

Eddie's mind spun as he absorbed all the news. The silence and warmth in the kitchen wrapped around him like a blanket. Only one thing was clear. "I gots to get out to the plantation," he stated. "Can you help me?"

"I would," Carrie replied, "but it's not possible right now. There's not a road that could take you to Cromwell that isn't crawling with soldiers. You would never get through." She understood the stubborn look on his face and reached out to grasp his hand. "Trust me," she said softly, waiting until he gazed into her eyes. "I'll find you someplace safe, Eddie. The war can't possibly last much longer. There's no reason to risk getting caught again when you'll see your children soon."

Eddie stared at her. "You really think it will end soon?"

Carrie nodded. "Lee made a final attempt to break out of Grant's stranglehold on the city yesterday. The attempt failed miserably and resulted in thousands more wounded or captured troops. Grant is getting reinforcements soon."

"You don't seem too upset," Eddie said, staring at her intently.

"I'm not," she said. "Oh, I worry about what will happen to Richmond, but all I want is for this war to be over. We'll all deal with what comes afterwards, but I want it to end."

Carrie took a deep breath. "I have to get up to the hospital. I have patients who need me." She looked at May. "I'm putting Eddie in my room. It's not safe for him to be out during the day." She looked back at Eddie. "I'm assuming they are probably looking for you."

"Probably, though I may not be real important right now since they moving all the prisoners."

"Still, we will take no chances," Carrie said, turning back to May. "Give Eddie all the food he can eat today, and make sure you fill a big crate of food for him for later. When it gets dark again, he can slip down to the black hospital."

Thinking quickly, she outlined the rest of her plan. "There is a room in the back of the hospital no one is using. I can't take you myself, but you're probably safer sneaking back the same way you got here. I'll have Spencer take the food down for you today and stash it away. No one but May, Spencer and I will know you're there. You'll find everything you need."

Eddie stared at her. "You gonna do all that for me?"

"You're Opal's family, which makes you my family," Carrie said. "I'll make sure you have food. You make sure you don't get caught. When the war is over, I'll find a way to get you to the plantation." She gazed out the window in the direction of Cromwell. "We just might all go out together," she said with a smile.

Chapter Twenty-Seven

Carrie took deep breaths as she walked slowly down the hill from the hospital, her heart heavy from the staggering casualties that had come in from the battle at Fort Stedman. She stared at the thick gray clouds massed on the horizon, and hoped for rain that would push down the smoke that had drifted over the city from the battle.

"And so another summer begins," Janie observed, staring at the clouds as Carrie was. "And it's still spring."

"I can't bear to think we'll have another whole summer of this," Carrie replied, her hands tightening into fists. "It has to end, Janie." She took another breath. "I'm praying Richmond will fall."

Janie looked at her sharply. "Do you mean that?"

"I do," Carrie said, hoping Janie could understand. "Too many have died. Too much has been destroyed. It has to stop."

"Even if it means you lose everything? Even if it means the people you love lose everything?"

Carrie gazed at her, knowing she could be honest. "We lost everything the day the war started. There was never a chance we would win this war. The only thing the South has accomplished is to kill or maim hundreds of thousands of men who did what they were told was the right thing to do." She stopped and looked over at Janie. "Do you disagree with me?"

"No," Janie whispered, meeting her gaze levelly. "We lost six more soldiers today in our ward."

Carrie gazed at her, recognizing something in Janie's eyes that sparked a quick alarm, something that went beyond concern for her patients. "Clifford? Is everything okay?"

Janie's eyes fell. She twisted her hands as she stared at the ground. "He's so conflicted. Losing his arm...wondering whether he'll ever be able to practice law again." She looked up. "His parents' plantation on

St. Simons Island was completely burned and destroyed when Sherman went through. He just found out. They've lost everything."

Carrie gasped and reached out to grab her hand, while trying to block images of their own plantation burning. She had to focus on her friend. "I'm so sorry!"

"He's bitter," Janie admitted. "And every night he has such horrible nightmares. My heart is breaking for him."

Her eyes held a desperation Carrie had never seen. She knew there was nothing she could say to ease the pain, so she stepped forward, wrapped Janie in her arms, and stroked her back as her friend sobbed against her shoulder.

Long minutes passed before Janie stepped back and gulped down a weak laugh. "I'm usually the one to do that for you."

"About time you fell apart," Carrie teased gently. "I needed to pay you back for at least one of the times you've done this for me."

Tears still on her cheeks, Janie stared at her. "I want the war to end, but I can't imagine leaving here and not having you," she said. "You're the best friend I've ever had. I don't know that I want to go back to Raleigh," she cried suddenly. "I love Clifford so much, but I will miss you terribly."

Carrie pulled her back into her arms. "The war isn't over yet," she said gently. "Not one of us knows what will happen when it finally ends. Let's take one day at a time." Tears filled her own eyes, and she gripped Janie in a tight hug. "I'll miss you so much, too," she whispered fiercely.

꧁ ꧂

Thomas and Jeremy were sitting down to dinner when Carrie and Janie arrived. The other boarders had eaten earlier and retired to the parlor. Janie settled in her seat while Carrie headed into the kitchen and called back that she would join them in a few minutes.

May stood by the stove when she swung in through the door. She nodded when she saw Carrie's raised eyebrows. "Spencer done took the food down already," she said quietly, watching the door to make sure no one else walked in. "Eddie has been waiting for dark out in the barn with Granite, so that he can slip on down to the hospital. He got some good sleep and ate more than I ever done seen a man eat," she finished with a smile. "Spencer will go down tomorrow to make sure he got there okay."

Carrie sighed with relief. "Thank you, May."

"No," May shook her head firmly, reaching out to grab her hand. "Thank *you*, Miss Carrie. Ain't many white people care about us black people the way you do. I'm real grateful."

Carrie squeezed her hand tightly and headed back to the dining room, before she had to explain what was taking her so long. Her father was talking as she entered the room and slid into her place. She reached gratefully for the hot cornbread sending up little puffs of steam.

"According to my source, Lee told congressional questioners back in January that leaving Richmond would not necessarily end the struggle."

Carrie stiffened, almost dropping the cornbread she had picked up. "What do you mean?" she asked.

Thomas shrugged. "All I know is General Lee told a senator that evacuating Richmond would make him stronger than before. Lee did concede that losing Richmond would be a serious calamity from a moral and political viewpoint, but he also believed, at least then, that he could prolong the war two or more years on Virginia soil. He said that, since the war began, he's been forced to let the enemy make strategic plans for him because he had to protect the capital. If Richmond falls, Lee will be able to make them for himself. "

Carrie gasped and dropped the cornbread. "No!" She stared at her father, a wild pounding starting in her head. "The war has to end," she murmured. Anger surged through her, making her voice rise. "The war has to end," she said louder. She met her father's eyes squarely. "How many more, Father? How many more have to die? How many more men have to sacrifice their lives? Their futures? How many more families have to lose the ones they love?"

"And how much more of Virginia has to be ransacked and burned before it's over?" Jeremy added, his own eyes burning with anger.

Carrie looked at him, grateful he shared her outrage, and then turned back to stare at her father.

Thomas looked back at her steadily. "I just report the news," he said, his eyes and voice strained. "There's no need to kill the messenger. Besides, you'll be very surprised to discover I agree with you."

Carrie gaped at him. "You do?"

Thomas nodded. "If I thought there was any hope of a victory, I would be the first to applaud his commitment to fight on. There is none. I can't imagine what my life will be like if Richmond falls, but I do know we can no longer demand the sacrifice of any more lives."

Carrie stared at him for a long moment and then stood to wrap her arms around him. "I love you," she whispered. "Somehow we will find a way to move forward and create a new life."

Thomas nodded and picked up where Carrie had interrupted him with her outburst. "I hear Davis asked Lee earlier this month why, if withdrawal is inevitable, he wasn't leaving. Lee told him the horses were too weak to pull the wagons and cannons through the March mud, but that soon the roads would be passable."

"Soon, as in now?" Janie asked.

Thomas nodded his head heavily. "Yes."

Carrie recognized the look on his face. "What are you really wanting to say, Father?"

Thomas smiled. "You know me well," he admitted with a soft smile, and then reached to take her hand. "As soon as we receive word of Lee's withdrawal, the entire Virginia legislature will evacuate, along with the Confederate administration."

Carrie sat back heavily, a sick dread in her stomach adding to the pounding in her head. "Where will you go?" she asked quietly, knowing this had been coming but still not prepared for it.

"I understand we're going to Lynchburg. The Federal administration will go to Danville."

"And if the Federals follow you to Lynchburg?"

Thomas shrugged. "I don't know. I do know I have no desire to spend time in prison, and I suspect that would be my reward for what I've done for Virginia." He paused and shook his head. "That's not important now. Are all of you still determined to stay?"

Carrie nodded. Janie and Jeremy exchanged looks with her as they gave their own affirming nods.

Thomas sighed and ran his hand through his white hair. "I know better than to try to talk any of you out of it. All I can do is try to prepare you."

"Prepare us for what?" Carrie asked unsteadily, dreading the thought of her beloved father on the run.

"We have to make plans now while we have the time to do it," he said.

Only the strain on his face and in his voice told Carrie how much this was costing him. She knew how devastating it would be for him to leave her behind, but he also respected her enough to understand why she couldn't—*wouldn't* leave. The only thing she had left to give him was to make this time as easy as possible. "Then let's do it," she said equally as firmly, smiling when his eyes met hers with relief.

"You must keep Granite in the stable," he said quickly. "Ever since Sheridan destroyed a huge chunk of the James River Canal, it has been almost impossible to get food into the city. It was horrific before. Now it will get worse. Butter is up to twenty dollars a pound."

Carrie opened her mouth to ask what the cost of butter had to do with Granite...

"Listen to your father," Jeremy warned. "The government is so desperate for horses they are snatching them off the streets. Farmers are refusing to bring food into the city because they're afraid they will lose the horses pulling their wagons."

"How horrible!" Janie cried.

Carrie tightened her lips and stared in the direction of the stables. "They will not get Granite for any more of this war." She thought of the Union Army taking

Richmond and was quite sure how they would feel about her beautiful Thoroughbred. He was thin, but it was easy to tell what a remarkable animal he was. "Father, how will you get out of the city?"

Thomas shrugged. "I'm not sure yet. Trains will take some of us. Others will go in wagons. I'm sure some will ride on horseback because it won't be possible for the train to carry everyone."

"Take Granite."

"Carrie, I..."

"Take him," she repeated, blinking back her tears. "I'll know you have a horse that can help you get away, and I'll also be sure the Union Army won't get their hands on him."

Thomas nodded slowly. "Thank you," he said, his eyes saying he knew how much this meant to her. "I'll bring him back to you."

Carrie forced a smile. "I'm counting on it," she managed to say, swallowing back her fear and pain. "What's next?"

Matthew stared around at the massive Union encampment. Men, artillery and cannons poured in from what seemed every direction. The feel of battle hung heavy in the air. He had arrived the day before. He'd seen a lot of battle camps, but never one that had quite this feeling of *finality*.

"It won't be long," Peter said. "Sherman's sixty thousand soldiers have arrived. Sheridan is already here. His cavalry did massive damage outside of Richmond and then crossed the James River to join Grant."

"There are close to two hundred and fifty thousand troops here," Matthew said, shaking his head as he looked in the direction of Richmond.

"To take on an army of less than fifty thousand men who are starving to death," Peter acknowledged. "It will be hard to call it a battle."

"Lee has pulled off miracles before," Matthew said, though he knew this time nothing would stop the inevitable.

"Not this time," Peter predicted. "Richmond will fall within the next few days. Lee may stretch it out. If he's as smart as I think he is, he'll run. He knows he can't win, but I do think he might believe he can continue fighting if he gets out of those trenches. He was trying to get away when they attacked Fort Stedman. My guess is he was trying to join up with General Johnston so he would have more of an army."

Peter stopped to confer with a messenger who ran up and then turned back to Matthew. "Why are you here?"

Matthew looked at Peter for a long moment, respecting their friendship too much to give him the line that *'he had a job to do and he was here to do it.'* "I'm worried about Carrie," he admitted. "If I can be one of the first into the city, I can possibly help her."

"You still love her," Peter said, a note of sympathy in his voice.

"I reckon I always will," Matthew replied. "It runs in my family. Once a Justin man falls in love, it seems to stick for life. I just happened to fall in love with a woman who is now married to one of my closest friends," he said ruefully.

"Wouldn't it be easier to stay away?"

"Maybe, but it wouldn't change how I feel, and Robert knows I would never do anything to betray our friendship. Besides, I couldn't live with myself if I had a chance to help her and didn't take it." He looked hard at Peter. "Without Carrie, you and I would probably still be rotting in Libby Prison, hauled back with the others who tried to escape but were recaptured."

"You're right. That's why one of the first things I planned to do when I reached Richmond was to make sure she was okay," Peter admitted with a smile.

Matthew smiled in return, grateful to have such a good friend. "We'll find her," he said. "When the Union takes Richmond, we'll go in and find her."

"It won't be long," Peter stated. "My source just told me the battle will start in the morning."

Carrie and the rest had stood up from the dinner table after a long session of planning when Hobbs entered wearily, his face caked with sweat-streaked dust, fatigue making his limp more pronounced. "What happened, Hobbs?" she exclaimed. "You didn't get all that dirt on you from the hospital."

"No, Miss Carrie, I reckon I didn't," Hobbs agreed as he gave her a tired smile. "General Ewell figures there should be some men to protect Richmond, even if Lee has all the regular soldiers out on the lines."

"They're calling you to fight again?" Carrie asked sharply.

"I volunteered, Miss Carrie. I reckon Richmond is pretty ripe for cavalry attacks from the likes of Sheridan. Them boys been out wreaking some mighty bad havoc. A bunch of the hospital attendants and patients who can still shoot a gun have been assigned to battalions. There's a pile of rifles and ammo stacked up between the wards now." He pulled himself up proudly. "While we were marching, a bunch of clerks and stewards came out to join us. We ain't going to lie down and let them Bluecoats run over us. We intend to protect what is ours."

Too sick at heart to know what to say, Carrie stared at him. "Stay safe," she finally managed as she turned to go upstairs.

Her father stopped her with a hand on her arm. "I know you're tired, but can you come up to my room for a few minutes?"

Carrie, exhausted to the bone, started to shake her head and ask whether they could talk in the morning, but she caught the look in her father's eyes. Swallowing her refusal, she nodded and hooked her arm through his. As they walked up the stairs together, she wondered whether there would be many more times they could do something so simple. Suddenly, it became very important to savor every moment with this man she loved so much.

Thomas turned to her as soon as he had closed the door. "I'm going to be broke, Carrie." He waved a hand at the sumptuously decorated bedroom with its high four-poster bed and elegant wardrobe. Beautiful pictures adorned the light blue walls, and a gentle breeze had the soft white curtains puffing back from the window. As beautiful as it was, it still held a distinctly male feel that suited her father. "All of this may be gone soon. I will have no money."

"You've spent it all?" Carrie asked, wondering why this eventuality hadn't dawned on her.

"No, but all I have is worthless now. I converted it all to Confederate currency when the war started. It will have no value when the war is over."

"I see," Carrie murmured, her thoughts spinning. "The plantation?"

"It belongs to us free and clear," Thomas said. "Assuming it's still standing and the federal government doesn't take it as retribution."

Carrie stared at him with burning eyes. Such a thought had never entered her mind. She had been so worried about its burning, that she never stopped to think about what would happen after the war. "You can't go back home, Father?"

"I'll be a man on the run," he said shortly. "I don't know what will happen."

"I'll go back to the plantation and wait for you," Carrie said, knowing it was the right thing to do as soon as the words passed her lips.

Thomas smiled. "Your husband may be eager to get back home to Oak Meadows," he reminded her.

"His mother is there," she insisted. "He will not want you to lose the plantation, and I certainly don't want to lose it. We'll wait for you, and then we'll go to Oak Meadows." She wondered briefly when her plans would include medical school, but she knew the country would have to settle down first.

Thomas reached for her hand. "Thank you. No one knows what will happen, but I appreciate what you want to do. I'm afraid there is nothing but darkness ahead for us."

"Perhaps," Carrie acknowledged gently, "but the darkness always ends, and the light always shines again." Her eyes glittered with confidence. "This long, dark night will end."

Thomas stared into her eyes and shook his head. "I wish I had your confidence. I've leaned on you so much in the years since your mother died. I don't know how you have borne the weight."

Carrie squeezed his hand. "There have been many more times you've been there to help *me* bear the weight," she replied. "It's what family does."

"Yes," Thomas agreed, a catch in his voice as he gazed at her lovingly. "I am indeed a lucky man...but I'm also a man running out of time." He walked over to the wardrobe and beckoned her to join him.

Carrie watched as he pushed a button hidden at the back of the wardrobe. She stared in astonishment as a small door swung slowly open to reveal a cavity in the wall.

Thomas smiled at the look on her face. "Not nearly as impressive as the tunnel, but it's come in handy. I want you to know it's here."

"What's here?" Carrie asked, still bemused as she stared into another hidden place she'd had no idea existed.

"Gold," Thomas replied. "It's too heavy for me to take to Lynchburg, so I'm entrusting it to you. I want you to know it's here. If you have a chance to get it out to the plantation and hide it in the tunnels, it might be enough to help me get started again. If something happens to me, it will be yours."

"Gold?" Carrie echoed, choosing to block out the suggestion her father would not return.

"There's not much," Thomas admitted. "Certainly nothing that would replace the fortune I've spent these last five years, but it might be enough to survive and start over."

Carrie stared at the glistening bars and nodded, tears shining brightly in her eyes. "I'll do the best I can, Father. Your job is to stay safe and come home. I will not go to Oak Meadows with Robert, until I know you are safe."

"And then?" Thomas asked, fixing her with his eyes. "Your dream is not to be a plantation wife. You've spent the last three years working as a doctor. What are you going to do about that?"

Carrie looked at him as he asked the question that had been pounding in her heart and head for weeks, and then she shook her head. "All we can do is take one day at a time and see what happens," she said, the exhaustion completely swamping her as she faced a question she had no answer to.

Thomas squeezed her hand, his eyes saying he understood the struggle she was enduring. "He loves you, Carrie. The two of you will find your way together."

"All I care about is my two favorite men coming home to me safely," Carrie said, willing away the tears she knew would fall as soon as she was back in her room.

Chapter Twenty-Eight

Matthew sipped hot coffee while he stared in the direction of Richmond, fog blanketing the ground and floating up into the cool air. Heavy smoke from the night's bombardment mixed with the fog stung his lungs. He nodded briefly as Peter strolled up to join him. "I'll be glad when this war is over and I don't have to get up at two o'clock in the morning," he grumbled, feeling the ache of sleeping on hard ground. "Especially when all the bombing didn't stop until midnight."

Peter blinked his bleary eyes and reached for the coffee pot. "You and me both," he growled. He stared out over the battle preparations happening in every direction. "I wonder whether Lee knows what is about to happen," he mused.

"I'd be surprised if he doesn't," Matthew murmured. "The question is, whether he is pragmatic enough to realize he doesn't stand a chance, or if he is foolhardy enough to fight back and risk his entire army." He looked northward again. "Quite a concert last night," he commented, wanting to think about something other than war.

Peter smiled. "I was thinking last night that it might be the last concert I hear on the battlefield. They have been going on for the last four years—each band, Yankee and Rebel, trying to outdo the other with their renditions of 'Dixie,' 'Hail Columbia' and 'My Maryland.'"

"Don't forget 'The Star-Spangled Banner,' our national anthem," Matthew said, mesmerized as always that war could produce such moving music. "My most vivid memory is a battle of the bands last winter on either side of the Rapidan River that finally ended in both bands playing 'Home Sweet Home.' I watched Union men cry, and I'm quite sure there were tears on the Rebel side as well."

Peter nodded. "I remember. I also remember wondering how many of the men on either side of the river were related, and whether they would kill their brother or father the next day."

Matthew tightened his lips as he stared at the Confederate lines. He was certain Robert was standing in one of those trenches right now—if he had lived through the night. He was grateful, as he had been throughout the war, that he would never have to shoot a gun at his friend. Now his only hope was that Robert would live through what was coming. "I'm wondering whether there are any Rebels left after the bombardment last night."

"It was after midnight before the shelling stopped," Peter said grimly. "I'm sure it was the heaviest exchange of artillery since the battle for Petersburg began. Grant is serious about taking Richmond."

"It felt like an earthquake from all the explosions. I don't know how there can be any Rebels left to fight us." He glanced back at the masses of men taking their position in the early morning darkness and then stared toward Richmond and thought of Carrie.

"The Rebels are there," Peter replied as he took Matthew's arm. "Time for us to get behind the lines," he said. "The battle should start soon. I'd rather be *behind* the bullets than in front of them."

Robert woke up coughing, his lungs burning from heavy smoke as he struggled to take deep breaths. It had been after midnight before the barrage of artillery shells finally stopped. He had no idea how many were killed, but he was certain it had been only the prelude to a much bigger battle. Every quivering nerve, still exhausted after a couple hours of sleep broken by coughing fits, told him this would be the day. A mist combined with darkness completed a curtain that Robert felt separated his position from the rest of the world.

"They're coming ain't they, Captain?"

Robert glanced at Alex staring over the top of the trench. "I believe they are," he agreed.

"I've been watching the last few days," Alex said nervously. "They've sure been getting a lot of reinforcements." He squatted down beside Robert. "We don't stand a chance."

Robert wanted to deny that statement, but he opted for honesty. "I believe you're right."

Alex took a deep breath. When he spoke, his voice was both hard and vulnerable. "I heard Pickett's boys took a mighty beating yesterday from that Yankee Sheridan."

Robert hesitated. He wasn't sure truth was the best option this time. "There was a battle," he agreed, searching for words.

"You can tell me how bad it was, Captain," Alex said quietly. "I was sure hoping our boys could whup Sheridan and make up for everything he did up in the Shenandoah, but I'm thinking that didn't happen."

Robert could hear a maturity in the battle-hardened youth that demanded his respect. "It was a complete rout," he admitted. "Close to five thousand prisoners were taken."

A long silence gripped the night. "You really think them Yankees can get past all our fortifications?" Alex asked.

Robert knew every inch of the ground in front of their trenches. He could envision the layers of wooden barricades that protected them, but he knew the brute force of far superior numbers could overwhelm them. He remained silent.

Alex interpreted his silence and swallowed hard. "You reckon we gonna live through this one?"

Robert laid his hand on Alex's thin, muscular shoulder. "That's the plan," he said confidently. "Lee will try to hold them off, but his bigger plan is to allow all of us to evacuate and move out of these trenches."

"We're getting out of here?" Alex asked with almost pathetic hope in his voice.

Robert nodded. "Yes. We tried that with Fort Stedman. Since we couldn't break through, we're going to swing around them and go down to join General Johnston in North Carolina. Lee has supplies stockpiled for us southwest of here. The general figures, once we're out of these trenches, our superior fighting ability will turn the tide."

Alex brightened, his shoulders squaring as his eyes flashed with pride. "General Lee has that right! Get us out of this mud, and it won't matter how many Yankee soldiers come after us. We'll handle them with no problem," he boasted.

Robert smiled, knowing Alex needed confidence more than anything, but he knew exactly what bad shape the Confederate Army was in. He was terrified to evacuate and leave Carrie and Thomas to Union occupation, but he knew desertion was not an option for him. He would continue with Lee's army for as long as there was an army, but his heart would remain in Richmond.

Alex read his mind. "It's going to be right hard to leave your pretty wife isn't it, Captain?"

Robert nodded, staring into the darkness beyond the trench. The tightening in his gut said something would happen soon. He'd learned to sense battle before the first shot was ever fired.

Boom!

The first shot of the battle sounded at close to half past four o'clock in the morning. All around him his men stood to their feet, aimed over the trench tops, and began to fire. The rain of artillery shells that descended on them was like nothing they had ever experienced. The whole sky pulsed and shuddered with great sheets of light. Jagged flames lit the horizon as the Confederate guns replied. The battle smoke piled up in monstrous thunderheads, fitfully visible in the flash of exploding shells, like a dark canopy of impending doom.

Robert gritted his teeth and sank down to the bottom of the trench as he motioned his men to join him, knowing none of them could fire into that kind of barrage, and also certain the Federals wouldn't advance under that kind of fire.

He didn't know how long the firing continued before silence finally swallowed them again. Robert looked down his line, the gray sky of dawn giving him enough light to see most of his men staring back at him. The shells, for the most part, had gone over their trenches. He would mourn the dead later.

He was suddenly alerted by another mysterious sound. He raised his hand to keep his men silent and strained his ears to determine what it was. It sounded like a deep distant rustling, like a strong breeze blowing through the swaying boughs and dense foliage of some great forest.

Curiosity got the best of him. When Robert peeked over the top of the trenches, his blood froze. The sound of rustling was the noise made by thousands of Federal soldiers tramping toward his position over soft, damp ground.

Matthew stood next to Peter on the parapet of the Union's Fort Fisher and watched the attack unfold. It was still too dark to see much except the flash of cannon and rifle fire, but he could clearly see a half-mile of twinkling, flashing light, the rim of the Confederate works lit by musketry. They were putting up a valiant fight, but Matthew knew the dark wave he could see in the distance was the massive Union force moving toward them.

He and Peter watched silently as the drama played out before them.

"Peter, look!" he shouted suddenly. "Do you see that black gap in the Confederate line?"

He could feel Peter's body tense next to his. "I do," he said. "And look, there is another one to the right, and another farther down to the left!"

"They're taking them!" Matthew knew the dark gaps reflected positions the Rebels had abandoned. The sheer exultation of the moment after almost a year of siege warfare had Matthew's heart pumping with excitement.

As they watched, the black spots in the line grew and multiplied until finally the whole line went dark. The Confederate line had been captured.

The men from the Sixth Army Corps were still celebrating when Matthew and Peter, along with other journalists eager to document the historic happening, topped the last of the trenches.

Matthew couldn't help smiling when a burly buck private donned a tinseled, gray uniform dress coat left behind by a Confederate officer. Another soldier wrapped a Confederate flag around his shoulders as if it were a toga. The area was an anthill of activity as soldiers swarmed around bombproofs, huts and tents exploring the camp they fought so hard to capture.

They deserved to celebrate. It didn't matter what he thought of the war—these men had suffered, watched their friends die, and given everything they had to accomplish this moment.

A movement from behind caught his attention. He watched as General Grant, General Meade and General Wright topped the trench on their horses and paused to stare out over the captured camp, their eyes taking it all in.

The troops looked up and saw them, and they all took a moment to gaze up and down the broken line. The sun topped the horizon and shone through the haze of smoke, casting a golden glimmer on the scene.

Matthew caught his breath and knew he would never forget this moment. He was even more certain when, almost as one, a wild shout rose from every Union man present and rang through the air, announcing their celebration of a victory they had fought so long to gain. Matthew stood quietly, choosing to believe the shout rose to heaven, and announced the victory to all those who had given their lives before. He also prayed the victory would mean the dying would stop on the Confederate side.

Minutes later, Matthew and Peter followed Grant's lead as he headed into Petersburg. While the two walked behind him, Carter, another journalist, fell in line with them. "Did you hear what happened at the stockade this morning?"

Matthew glanced at him. "The prisoner-of-war stockade?"

"Yes. Those Rebel boys aren't planning to give up."

"What happened?" Peter asked.

"There are about five thousand men there who were captured at Five Forks yesterday. Our provost marshal made a little speech to them and pointed out their cause was doomed."

"I can imagine how they took that," Matthew said wryly.

"He invited everyone to step up, take the oath of allegiance, and then go home and fight no more," Carter continued.

"And?" Peter asked.

Carter shrugged. "About one hundred of those five thousand took him up on it. I'm sure they regretted it immediately, because the rest of the prisoners bitterly derided the ones who stepped forward, calling them cowards and traitors."

"I wonder where General Lee is now," Matthew said, looking back at the captured lines.

"Running," Carter crowed.

"Not running," Peter corrected. "Lee doesn't run, not even after a massive defeat. I can guarantee you he is trying to move into a new position he can fight from."

Matthew saw the corps swing into formation, unfurl their flags, and strike up the music from their band. The Union forces were eager to show themselves as the conquering heroes. Matthew frowned as they reached the edge of Petersburg and moved into the city. The music echoed through desolate, deserted streets that seemed to absorb the music and swallow the joy. The houses lining the streets all had drawn blinds. Here and there, he spied expressionless faces peering through parted curtains.

As the morning progressed, Matthew saw not a single woman. The only inhabitants of Petersburg after months of siege seemed to be old men, cripples and a large contingent of blacks that cheered the arrival of the army and looked at Grant with awe.

Puffing on his ever-present cigar, Grant, on the other hand, was all business as he stood waving his arms in a doorway and dictating orders to his staff.

"Grant knows he really hasn't won anything yet," Peter announced dryly.

Matthew nodded his head. "He has an empty city, and the trenches now belong to the Union, but he certainly hasn't destroyed Lee's army."

"He'll capture Richmond tomorrow," Peter said in agreement, "but as long as Lee's army is out there, the war will continue."

Carter joined them again and overheard their conversation. "He's already sent his army after them," he announced. "Lee seems to be headed southwest, going north of the Appomattox River."

"If he expects to join up with Johnston, he has to," Peter observed.

"That's right," Carter replied. "My sources tell me Grant already has troops as far west as Lee, and quite a bit farther south. The plan is to head him off before he can connect with Johnston. I'm going down to join them. I want to be there when this war actually ends. It won't end until Lee surrenders, and I don't intend to miss it."

Matthew listened, but his thoughts were already in Richmond. "Who is Grant sending in to occupy Richmond?" he asked brusquely.

Carter shrugged. "I hear he's sending in some of the black corps. The people of Richmond should love that."

⁂

Robert gritted his teeth and continued to plod down the dusty, rutted road. He fought to ignore the fever burning in his body and struggled to breathe in between the coughing jags. Lee had called for their retreat and evacuation that afternoon. It would take all night to get his troops through Richmond and headed southwest. Robert's unit was one of the first to start the march.

Alex moved up to march beside him. "You ain't sounding too good, Captain," he said, worry shining in his eyes.

Robert shrugged. He was sure he didn't look much better than he sounded, but he knew none of them did either. He knew he was sick, but hoped the warmth of spring, as well as the chance to find food in the countryside, would begin to restore his strength. He resolutely blocked the idea of Carrie taking care of him from his mind. It did no good to imagine her tender smile and gentle hands. It only increased his misery. "It's nice to be out of the trenches," he said, feeling no need to talk about his health.

"You got that right!" Alex said enthusiastically. "I haven't seen anything resembling green grass or a flower for so long I was about to think I'd made them up." He waved a hand at the pasture they were passing. Bees swarmed over daisies and buttercups, and beautiful dogwood trees watched over the scene like cheerful sentinels. "The world is still a right pretty place," he said with something akin to wonder in his voice.

Robert smiled with understanding. Months spent freezing in dirt trenches followed by weeks standing in deep mud could wipe anything beautiful out of a man's thoughts. When survival was the primary need, Robert knew everything else seemed to fade away. He watched as a hummingbird dipped into a blooming poppy and then zipped away, following the path of a bright yellow finch skimming low over the grasses. The moment of beauty eased a bit of the ache in his soul.

"What do you reckon is happening back there?" Alex asked. "Do you reckon they're in Richmond right now?"

Robert frowned, his stomach clenching as he thought of the Union Army marching into Richmond. Would they destroy it like they had Columbia, South Carolina? Would Carrie or Thomas be harmed while he was marching away from them? For what seemed the thousandth time, he forced the images from his mind as he shook his head. "I don't think so. I imagine they're in Petersburg right now. Some of them will head into Richmond tomorrow, but..."

Alex looked up sharply as he hesitated. "But what, Captain?"

"I figure most of Grant's army is coming after us," he said. "Grant wants Richmond, so he'll take it, but what he really wants is Lee's army."

Alex was silent for several minutes as he stared up and down the line. "We probably can't move as fast as Grant's army," he stated.

Robert snorted out a laugh. Starved men, and starved animals straining to pull wagons, were certainly no match for Grant's well-fed, sleek army. Once again, he chose to give the only thing he had to give—confidence. He would live with the fact that it was false. "They may march faster than us," he said dismissively, "but they can't fight as hard as us. The odds have been against us for a long time, but we're still here, aren't we?"

Alex's eyes lit with passion. "You got that right!"

Robert smiled. "Be sure to encourage the men," he urged him. "You're a natural leader, Alex. I'm sure everyone feels bad we lost the trenches, but we still have a war to fight."

Pride joined the passion glowing on Alex's face. "Yes, sir!"

Robert watched as Alex began to move up the line, speaking to men as he went. He had no idea what Alex was saying, but he could tell by the soldiers' straightening shoulders and heads held higher, that the young man's words were hitting the mark.

Chapter Twenty-Nine

Carrie felt the tension in the house when she dressed and went down for breakfast. In spite of the pressing need she felt to be at the hospital, she had promised her father she would attend church with him—something she was rarely able to do with all the demands on her. She didn't feel she could spare the time now either, but something in the air demanded she be in church, and one look at her father's strained face when she reached the table confirmed her feeling.

She managed a calm smile as she slipped into her seat, enjoying the spring breeze puffing in through the open windows that coaxed tinkling music from the slightly swaying chandelier. "It's such a perfect spring day," she said lightly, laying her hand over her father's and smiling around at everyone.

"Perfect except for the sound of battle coming from Petersburg," her father growled, casting anxious looks south.

Carrie was well aware of the echoes of cannon fire that had ridden in on the air early that morning, long before the sun came up. "Do we know what has happened?" she asked.

"This morning?" her father asked. "No. But we do know General Pickett suffered a terrible loss on Saturday. Over five thousand men were captured."

Carrie whitened as she thought of Robert, though she knew he was under General Gordon's command. "I can't hear anything coming from Petersburg now," she said hopefully.

Thomas shook his head. "I fear the absence of any official report means the worst." He paused for a moment. "Hobbs was called out this morning to guard the city."

Carrie tightened her lips and clenched her hands in her lap, but remained silent, her thoughts still with Robert. "Do you need to go to the Capitol?

"No. I don't know what is coming tomorrow, but I know that for today I want to be in church with my family—*all* of my family," he said as he gazed around at Jeremy, Janie and Clifford.

"Where are the rest of the boarders?" Carrie asked. "I expected they would be here for breakfast since it's Sunday."

"They're at the Capitol boxing up our records."

Carrie ached at the lost look in his eyes but knew nothing she could do would change anything. She merely smiled at him and hoped the end of Richmond would not be too painful.

⁘⁘⁘

"It's hard to imagine a war is going on at all," Janie murmured, "much less believe Richmond is about to fall."

Carrie agreed as she gazed around at budding trees and glorious daffodils swaying beneath a soft, hazy sky. There were thousands of Richmonders strolling to church, either defying the inevitable by refusing to acknowledge it, or perhaps knowing they needed the comfort and strength of their faith to face what was coming. "I so wish people knew how to connect with God outside of the emergencies that send even the profane flocking to church," she murmured.

"And you know how to connect with God?" Thomas challenged as he overheard her.

Carrie flushed but met his eyes squarely. "I believe so. I struggle with fear and worry like everyone else, but I believe we can all feel and connect with God's heart and love." Her mind flew back to her special place on the banks of the James River where she had connected with God for the first time as she wrestled with the issue of slavery.

Her father stared at her with defiant eyes that suddenly softened. "How?"

Carrie took a deep breath, understanding how much was behind that simple question. "I find Him when I stay still," she said, struggling to find the right words that would carry her father through what was coming. "I've learned what it means to listen during the last four years."

"Listen for God?" Thomas asked skeptically. "You believe you can hear God?" His eyes, no longer defiant, begged for something to hold on to.

"I believe God wants his children to hear his heart. It's just that most of us never get still long enough to listen. I'm not saying I hear a real voice—it's more of a whisper in my spirit that carries me through, and lifts me up beyond the hard times."

"That's what you're doing when you wake up early and go sit on the windowsill," Janie said.

"Yes," Carrie admitted. "There are times I only hear the clamor of my own fears and thoughts, but if I can silence those, then I can hear God's heart."

"How do you know it's God?" Thomas asked.

Carrie smiled. "Usually because what I hear is so totally opposite from what I'm thinking or what I *want* to hear." She reached over to take her father's hand. "There are so many times pain and fear are rocketing around in my head and making so much noise that it's all I can focus on. But then I listen..."

"And you hear God."

Carrie prayed for her father to understand. "Or maybe I'm able to understand God's heart in the midst of all of it," she said. "It's hard for me to accept sometimes that God has only love in his heart for me, but I really do believe it's true."

"Love that would take everything I've ever worked for?" Thomas asked. His voice wasn't bitter, just full of painful question.

"God didn't take it," Carrie said. "The choices people made before the war started, and then all through the war, took it. I believe God has wept so many times through these years as he watched men kill and maim each other...as he watched beautiful things be destroyed." She squeezed her father's hand. "But none of that changes his love. Now he wants to help all of us walk through whatever is ahead." She took a deep breath. "No matter what it is."

Thomas stared at her as they neared the entrance of St. Paul's Episcopal Church. "How did you get so wise?" he asked. He reached out to lay a hand on her cheek. "You have become a remarkable woman," he murmured tenderly.

Carrie leaned into him. "Because my father has always been a remarkable man."

"No." Thomas shook his head. "This wisdom came from somewhere besides me. Where?" His eyes demanded an answer.

Carrie thought back. "Sarah taught me so much. And Aunt Abby. But the real lessons came when Robert was missing for almost ten months. I learned to listen because it was the only thing that kept me from going stark-raving mad."

"And God told you Robert would come home?"

"No," Carrie said slowly, "but I did keep hearing that God's love would carry me through whatever happened if I would trust him."

"I see," Thomas murmured, something hopeful coming to life in his eyes.

The church bells clanging through the morning air made Thomas grab her hand and pull her into the church. As they settled down in their pew, she saw President Davis sitting alone at the front. Carrie knew he had sent his wife and children off to protect them from the revenge of the Union Army.

Carrie gazed around the full church and realized just how many were searching for comfort. She suspected every church in Richmond was full. Reverend Minnigerode, still speaking with his slight Hessian accent, performed the service. It was impossible to focus on his sermon because her thoughts were far south with Robert. She prayed he was still alive, and then her prayers turned to Hobbs and Georgia. Finally, she thought of Moses and prayed he was still alive as she thought of the tens of thousands of Union soldiers who were paying the price to make Richmond fall.

Then, as always, her thoughts spun to Rose and Aunt Abby, hoping and praying the fall of Richmond would also signal the end of the war. She could handle whatever would come next as long as she could have Rose and Aunt Abby in her life once again.

A sudden motion at the back of the church grabbed her attention. Carrie felt her father stiffen beside her as they watched the pompous sexton move down the aisle, touch the president on his shoulder, and hand him a message.

Davis rose immediately. His face was grave and determined as he strode quietly from the church, his hat in hand, refusing to look at anyone.

Carrie knew from the look on the president's face, and from the expression on her own father's face, that it had to be very serious. Her own alarm grew as she watched the sexton return to summon another high official, then another and another.

Thomas leaned over to whisper in her ear. "I'll come back to the house as soon as I can." He rose quietly, slipped from his pew, and hurried from the church.

Carrie stared after him and hardly heard Minnigerode urge the congregation to sit calmly. He managed to keep them in place a few minutes longer before they all rose and rushed from the building.

"Carrie?" Janie slid up next to her and grabbed her hand, her arm hooked through Clifford's.

Jeremy fell in on the other side of her.

Carrie smiled at all of them, loving them for the support they offered, but her worries were for her father who would soon be on the run from the Federal government, for doing what he had believed was the right thing to do. She knew she was needed at the hospital, but she was going home to wait for her father.

A thin lady, well-dressed in spite of her hunger-pinched face, pushed past her crying, "Oh! The city is to be evacuated immediately, and the Yankees will be here before morning!" She raised her eyes to the sky and then whimpered, "What can it all mean? And what will become of us poor defenseless women, God only knows!"

A younger woman hurried to grab the distraught woman's hand. "Don't you worry," she said soothingly. "I don't believe they will evacuate. That has been the false report so often over the years of this war." Her voice was confident. "This is nothing but another of our Sunday rumors."

Carrie stared at the young woman whose eyes were full of burning defiance but didn't bother to correct her. She would discover if it was more than rumor soon enough.

"I'll go to the Capitol," Jeremy said, "and see what I can find out."

Carrie turned up the hill through the throngs of people and hurried for home. She knew it would probably take a while before her father could return to the house, but there were things to be done to help prepare for his departure.

Almost three hours later, Jeremy returned, his eyes and face grave with concern.

"They're evacuating," Carrie said flatly, having accepted the truth the moment the sexton tapped President Davis' shoulder.

"Yes. The city is in chaos. The banks just opened, telling all their customers to come get their money."

Carrie gasped. "I hadn't thought about that!"

"You have money in the bank?"

"No, thankfully. Father took me and Janie down to withdraw everything last week." She didn't add that it was hidden away in her father's wardrobe. Just as with the mirror, she would keep her father's secret and let him reveal it to those he chose.

Jeremy smiled grimly. "I'm glad you have it, though I doubt there is any value in Confederate currency any longer."

Janie came into the room, her blue eyes wide with worry. "Will they burn Richmond like they did Columbia?"

Jeremy frowned. "The reports are unclear as to who actually burned Columbia, but we are certain liquor played a crucial part in it. I attended a special meeting of the city council. Governor Smith was there. He promised to leave two militia companies behind to maintain order."

"Two militia companies for this whole city?" Carrie asked in dismay, imagining the chaos that would certainly erupt.

Jeremy nodded briefly. "I know what you're thinking, but they have taken steps to keep things under control. The council appointed twenty-five men in each of the three wards to destroy all the whiskey barrels and liquor supplies." He hesitated. "The mayor and a citizens' committee were authorized to meet the Federal Army and arrange for a peaceful surrender of the city."

"Do you know where my father is?" Carrie asked.

"I saw him boxing papers in his office," Jeremy reported. "He said he would be here shortly."

Just then, Thomas strode through the door, his face tight with worry and his eyes burning with anger. They softened when he saw Carrie standing next to the window.

Carrie fell into his arms, the reality of evacuation hitting her for the first time. Thomas held her closely for several moments and then set her back gently. "We must talk."

Carrie swallowed hard and joined Jeremy, Janie and Clifford on the sofa. Her father remained standing, obviously fighting for control.

"Petersburg has fallen. The Union Army will be in Richmond tomorrow morning."

Carrie stifled a groan. She had wished for this, but now that it was actually here, she fought the fear that swept through her, realizing she had no idea when she would see her father again. Although her hatred for the war intensified, she remained silent, letting her father talk.

"Grant is sending enough men to take the city, but most of his army is in pursuit of Lee, who is headed southwest along the Appomattox River."

Carrie could only hope Robert was part of the marching army, but she also knew the agony he must feel having to march away from Richmond and leave her. She suddenly felt more alone than she ever had in her life. "Are you certain you must leave, Father?"

Thomas hesitated and looked at her squarely. "Do you remember Dahlgren's failed attempt to take the city last year?"

"Of course." Carrie's face whitened as she remembered the letter that had been found on his body reporting his intention to kill high Confederate officers.

Thomas' eyes said he knew her thoughts had followed his. "We don't know how far they will go. We do know that people close to positions of power are in danger of capture and imprisonment. I will admit I have no desire to spend time in a Yankee prison."

Carrie shuddered at the idea of her beloved father locked away. "You must go," she said urgently. "I have everything ready for you. Granite is already saddled in the barn. I fed him all I could and hung a bag of grain on the saddle. I had May fix you some food that is already in the saddlebags. It should hold you for several days."

Thomas reached out to stroke her hair, his eyes speaking his gratitude. "Thank you," he said. "I love you, Carrie."

"I love you, too," Carrie cried. Then she whispered, "You'll get word to me?" Her throat constricted as she thought of watching her father ride away.

"As soon as I can," Thomas promised. He crushed her to him in a smothering hug and stepped away to grab Jeremy into a warm embrace as well. He did the same with Janie and Clifford.

"I'll take care of Carrie, Thomas," Jeremy promised.

Thomas managed a smile. "I know you will. Thank you. I'm trusting all of you will take care of each other. I would still try to convince you to come with me, but I know it would be futile. Even if I had a way to get you out of the city, I know each of you believes your place is here."

"For now," Jeremy agreed.

Carrie, watching Jeremy's face closely, realized he was staying for her. Her heart swelled with love and gratitude. She knew she should urge him to go, but she couldn't. Despising her weakness, she leaned against his side. Grateful for Jeremy's solid strength, she watched her father run upstairs to grab a few clothes and then move toward the back door.

All of them were with him when he led Granite from the stable. Carrie stepped forward to give him another fierce hug. She laid her face against Granite's for a long moment as her father mounted, certain her heart would explode from the pain. Thomas smiled down at her and turned his eyes on all of them for a long, burning moment before he swung Granite around and joined the throngs of people on the road.

*   *   *

Jeremy and Clifford saw Carrie and Janie off to Chimborazo before they headed into town.

The streets were filled with men waving farewell to families that had taken them in. Wagons and carriages bounced away with trunks and boxes, while servants carried bundles toward the rail stations. People with tear-streaked faces tight with fear and grief lined the roads and filled the porches. Women pressed their faces against windows as they watched the men they depended on for safety ride away.

Jeremy winced as he saw several stretchers bearing pale, sick soldiers carried down the road. He had no idea where they were being taken, but he was sure they had begged to be removed from the city before the Yankees arrived and took them as prisoners of war.

"You there!"

Jeremy watched as a gentleman stepped in front of a man on a horse heavily laden with baggage.

"How much will you take for that horse?"

The mounted man shook his head. "He's not for sale. Not to you and not to the dozen others who have asked me."

The wealthy man reached into his pocket, pulled out a bag, and opened it enough to show its contents.

Jeremy's eyes widened as he recognized the glisten of gold.

"I'll give you the contents of this bag," he said earnestly, obviously trying to hide his fear. "There is over one thousand dollars here. It's yours."

The mounted man shook his head, though his eyes shone with compassion. "Your money will do me no good in a Yankee prison," he said shortly, moving his horse past the man and breaking into a rapid trot.

His shoulders rounded in defeat, the elegant man stared after him.

Jeremy stepped up to him. "What about the train?" he asked. "Might you get a seat on a train out?"

The man shook his head dejectedly. "The train station is a madhouse," he stated. "Only high officials are able to get a seat. They're going to let the rest of us go to the devil." He scowled and turned away, his eyes once again scanning the road for another horse an owner might be persuaded to part with for enough gold.

Jeremy stared after him and turned to Clifford. "Let's go to the train station. I want to see what is happening."

Clifford nodded and fell in step beside him. "Things will get bad," he said as he looked at the hordes of terrified people thronging the roads.

Jeremy knew he was right. "These people have endured too much," he said quietly. "Now those who have sacrificed and served the Confederate cause so unselfishly are being left to fend for themselves."

"You could have left with the other officials," Clifford observed. "Your position would have allowed that."

Jeremy shrugged.

"You're staying behind to take care of Carrie," Clifford said.

"I suppose I am," Jeremy admitted. "There is no other option for Thomas. He would be one of the first imprisoned if he chose to stay. There is less chance I will be. Carrie has given so much to so many. My father... Me..." He glanced around the chaotic streets. "I couldn't leave her here alone."

Carrie and Janie felt the tension and fear vibrating through the air from Chimborazo Hill. The air was still soft and balmy, but the feelings ran harsh and cold—tight faces and frantic eyes were on every person they passed. The chaos grew as they drew closer to the hospital wards. Everywhere they looked, they saw patients with casts and bandages standing in little groups outside.

Carrie saw several of the patients she had helped settle the night before. Without stopping to think, she walked up to the group they were standing in. "What's going on here?"

The men glanced at her, but their eyes were too busy scanning the horizon to pay her much attention. Carrie stood quietly while they continued to talk.

"We've got to get out of here!"

"The Yankees broke through our lines and are on the way to take Richmond. They'll take all of us as prisoners."

"I ain't fought through this whole war to end up in some Yankee prison," another snapped.

One of Carrie's patients turned to her. "Are we hearing what's right? Did the Yankees break through our lines?"

Carrie took a breath, knowing if she told them the truth, they would walk away from the medical care they needed, but having far too much respect for what they had done for four years not to be honest with them. "Yes, it's true," she said quietly. "They have taken Petersburg and are on their way to Richmond."

"And the president and the cabinet are running away?" another asked in disbelief.

Carrie knew belief was the only thing that had kept them alive for four years. She wasn't about to take it from them now. "They are headed to Danville to set up another government," she said. "President Davis said the fight will go on."

Faces brightened around her.

"Where's Lee?" another asked. They had obviously decided Carrie was a valid source of information.

"We heard about you before we got here," one of her patients added. "Ain't your husband a captain? Captain Robert Borden?"

"Yes," Carrie replied.

"He's a fine officer," one of the men said earnestly. "And we hear you're a real fine doctor."

Carrie didn't bother to explain that she wasn't really a doctor, but she did decide to take advantage of her influence. "Then I hope you'll hear me when I tell you that you all need to be back in bed." She looked around and remembered tending the gunshot wounds and broken limbs on their emaciated bodies. "You won't get far in the condition you're in."

"You think we're going to lay here and let the Yankees take us as prisoners?" a young boy exclaimed. One of his eyes was heavily bandaged. The one that wasn't gleamed at her from beneath stringy brown hair.

"Where are you planning to go?" Carrie asked. "There are no trains, available wagons are trying to get supplies to Lee, and you can't find a horse anywhere in this city."

"We'll walk if we have to," one insisted, fear blending with the pain twisting his face.

"And how far do you think you'll get?" Carrie asked. "Every one of you is gravely wounded. Without care, you will end up with massive infections that will kill you. There is nowhere you can go to get care. You may escape the Yankees, but you'll likely die," she finished. "Is that better?"

The men grumbled among themselves while Carrie walked away. She'd done all she could. As she opened the door to enter her ward, she looked back and sighed with relief when all but one of the men turned back into their hospital wards. Three of them smiled at her weakly as they hobbled in and lay back down in their beds.

Carrie felt a wave of relief until closer inspection revealed about a fourth of her patients were gone. The beds had been full the night before. Now there were many empty beds.

A nearby patient gazed up at her with feverish eyes, his jaw clenched against the pain from his leg amputation. "They didn't figure they wanted to wait around for the Yankees."

Carrie nodded briskly. There was nothing she could do for them now. She would rather focus on her remaining patients. She knew caring for them would help her work through whatever was coming in the days ahead. "Let's take a look at that wound," she said kindly, beginning to pull back the bandages to check for infection. She looked up for an orderly to bring him some water but realized no one was there but her.

Her patient interpreted her look. "All the orderlies were called out this morning to defend Richmond."

Carrie's lips tightened as she hurried to get a pitcher of water. She took it up and down the rows, filling it several times, until all her patients had water. Then she began to move up and down the aisles checking bandages and administering herbal medicines to combat fever and infection. With or without help, she had patients who needed her.

She knew it wasn't long before Union soldiers would take over the hospital, but there was nothing she could do about that.

Chapter Thirty

Jeremy's eyes widened as he saw the hundreds of anxious people crammed into the R&D depot. He watched as people pressed tight against the doors in an effort to get a seat on a train—*any* train—heading out of Richmond.

"I don't see the president," Clifford yelled over the noise.

Jeremy shook his head. "His train isn't due to leave until later tonight. He's still at the Capitol working," he hollered back.

He watched as a Home Guard soldier shook his head at a well-dressed gentleman. "I'm sorry, sir, but I'm not allowed to let anyone come through that doesn't have a pass from Secretary of War Breckenridge."

"I assure you," the man said pompously, "that Breckenridge intends for me to have one. He just ran out of time to issue it." He turned pleading eyes on the soldier. "I have to get on that train," he insisted.

"You and hundreds of others," the soldier said, compassion shining in his eyes even as he delivered the words with a clipped voice. "I'm sorry, but you'll have to find another way out of Richmond."

Jeremy continued to watch as the man scowled angrily and walked away, and then he exchanged an understanding look with the soldier. "Don't worry. I don't want on the train," he said with a slight smile.

"Good," the soldier said shortly. "I've been turning people away all night." He sighed and straightened.

Jeremy stepped back as another man walked up. His mouth gaped open as he saw what the man had attached to him—a group of what looked to be fifty blacks all chained together, their eyes wide with fright and fury. Jeremy's stomach clenched as he turned to see how the soldier would handle it.

"...so as you can see, it is imperative I get these men on that train."

"Because you might lose your investment?" the soldier asked.

"Now see here," the slave trader snapped. "You fought this war so that I could have these slaves. The least you can do is make sure I keep them."

The soldier scowled, his thin face growing cold and hard. "I most certainly did *not* fight this war so that you could trade slaves," he snapped. "I didn't lose my father and all three of my brothers so that you could take away the seats of government men with your slaves." He scanned his eyes over the crowd. "I'll give you some free advice...let your slaves go. The Union Army will be here tomorrow and will set them all free anyway. I'd say your days as a slave trader are over."

Jeremy continued to watch as the muttering slave trader turned away and yanked the line of slaves after him. He could at least be glad all of them would soon be free. "Well spoken," he said to the soldier.

The soldier turned burning eyes on him. "This country is going to be in for a lot of trouble," he said harshly as he stared after the line of slaves being led away. "I didn't fight this war for slavery, but I sure ain't looking forward to living in a place where all the slaves are free. Ain't nobody gonna be safe then."

Jeremy recognized the fear in his eyes. "Those men don't want to hurt anyone," he protested. "They just want to be free and not chained up like animals."

"You one of those abolitionists?" the soldier asked, eyeing him suspiciously.

Jeremy smiled easily. Spouting his beliefs in the midst of a fearful, panicky situation was probably not wise. He shrugged casually. "I've been working for the Confederacy," he said. "But I know we're all going to have to figure out a way to get along."

Another want-to-be passenger demanded the soldier's attention.

Clifford tugged at Jeremy's arm. "Let's get out of here and see what else is happening in the city."

Jeremy nodded and fell into step. It didn't take long to determine that law and order had departed along with the trains carrying their government officials. He still saw faces tightened with fear and grief, but as the afternoon sun dropped lower on the horizon, he saw as many faces glazed with greed and the lure of opportunity.

"Jeremy! Look..." Clifford gasped.

Jeremy's face whitened as he looked down the road toward one of the liquor warehouses. The city council's resolution to destroy all liquor had backfired. Militia were busily knocking in the heads of whiskey barrels and throwing bottles into the streets where they shattered. As they poured kegs into the gutters, the smell had attracted what seemed like every thirsty roughneck in Richmond.

Jeremy and Clifford jumped up onto a porch and watched the chaos. Both men and women rampaged ahead of the official ax-wielders to grab casks and cases. There wasn't enough of the militia to stop them. Jeremy was relieved the men designated to maintain order were wise enough to know that. They simply stepped back and watched helplessly.

Jeremy watched as one woman pulled off her tattered hat and dipped it into the spilled liquor, holding her mouth wide to let it pour in, dark gaps indicating missing teeth. He felt sick as several men threw themselves on the ground and began to lap the liquor from the gutter like animals. He knew the drunkenness would soon make a bad situation even worse. "Let's get out of here," he muttered.

As he and Clifford forced their way past the hordes trying to reach the alcohol, he saw another stream of people heading toward the commissaries. He dreaded what new thing he would find, but he was compelled to follow the crowds.

"Good grief!" Clifford gasped as they rounded the corner and saw the swarm of people piling into the commissary.

"There's plenty of flour and bacon in that building," a woman as skinny as a skeleton yelled, pushing her way forward. "We been starving while they been hiding away all this food!"

"It ain't right," another yelled. "We've given up everything for the cause and now they're going to leave us. I'm done sacrificing for the South. I'm going to take care of my family now!"

"I want bacon!" another woman screeched as she clawed her way forward, her face twisted with hunger and despair.

Jeremy and Clifford were pushed back against the side of a rough brick building. Jeremy felt a moment of panic as he wondered if they were going to be trampled.

"Up here, Jeremy!" Clifford shouted as he reached up with his remaining arm and pulled himself onto the porch.

Jeremy followed quickly and breathed a sigh of relief as the door pushed open and they fell back into an empty office building. Only scattered papers remained to indicate this room had at one time been the scene of busy government work. File cabinets hung open, left that way in the frantic rush to gather important papers.

Clifford pointed upward. "Let's get higher."

Jeremy nodded and followed him up the curved wooden stairway. When they stepped out onto the third-floor balcony that allowed them to see across town, they realized how terrible the situation in Richmond was. The crowds that had swarmed into the commissary, ignited by a terrible anger and despair, had now turned their fury and greed toward every shop and warehouse in the business district. They watched in horrified fascination as doors were busted in and front windows were smashed. Looters hurried by, their arms full of everything from clothes to shoes to candy to food.

"It's every man for himself!" one yelled as he hurried by. "Get everything you can because the Yankees will own it tomorrow!"

City gas lines and the light they provided had all been cut off. As the sun sank below the horizon and the streets grew dark, looters desperate to find anything they could, lit paper torches and tossed the burning paper aside when they left buildings with their arms full. The glow of bonfires set to burn government documents shimmered against the side of buildings and threw flames high into the air.

"Things are out of control," Clifford snapped. "Where are the militia units?

"General Ewell doesn't have enough men to handle things," Jeremy said. "He asked weeks ago for a volunteer force to be raised in the event of an evacuation, but his request didn't get anywhere." He gazed around at the angry scene. "It's too late to try to stop it," he said sadly. "Besides, the general has more important things to do tonight."

Clifford stared at him. "It's true then? They're going to burn the cotton and tobacco warehouses?"

"He has orders," Jeremy responded. "I do know he inspected the warehouses and had everything moved into buildings he believes can burn without endangering the city. Officers have been assigned to carry out the burning, and he has asked the fire department to have crews ready to keep the blazes from spreading."

Clifford gazed down at the out-of-control crowds fueled by drunkenness, fear and greed. "You figure that's going to work?"

Jeremy had decided he wanted to be available if the fire crews could not contain the fires that were to be ignited. He had sent Clifford back to protect Carrie and Janie. He could only hope they would be high enough to escape the danger of spreading flames if the worst were to happen.

The chaos had only increased as the sun sank below the horizon, signaling a long night that would end with occupation by Union forces. Wagons and drays created a loud rumble as they were driven as swiftly as possible, too often being forced to a standstill. Drivers' curses and shouting joined in with the sounds of screaming women and crying children. People thronged the streets searching for information that would tell them what to do—only none existed. Neighing horses and shrieking train whistles added to the cacophony of noise.

Jeremy pushed his way through the crowd and headed for the warehouse district down by the water. His path led him once more past the train station, which even at this late hour was still thronged with people. He noticed huge piles of supplies next to the tracks and edged close enough to hear two men arguing as they stood over the piles.

"Lee said he wanted these supplies to meet his army."

"And I'm telling you there are no trains available to put them on!" another man shouted. "We're not even going to get all the officials and archives out. There is certainly no room for blankets."

"Or food? Or ammunition? Just what is Lee supposed to do when he gets to Amelia Courthouse and has no supplies?"

"That's not my problem tonight. I'm under orders to get President Davis and his cabinet out of here, along with all the governmental archives. There are going to be a lot of people who don't get what they want," he ended with a heavy sigh, rubbing a hand over his thin, bearded face.

Jeremy was quite sure he was right about that.

"The president is leaving!" he heard a woman scream. Jeremy glanced at his watch. Eleven o'clock. He'd heard the president was supposed to leave three hours earlier, but he well understood the delays caused by such chaos. He watched as the train full of the Confederate government pulled slowly out of the station, gathering speed until it disappeared from sight around a bend.

For those few minutes the chaos calmed as people watched the train depart...

"We're now totally on our own!"

Jeremy heard the screech and whipped his head around to see a mob of people surge down Cary Street. A sudden howl rose in the air as the last thread of constraint was broken.

Jeremy moved down the road, both horrified and fascinated by the madness swirling around him. Tens of thousands of suits of clothing were thrown from the Richmond Clothing Bureau. The remaining food stores in the commissary were being fought over by thousands of poor women. Store owners desperate to save their buildings opened the doors and tossed out dry goods, shoes, and every manner of provision. The crowd fell on them like wild animals.

Jeremy felt sick but had a sad understanding of the strain and deprivation these people had felt for so long. He was sure they thought they were only taking what they had rightfully sacrificed for. He also understood the power of the mob mentality. If somehow the city could be held together until the Union troops arrived, all these people would be driven back indoors to peer through their windows and think with astonishment of what they had done the night before.

It was after midnight when he successfully worked his way down to the warehouse district. Men were hard at work building bonfires in front of the tobacco warehouses with chairs, tables and desks taken from government offices. They were broken up and piled high in front of the wooden buildings.

He caught sight of a familiar face coming toward him on the street. "Hobbs!"

Hobbs looked up wearily, his face brightening immediately. "Jeremy!"

"What is going on?" Jeremy asked. "Where are you going?"

"Back up to the hospital."

"You can't make your way through this mad crowd with that bad leg."

Hobbs managed a grin. "Oh, it might take me a while longer than most, but I figure I can handle it."

Jeremy shook his head, knowing he was probably right. "What have you been doing since this morning?"

"Pretending to be a lot more people than I really am," he said.

"Excuse me?"

Hobbs nodded his head. "Lee had some of us occupy the picket lines outside the city. We've done a lot of moving around and made a whole lot of noise so it would sound like there were a whole bunch of us. We kept the fires burning bright." He drew himself up proudly. "Lee wanted us to give him time to get away with his army.

Word just came to us that Lee's last troops departed the city. The last cavalry brigade is supposed to leave at two o'clock this morning, act as a rear guard for the army, and then burn Mayo's Bridge."

Jeremy's lips tightened again thinking of all the frantic citizens who were hoping to use that bridge as a means of escaping the city.

"What are you doing down here, Jeremy?" Hobbs asked, staring at the growing bonfire piles in front of the warehouses.

Jeremy brought him up to date, informing him that Thomas had left, and telling him what was happening in the city.

"Jumping Jehoshaphat!" Hobbs breathed, looking over Jeremy's shoulder with horror.

Jeremy turned around and groaned when he saw flames begin to illuminate the sky from downtown Richmond. "There are mobs down there looting every building of whatever they can take. I saw them lighting torches so they could see into the buildings. Combine that with huge piles of burning documents, and I'm surprised things are only now starting to burn. Let's hope the fire crews can put them out quickly."

The activity behind him continued at a fevered pace, the bonfires growing steadily in front of all the buildings to be torched. Jeremy lifted his face, glad the night was calm and still, and praying it would stay that way.

"Go, Hobbs!" he said urgently. "I sent Clifford to be with Carrie and Janie, but I'll feel better if you're there to protect them as well."

"And if the city begins to burn?" Hobbs asked.

"I'll do what I can, and then I'll go home."

Jeremy was still waiting for the lighting of the bonfires when he saw a colleague from the Capitol coming down the street. "Franklin!"

Franklin Ash, spectacles covering exhausted brown eyes, glanced up and managed a weak smile. "Jeremy. What are you doing here?"

"I figured I would be on hand to help if the flames start to get out of control."

"Good luck," he growled, looking back over his shoulder at the bright light of flames coming from the downtown area. "Someone cut the water hoses," he said grimly.

"What?" Jeremy gasped in disbelief.

"Oh, there are a few men trying to put them out, but they've got a battle on their hands." Franklin sighed. "Quite frankly, I don't think they can stop them. Most people have been trying to loot as much as they can from the buildings before they completely burn." His voice was tight with frustration. "I'm on my way home to make sure my kids are safe. My wife is very ill and I'm afraid of what will happen if things get out of control."

"Is that why you're still here?"

Franklin nodded. "There was no way I was going to leave my family behind. If I end up in prison, so be it." His eyes sharpened. "What about you, Jeremy? You should be gone."

Jeremy shrugged casually. "I have things to take care of here," he said and then changed the subject. "Are things still as chaotic downtown? Have they gotten control of the mob?"

"Mostly, at least for now. The police and soldiers moved in and made some arrests of the worst offenders. That and the spreading fires seem to have driven most people indoors. The ones still out there are trying to fight the fires."

Jeremy drew a breath of relief. "Good luck with your family," he said as he reached out to grasp Franklin's hand.

Franklin shook his hand firmly and exchanged a long look that showed exactly how worried he was, before he hurried away.

Just then, the first torches were used to light the bonfires. Jeremy watched as the fire spread through the warehouses, thankful for the calm night air that sent the smoke and flames straight upward. He joined the crowd of men who stepped back to watch them burn, the aroma of tobacco pervading the night air as the buildings and their contents began to flame brightly.

"This is craziness," one snapped. "General Lee has been telling Davis for months there would be an evacuation."

"Why Davis waited until the last minute is beyond me," another said as he scowled at the flames lifting high over the city. "People are terrified, and they're going wild."

"The evacuation should have started days or weeks ago," another said bitterly. "Everyone would be gone, and the Yankees wouldn't have much to lord over. If the government wanted to stay, fine, but they should have emptied the city of everyone else."

Another man shrugged pragmatically. "I don't reckon it does any good to talk about what *should* have happened. All we can do now is deal with what *did* happen."

Jeremy agreed with all of them. He stood quietly but grew more concerned as he felt a slight breeze whisper at his hair.

"If the wind starts blowing," the man standing closest to him said, "I don't think there's anything anyone can do to control these flames."

Unfortunately, his fears materialized as the light breeze increased to a brisk wind. Flames, fanned to burn hotter and brighter, began shooting out sparks in every direction.

Jeremy watched as the buildings around the warehouses began to catch fire, their flames adding to the heat and intensity. He looked down the glowing streets and feared for the whole of Richmond.

He sprang forward with the rest of the firefighters, but it didn't take long before everyone there understood there were not enough of them to put out the fires.

Jeremy joined them as they ran for the center of town, looking for help.

Carrie, Janie and Clifford watched from the bluffs near the hospital, knowing it would give them the best view of the city. The bluff was crowded with patients and medical staff staring down at the burning city with shocked and stunned faces.

Carrie moved over to the edge and peered down, sick at what she saw unfolding below. Flames shot up from the business district, but those were dwarfed by the raging inferno creeping toward town from the warehouse district.

"Jeremy is down there!" she cried to Clifford, tears filling her eyes.

She felt an arm circle her waist. "He said he would leave if it got out of control."

"Hobbs!" Carrie grabbed him in a fierce hug. "You're safe!"

Hobbs flushed with pleasure. "I reckon I am, Miss Carrie. I saw Jeremy down by the warehouses an hour or so ago. He was fit as a fiddle then. He told me if things got out of hand, he would go back to the house."

Carrie nodded in relief.

Hobbs frowned. "You reckon it's a smart thing to leave the house empty with all the people looting?"

Carrie shrugged. "From what I could tell, nothing was going to stop them if they came. They may take our things, but at least no one will be hurt." She also knew no one would find the money hidden away. She could only hope the house was far enough away from the fires. At least she didn't have to worry about Granite locked away in the barn.

Janie groaned. "Feel that wind," she said with dismay. "There is no way they are going to get those fires out."

Carrie stared down at the orange glow. Would there be anything left of her beloved city for the Yankees to conquer?

"They're burning the boats," Clifford said, waving his hand toward the river.

Carrie looked down at the orange blazes shimmering against the water of the James River. She could almost appreciate the beauty if she wasn't so aware of the destruction being wrought.

Boom!

Carrie was thrown to the ground, perilously close to the bluff ledge as an explosion rocked the air and shook the earth.

The initial explosion was followed by what sounded like a hundred cannons discharging at once, and the sky lit up as shells from the gunboat shot into the air in a huge pyrotechnic display. Into the midst of the firing missiles came three more massive explosions as other gunboats were fired.

Hobbs still had his arm around Carrie, holding her close to the ground. "Stay down!" he yelled.

Carrie lifted her head just enough to see the entire bluff littered with prone bodies. "Are they hurt?" she gasped, struggling to get up and go to her friends.

Hobbs pressed her down firmly. "I don't think so. The explosion threw everyone to the ground. You're lucky you didn't go over the edge," he said. "The best way to miss all those exploding shells is to stay low. It won't last for long."

Carrie nodded and peeked over the edge again. "Oh my..."

"That's one way to put it," Hobbs growled. "We're blowing up our whole fleet so the Yanks can't get them."

※

Once Jeremy realized there was nothing that could be done to stop the fire, he was anxious to get back home. He thought about helping to fight the fires, but he had promised Thomas he would take care of Carrie. The streets were almost deserted now, with the exception of soot-covered men trying to fight the flames. He was certain the frightened citizens would hide in their homes until morning.

He was at the bottom of Church Hill when the explosion of the gunboats rocked the streets. He grabbed a lamppost to remain standing, listening to the tinkle of glass that said windows were being shattered all over the city. He could only imagine how many buildings on the waterfront had been leveled, or how many new fires had been ignited. He stared up as missiles lit the air, but he continued to move toward home.

Would this night ever end?

As he crested the hill and turned toward the house, he looked back, his heart surging with sadness. A stormy sea of smoke, shot through with crimson arrows of fire, covered the city. The brisk wind caught spiraling flames and sent them leaping onto the next building, and the next, and the next.

Jeremy could hear screams from women and children rising in agony above the cloud. Crashing buildings and pounding feet added to the chaos.

He tightened his lips and hurried on.

He was halfway up the hill when another explosion threw him forward off his feet, slamming him into the ground violently. Jeremy lay still, his heart pounding as he tried to identify the newest explosion.

He heard the sound of running feet coming up the hill. "They blew up the arsenal!" a man yelled frantically. "They blew up the arsenal!" The man sprinted past him and disappeared.

Jeremy groaned. No wonder the explosion had been so violent. The arsenal stored close to three-quarters of a million shells that were now exploding into the sky, lighting it up like fireworks. The very earth seemed to be writhing in agony.

Jeremy struggled to his feet, gasping when he saw shattered windows everywhere. Doors were torn from hinges, and chimneys were caved in all around him.

"What's happening out there?" a woman screamed.

"Are the Yanks destroying our city?" another screamed.

"Mommy! Mommy! Are they going to kill us? Are the Yankees going to kill us?" A child's shrill scream rose to the sky above the explosions.

"They won't need to," Jeremy muttered. "We're going to do it ourselves." He gritted his teeth and continued forward, his only thoughts now of reaching home.

"Will this night never end?" he groaned.

Carrie stared in fascinated horror at the scene below her. "The whole city is on fire," she whispered, trying to control the shaking in her voice. "Is no one going to put it out?"

Dr. Wild joined their group on the edge of the bluff, overhearing her question as he walked up. "They tried, but the fire hoses were cut."

"Cut?" Carrie gasped, turning horrified eyes back to the spreading orange glow beneath her. "Why?"

"The city is being looted," Dr. Wild said. "I suspect they were cut by those who wanted the chaos to cover their stealing."

"Where will they take what they've stolen if the whole city burns?"

"I'm quite sure their drunken brains didn't think through things that clearly," he snapped, putting his arm around Carrie's waist.

Wedged between Dr. Wild and Hobbs, Carrie couldn't turn her eyes away from the devastation. "The bridge!" she cried. She saw men moving across it with flaming torches.

"The last of the retreating troops have just crossed it," Dr. Wild said. "They have orders to burn it now."

Carrie's thoughts flew to Robert. Where was he? Was he out of Richmond? How torn he must be to see the city in flames and know he was leaving her there. For a moment, she wished he would desert and come to her, but she pushed the thought aside impatiently. One of the things she loved best about Robert was his integrity. He would never be able to live with himself if he deserted his men.

"Burn the bridge?" Janie murmured. "What about the people still trying to get out of the city who have been waiting their turn for the troops to cross?"

"They will be staying," Dr. Wild said flatly.

Carrie watched as a golden glow joined the orange shimmer below. "The sun is coming up," she said in wonder, hardly able to believe a new day could begin on the heels of such destruction and devastation.

"Which means the Federal troops will be here soon," Clifford stated quietly. "They can hardly do more damage than we have done ourselves—if there is even a city left to conquer."

Chapter Thirty-One

Matthew was almost crazed with worry for Carrie. Word of the evacuation of Richmond had reached behind the Union lines, so he was almost certain Thomas was no longer in the city. The idea of Carrie there alone, without Robert or Thomas, was causing his heart to pound. He fought to remain calm as he and Peter moved down the road on horseback.

"It's quite an honor to be one of the few newsmen they are allowing to come into Richmond this morning," Peter said with a broad grin.

Matthew nodded. "Quite a switch from the way we left it a year ago," he replied.

"You got that right!" Peter laughed. "It's going to make a great story. I can just see the headline: *Former Libby Prison Inmates There for the Fall of Richmond.*" He glanced over at Matthew's somber face and reached out to squeeze his arm. "We're going to find Carrie," he said.

They rode in silence for a few minutes, watching the excited expressions of the black corps given the honor of being first into the city. The rest of Grant's soldiers were in fast pursuit of the ragged remnants of Lee's army. Major General Godfrey Weitzel, commander of all the black troops, was in charge of the occupation of Richmond. The symbolism of ex-slaves being the first to enter the conquered Confederate capital would not be lost on anyone.

Matthew thought it fitting that the city built on the backs of slaves, would be claimed back into the Union by former slaves. He could appreciate the justice while also envisioning the bitterness of Richmonders who would be forced to accept the authority of the people they had once owned. Nothing was going to be easy about any of this.

"At least there have been no more explosions for the last couple hours," Matthew said with relief. The fires and explosions had kept him awake all night. Watching the growing orange glow on the horizon had been terrible. Imagining Carrie in the madness had almost driven him mad himself.

"It didn't take our boys long this morning to discover all Lee's troops are gone," Peter said with satisfaction. "You should have heard their hollering when they realized the last line of trenches was empty. They evacuated sometime last night."

Matthew nodded and stiffened. "Someone is coming out of the city," he announced. "It's a rickety, old carriage with a white flag of surrender flying."

"I bet it's the mayor," Peter said. "The same thing happened in Atlanta and Savannah. Once they realized there was no escape, the mayors came out to surrender the city."

They watched as the leading officers, Majors Stevens and Graves, rode forward to meet the carriage bearing six men who might have looked distinguished if they weren't so disheveled and exhausted. Matthew felt pity for these men who fought so hard and so long to protect their city.

"What will happen now?" Matthew murmured.

"The Union commanders have been given strict orders to protect the city," Peter said. "President Lincoln met with them earlier and said they were to treat the citizens with respect and compassion—that there was to be no revenge or retribution."

"Thank God for Lincoln," Matthew said. "I know there are many in positions of power who feel quite differently. They believe the South should pay heavily for what has been done."

"And Lincoln understands they have *already* paid a horrible price," Peter said. "He simply wants the country to reunite."

The word passed back down the procession until it reached Matthew and Peter. The man now riding with Major Stevens was indeed Richmond Mayor Joseph Mayo. He had requested the Union take possession of the city to preserve order and protect women, children and property.

"Carrie! Thank God I found you."

Carrie, bleary-eyed with exhaustion, turned away from watching the city. "Jeremy," she murmured, moving into the strong arms he held out. "I'm so glad you're safe."

They turned together to watch the scene unfolding below them as the sun topped the horizon. Now that daylight had returned, looting was once more rampant.

"Is no one trying to put out the fires?" Carrie asked in disbelief. "Are they going to let the city burn?"

Jeremy shrugged helplessly. "The city is such a madhouse that I don't think anyone knows what is going on. It all happened so fast... Things are totally out of control. A group of men tried to put out the fires, but they couldn't."

Carrie pointed down to the bridge. "Look! Our soldiers have been crossing all morning. They've been down there with torches for a while. Are they setting it on fire now?"

Jeremy nodded. "And just in time," he muttered. "That's the last of the cavalry crossing over."

Carrie rubbed her eyes and stared harder. "Are those Union soldiers riding up Main Street?"

"Yes. Mayor Mayo rode out this morning to surrender the city."

Carrie took a deep breath as flames began to devour the bridge. Shots rang out from the Union troops as the last of the Rebel soldiers disappeared into the woods on the other side. "I'm so glad Father isn't here to see this. It would break his heart to watch Richmond burn."

She watched as the Confederate flag was lowered from the dome of the Capitol and replaced with the Stars and Stripes. Her relief that the war was closer to being over was mixed with the horror and grief she felt from a long night of watching the city burn and implode. She was simply too exhausted to know how she felt right now.

Suddenly, she wanted to be with the people of Richmond. Whatever she thought of the war, they had stood and survived together for four years. She belonged with them. "Let's go down to the city," she said, turning away and tugging at Jeremy's arm. Janie and Clifford had gone back to the house earlier, and Hobbs had been called away for something. None of her patients needed her right now.

Jeremy frowned. "It's not safe down there. It's a madhouse."

Carrie nodded calmly. "Yes, and I'm a part of this city. I want to know what is going on. I've watched enough from on top of this hill, and now I want to be down there."

Jeremy opened his mouth to protest but closed it, obviously knowing it would do no good. He merely held out a small bundle. "I was at the house, and May gave me some biscuits for you." He reached into the bag he was carrying. "Along with this canteen of water. If we're going into chaos, you need to eat something."

Carrie smiled and reached for them hungrily. "You're my hero," she sighed as she bit into the biscuit. "I guess having you for an uncle isn't so bad after all."

Jeremy laughed and started down the hill.

Matthew was close to the front of the procession as they entered the city, the regimental bands out front playing "Yankee Doodle." Hordes of well-wishers, almost all of them black, lined the roads and handed them fruit and whiskey. The former slaves danced, shouted, waved their rag banners, laughed, cried and called out thanks to God. Matthew made no attempt to hide the tears in his eyes. This was the first true day of freedom for people who had paid a horrific price.

Following the lead of the officers, Matthew grabbed every bottle of whiskey and smashed it. The Union soldiers were under strict orders not to touch one drop of alcohol while they were in the city, and to destroy all they could. He wasn't sure, though, how anyone could merely stand on the side of the road and watch them ride in when their whole city was in danger of burning to the ground.

Heat seared his lungs as he coughed in the smoky air. As they neared the Capitol, he felt tears sting his eyes. He could hardly believe this was the elegant city he had visited so often. Buildings threatened to collapse from all sides. Hundreds of Richmonders were huddled on the square, their red-rimmed, swollen eyes staring up at them as they sat surrounded by bedding and household items piled on the grass.

"They must have all been burned out of their homes," Matthew said, his heart going out to them. He relaxed some when he saw the same look of compassion on General Weitzel's face. From everything he had heard, the twenty-nine-year-old graduate of West Point was a fair and compassionate man. He could only hope Weitzel had a plan to save the city.

"I understand he is putting Colonel Ripley in charge of the city," Peter said quietly, his gaze also settled on the miserable, displaced people staring up at them with fear and misery.

"A twenty-five-year-old?" Matthew asked in astonishment.

"I'd say four years of war has matured him far beyond any twenty-five-year-olds we've known," Peter observed. "He's a natural leader. His black regiment loves him."

Matthew nodded. "You're absolutely right." His attention was caught by a small train of wagons rumbling their way down the road, a contingent of black soldiers surrounding it. "What's that?"

Peter glanced over and frowned. "There was a group of black soldiers wounded during the last few weeks who were still in the hospital. I understand the commanding officer demanded they be brought to Richmond to try to save their lives."

Matthew thought immediately of Carrie—not that his mind had thought of much else the last few days. "Where are they taking them?"

"I don't think they know. They're just bringing them into the city, hoping someone will help them."

Matthew pursed his lips. "Bringing black soldiers into Richmond who need help might not be the wisest thing right now. Every medical person is white. I don't think most of them will be sympathetic toward black Union soldiers who are former slaves."

Peter shrugged. "I don't think their officer felt he had any other options."

A sudden shout caught Matthew's attention.

The holler came from a young Union officer standing on top of the Capitol stairs. "Every able-bodied man is being called to fight the fires!" he yelled above the noise. "I don't care if you're black or white. We want to help you save your city, but we're going to have to work together!"

As he spoke, the wind shifted, sending sparks flying onto the roofs of more surrounding houses and buildings. New flames shot into the air. His call to action mobilized all those who had been merely standing around as their city burned. They may be occupied now, but they still had some of their city left.

When it was discovered the fire hoses were useless, buckets appeared from every direction. Young boys leapt forward to join the older men. Even women snatched up buckets and began to haul water to the flames. Many buildings were completely gone, but now they needed to work together to save the ones still standing.

Matthew and Peter jumped from their horses and joined in the effort.

⁂

Carrie and Jeremy reached downtown just as the call went out for firefighters. It was hard to see through the thick smoke and haze. "Go!" Carrie urged Jeremy as she saw his eyes shift toward the throng of men headed into the flames.

"I don't want to leave you down here alone," he protested.

"I'm hardly alone," Carrie said lightly, secretly alarmed by the chaos and fear permeating the air. "There is a town full of Union soldiers. I hardly think I'm in any danger." She pushed Jeremy in the direction of the fire. "Go. I'd hate to think of our house burning. And stay safe," she added.

Jeremy hesitated again for a moment and then turned to disappear into the smoke.

Carrie stood uncertainly for a few minutes and then decided to move closer to the Capitol building. Whatever happened, she was quite sure those fighting the fire would keep the flames away from it. As she walked through the thick smoke, she was once again thankful her father did not have to see what was happening. She settled down in a small space next to George Washington's statue and watched the action around her, listening to the frightened women surrounding her.

"The horrible Stars and Stripes are over our beloved Capitol," one woman cried. "Oh, the horrible wretches! I can't think of a name dreadful enough to call them! It makes me fifty times more Southern in my feelings."

"My sons gave their lives for this city," one woman whimpered piteously. "And now it's all gone. I lost my three boys for nothing..."

Carrie's heart ached as she looked into the woman's wooden, stunned face.

"That horrible Yankee officer has dared to take office in our Capitol," another said bitterly. "What is to become of us?"

"My house has burned. It was a pitiful excuse of a house, but it was all me and my five children had," another said, pain and bitterness mixing in her voice. "My husband is dead, and we have nothing. What are we to do now?"

Carrie couldn't hear another word. She understood the pain, but she certainly had no answers, and she didn't think her heart could stand even one more story of pain and loss.

She stood restlessly and gazed around, her attention drawn to a group of wagons parked over to the side. Her curiosity grew when she saw a cluster of doctors and nurses standing close by, obviously arguing as they shook their heads at each other. "What is going on?" she asked as she drew near.

"Can you believe it, Mrs. Borden?" one of the nurses asked, her eyes flashing with anger. "Those soldiers dared to bring wagons full of wounded black men. They seem to think we should care for them! Imagine the audacity."

Carrie didn't bother to mention the hospital was now under Union control and would probably soon be full of wounded Union soldiers, both black and white.

She moved toward a doctor from another ward. "Are we going to help them?" she asked.

"Certainly not!" he said indignantly. "They have taken our city."

Carrie looked out over the swarms of blue uniforms carrying water to fight the fires set by Southern citizens, but she decided now was not the time to point out the obvious. As she looked up and caught Dr. Wild's eyes, she felt a flash of hope. They began to move toward the wagons in unison, ignoring the angry muttering that came from behind them.

Carrie's heart melted with pity as she stared down into the first wagon full of wounded black soldiers. It was obvious by the glaze of fever in their eyes that the wounds were old and had become infected. Their dusty skin was damp with sweat as they gazed up in mute appeal, their eyes shifting away when they realized she was white.

She reached out a hand immediately and grasped the nearest soldier she could reach. "We'll get you help," she promised. His eyes widened with surprise and then softened with gratitude. "Thank you, ma'am," he whispered. He nodded toward the wagon at the front of the line. "Them boys up there need help more than us. That's why they be at the front."

Carrie squeezed his hand and moved with Dr. Wild to the first wagon. When she looked in, her heart stood still and her shocked voice burst forth in a whisper.

"Moses!"

Chapter Thirty-Two

Dr. Wild looked up sharply. "You know this man?"

Carrie nodded. Tears blurred her vision, but her first look had told her how close to death Moses was. "He's one of my best friends," she managed in a choked voice. "He saved me when I escaped from the plantation and came to Richmond." She took a deep breath and brushed the tears from her face. "We've got to save him."

"Carrie..."

"No," Carrie cried fiercely. "Do not say it. Do not say he cannot be saved. We have to try. We have to try!" She reached down and grabbed Moses' limp hand, shuddering at the burning dryness of his skin.

Dr. Wild gazed into her eyes and nodded. He turned to the driver of the wagon. "Get this wagon up the hill to Chimborazo immediately," he snapped. He quickly gave him directions for how to get around the fires, calling out to the other drivers to follow him.

He turned to the rest of the medical personnel milling around while they glared at him and Carrie angrily. "Whether we like it or not, Richmond is now under Federal control, and our hospital will soon be full of Union soldiers. We are going up to do what we do—care for sick people. You can join us or not. If we have to, Mrs. Borden and I will care for every one of them." He allowed his gaze to sweep across their faces. "If you care to join us, we will welcome your help." Then he swung onto the seat of the second wagon.

As Carrie moved to join the driver on the seat of Moses' wagon, a kind-faced Union officer with tired eyes stepped up to her.

"Thank you," he said gratefully.

"You're welcome," she said. "Are these your soldiers?"

"Some of them. My name is Captain Jones."

Carrie gasped. "You're Moses' commanding officer!"

Captain Jones gaped at her. "You know Moses? How is that possible? How could he have told you about me?"

Carrie smiled and reached down to press his hand. "Let's just say I wasn't ready for you to take my horse."

Captain Jones' eyes widened with disbelief. "Carrie Cromwell? The woman who escaped on that glorious Thoroughbred by jumping a fence I would have been afraid to attempt?"

Carrie smiled again, her earlier suspicion that she would like the young officer confirmed. "It's Carrie Borden now, but we'll exchange stories later," she said, fear striking deep into her heart as she looked back into the wagon. "I'm taking Moses to Chimborazo along with all these men. We'll do the best we can."

"Moses saved my life, Mrs. Borden. Please save his," Captain Jones beseeched her before he stepped back.

Sparks and ash flew around them as they navigated the smoky roads. As they rounded the corner to head up the hill to the hospital, a building collapsed behind them, and another burst into flame.

"Run!" Carrie yelled, grabbing onto the sides of the seat as the horses broke into a gallop, the wagons behind them following their example.

Dr. Wild jumped out and motioned her over as soon as they reached the hospital. "Give me a few minutes to move the soldiers in our ward over to another ward."

Janie hurried over. "What in the world is going on?" she asked.

Carrie squeezed her hand. "I'll explain later. Is there room in your ward for thirty-five more men?"

Janie nodded. "There is, since so many left this morning when they knew the city was being taken."

"Call all your orderlies that are not down fighting the fires to move the men," she said quickly, motioning for her own orderlies to begin to do the same thing.

The fact that Janie did what she asked without a question added one more reason why Carrie loved her so much.

It took only twenty minutes to move all the men. No one answered their questions, because no one had the answer. Carrie and Dr. Wild had already decided not to broadcast what they were doing. There was no telling what would happen if the rest of their soldiers knew one of the wards was full of black Union men.

As soon as the ward was empty, Dr. Wild called the orderlies inside. While he gave them stern instructions on secrecy, Carrie hurried back outside to the wagons. She reached down and took Moses' slack hands, her heart pounding as she saw the gray pallor of his face and skin. "What happened?" she asked one of the soldiers who was conscious.

"Moses done caught a cannon shell right in the chest," he said hoarsely, his own eyes glistening with pain. "I reckon it would have kilt any other man, but our Moses ain't like no one else."

"He is your commanding officer?" Carrie asked.

"Yessum. The real officers all be white, but Captain Jones done put Moses in charge of all of us."

Carrie nodded. "When did his injury happen?"

"Back at Fort Stedman, ma'am. Back on what I think be the twenty-fifth."

Carrie controlled her groan as she realized he'd been shot eight days before.

"You be knowin' Moses?"

Carrie smiled softly. "He's one of my dearest friends."

The man whistled. "I bet that's a story, sho 'nuff!"

Carrie managed a smile as memories of her strong, vibrant friend filled her mind, followed closely by images of Rose's grief if her husband died. "You can be sure I'll do everything I can to save him."

The first orderlies streamed out of the building and moved toward the wagons. "Take this man first," Carrie called sharply, holding on to Moses' hand as they carried him into the building.

As soon as he was on the bed, Carrie pulled aside his shirt and peeled back the bandage on his chest. She made no effort to control the noise that escaped her lips as tears filled her eyes. Angry, swollen skin surrounded a gaping five-inch hole. A spider web of infection spread in every direction. A weaker man would already be dead. Despair swamped her.

"Let's get him into surgery."

Carrie looked into Dr. Wild's eyes. "Is there any chance?" she whispered.

"He's not dead yet," he replied. "As long as he is breathing, there is hope." He grabbed Carrie's hand. "We've saved lots of men who should have died. Now is not the time to lose hope."

Carrie stared at him, gaining strength from his shining eyes. "You're right," she whispered. Her voice was stronger when she straightened. "We're going to save Moses."

Carrie stood ready as Dr. Wild examined the wound carefully. "They did a good job on this," he said finally. "That tells me there must be a shell fragment they left behind that is causing all the infection. Now, all I have to do is find it."

Carrie could only be grateful Moses was unconscious as Dr. Wild probed around in the red, raw flesh. They had run out of morphine long ago.

Sweat dripped from his face, but after long minutes, Dr. Wild held up the jagged shell fragment he had been searching for. He glanced down at Moses. "As long as he's still unconscious, I'm going to make sure I got it all."

Carrie winced and gritted her teeth as he went back to digging. Holding Moses' hand was all she could think to do, hoping beyond hope that he had no awareness of her presence, but also praying her love would somehow penetrate the darkness.

Dr. Wild straightened. "I got it all," he announced. He looked at her sharply. "I've got other patients to treat. Can you finish with Moses?"

"I'll take care of him, and then I'll be out to help you." She reached over for the basket of onions sitting on the shelves, grateful a new crop had been harvested the week before. She quickly crushed two small onions and tenderly applied the poultice to the gaping wound, knowing the juice from the onion would draw the infection out.

When it was completely covered, she called for two orderlies. "Carry him to his bed," she ordered. "I will wash off the onion in an hour and wrap the wound. Be sure to drip as much water into his mouth as you can."

They said nothing, though the stoic looks on their faces said they were not pleased with their new assignment. Normally, Carrie would have assigned them to wash the wound for her, but she was taking no chances that Moses wouldn't get the best care he could get. When Moses was settled in his bed, a light covering over the wound and a blanket laid over him to protect from further shock, she wiped a hand over her exhausted face and turned to the other patients filling her ward, thrilled to find a few of the other doctors and nurses had changed their minds and joined her and Dr. Wild in their efforts.

It was going to be a long day...

Matthew and Peter fought side by side to control the flames threatening to devour the city. The fierce updraft of the blaze blew flaming brands across the city that dropped on roofs many blocks away. Both men stood at the front of a water brigade heaving buckets up to men standing on porches and roofs, dousing flames with both water and wet blankets.

"It's coming down!" Matthew heard someone yell as a cluster of men broke apart and ran from the collapsing building a half-block away. The fire continued unchecked as it raced to the next building.

"Help! Help!"

Matthew heard the screams over the roar of the flames. He searched the houses a few doors down with blurry eyes until he saw a servant standing on the porch frantically calling for help. He watched as a soldier moved up to talk to her, then beckoned to General Weitzel who conferred with a young lady who appeared on the porch for a few minutes.

"That's General Lee's house!"

"What?" Matthew asked.

The young boy handing him the bucket nodded earnestly. "That's where General Lee's wife lives."

"Why is she still there?"

"She's too sick to leave," he explained. "She's in a wheelchair. I heard General Lee tried to get her to leave, but she insisted on staying."

General Weitzel stood on the porch and called to everyone who was close enough to hear. "Keep this house from burning!" he hollered and then stomped down the stairs to confer with Major Ripley. Minutes later, an ambulance appeared and took position at the bottom of the steps. If Mrs. Lee had to evacuate, she was going to have a way to do it.

Matthew nodded with satisfaction. The war had wrecked their country, but there was still compassion and respect for the man who had evaded Union forces for so long. He paused long enough to appreciate the swell of hope that sprang into his chest and then turned back to swinging buckets of water.

He understood when the firefighting efforts became purely defensive. The only way to stem the flames was to tear down threatened buildings, creating a firebreak before the flames devoured more buildings. Slowly, the battle was being won as they fought to contain the fire.

"She's under control!" someone finally yelled. "Everyone take a break."

It was almost two o'clock before Matthew and Peter were able to step back and use a bucket of water to pour over their heads and wash their hands.

Peter looked at him through gritty, raw eyes. "Well, this is certainly one way to get a story," he said ruefully.

Matthew nodded, grateful for the cool water pouring over his face and soaking his shirt. "Let's get the rest of it," he said grimly as he moved toward the wreckage blocking the streets. He glanced up the road in the direction of Carrie's house, but knew he had to do his job first. At least he was certain Carrie's house was safe.

⁙

Carrie was exhausted to the bone when the last of the black soldiers was treated at about six o'clock that evening. They had lost two of them, but the outcome looked good for the rest. Word had spread rapidly through the ward that she was Moses' friend. The men treated her like she was an angel. Carrie was both flattered and embarrassed, but mostly thankful for the trust they gave her because of Moses.

"Miss Carrie," a young man murmured.

"Yes, Charlie?" Carrie asked, relieved when a hand on his forehead said his fever was broken.

"I reckon Simon gonna come up here real soon."

"Who is Simon?"

He looked at her closely. "You ain't be knowing Simon?" His look changed to one of suspicion. "I thought you said you be good friends with Moses."

Carrie smiled. "We haven't seen each other in almost three years," she said sadly. "I'm sure there are a lot of things we don't know about each other now."

"Simon be Moses' brother-in-law," Charlie revealed.

Carrie stared at him as her mind absorbed the implications and then a smile exploded on her face. "Moses found one of his sisters?" she cried.

"Yessum, I reckon he did," Charlie said. "Simon be June's husband. She be over at the contraband camp with Miss Rose."

Carrie gasped and sank down in the chair next to the bed. It hadn't dawned on her that Moses' men might know Rose. "Rose..." she whispered, tears filling her eyes and clogging her throat, "...she's okay?"

"Oh, yessum," Charlie replied. "Miss Rose be a teacher at the contraband camp. She's a real fine teacher." He peered at her closer. "You be knowin' Miss Rose, too." This time it wasn't a question.

Carrie nodded, full of questions until she saw Charlie wince and grit his teeth against the pain. She stood and tucked the blanket in around him. "We'll talk later, Charlie. Right now, you need to get some rest."

Charlie closed his eyes, and seconds later was asleep.

Carrie went in search of Dr. Wild. She didn't find him in the ward, so she stepped outside to continue her search, slightly startled when a large black man, almost as big as Moses, stepped toward her.

"Miss Carrie?" he asked tentatively.

Carrie moved forward and took one of his hands. "You must be Simon."

Simon didn't bother to ask how she knew. There would be time for all that later. "How is Moses?" he asked earnestly, his eyes shining with worry.

"He's not good," Carrie said, "but he's a fighter. We've done everything we can." She explained about the shell fragment they had extracted. "I need your help with something—you and some of the men in your unit."

"We'll do anything you want," Simon said.

Carrie nodded gratefully. "I don't want Moses to stay here in the hospital. I want him in my home where I can be sure he will receive around-the-clock care." She frowned in the direction of the city. "That is, if my house doesn't burn."

"We got the fires under control, Miss Carrie," Simon assured her. "It did a heap of damage, but the fires are all out."

Carrie breathed a sigh of relief and signaled for a wagon. "How long will it take you to get enough of your men to carry Moses? I'd rather we not broadcast where we're taking him." Occupied or not, she knew there were many Richmonders that would resent her having a black soldier in her home. She didn't care what they thought, but she also didn't want to do anything that would put Moses in danger.

Simon grinned, lifted his arm, and beckoned to a group of men waiting quietly in the patch of trees along the drive. "Captain Jones said it would be okay if some of us came to check on Moses."

Carrie smiled at him, seeing the deep love shining in Simon's eyes. "Moses is lucky to have you," she said softly.

"I'm the lucky one," Simon said. "Me and June."

Carrie smiled again, the weight of the day lifting from her. "I can hardly wait to hear that story, but first we have to get Moses to where I can care for him."

Carrie had just settled Moses into the room next to hers when she heard a light knock on the front door. May was in the kitchen getting water, and she had sent Micah out to dig some fresh onions from the garden, so she went to answer the door herself. When she opened it, she could only stand and stare.

"Don't I even get an invitation inside? I'm not an escaping prisoner this time."

Carrie found her voice. "Matthew!" She laughed happily and moved forward to give him a warm embrace. Then she stepped back to look into his face. "How?"

"I'm in Richmond as a journalist," he explained. "I came in with the army this morning, but I've been busy putting out fires in the city."

"I see," Carrie murmured, thinking about the horrible smoke, flames and explosions. "How bad is it?" she asked.

Matthew frowned. "It's bad," he admitted. "We can talk about this when you're not so tired, though."

Carrie shook her head and pulled him into the house. "I'm sorry I'm being such a terrible hostess. Please, come in." She motioned to May when she moved through the parlor. "May, when you're done upstairs, will you please get us some tea?" She turned back to Matthew. "Please tell me the truth about the city so we can move on to more pleasant things," she said.

"Nine hundred homes and businesses were destroyed."

Carrie stiffened and turned white, but she remained silent and let him continue.

"All the banks are burned. So are two of your hotels, all the newspaper offices, the General Court of Virginia and the Henrico County Courthouse, the arsenal and the laboratory, almost all the warehouses along the river, the Danville and Petersburg railroad bridges and depots, Mayo's Bridge, a dozen drugstores, two dozen groceries..." Matthew frowned deeply. "All, or at least part, of fifty-four blocks are gone."

Carrie couldn't find her voice as she stared at him with shock. Her beloved city...*burned.* She began to tremble.

Matthew reached forward to grab her hand. "The fires are out, Carrie. General Weitzel has already started the cleanup. I know it seems impossible now, but Richmond will rebuild."

"Yes," Carrie murmured, struggling to remind herself she had wanted the city to fall. She never imagined it would mean such destruction. The fact they had inflicted the destruction themselves made it all the more difficult to bear. She took a deep breath and managed a smile. "Thank you for helping to put it out."

She stood and went to stand beside the window to look out at the magnolia tree. Suddenly, she very much needed to see something alive and growing. She stared out at the tight buds holding the promise of glorious white blooms and thought of Robert. "Please tell me this war is almost over," she whispered.

Matthew rose to stand beside her. "Grant is in pursuit of Lee now. Your army can't survive much longer."

Carrie smiled up at him through tears. "That makes me very happy, you know. All of this madness has to stop."

Matthew nodded and gazed at her more closely. "You're exhausted," he stated, taking her arm and leading her back to a chair. "I can come back tomorrow. You need to get some sleep."

Carrie smiled wearily and shook her head. "I won't be going to bed right away," she said. "I have a very important patient upstairs. Someone I know you'll want to meet," she said with a smile. "There are so many things I want to talk to you about, that I hardly know where to start."

May appeared in the doorway, her eyes wide, and a brilliant smile on her face. "He be awake now, Miss Carrie. He still be right out of it, but least ways his eyes are open."

"Thank God," Carrie breathed as she jumped to her feet, her exhaustion forgotten. She reached the bottom of the stairs, and then remembering she had a guest, turned back to Matthew. "Come with me," she urged. "You're going to want to meet this patient," she added, enjoying the confused look on Matthew's face.

Carrie entered the room quietly, smiling when Moses turned exhausted, confused eyes to her.

"Where am I?" Moses' eyes widened with disbelief, pain etching lines on his face. "Carrie?" he asked hoarsely, staring at her as if she were a ghost. "Carrie... Am I dreaming? Am I dead..."

His voice trailed off as she took one of his hands gently and laid her other hand on his face, frowning a little when she realized the fever was still burning in his body. "*Shh...* You're going to be okay now."

"How—"

"The Union has captured Richmond," she explained. "You were shot at the Battle of Fort Stedman. Simon got you off the field and back to a hospital, but you've been terribly sick with an infection. Captain Jones had you brought into Richmond this morning to get medical care. I found you." She stroked his cheek. "Your Captain saved your life."

Moses closed his eyes for a long moment.

Carrie thought he had drifted back off, but he forced them back open. "What..."

Carrie understood the frustration that he couldn't speak. "*Shh...*" She laid a finger to his lips. "You'll get all your questions answered soon. You're going to be okay. They missed a shell fragment in your wound."

Moses frowned and tried to raise a hand to his chest.

Carrie held it down. "We got it out," she assured him. "Now we have to fight down the infection." She made her voice stern. "You're still very sick, Moses. For once in your life, you're going to do exactly what I tell you to do."

Moses smiled fleetingly.

"If I were you, I would do what she says."

Moses' eyes flew to the doorway. "Matthew?" he whispered faintly, more disbelief showing on his face.

Now it was Carrie's turn to stare at Moses. "You know each other?" She swung back to look at Matthew.

Matthew smiled easily. "We met on the battlefield last summer."

Carrie's eyes glistened with tears as she thought about all the events she had missed in her friends' lives over the last four years. She felt Moses' hand squeeze hers, and she looked down at eyes warm with understanding.

"Time..." he murmured.

"You're right," she forced herself to say. "We're all going to have time to catch up, but right now you need to get some rest. Either May or I will be with you all the time. I want you to focus only on getting well."

He closed his eyes in relief, and then they flew back open. "Rose..."

Carrie ached to tell him what he was asking, but she knew she couldn't. "I know she's in the contraband camp, but it's almost impossible to get communication out of the city right now. I promise we'll let her know as soon as we can."

Moses nodded once and then his face went slack, his breathing shallow.

Matthew frowned and moved to stand next to the bed. "Is he going to get well?" he asked, his eyes demanding the truth.

"I don't know. It's a miracle he woke up, but his fever is still high." She paused and thought of the high fever, sustained too long, that had killed her mother. "We'll keep working to bring his fever down and keep putting on poultices to drain the infection. Only time will tell if he's strong enough to make it." She took a deep breath, praying her next words were true. "I believe he is. He has so much to live for."

Matthew stared back at her, his face full of admiration. "It's no mistake Moses found his way to you," he said quietly. "I don't believe God is going to let him die now."

Carrie looked at him. "I hope you're right, but I've seen way too much in this war that doesn't make any sense. I do know, however, that the darkness will always end. This war is going to end and all of us are going to have a chance to rebuild our lives. That's what I hang onto every single day."

She heard the clatter of boots on the steps and looked up as Jeremy walked in the room.

He stared down at Moses, whose massive body dwarfed the bed he was in. "Carrie...what?"

Carrie rose to take his arm and lead him from the room. "I'll explain downstairs," she said. "Moses needs his rest."

"Moses?" Jeremy spun around to stare at him.

Carrie gripped his arm tighter. "Downstairs," she repeated. "The most important thing for him now is sleep."

Jeremy nodded, noticing Matthew. "I saw you downtown fighting the fires."

Carrie smiled and tucked a hand in each of their arms. "I suspect we won't get a lot of sleep tonight, either." She smiled when she saw the plate of cornbread and biscuits May had placed beside the fireplace in the parlor. "We have a lot of talking to do."

Chapter Thirty-Three

Carrie woke to singing birds and a soft breeze the next morning. She stretched and yawned. She was still tired, but the few hours of sleep, after hours of talking, had refreshed her—or perhaps it was having Matthew and Moses here that breathed new life into her.

She hurried over to the window and sank down to her knees, watching the golden orb of the sun slowly rise through the mist and the smoke that had not yet dissipated. Yesterday, it was as if she was walking through a haze. Today, she could feel the joy of having Moses alive in the next room. Matthew, knowing Peter would be concerned, had returned to his lodging after the long hours of talking. She hoped he was still sleeping.

There was a light tap on her door. "Come in," she called.

May stuck her head in the door. "Moses be asking for you," she said, excitement shining in her eyes.

"His fever?"

"His fever be almost all the way down," May said with quiet satisfaction. "Those wet wraps you put on him must have done the trick. He even ate a little bit of my soup."

Carrie smiled with delight. "I'll be right there." She quickly dressed and slipped into the room, her delight increasing when he turned clear eyes on her.

"Carrie," Moses breathed. "I didn't dream this after all."

Carrie laughed and grabbed his hands, thrilled to find them cool to the touch. She laid a hand on his forehead, relieved beyond words to find almost all the fever was gone. "It's a miracle you're alive," she murmured.

Moses squeezed her hands. "You saved my life," he said.

Carrie shook her head. "Captain Jones and Dr. Wild saved your life," she corrected.

Moses continued to gaze at her. "Micah just left. He was downtown yesterday. He told me how you saw the wagons and came over to help, shaming the other doctors and nurses into helping."

Carrie shrugged. "The important thing is that you're going to get better," she said happily. "Just in case you get any ideas of getting out of bed, I want to show you something." She pulled the blanket down and gently peeled back the bandage that lay loosely on his chest.

Moses' eyes widened, and he looked a little sick as he stared down at the gaping wound.

"It's going to take weeks for that wound to heal. If you decide to be stupid, the infection could come back. The next time, it could kill you."

Moses continued to stare at the wound and then looked up at her. "I hear you," he said. "I'll do whatever you tell me."

Carrie nodded in satisfaction. "It's so nice when men know how to listen," she said primly, smiling when Moses attempted a laugh. She was glad he was feeling so much better, but she knew exactly how much the fever had weakened him. It was going to take his body a long time to heal. It would take a lot of good food to make him strong again, and thankfully, the garden was beginning to produce.

"For at least the next two weeks, you are not to leave this bed except to go to the restroom," she said firmly. She saw his eyes widen in protest before he nodded meekly.

"Yes, ma'am."

"So, she's already pushing you around, is she?" Jeremy entered the room, a cheerful smile on his face. "You have to be careful—she can be extremely bossy."

"You're telling me," Moses agreed, eyeing Jeremy with curiosity.

Carrie scoffed. "If men weren't so obstinate and hard-headed, I wouldn't have to treat you this way."

Jeremy laughed and held out his hand to Moses. "My name is Jeremy. I couldn't wait any longer to meet my twin sister's husband."

Carrie grinned as the words sank into Moses' head. His eyes were first puzzled and then grew wide with astonishment. "A lot has happened in the last few years," Carrie teased.

Moses was still staring at Jeremy. He nodded slowly. "I see it," he murmured. "I didn't think I would be able to see Rose in a white man, but I do."

"Yes, I hear she is as beautiful as I am handsome," Jeremy said modestly, throwing his head back in a joyful laugh.

Suddenly, Moses and Carrie both joined in the laughter, years of pain and loss beginning to fade away.

Moses grimaced with pain from laughing too much, and worked to calm himself. "Robert? How is he?"

Carrie grew serious with him. "I don't know. There's been no word since Lee left Richmond. I haven't seen or heard from him in over a month."

"But he recovered fully?"

Carrie looked at him with confusion. "Recovered from what?"

"He was badly wounded when I found him," Moses answered, and then he understood her confusion. "Matthew didn't tell you?"

Carrie's confusion was growing. "Didn't tell me what?"

"I was the one who found Robert on the battlefield a couple years ago, and took him to a nearby family."

"You're the one who saved Robert?" Carrie whispered, sinking down in a chair. "And Granite?" She could barely breathe as she stared at Moses. "After what you knew Robert did to his slaves?"

"I did it for you, Carrie," Moses said tenderly.

Carrie rushed over to kiss his face. "You saved more than his life, Moses! What you did made him into a new man." She settled down to tell him the story.

Abby held her face up to drink in the glorious sun, holding the rail tightly to steady herself against the rolling waves as she enjoyed the feel of the wind whipping her body. What a wonderful day to be traveling via boat.

"You seem to be enjoying this."

Abby opened her eyes when an amused voice sounded beside her. "I most certainly am," she said cheerfully as she looked into warm brown eyes under dark hair streaked with gray. She continued a casual inspection that approved of the man's impeccably tailored suit. "And who might you be?"

"Dr. Lucas Strikener," came the immediate response as he bowed slightly. His voice had a warmth that matched his eyes. "And with whom do I have the pleasure of speaking with?"

"Abigail Livingston," Abby responded cordially. "What takes you to Fort Monroe, Dr. Strikener?"

"Richmond, actually," he replied.

Abby eyed him more closely, her curiosity piqued. "And what is in Richmond?"

"The hospitals that will soon need to care for Union soldiers too ill to transport north. My job is to inspect them and make sure they meet our standards."

"I see," Abby murmured. "I imagine that will include Chimborazo?"

Dr. Strikener's eyes widened with surprise. "You know about Chimborazo?"

"I have a young friend who has been serving there as a doctor," she replied. "I'm on my way to Richmond myself now that it is under Union occupation."

"What is his name?"

"*Her* name is Carrie Cromwell—actually, Carrie Borden now. She has married since the beginning of the war." Abby enjoyed the way the doctor's eyes widened with surprise.

"A woman doctor?" His next words were even more incredulous. "In the *South*?

"Well, she's not official, but she has been serving as a doctor. In fact, she has been responsible for the introduction of herbal medicines since our embargoes so successfully blocked medicine from Richmond."

Dr. Strikener eyed her more closely. "I thought there was no communication with Richmond," he said.

"It helps to know the right people," Abby said with a hearty laugh. "I suppose I should admit I have an agenda for this conversation."

The amused glint came back into the doctor's eyes. "And what might that be?"

"Carrie Borden is like a daughter to me. I have kept up with her in much too small a way through a journalist who escaped Libby Prison." She quickly explained how Carrie and Robert had helped Matthew, enjoying the way Dr. Strikener's eyes widened as she told the story of two Rebels helping a Yankee journalist. "I have already made connections with Dorothea Dix and Dr. Blackwell." Her smile grew broader as his eyes narrowed with intensity. "I told you I had an agenda," she teased.

"One you seem quite determined to achieve."

"Oh, yes. Carrie was to come live with me and start college in Philadelphia just before the war broke out and separated us. I'm quite determined that she get her chance now. I imagine the more contacts and connections I have with the field of medicine, the more I will be able to help her."

Dr. Strikener gazed at her for a long moment. "And what makes you think I would help a woman enter the field of medicine? You do know it's considered a profession for men, don't you? There are many men working to block what you're suggesting."

Abby stiffened and stared into his eyes, relaxing when she saw the easy humor lurking there. "No one with eyes as kind and warm as yours would block anyone from the medical field who really wants to help make a difference."

"You're sure of that, are you?"

Abby nodded and grinned impishly. "Are you going to tell me I'm wrong?"

Dr. Strikener laughed and moved to stand beside her on the railing. "No. Why don't you tell me more about this young woman?"

Abby happily obliged and then let silence lapse between them, content to watch the bow of the boat plow through the waves. She knew the doctor was processing everything she had told him.

Seagulls soared and swooped overhead. She gave a gasp of delight as a dolphin leapt from the water in greeting. "It's a beautiful day," she murmured.

"Yes, it is," Dr. Strikener agreed, "and I want to assure you I will do everything I can to help Carrie when she comes to see me."

Abby smiled gratefully. "Thank you."

"Are you going to Richmond just to see her?"

Abby shook her head. "It would be enough of a reason, but it's not the only one. It won't be long until the war is over. Richmond fell four days ago, and I understand the Confederates surrendered another eight thousand men when Sheridan cut them off at Sayler's Creek yesterday. They simply can't resist much longer."

"You are well informed," Dr. Strikener said, respect and amazement shining in his eyes.

"I have to be in my business," Abby said.

"Your business?"

"I'm one of *those* women who took over her husband's manufacturing business in Philadelphia when he passed away." Somehow she knew he wouldn't be appalled. "I've done well over the years. The South is going to need help to rebuild. I want to play a part in it. I plan on placing a clothing factory in Richmond to help provide jobs—if there are any buildings still standing after the massive fires," she said, still horrified by the destruction she had learned about. "I'm also involved in helping form schools for the freed slaves. There is going to be a huge need."

"A busy woman," Dr. Strikener commented. "I respect people who take action."

"Yes. I've discovered there are more ways to make a difference than I could possibly provide, but I'm also quite determined to do everything I can. Imagine if everyone felt the same way..."

"You mean if everyone did what they could, knowing the accumulative effect would make a massive difference?"

Abby gasped with delight. "Exactly!" She leaned back against the railing to look more closely at her traveling companion. "I was right about you," she murmured.

Dr. Strikener smiled. "You could have taken a train into Richmond. They've reopened enough of the lines to Washington."

"I'm going through Fort Monroe to connect with a very special young woman who is a teacher in the contraband camp. She loves Carrie as much as I do. I wouldn't dream of going to Richmond without Rose."

"Did Carrie and Rose meet up north?"

Abby chuckled. "No. Rose was Carrie's slave until Carrie helped her escape. They are the closest of friends." She decided to leave out the part about their being related. The poor man could only take so much.

Dr. Strikener leaned back and stared at her. "This story gets better and better," he murmured.

"It's a story that gives me hope," Abby said, sensing he would understand. "The last four years have ripped apart our country, but it has not ripped apart the hearts of the people within it." She groped for words now. "If our country has any chance of uniting, it will be because people choose to look beyond North and South, black and white, to see the people who are beneath the labels."

"You don't think the South should pay for what they've done?"

Abby looked at her companion sharply but kept her voice calm. "I'd say they have already paid a heavy price for the choices they've made. Do you suggest they go on paying? How will that create a reunion or healing?"

"Whoa." Dr. Strikener held up his hands in mock surrender and took a step back before he grinned. "It so happens I agree with you." Then he frowned. "I'm not sure that what we want is going to be easy to make happen, though."

"President Lincoln feels the same way," Abby protested, though she knew everything would not revolve around one man, no matter how powerful he was.

"Yes," he agreed. "Thankfully, he does feel the same way, but there are far too many men in our government who feel differently. It's going to be difficult to push his agenda forward."

"He was able to get the amendment to abolish slavery passed," Abby reminded him.

"Yes, but that was partially because he pushed hard on it being necessary to win the war. Now that Richmond has fallen and the Confederacy is close to defeat, he has only the goodwill of men to fall on. I fear there is not enough there."

"But surely the politicians in the North want to see our country reunited?" Abby asked, her heart sinking as she thought about many of the things she read that disputed her conclusion. "It's what we have fought so hard for the last four years."

Dr. Strikener merely smiled sardonically.

"So it always comes back to this," Abby said heavily. "We wouldn't be in this war if it weren't for the politicians, and now that we have a chance to create a unified country again, they are once again going to stand in the way."

"President Lincoln is a powerful man, and he's also very politically savvy," the doctor replied. "I have hopes he can hold things together and fight for true unity."

Abby fought the tears that blurred her vision.

Dr. Strikener moved forward and took hold of one of her hands. "I'm so sorry to have distressed you," he said.

Abby managed a short laugh. "I have been *distressed* for years," she murmured. "I just thought if I kept trying..."

"That you could make a difference in black students getting educated?" the doctor asked. "You have. You hoped you could make a difference by helping Carrie become a doctor. You're taking every step you can to do that. I suspect you were very involved with the abolition movement." He smiled when Abby looked up sharply. "So was I, and now the slaves are free."

He gripped Abby's hands tightly until she looked in his eyes. "We've had to fight politicians every step of the way," he said. "There are politicians who do wonderful things, and there are those who serve in order to promote their own selfish agendas. I suspect that will never change. Human nature is a powerful thing, but that doesn't mean we can't do something about it. We simply have to be determined enough to continue to fight."

Abby felt a sudden blaze of hope, and her determination strengthened. She straightened her shoulders and took a deep breath. "You're right. Enough of us fighting for the right thing will make a difference. It may take a long time, but we simply have to continue to fight."

"That's the spirit," Dr. Strikener cheered. "You also can't give up on women having the ability to vote."

Abby stared at him. "You are indeed an unusual man," she said. "Your wife is a lucky woman."

"She was..." he said quietly, a flash of pain shooting across his face.

"I'm so sorry," Abby said quickly.

"Don't be. We had thirty wonderful years together, and she gave me five fine children who are busy producing the next generation. She died eight months ago from pneumonia. Rebecca insisted on helping our wounded soldiers. She was exhausted after they all poured in from the battles around Richmond last summer. She couldn't fight the pneumonia."

Abby reached over and put a hand on his arm.

Dr. Strikener shook his head and forced a smile. "She was fighting for a woman's right to vote. I promised her before she died that I would do everything I could to carry on her fight."

Abby's eyes widened. "Rebecca Strikener...of course. I remember her from a meeting in New York City. She was quite a beautiful and intelligent woman. I hadn't heard she passed away."

"Her body is gone, but her spirit remains," the doctor assured her. "All three of my daughters have joined the fight."

Abby smiled and gazed out over the water as Fort Monroe came into view. "It won't be easy, but this country is never again going to be the same. Women have had to carry the weight of responsibility since men were called to battle. They have also experienced freedom. They will never go back to the way things were before the war." She thought of Rose. "And we have millions of people who are now free to live their lives. I think most of them have no clue that the ending of slavery is the beginning of their fight for true freedom, but they will realize it soon. They will need a lot of help."

"It's quite a privilege to be alive at a time like this," Dr. Strikener replied. "I doubt any of it will be easy, but I'm glad to have a chance to be part of the solution."

"Yes," Abby said thoughtfully. "I'm glad I am here to play a part in how history will unfold in this great country. We're all a part of it, you know…"

"Part of the braid of life," Dr. Strikener agreed. "Every single thing we do will have an impact somewhere in the future."

"That's it exactly," Abby said eagerly. "I can't help believe that if more people understood the truth, they would choose their actions more carefully. Nothing we do stands alone in the world. Nothing!"

The clanging of bells from Fort Monroe said they were drawing close to shore. Silence fell between them as the boat slid into its slip and was secured.

"It's full circle, you know," Abby said quietly.

"What is?"

"Fort Monroe," she answered. "It was in 1619 that a Dutch ship carrying slaves arrived on American shores. They were brought right here to Point Comfort. Two hundred years later, it was slaves that constructed Fort Monroe, just a few hundred feet from where the first slaves landed. And now Fort Monroe was the first one to conscript slaves, opening the gates to freedom for millions."

"It has indeed come full circle," Dr. Strikener agreed, "and none of those involved will ever fully comprehend the consequences their actions had. They probably never thought about what they were doing. They were simply driven by the need or the greed of the moment. I pray every day I will be aware of the long reach of my actions through the ages."

The gangplank dropped and the call rang out for everyone to disembark. Abby and Dr. Strikener exchanged a long look.

Dr. Strikener squeezed her hand. "Perhaps we will meet again."

"Perhaps," Abby agreed, accepting his arm as they moved off the boat onto the dock. "I hope so."

***

Rose had struggled to concentrate on her students all morning. She had been expecting a letter from Moses for several days. She knew a warfront was unpredictable, but he had managed to get at least a few lines off to her every week since he joined in the siege of Petersburg. Now Richmond had fallen, but she still had received nothing from him. She was sick with worry for both him and Carrie. She was trying her level best to stay calm and trust God, but she was honest enough to acknowledge she was failing miserably.

"Did I say that right, Miss Rose? Miss Rose?"

Rose jerked her attention back to the classroom when Carla stepped up and tugged the sleeve of her dress. "I'm sorry, Carla. What did you say?"

"I asked you if I said it right."

Rose stared at her, unable to remember Carla even saying *anything*. She was obviously not doing her students any good. She shook her head and then saw June slip into the back of the school. She breathed a sigh of relief, certain June had brought her a letter from Moses, because she knew June had gone down to collect mail that morning.

As she drew closer, Rose saw the look on June's face and froze in mid-stride, her breath catching in her throat as her heart began to pound. All she could do was stand and stare at her.

June hurried forward, grabbed her arm, and turned to the class. "Y'all can go home early today," she called.

Rose was aware her students were looking at them with frightened faces as they grabbed their supplies and began to file slowly from the room. "Moses?" Rose managed to whisper, tears already forming in her eyes.

June nodded and handed her the letter. "It's from Simon."

Rose forced the words to come into focus.

Dear June,
We had a mighty battle yesterday at Fort Stedman. I'm okay, but Moses was shot.

Rose gripped the letter tighter and willed herself to continue reading.

The doctors are doing everything they can, but it was a real bad wound. It's been three days, and he is still unconscious. Captain Jones lets me go check on him every day, but no one can tell me anything.
Moses is real strong, June. If anyone can come back from this, he can.
I don't think it will be long before we take Richmond. I'll write again soon as I can, and let you know how things are.
I love you so very much,
Simon

"Moses has been shot..." Rose made no attempt to hide the tears falling down her face as she turned into June's arms. The two women held on to each other as sobs shook their bodies. Once the tears had run their course, Rose sat back and straightened her shoulders. "When Simon wrote this letter, Moses was still alive," she said. "He probably still is." What her voice lacked in confidence, she was sure her heart made up for in fervent hope.

June remained silent, her frightened look saying it had been almost ten days since Simon wrote that letter. Why hadn't another one come through?

Rose felt June's fear grab her and pull her in. Tears filled her eyes again. Suddenly, her mama's face was clear in her mind. Rose could hear her voice almost as if she were right there. *Girl, you be borrowin' trouble 'fore trouble be here. That Moses of yours be a real strong man. And I don't reckon God be done with him just yet. You gots to hang on, Rose girl. You gots to hang on and send lots of love right through the air to him. Don't you be lettin' those fears of yours swallow you up. You done come too far. Hang on!*

Rose took a deep breath, willed the fear away, and swallowed back her tears. "We don't know anything yet, June. He could just as likely be alive as dead. Until someone tells me he is dead, I'm going to believe he's alive."

June nodded slowly, some of the fear receding from her eyes. "You're right," she whispered.

Rose knew the Union Army had taken Richmond. The news had been swirling through the camp for the last four days, with wild celebrations in every house and dancing in the streets all through the lengthening spring days.

"I wish I could go to Richmond," she said fiercely. "I want to find Moses."

"I might be able to help with that," said a soft voice behind her.

Rose whirled around. "Aunt Abby!"

Abby held out her arms, and Rose collapsed into them, her body trembling.

"Moses..."

"I heard," she said gently. "I got here a few minutes ago."

Rose blinked her eyes at her. "Why are you here?"

"To get you," Abby replied. "I'm going to Richmond. I came to take you with me."

"To Richmond?" Rose gasped with disbelief. "Are you serious?" Her thoughts spun in dizzying circles.

"I'll keep John here with me," June offered.

Rose shook her head. "John will stay with me." She couldn't imagine leaving the warmth and love of her little boy. And when she found Moses, she knew he would need his son. She peered at Aunt Abby. "Will that be okay?"

"Absolutely. We're catching the train out tomorrow morning. We'll be there by the afternoon."

Rose stared at her. "Carrie," she said softly. Then her eyes swam with tears again. "And I can find Moses."

Chapter Thirty-Four

Carrie stepped back from her final patient and rubbed the small of her back. The last few days had been complete chaos as Richmond struggled to deal with the occupation. The Union had moved all Confederate soldiers to Jackson Hospital and taken control of Chimborazo for their own. Carrie was the only Confederate medical personnel still at Chimborazo, retained because the black soldiers had begged for her to stay with them. She'd heard that Captain Jones had stepped in to make the odd request a possibility.

"I'm real glad you stayed with us, Miss Carrie."

Carrie smiled down at Charlie, his eyes clear and free of fever. "I'm glad, too," she said sincerely. Many of the soldiers had shared their stories with her over the last few days. Her love for these men who suffered for so long in slavery, and walked through the agonies of war had grown. She had mixed feelings about losing her patients from Chimborazo, but now she was simply glad she had the opportunity to care for these amazing men.

"Them doctors from the Union took care of us back at the camp," Charlie continued, "but it's like you done care about us like real people."

"I do," Carrie said. "I know you've got a lot of challenges ahead of you now that you're free, but at least you're free. I'm so glad for you."

Charlie gave her a huge grin. "Yessum, we all be free now!" He paused, his expression serious. "Have you heard any word from the armies, Miss Carrie? I realize we be on different sides," he said hesitantly.

Carrie smiled. "I want this war over as badly as you do, Charlie. I accepted a long time ago that we're not going to win it."

"That bother you, Miss Carrie?"

Carrie struggled to find the right words. "I never thought this war should have happened in the first place. There are times I wish the North would have let us go in order to form our own country, because it would have spared so many lives and stopped so much destruction, but in the end I'm glad I'm still going to be a citizen of the *entire* United States of America." She paused. "And I can be nothing but glad that the slaves are free. I know that would not have happened if we had won the war." She managed to smile at Charlie. "I'm sad because of everything that has happened, but I'm not bothered. We never had a chance of winning this war."

Charlie watched her closely. "So you don't mind telling me what is happening?" he asked eagerly.

Carrie laughed. "My understanding is that Grant and Sheridan are in relentless pursuit of our army. There was a serious loss for the Confederacy two days ago when Sheridan forced over eight thousand men to surrender."

Charlie whistled. "That be a lot."

"Close to a sixth of Lee's army," Carrie confirmed. "There was another battle at High Bridge. Our troops had set fire to the bridge to keep the Union from pursuing them. Your troops put out the fires and caught up with them. I think our troops managed to hold them off, but your soldiers are after them again."

Charlie nodded. "I reckon the war about over sho 'nuff."

Carrie didn't want to talk about the battles anymore. Every thought of it increased her fear of whether Robert would come home to her. "What are you going to do when the war is over?" she asked.

Charlie stopped grinning and frowned. "I don't reckon as how I got an answer to that yet. I joined up with the army when they came through my plantation down in Mississippi. I was real happy to fight to help set everyone free, but I ain't thought much beyond that. I reckon I'll figure it out, though."

Carrie nodded. She had heard the same story over and over. She was happy beyond measure that the slaves were free, but she knew they were going to need a lot of help to create new lives. She hoped there were enough people who cared about them to make it possible, and that those who fought for their freedom would fight just as hard to help them create a new future full of justice and opportunity.

"You were a fine soldier," she said. "I imagine you'll do well with whatever you decide."

Charlie stared at her for a few moments and then nodded. "I reckon you're right, Miss Carrie. Did you know the doctor said I was going to get out of here tomorrow?"

"Tired of my company, are you?"

"Of course not..." Charlie broke off when he saw the laughter in her eyes. "I'm gonna miss you, Miss Carrie, sho 'nuff."

Carrie squeezed his hand. "I'm glad you're better, Charlie. You keep taking care of yourself," she added as she pulled off her smock and prepared to leave.

The sun was sinking low on the horizon when Carrie stepped from the ward, looking for Janie out of habit until she remembered she was now at Jackson Hospital. Oh well, they would have dinner together. All of them were now crowding into Moses' room to eat so they could share that time with him. May cared for him during the day, treating him like he was a hero.

So many gaps had been filled in with hours of conversation, but it had also increased her ache to see Rose. Surely it wouldn't have to be much longer. She had sent a letter to Fort Monroe for Moses just the day before, but she didn't know how long it would take to arrive. Simon had told her about the letter he had sent June, so she was sure Rose was sick with worry and fear. She frowned as she thought about what her best friend must be feeling.

"Sure is a nice day for a frown."

Carrie heard the words and registered the voice but was sure her thoughts had conjured them up. She continued moving down the hill.

"Maybe she didn't hear you."

Carrie froze. How could she have conjured up Aunt Abby's voice, too? She hadn't been thinking about her just then. Slowly, telling herself the whole time that she had to be imagining it, she turned toward the voices. She gasped when she saw the two women silhouetted against the woods, the setting sun casting a glow over their bodies.

"Carrie!" Moments later, Rose rushed into her arms, laughing and crying.

Carrie stared in disbelief and burst into joyous tears. Her heart swelled until she thought it would surely burst from her chest. "Rose! Rose!"

"Carrie!"

They went back to rocking and hugging, ignoring the stares of medical personnel passing by.

"You're two intelligent women, so I know you can say more than each other's names," came a teasing voice.

Carrie remembered the other voice she had heard. She froze again, her eyes growing wide.

Rose laughed with delight. "It's not a dream, Carrie."

"Aunt Abby?" Carrie whispered, turning slowly to see Abby standing with her arms open. Carrie rushed into her arms and began to cry and laugh all over again. "How... Where did you... When..."

Abby laid a finger over Carrie's lips as she held her back to stare into her face. "You'll get your questions answered," she said softly. "I just want to look at you."

Rose moved up to stand beside Carrie and wrap an arm around her waist.

"Both my girls together," Aunt Abby said quietly, struggling to control her emotion. "We've all waited so long..."

Carrie stared from one to the next, struggling to capture her breath. Finally, she shook her head. "I don't care how you got here. I'm just so glad you're real and that I'm not hallucinating."

"Mama!" A wail of protest split the air. A nurse stepped forward, a toddler squirming in her arms.

"I'm sorry, miss. I couldn't keep him quiet any longer."

Rose laughed and reached for the little boy.

Carrie put her hand out and stroked her finger down his tear-stained cheek. "John... You're so beautiful. You look just like your daddy."

"Thank you, he—" Rose's brilliant smile faded as she fell silent, confusion clouding her face. "How did you know about John, Carrie? He hadn't been born when Moses saw you at the plantation."

Carrie smiled, joy exploding in her heart, and held out a hand to each of them. "To quote a friend, *'You'll get your questions answered.'*" She began to walk rapidly down the hill. "We have so much to talk about, but first I have something to show you." She shook her head when she saw both of them open their mouths to ask questions. "Not another word," she said playfully as her heart threatened to burst wide open again.

⁊ ⁘ ⁖ ⁛

Carrie was laughing as she hurried up the stairs to the house. "This is my home," she explained quickly, not bothering to say anything else. She waved at May and Micah when she strode into the house, again not bothering with explanations. Instead, she pulled Rose and Aunt Abby up the stairs, John grinning happily as he bounced on his mama's hip. If Moses was sleeping, the clatter of footsteps was sure to wake him.

She slowed when she reached his door and put a hand out to stop Aunt Abby. She smiled and nodded at Rose. "There is a surprise in there for you," she said, hardly able to contain herself.

Rose walked into the room. Her scream sounded a moment later. "Moses!" A sound of joyous laughter exploded from the room. "Moses!"

"Rose! My Rose!" Moses' booming voice vibrated through the house.

Only then did Carrie walk into the room. Rose was down on her knees beside the bed, her head nestled on her husband's shoulder, John dancing around on the floor with excitement.

Carrie scooped him up where he could stare down at his father.

"Daddy! Daddy!"

Moses' face was split with a grin as he looked up at Carrie. "I know...I know..." he said. "I'll get my questions answered soon."

"*Your* questions?" Rose breathed. "I can hardly believe I'm really seeing you. I've been so worried."

"Me, too!" Aunt Abby said as she walked into the room.

Moses' shout could be heard through the house again.

Carrie was laughing so hard tears were pouring down her face. John was bouncing in her arms, straining to reach his daddy.

Carrie sobered long enough to take control of her patient. "I'm sorry, John, but your daddy can't hold you right now."

"Not hold?" he asked sadly, his face puckered with confusion.

Rose looked up at Carrie then reached to take John and draw him close. "How bad is it?" she asked.

"He'll get well," Carrie said, "but his wound was serious."

"Carrie saved my life," Moses said gruffly. "I was almost dead when they brought me into Richmond."

Rose lifted shining eyes of gratitude.

Carrie squeezed her hand tightly. "He can't get out of this bed for at least ten more days. His wound has to have time to heal, or the infection could come back. I don't suppose," she added teasingly, "that he'll care about moving as long as he has you and John to look at."

Her mind turned to practical matters. "All our boarders are gone. They left when Richmond was evacuated. You, John and Aunt Abby will stay here."

<hr />

Rose fought to bring her swirling thoughts into place. She wasn't sure a heart could contain so much joy. She simply couldn't believe she was in Carrie's house holding Moses' hand and looking at her best friend. Yet, after almost four years apart, it was as if they had never been separated. And Moses was alive!

Aunt Abby understood the intensity of her feelings. "How about if we give you some time alone with Moses? Then you and Carrie will be able to talk."

Rose nodded automatically and turned toward the door when she heard a shuffling noise. She gazed at the man staring at her with a burning look in his eyes. Why was he looking at her that way?

She glanced over and saw Carrie staring at the man with a huge smile on her face. Then she turned back to the stranger whose eyes had never left her face, taking in his handsome features, and not understanding the sudden, mysterious connection she felt with someone she had never seen. "I'm sorry, do I know you?" she asked in confusion.

"Take a good look, Rose," Moses said.

Rose was stunned to see Moses smiling as well. "What's going on here?" she asked, her thoughts spinning even faster. She turned back to the man at the door. "Who are you? Am I supposed to know you?"

Jeremy smiled and stepped forward. "Probably not. I imagine I have changed quite a lot from the day I was born."

Rose stared at him, her mind not registering what he was saying. "The day you were born? What does that—" Her question broke off as she stared in shock, realizing she was looking at a white, male version of herself. Her mouth opened and closed, but no sound came out.

Carrie laughed and stepped forward. "Rose, I would like to introduce you to your twin brother, Jeremy."

"Jeremy?" Rose whispered. She stood slowly, taking in every feature that told her it was true, but her mind simply couldn't absorb it. Her eyes swung back to Carrie.

"I promise we'll answer all your questions," Carrie assured her. "It's true. Pastor Anthony, the man who set up your escape through the Underground Railroad, was Jeremy's adoptive father. I figured it out after I went to the plantation two winters ago. It's quite the story."

Rose swung her eyes back to Jeremy and stepped forward. "You're my twin?" she said unsteadily, her eyes burning into his, her heart telling her it was true. A smile exploded on her face. "And you're okay with me being black?"

"As long as you can put up with me being white," Jeremy assured her and then reached out to take her hand. "Hello, sister. It's been a long time."

Rose gave a cry and flung herself into his arms. "Jeremy! My brother!" Great sobs of joy ripped through her body as she clung to him. Finally, she stepped back. "How can one person take so much joy?" she murmured, her eyes traveling around the room.

"I'm asking myself the same question," Carrie responded.

"As am I," Aunt Abby said in a voice thick with tears.

"Even men can't take this much joy," Moses said, his eyes shining wetly.

May stomped into the room just then with a huge platter of food. "Ain't never heard so much noise in this house as long as I been here," she stated in a voice full of happiness. "I reckon all of you done built up a right big appetite. I got Micah bringing up some more chairs. We ain't got nothing fancy to eat in this beat up old town, but I reckon I can fill your stomachs."

<hr />

It was almost midnight before Carrie and Rose were alone. Carrie knew the celebrations and talking would go on for several more days, but she had shooed everyone out of Moses' room so he could get some rest, assuring Rose she could sleep with him again in a few days. John was asleep in a corner of the room, snuggled in a crib May found in the attic. Rose and Aunt Abby had met Janie and Clifford, and Hobbs had stumbled in shortly before midnight, exhausted from a long day at the hospital. She sent him to bed, telling him she'd fill him in on everything the next morning. He had been too tired to protest. Aunt Abby was tucked into the room next to theirs with a promise Carrie would have her all to herself for a while the next day. Carrie was holding the secret of Matthew being here, wanting to enjoy the renewed celebration when he arrived for breakfast the next morning.

Rose settled down in the bed next to Carrie's and just stared at her.

Carrie stared right back, letting the silence linger as cool air swirled in through the filmy curtains. She took a deep breath, thankful there was no longer the smell of smoke. "You don't seem real to me yet, either," she finally said, breaking the silence.

Rose smiled. "You always know what I'm thinking," she said softly, her eyes filling with tears. "I've missed you so badly. There were times I was afraid things wouldn't be the same again..."

"...That we both would have changed too much," Carrie finished for her. "I know. I felt the same thing. But it's like..."

"...we were never apart," Rose said with a laugh. Then she sobered. "We haven't talked about Robert."

Carrie sighed heavily. "He's with Lee's army. At least, I hope he is. There is so much chaos since the city was occupied that we haven't been getting any reports. I don't know if he's dead or alive, or perhaps a prisoner of war."

Rose gasped. "That's horrible!"

"I suppose I should say I'm used to it," Carrie said, "but I don't suppose you ever get used to not knowing if someone you love is dead or alive. But you know that..."

Rose nodded. "Yes," she whispered as she looked at the wall. "I can still hardly believe Moses is right next door." She swung her eyes back to rest on Carrie's face. "Matthew told me Robert was missing for ten months."

"Yes," Carrie said, a smile finding its way to her face. "I know Moses was the one who saved his life and took him to the black family who so changed him," she said. "I will forever be grateful. The months he was missing were the most difficult time of my life, but it also made him into the man I could marry. You'll find he's very different."

"All I need to know is that you love him," Rose said. "Your father?"

Carrie told her what she knew. "I know he's going to try to get a message through to me, but I don't know when I'll see him again, or if he'll have to go to prison."

Rose frowned. "I don't think Lincoln is planning on putting officials in prison," she protested.

"Perhaps not," Carrie replied, "but everyone is terrified, and no one really knows what is going on. The last week has been rather difficult."

Rose laughed. "You've always had the gift of understatement," she teased. "I was horrified when we came into the city. There is only one train depot that isn't burned. So much of the city is ruined."

Carrie nodded sadly. "It was horrible to watch."

Rose finally waved her hand. "We have days to catch up on what has happened. Aunt Abby has promised we'll be here for at least two weeks."

"Two weeks!" Carrie gasped, joy exploding in her heart again. "That's wonderful."

Rose moved over to sit on the bed next to her and grabbed her hands. "Who have you become, Carrie?"

Carrie sobered instantly, looking deep into the brown eyes regarding her with so much love. "Who have I become?" she murmured, knowing Rose wanted nothing but the truth. "I've grown up," she said slowly. "I've been through four years of war that have taught me how strong and capable I am. It's given me opportunities I would never have dreamed of. I've learned I want to be a doctor just as much as I thought I did. I'm married to a wonderful man who supports my dreams, and whom I love with all my heart. But mostly," she took a deep breath, "I've learned that nothing ever lasts."

"What do you mean?"

"Nothing ever lasts," Carrie repeated softly. "No matter how difficult a time is, it will pass. No matter how wonderful a time is, it will pass. Life is like the tides in the ocean. It's a continual ebb and flow. I've learned not to hang on too tightly. If I hang on to the pain, I can't see when it's gone, and I miss the joy. If I hang on too tightly to the joy, I am devastated when something else difficult or painful happens." She stopped to see if Rose understood what she was saying.

"Keep going," Rose said gently.

"How I live life is my choice. Always. I can choose joy and peace in the midst of any circumstances because I know things will always change. I've learned that, like the tides are necessary in the ocean, they are necessary in my life. I wouldn't be who I am without the hard times, and life would hardly be worth living without the times full of joy."

Rose nodded. "Times like these."

Carrie smiled. "Exactly! I'm learning to embrace both of them." She squeezed Rose's hands. "Your turn. Who have you become?"

"Exactly who I wanted to be," Rose said with a wide smile. "I love being a teacher, and I'm very good at it."

"That I'm sure of," Carrie said proudly.

Rose grinned. "I love being a wife and mother. Most of the time, I can move beyond the fears Mama told me always held me back. I feel them, but I know I can banish them by taking action. There are so many times when I feel she is still with me, looking at me with her loving, wise eyes."

"I know exactly what you mean," Carrie exclaimed. "She may be gone, but all she taught me is still in my heart and mind. It pops up when I need it."

Rose nodded and looked off into the distance. "Mostly I've become someone who knows I have to be so much more." She paused while Carrie waited quietly. "Black people are free now. They believe they have accomplished so much, but all they've really done is received the *freedom* to accomplish something." She struggled to find the right words. "I know my job is to help them become all they've dreamed of being. I've known for a long time that I *want* to be a leader for my people, but it's been only recently that I've realized I'm *meant* to be a leader for my people."

"And the reality of that responsibility is scary," Carrie added.

"Yes," Rose whispered. "I'm afraid I won't be enough."

"Now what would your mama say?"

Rose laughed. "You're right. Remember, I said *most* of the time I can move beyond the fears. This is a big one."

Carrie nodded. "I understand. I know I'm meant to be a doctor. I also know I'm meant to be a role model for women who will follow after me in the years to come. Most of the time it excites me, but there are those times when it terrifies me, and I want to run back to the plantation and raise tobacco."

Rose looked at her. Suddenly, they were both laughing hysterically, holding their sides at the image of either of them back on the plantation for good. Their laughter died away, the air cleansed of fear by laughing in the face of it.

"The war is almost over," Carrie said. "The last four years have almost been mandated for us because of the reality of the war. Now it's going to be up to us to decide what we want for our lives."

"We thought we knew what we wanted four years ago," Rose agreed. "Then life happened and turned everything upside down." She stared off into space. "I'm glad it did," she said. "Oh, I hate that the war happened, and I hate all the pain and loss. I would have stopped it all if I could, but I couldn't, so I've decided to be grateful for what I've learned and for who I've become. I don't think I would have grown up so quickly without everything."

"We're so blessed," Carrie said softly. "So many people have lost everyone they love. You have Moses and John, June and Simon. As far as I know, I still have Robert and Father. And now I have you and Aunt Abby and Matthew back in my life..."

"And we have Jeremy," Rose whispered, tears brimming in her eyes again. "You're right. We're so very blessed."

<hr/>

Robert gasped for air as another coughing attack seized him. His stomach was pinched with hunger, but he didn't think he could have eaten even if someone had arrived with a meal—not that it was likely to happen. His gut told him things were almost over.

General Longstreet had tried to escape by setting fire to the bridges the Confederate troops had crossed. Grant's infantry managed to put out the fires, cross the bridges, and catch up with them in Farmville. Fitzhugh Lee's cavalry had managed to hold off Grant's infantry until nightfall, but the Rebels had been forced to continue marching westward to avoid capture. The promised food had been left behind.

"Captain?" Alex appeared by his side, his emaciated face lined with worry. "I got you some water."

Robert nodded his thanks and drank down the water. As soon as he had swallowed it, the dry dust caked his lungs once more, and the coughing resumed. He knew his fever was going higher, but he refused to give into it.

"I thought we were going to eat in Farmville," Alex said quietly. "I ain't complaining. Just wondering."

"We were supposed to," Robert replied. "When Grant caught up with us, we had to march right past where the rations were. I believe Lee has rations stored at Appomattox. It should only take us another day to reach them."

Alex stared around at the men marching down the road, some of them stumbling in the ruts. "I hope they can make it that far," he murmured. "Some of them ain't doing so good." He gripped Robert's arm when he stumbled sideways. "Like you, Captain."

Robert gritted his teeth and moved forward. "We keep moving, or all is lost."

"It's all lost anyway, ain't it?" Alex asked.

Robert chose to not answer.

Chapter Thirty-Five

The clatter of boots on the porch woke Carrie. A quick glance at the sun streaming in the window, told her she and Rose had slept much longer than she intended. No surprise, since they had talked almost all night. She looked over, saw Rose open her eyes, and shrugged. "I guess I botched that surprise," she said ruefully.

Rose looked at her, blinking sleep out of her eyes. "What are you—"

The scream floated up the stairways. "Matthew!" Aunt Abby's delighted laughter followed right on the heels of the scream.

"Aunt Abby!" came the booming reply, followed by a laugh that Carrie didn't recognize.

Rose sat straight up in bed, fumbling to throw back the covers. "Matthew?" She turned to stare at Carrie with open-mouthed astonishment. "You knew he was here?"

"He's been here almost a week," Carrie admitted cheerfully. "I decided to keep it a secret, but I had planned to pull off a better surprise than this one."

"God help us if you had," Rose said fervently. "I don't think my heart can take much more!" She laughed as she sprang up and reached for her dress. "Moses knows he's here?"

"They've spent hours talking over the last few days when Matthew hasn't been working. He was sent here to cover the occupation of Richmond. Moses has been able to make amazing connections for him. Captain Jones comes by to check on him most days, which means Matthew is getting information before any of the other journalists. They are almost green with envy."

"I heard another laugh I didn't recognize," Rose said as she buttoned her dress, quickly pulled her hair back, and moved over to wash her face and brush her teeth.

"So did I," Carrie replied, moving as quickly as Rose to go down and join in the fun. "I'm guessing that was his friend Peter. I haven't seen him since we helped him and Matthew get out of town after the prison break."

Rose grinned. "This is going to be another day full of joy. I intend to embrace it."

Carrie laughed as she rushed over to give Rose an exuberant hug. "You and me both! And get used to a lot of hugs. I have a lot of years of lost ones to make up for."

Rose squeezed her back tightly. "I plan on a *lifetime* of hugs," she promised, her voice choked.

"Don't start crying again," Carrie scolded, blinking back her own tears.

Rose laughed, finished poking the last pins in her hair, and turned toward the door.

"Oh bother!" Carrie scowled as she tried to tuck stray hairs into her bun. "I don't have time for this right now."

Rose laughed. "You never were very good at that." It took her moments to pull Carrie's hair back into a smooth bun. "Now, let's get down there before we miss something."

"Mama?"

Carrie smiled as she looked over at John peering sleepily over the edge of the crib. "It looks like John is ready to go join in the fun, too."

John stared at Carrie for a long moment before his confusion melted into a lopsided grin. "Kaywee..."

Carrie grinned and leaned down to scoop him up, nuzzling into his warm, soft neck. "That's right, John. I'm your Aunt Carrie." She smiled as she looked over his head into Rose's eyes. "I think that will be easier than trying to explain we're really cousins."

"Thank goodness that conversation is a long time away," Rose exclaimed. "I can barely make sense of it myself. It's also going to be fun to explain his white uncle."

"Never a dull moment," Carrie agreed. The sounds of laughter from downstairs floated up the stairway. "Go on into Moses' room, and I'll bring everyone else up. May will have breakfast ready soon. I'll change his bandage before I head to the hospital."

Moses' room was soon crowded with everyone in the house.

"We're going to have to move you downstairs into the parlor if this keeps up," Carrie said, staring around with delight. "I don't think this room could hold one more person."

Little John alternated between walking and crawling, moving from person to person to make his inspection. He stopped often to give a smile like sunshine, or reach up his chubby hand to pat a cheek or arm.

May and Micah, their own smiles as bright as sunshine, walked into the room with huge platters of food. "Mornin' everyone!"

Micah laid his platter down and turned to look at Carrie. "And I got some news for you, Miss Carrie."

Carrie looked up quickly. "What is it, Micah?

"Spencer was by this morning... Eddie is back living with Frank somewhere. He's safe. Most of the black section of town was burned out, but there weren't many that were hurt. They're making do."

Carrie sagged in relief. She knew the black hospital had burned, along with the church, and she hadn't been able to learn anything about Eddie. "I'm so glad!"

Micah nodded. "Eddie knows things are real chaotic right now, but he said he would come to the house when he thought you might be able to go out to the plantation. He's real anxious to see his kids."

"Of course he is!" Carrie exclaimed, fighting her own passionate desire to discover if Cromwell Plantation was still standing.

When Carrie looked around, the curious expressions made her realize most of the people in the room didn't know what she and Micah were talking about. She explained quickly and motioned everyone to eat while it was still hot.

Carrie tried to not let it bother her that breakfast was beans and cornbread, the only staples left in the house. It had been bad before, but now that the fires had destroyed almost every grocery store in town, the only food to be found was what was coming from the garden, and that was very little considering the season had just started.

She sighed with relief when she realized no one cared. They were simply happy to be together. Laughter and talking swirled through the air as the food disappeared. No one even seemed to mind the strong onion aroma that permeated the air. Carrie was still changing Moses' poultices three times a day. The swelling and redness were almost gone and the wound was shrinking, but she was taking no chances of the infection returning.

She relaxed back against the wall and let her gaze rove around the room. Jeremy was laughing with Rose over something little John had done. Moses and Matthew were deep in conversation, while Clifford talked with Peter and Hobbs. Aunt Abby and Janie had their heads close together over something. Suddenly, the tears welled in her eyes. She blinked them back as thoughts of Robert tore through her, leaving her raw and vulnerable. *If only...*

Carrie looked up to discover Aunt Abby's eyes locked on her from across the room, compassion and understanding shining in them. Just that one look steadied her and gave her the courage to take a deep breath, and then another.

Matthew cleared his throat and stepped away from Moses' bed. "Anyone care to know what is going on outside this room?" he asked.

Carrie wanted to say no. She wanted to preserve what they had and never let anything else touch it, but she already knew that was impossible. She would embrace the joy, but she wouldn't hide from the challenges that were surely coming. The war had not achieved anything. The real achievements would come when people began to rebuild their lives and their country.

"Let's have it," she said firmly, feeling Aunt Abby's warm approval radiating from across the room.

Matthew sent her an understanding smile. "If my sources are correct, Lee will be forced to surrender today."

Carrie gasped. She'd known things were going badly for the Confederates, but she hadn't realized just how badly.

"Two nights ago, after the battle at High Bridge, Grant sent Lee a letter proposing the Army of Northern Virginia surrender. I'm told Lee sent him back a noncommittal letter asking about the surrender terms."

"We suspect Lee was hoping they could reach their ration train at Appomattox Station before he was trapped," Peter added. "He was trying to buy some time by pretending interest in negotiation."

Matthew nodded. "Lee didn't reach his rations. Major General Custer seized a supply train and twenty-five guns, blocking Lee's path. He burned the three trains loaded with provisions for Lee's army."

Carrie stiffened. She didn't care about losing the war, but she cared very much that Robert was continuing to go hungry. He had been so thin the last time she'd seen him over two months ago. What condition was he in now?

"Grant sent Lee another letter last night offering the generous surrender terms Lincoln has proposed. He offered a meeting to discuss them," Matthew finished. "We haven't heard anything yet, but Lee simply has nowhere to go and no other options."

Carrie fought to keep her voice calm. "Do you know the terms of surrender?" she asked. "Will Robert be taken as a prisoner?" She knew her voice was not hiding her fear, but she couldn't help it. She also knew every eye in the room was on her, but she felt cradled by their unconditional love and warmth. There was not one person there who judged Robert for fighting.

"Absolutely not!" Matthew said quickly, walking over to take her hands. "I don't know the actual wording of the terms, but I do know that as long as every soldier agrees to never take up arms again, and then leaves their gun on the battlefield, they are free to go home and live their lives. The war will be over for them."

Carrie's eyes filled with tears of relief. "Thank God," she whispered, not trying to stem the flow of tears down her cheeks.

Now the question was whether Robert was alive to take advantage of Lincoln's generosity.

Carrie gave Aunt Abby a warm hug before she hurried down the stairs. "I'll be back this afternoon," she promised. "And then I'm going to claim you all for myself!"

"I'm going to hold you to that," Aunt Abby responded, her expression full of love.

Carrie fought the emotion swelling in her chest as she looked into the eyes of the woman who was more her mother than her own had ever been. The four years of separation had been agony. To have her right here in the house was almost more than she could absorb. She turned and raced back up the stairs to give her another big hug. "I love you so much!" she cried. "I'm so very happy you're here."

Aunt Abby laughed joyously and kissed her firmly on the cheek. "It's a dream come true, Carrie. I'll be counting the minutes until you're done at the hospital today. We have so very much to catch up on. I know we'll only touch the surface today, but I intend to make the most of it."

"Embrace the joy..." Carrie murmured. "I'll explain that later," she promised as she ran down the stairs and headed up the road.

The day was almost over before Carrie noticed a very distinguished looking man standing inside the door, watching her change the bandage on one of her patients. She gave him a courteous smile and went back to work.

"Your wound is almost healed, soldier."

"Yessum, I reckon it is. All because of you."

Carrie smiled. "You were a good patient. It's always nice when patients do what I tell them to do."

"I's real smart," the soldier said, his eyes twinkling. "I ain't aimin' to cross Moses. He may be sick right now, but I don't want him after me when he's well again."

"Moses?" Carrie asked. "What does he have to do with it?"

"He done sent all of us a letter. Captain Jones done brought it some days ago and read it to us."

"A letter?" Carrie had heard nothing about a letter. "And what did this letter say?"

"It tole us that if we didn't do what you tole us to, we was gonna have to answer to him. Tole us you be the best doctor he knows about, and that we weren't to give you any trouble."

"Is that right?" Carrie murmured, fighting the laughter that wanted to burst forth. No wonder everyone had been so compliant. They had been almost pathetic in their desire to please her.

"You be mad, Miss Carrie?" he asked, his face suddenly tight with concern. "Maybe I shouldn't a said nothin', but I figured since I was leavin'..."

Carrie let the bubbling laugh break forth. "Of course I'm not angry. I wish I had someone like Moses to make all my patients so easy to work with!" She finished wrapping his bandage and stepped back. "Your wound is almost healed, but I want you to keep a covering on it for at least five more days."

"Yessum," he said meekly, impudent fun once more shining in his eyes.

Carrie laughed again and turned to the door, surprised to see the man still standing there. She pulled off her smock and moved toward him. "May I help you?" she asked.

"Your reputation precedes you, Mrs. Borden, but I wanted to come see for myself." The man stepped forward, sun from the open door glinting on the gray streaks in his dark hair. "My name is Dr. Strikener."

Carrie nodded quickly. "I heard you were coming through to inspect Chimborazo and make sure it was adequate for the Union troops. It's nice to meet you, Dr. Strikener."

"It's a pleasure to meet you as well, Mrs. Borden."

Carrie stepped out into the bright sunshine with him, feeling comfortable as soon as she gazed into his warm brown eyes. "What can I do for you, Dr. Strikener?"

"You can tell me where you learned so much about herbal medicine."

"How did you..."

"How did I know you're the one responsible for the herbal medicines I found in our supply room?"

Carrie frowned. "I thought that all went down to Jackson Hospital. They have no medicine down there." Her mind spun as she thought of the implications. She had to find a way to get some down to them.

"It's there now," he assured her. "I had it sent down as soon as I found it. It was overlooked somehow in the move. Our medical personnel isn't interested in it, though I suspect it works as well as our more accepted medicines." He stared at her with open admiration. "She told me you were quite unique, but until I saw the vast collection of herbs in that storeroom, I didn't really understand what she meant."

Carrie blinked at him in confusion. "She? Who are you talking about?"

Dr. Strikener laughed. "I imagine I do sound like I'm talking in riddles. I met a friend of yours on the boat ride down from Philadelphia."

"Aunt Abby," Carrie whispered.

"Well, she identified herself as Abigail Livingston, but I imagine that must be your Aunt Abby. She is quite fond of you."

Carrie flushed. "And I am quite fond of her," she replied. "She is a remarkable woman."

"That she is," he agreed instantly. "Remarkable enough to make sure I help you with a reference to medical school when you are ready."

Carrie gasped and looked up at him.

"That's the real reason I was lurking in your ward today. I had to see for myself if you're as good as she thinks you are." He paused. "I would say you're better," he said quietly. "I have rarely seen a doctor so proficient who has as good a bedside manner. Your patients obviously trust and love you."

Carrie managed to chuckle in spite of the choked feeling in her throat. "They were under orders."

Dr. Strikener laughed again. "Yes, I heard what that patient said. The other thing I learned is that the people who love you are quite loyal to you. That's good to know."

Carrie flushed again, uncertain how to respond.

Dr. Strikener looked over the bluff down to the waters of the sparkling James River, watching as boats plied the water, carrying the destruction of the burned buildings as the massive cleanup continued. "What are you going to do after the war is over, Mrs. Borden?"

Carrie struggled for words. "I want more than anything to be a doctor," she replied. "I'm aware of the challenges I will face, but after four years of war, I doubt they can be more daunting than the ones I have faced so far."

Dr. Strikener looked at her, nodded, and handed her a folded slip of paper. "This is my address. I hope when you are ready to move forward, you will allow me to help you. I realize the benefits women can bring to medicine. I believe I can smooth the way for you a little. Don't kid yourself that it will be easy, but other women have proven it is doable."

Carrie smiled as tears shimmered in her eyes. "Thank you," she said fervently. "Thank you so much." She reached for the paper he held out to her, but he pulled it back with a teasing smile.

"You haven't told me yet how you learned so much about herbal medicine. Perhaps you would consider my contact information a fair trade?" His eyes were dancing.

Carrie looked at him with genuine delight. "Well..." she pretended to deliberate and then grinned at him. "I suppose it would be an adequate trade." She grinned again and settled down on a stump. "One of my father's slaves on the plantation where I grew up brought some of the herbal secrets over from Africa. They were passed down through generations. She learned about more of the plants once she was brought to America. She started teaching me when my mother was very ill..."

Dr. Strikener settled down on another stump, cupped his chin in his hand and listened intently as Carrie told her story.

"I'll be happy to teach you all I can while you're here," Carrie offered.

"I was hoping you would," Dr. Strikener responded. "I'll plan on some time spent with the herbs every day. The Union Army was confident they were cutting off all medical supplies. They just didn't know about you."

Carrie smiled as Sarah's face and voice filled her mind. *I done tole you all them days spent trompin' around in them woods learnin' the magic was gonna pay off. Didn't I tell you man couldn't make nothing better than what God already made? Didn't I, Carrie girl?*

⁙

Abby was walking toward her up the hill when Carrie started for home. She ran forward and threw her arms around the older woman. "You are an angel," she cried. "Thank you, Aunt Abby!"

Abby smiled and returned the embrace. "I'm always happy for a hug, but what am I being thanked for?" she asked.

"I just talked with Dr. Strikener," Carrie said excitedly. "He came over to visit me in the ward because of your talk with him on the ship. He has promised to help me when I'm ready to go to medical school."

"Excellent!" Abby clapped her hands together. "I knew it wasn't a coincidence that we met."

"And I bet you didn't even notice how attractive he is," Carrie teased. "Of course, his wife might object." Abby laughed and tucked her hand in Carrie's arm, but there was something about the way she avoided her eyes that had Carrie swinging her around. "Is he married?" Carrie demanded.

"His wife died eight months ago," Aunt Abby revealed. "She was quite a remarkable woman. I knew her from a women's voting rights convention. I didn't know her well, but she did so much for women's rights."

"And Dr. Strikener supported her?"

"He didn't just support her—he has vowed to carry on the fight. His three daughters have joined him."

"Attractive, intelligent *and* compassionate," Carrie murmured, laughing when Aunt Abby spun toward her with protest in her eyes. "He's quite the catch."

"Neither of us is looking to *catch* anyone, Carrie."

"Then you're not as smart as I thought you were," Carrie observed.

Aunt Abby stood back and laughed helplessly. "Why the sudden interest in my love life?" she asked.

"Because you're the most remarkable, beautiful woman I know," Carrie answered promptly, "and because Dr. Strikener seems to be quite remarkable as well. *And* because life is much too short not to embrace every moment of joy that comes your way. Come on," she teased, "are you telling me you didn't even notice?"

Aunt Abby stepped back to examine her more closely. "You have indeed grown up and are becoming the wise woman I suspected you would become. And, yes," she admitted with a grin, "I noticed."

Carrie smiled smugly and moved toward a bench under a leafy dogwood bursting into bloom. "Let's sit here to talk. The house is so full, and I don't feel like sharing you."

"That sounds perfect," Aunt Abby agreed. She held up a bag she had hanging on her shoulder. "I hope you don't mind, but I did a little grocery shopping while you were at the hospital."

"*Grocery* shopping?" Carrie echoed.

"Yes. The troops have converted two buildings into stores. The first trains are coming through from the North to restock them. Having so many people in your house has to be a strain."

"More like a total joy," Carrie protested, eyeing the bag with anticipation.

"That, too," Abby said, "but May tells me you're rather fond of fried chicken and mashed potatoes. I hope you don't mind that I brought a picnic."

Carrie stared at the bag with awe. "Fried chicken?" she breathed. "You really are an angel!" Then she frowned as she thought of the rest of the household.

Abby interpreted her frown and reached up to lay a hand on her cheek. "May is frying up chicken for everyone," she said.

Carrie smiled through her tears. "We haven't had chicken in more than two years," she admitted.

"I know it's been hard," Abby said tenderly. "My heart has been with you for every one of the years this war has kept us apart. It almost killed me to know how much you were suffering and not be able to do anything to help."

"I felt it," Carrie whispered, her heart overwhelmed with the love and care flowing from Aunt Abby. "Do you realize we've actually only ever spent a month together in all these years?"

"Yes, but our hearts were connected in a way that time, distance and a war couldn't touch."

"Yes..." Carrie whispered, as she laid her head on Aunt Abby's shoulder and let the woman hold her. "I missed you so much."

Robert fought to breathe steadily as he eyed Federals spread out before him across the field. An earlier battle that day had already resulted in heavy casualties. There had been so many times these two armies had paused to look at each other across empty fields, taking a final analysis before exploding into battle again. This was going to be another such time, but it was different. He could feel it.

The sparse Confederate lines were facing an enemy four times larger. They were facing an enemy that was strong and well-fed. Quite simply, they were facing an enemy they had no hope of beating. They had no trenches to hide in and no fortifications to protect them. They were going to be mowed down. Hemmed in on three sides by Union troops, they had nowhere else to run.

The Union bugles sounded, their clear notes spreading all across the field. All of Grant's brigades wheeled and swung into line. Every saber was raised high, shining silver as they reflected the sun.

Robert looked up and down at the tense faces of the men he had grown to love and felt sick. This was where it would end. He allowed only a brief thought of Carrie before he pushed it aside. It was too painful to envision her shining eyes and beautiful face. "I loved you with all my heart," he whispered almost silently.

Suddenly, as every muscle in his body stiffened in preparation, Robert saw an officer burst forth from their lines, galloping madly toward the Federals. He held a staff in his hand with a white flag fluttering from the end of it."

"Captain?" Alex had crawled over to his position.

Robert started to shake his head to indicate he didn't know any more than Alex, but he heard his name called.

"Captain Borden!"

"Yes, sir?" Robert stood quickly and looked up at his commanding officer.

"Have all your men stack their guns in the clearing to the right."

Robert was sure he had heard wrong. "Excuse me, sir?"

"Have all your men stack their guns in the clearing to the right," he repeated, his eyes dull with defeat, somehow carrying a spark of relief at the same time. "It's over," he said quietly. "Lee has surrendered."

Robert stared at him, and then swung around to watch the Federals disengage from their battle positions. He turned back to the officer, but he had already moved on down the line. "Stack your weapons, men," he called, still stunned. "There isn't going to be a fight."

"Today?" Alex asked.

"At all," Robert said, the reality starting to break through the shock. "We're done." He took a deep breath. "Lee has surrendered."

His men stared at him as if they couldn't comprehend what he was saying.

"We're done, Captain?"

"Yes, Alex. We're done."

Alex frowned and looked frightened. "What's going to happen to us? Are we all going to prison?"

"I don't know," Robert answered heavily. "Right now, you know as much as I do. Have all the men stack their weapons. I'll try to get some answers." He doubled over in a coughing attack and then walked slowly in the direction of the command tent. He was too weak to move faster.

When Robert reconnected with his men, they were all lined up along one side of the dusty road leading into Appomattox Courthouse. He was amazed to look over and see Union soldiers lining the road on the other side. Both sides were waiting quietly.

He called his unit together, knowing he had a few minutes before Grant arrived. Lee was already waiting in a house owned by Wilmer McLean. Robert found it ironic that McLean had fled Manassas after the First Battle of Bull Run to escape the war. Now it was ending right in his parlor. It was just one more oddity of a war that should never have happened.

Robert looked around him at the faces he knew so well. They were emaciated and exhausted, but spirit still shone in their eyes.

"We going to prison, Captain?" Alex asked quietly. "You can be straight with us."

"You are *not* going to prison," Robert said. "You're going home." He watched his men exchange astonished looks.

"Home, sir?" one ventured to ask, seeming to test the word on his tongue.

"Home," Robert repeated firmly, enjoying the looks of relief that replaced the dread on their faces. "I will be signing the parole for each of you. As long as you do not bear arms against the United States, and you observe the laws in force where you live, you will not be imprisoned or prosecuted for treason."

"That's good news," Alex said with relief, his eyes revealing it hadn't quite sunk in yet.

"It gets better," Robert said, thankful he could give the men some good news for a change. "Any of you that have horses or mules here will be able to take them home for spring planting." He knew most of them did, though it would take some time to make any of the animals strong enough to pull a plow. "And..." he hesitated because he wanted to play up the moment he was sure would make them the happiest. "...the Union is releasing a supply of food rations. You will eat tonight."

He knew his men would have broken into cheers if it had been a time for cheering. He was content with the looks of anticipation and gratitude on their grimy faces. He knew Grant's generosity in feeding Lee's army would go a long way toward reuniting the two sides.

A bugle call in the distance announced the arrival of General Grant. Both armies waited while a brown-bearded little man in a mud-spattered uniform rode up. He exchanged quiet greetings with his officers and then the little cavalcade went trotting up to the village where Lee waited for them in a modest brick home.

"I reckon I thought he would be bigger," Alex commented as they disappeared from sight.

"General Grant's power and strength are inside," Robert said quietly.

"Big enough to win this war," Alex agreed.

※

The feelings around the campfire that night fell on every spectrum.

"I'm right glad to be going home," one soldier commented. "My wife and kids been on their own long enough. I'm going home to plant my fields and grow food to eat."

"We should have taken another crack at them," another insisted. "I done heard about some boys that are going to take off for the hills and keep fighting."

Robert scowled. "I will have no talk like that in my unit," he ordered.

"Why not?" the soldier snapped with an angry scowl. "We done been fighting for four years. Don't seem right to give up now. We could all disperse and take to the hills. Let's see how them Yankees handle guerrilla warfare for a while."

Robert bristled with anger, but he fought to keep his voice calm. "So you want to create a state of affairs in the South that would take us years to recover from? You want Federal cavalry traveling the length and breadth of the South for no one knows how long, killing first and asking questions later, because they'll never know where their enemy is? You want to create a country where no one is safe, and we don't have a chance to rebuild our lives? You want to make certain your fellow soldiers end up in prison because you're too proud to admit we lost?"

Silence fell over the entire area as Robert's voice rang out strong and proud. "Is that what you want?"

The soldier hung his head and shook it slowly. "No. I guess I didn't think it through real good."

Robert nodded. The offending soldier was a good man who had lived through an unbearable four years. "It's hard to think when you're starving and have been marching for days with no food," he said generously, knowing creating goodwill would get him much further than casting blame. Robert hid his smile when the offending soldier relaxed again, reaching out to fill his plate with more bacon and beans.

"What you gonna do, Captain?" the soldier asked.

It only took Robert a second to give his answer. "I'm going home." He looked eastward to Richmond and smiled. "I've got the most beautiful wife in the world waiting for me. *I'm going home.*"

Late that night, his fever began to climb again and his coughing seemed as if it would explode his lungs. He could feel the life being sucked from him as the pneumonia he had fought for weeks took control with a vengeance.

"Captain?"

Robert looked up through burning eyes at Alex's young face peering down at him. He opened his mouth, but he was too weak to speak. "Carrie..." he managed to whisper. "*Carrie...*"

An Invitation

Before you read the last chapter of The Last, Long Night, I would like to invite you to join my mailing list so that you are never left wondering what is going to happen next. ☺

Join my Email list so you can:

-   Receive notice of all new books & audio releases.
-   Be a part of my Launch celebrations. I give away lots of Free gifts! ☺
-   Read my weekly blog while you're waiting for a new book.
-   Be part of The Bregdan Chronicles Family!
-   Learn about all the other books I write.

Just go to www.BregdanChronicles.net and fill out the form.

I look forward to having you become part of The Bregdan Chronicles Family!

Blessings,
Ginny Dye

Chapter Thirty-Six

Matthew was waiting on the porch when Carrie and Aunt Abby walked arm in arm through the gate. "Now that's a wonderful sight," he called. "Two of my most favorite women in the world together again."

"Just two *of* your most favorite women?" Carrie replied playfully. She turned to Aunt Abby. "Surely there must be something we can do to knock someone else out of the top positions." She laughed and looked back up at Matthew, not understanding the quick shadow that flashed in his eyes. She decided he must have news. "What is it?" she asked quietly.

"Lee surrendered his army this afternoon," he informed them. "Word came through over the telegraph. I came straight here."

Carrie stared at him and sank down on the step, her thoughts swirling.

"Carrie?" Aunt Abby asked gently as she sat down next to her and took her hand.

Carrie shook her head. "I'm trying to figure out my own feelings," she admitted. "I wanted Richmond to fall. I wanted Lee to surrender. I want the war to be completely over. I just know so many people are going to grieve." An image of her father caused her heart to squeeze with pain. She looked at Matthew. "What does this really mean? There are other Confederate forces. The last I heard, there are over one hundred thousand men still in units around the country."

"That's true," Matthew agreed, "but all of them have hinged their spirit and belief on General Lee. As long as Lee's troops were still fighting, all of them had the will to continue. Lee's surrender is going to deflate everyone. I predict General Johnston will surrender by the end of this month, and then it will spread west." He took one of Carrie's hands. "The war is over, Carrie. There will be a little cleanup, but it's over."

Carrie stared at him. "Over..." she murmured, not sure if she really believed it. Now, only one thought burned in her heart. "Lee's soldiers? Robert?"

"Everyone is free to go home," Matthew said. "Lee is talking to them today, and then they'll be free to go."

Carrie brushed at the tears on her cheeks.

"You don't seem excited," Matthew said quietly, peering into her eyes, his blue eyes dark with compassion.

"Last night I had a terrible dream," she admitted, and looked at Aunt Abby. "I haven't said anything about it because I didn't want to give any validity to it."

"That explains why I felt you were far away a few times this afternoon," Aunt Abby said gently. "What did you dream, Carrie?"

Carrie took a deep breath and felt their love embrace her. "Robert was very ill," she whispered. "He was burning up with fever and no one could get it down. When the dream ended, he was whispering my name." She shook her head. "I've learned I can't let my fears and dreams control me, but it seemed so very real."

Aunt Abby moved forward to enfold her in her arms. "I'll be here with you until Robert comes home..."

Carrie smiled gratefully, but noticed the unspoken sentence that said '*or until you receive word.*'

Three days later, the city was still reeling from news of Lee's surrender and the obvious collapse of the Confederacy, but the city was also full of joyous reunions as exhausted soldiers returned from the war. Some were coming home, some were making their way home. All their faces were a mixture of defeat and relief, their eyes still dull with disbelief that four years of agony had come to this.

Vibrant young men or boys when the war started, they were now caricatures of themselves—starvation, illness and wounds had sapped their energy and life, leaving them old men before their time. Confidence and joy had been replaced by numb acceptance. Hope had been eroded by pain.

Carrie watched every face, hoping for just one, but Robert did not appear. It was almost dark when she trudged up the stairs to the house, wishing for the easy happiness and celebration she was feeling days before when her house was full of friends and family. They were still there, but the cloud over her heart wouldn't lift. "This will pass," she murmured as she came onto the porch. "This will pass."

"It will, you know," Aunt Abby said tenderly.

Carrie sank down next to her on the porch swing and rested her head on Aunt Abby's shoulder. "I know that in my mind, but my heart can't feel it. I've dreamed all these years that if the war would end, everything could go back to normal. But nothing's normal."

"And it won't be for a long time, my dear."

Carrie gazed up at her. "I want it to be," she said.

Aunt Abby smiled. "And there's nothing wrong with you wanting it to be different," she replied. "It's what will keep you fighting through challenges to create change." She paused. "The end of the war is just the beginning. Our country is full of wounded soldiers who will never again be able to live independent lives. It's full of women who will never be content to go back to being wives and mothers, because they know what it's like to be responsible for everything, and to do it well. It's full of children who have grown up hating people they don't know and something they couldn't possibly understand." She took a deep breath. "It will take a long time for things to change. Perhaps even longer for the feelings to follow the actions."

"Robert..."

Aunt Abby squeezed her hand. "I won't insult you by saying everything will be fine. You've been through too much, so you know that's not true. Horrible things happen and pain must be endured. I will, however, tell you you're borrowing trouble before it is here," she said. "You're acting like Robert is dead, when he could just as easily be alive."

"I'm disappointing you," Carrie whispered, fatigue pressing down on her.

"Nonsense!" Aunt Abby snorted. "You couldn't disappoint me if you tried." She reached over and lifted Carrie's chin until their eyes met. "When you told me about your rainbow this spring, you told me that darkness never lasts. That the sun always comes out."

"Yes," Carrie murmured, fighting to see the rainbow through the fog of her fears.

"You are not alone, Carrie. No matter what darkness comes, or no matter how long it lasts, you are not alone. And you're right, the sun will come again."

Carrie stared at Aunt Abby, and managed a smile when Rose squeezed in beside them on the swing and took her other hand. She looked at both these women who loved her so much, and whom she loved so fiercely in return. No, she wasn't alone. Slowly, her heart steadied and her mind cleared.

Finally, she nodded. "You're right," she said, relieved to hear the strength back in her voice. "Thank you," she whispered.

"Carrie! Carrie!" She turned and shaded her eyes against the rays of the sinking sun, realizing Hobbs was hurrying down the road as fast as he could with his limp.

She stood, shielded on both sides by Aunt Abby and Rose, as Hobbs stopped at the bottom of the road, breathing in deep gasps. "Hobbs! What is it?"

"It's Robert," he said, leaning over to catch his breath. "He's at Jackson Hospital."

Carrie gasped, feeling arms come around her waist from both sides.

Hobbs stared up at her, his eyes wide. "He's alive, Carrie."

Carrie didn't need him to tell her it was serious. "Thank you, Hobbs." She fought to remain calm, wishing Chimborazo was still in operation. It would take her almost thirty minutes to walk to Jackson Hospital.

"Spencer is coming right now," Hobbs continued as his breathing slowed. "He went to get the carriage."

Carrie managed a smile. "Thank you." She turned to Aunt Abby and Rose.

Aunt Abby squeezed her hand. "We'll be here when you get back," she promised. "If I thought we could help, I would go, but I fear we would only be in the way."

Carrie nodded, her thoughts already in Jackson Hospital. She jerked her head up as the sound of carriage wheels announced Spencer was coming. "Please have May prepare my room to take care of Robert. He'll sleep in my bed. I'll need a cot next to him. I may not be able to bring him home tonight, but I will as soon as it's safe."

"Of course," Aunt Abby replied.

Rose threw her arms around her. "You saved my Moses," she said firmly. "I'm praying Robert will survive, too. He just has to, Carrie!"

Carrie managed to smile as she stepped into the carriage, squeezed both their hands, and settled back for the ride.

<hr />

Carrie forced herself to breathe evenly as Spencer drove into the city as fast as he could, swinging around groups of soldiers mingling on the streets, their eyes glazed with confusion and despair.

"Them poor men don't know what to do now that they ain't got nobody ordering their every move," Spencer said sympathetically.

Carrie gazed at them, but couldn't force her thoughts to move beyond Robert. Long minutes later, the carriage jolted to a stop. She was out of the carriage before Spencer could jump down to help her.

"I'll be right here waiting, Miss Carrie," he said quietly.

Carrie shook her head. "I don't know how long I'll be."

"Yes, ma'am, I know that. I'll be right here waiting," he repeated.

Carrie gave him a look of gratitude and hurried into the hospital. She gasped with relief when the first person she saw was Dr. Wild. He saw her at the same moment she spotted him.

"Carrie!"

"Robert is here," she said quickly. "Do you know where?"

He nodded and took her elbow. "He's right down here," he said. "As soon as I saw him on the list, I had him moved to my ward. He got here a little while ago. I sent Hobbs to tell you."

"Thank you," Carrie whispered, her heart full of gratitude. "How is he?"

"He got here last night with a load from Appomattox Courthouse. He had a high fever, but we're finally getting it down." He paused. "He has pneumonia."

Carrie groaned.

"I talked to some of the soldiers from his unit who came in with him. He's been sick for a long time, but he refused to quit fighting because..."

"...his men were counting on him," Carrie finished heavily, not sure if the feeling swirling through her was admiration or anger.

"Yes."

"What has been done for him?" Carrie asked, dreading his answer.

"I got to him in time," Dr. Wild said quickly. "They didn't bleed him."

Carrie sagged in relief. Many of the doctors still believed in treating pneumonia by cutting open a vein in an effort to cleanse the body of diseased blood. It didn't seem to faze them that the cure often proved fatal. Other common treatments were alcohol and quinine, but when the blockades stopped the drugs, Carrie had created different treatments that resulted in higher cure rates in her ward than anywhere else. Unfortunately, many of the doctors ignored the results because she was a woman, and instead continued their methods.

"I want Robert moved to my house where I can care for him."

"Yes, I already knew that was what you would want. I have a wagon ready to move him."

"Is it safe?"

Dr. Wild hesitated. "I don't know. He hasn't regained consciousness, so I don't know exactly how sick he is. His breathing is very shallow and he still has a fever, but it is starting to come down. We were able to get him to swallow a little garlic, onion and honey mixture, but there's not a lot we can do until he wakes up."

Carrie nodded, weighing the risks of moving him against the benefits. "Please have the wagon brought around," she said. "I want him at home. I'll have more control of what he is eating, and I'll have someone with him twenty-four hours a day."

"I believe it's the best place for him," Dr. Wild agreed, and then hesitated again, his eyes full of compassion. "He doesn't look good, Carrie. The fever and pneumonia burned him up."

Carrie took one look in his eyes and knew it was going to be bad.

"He doesn't look like the man you remember," he said kindly.

Carrie took a deep breath. "No matter what he looks like, he's my husband." Tears filled her eyes. "I love him. Please take me to him."

Dr. Wild nodded and led the way to Robert's bed.

Carrie swallowed the lump in her throat and clenched her fists as she stared at the caricature of her husband. His face was skeleton gaunt. Saggy skin hung on his body. His skin was a chalky gray, and stringy black hair hung limply. Shallow gasps came from him, along with an occasional shudder as his eyes twitched in what Carrie was sure were horrific nightmares.

Suddenly, she was down on her knees, her cheek pressed against his chest. "I'm here, Robert," she said softly. "I'm here."

Was it just her imagination, or did his breathing ease a little? Pushing herself up, Carrie watched as several men came down the aisle with a stretcher. "Move him carefully, please. And," she added, "I will be riding in the wagon with him."

No one bothered to remind her it was against procedure.

Everyone was waiting on the porch when the wagon pulled up. Carrie managed to give them a tremulous smile before she jumped down. No one said a word as Robert was carried into the house, though several of their faces whitened in disbelief.

Matthew gasped softly as he stared down at his friend. Carrie exchanged a long look with him before she followed the stretcher up the stairs, trying to push away the memories of her mother's face after her fever. She had saved Moses—surely she could save Robert. She pushed away the thought that Robert had been sick for months, letting the pneumonia sap all his energy and strength until he had nothing left to fight with.

"Micah, please bring up lots of water and rags," she ordered from the stairs. "And, May, will you please make a broth of onion, garlic, carrots and celery? Add in some radishes and some of the parsley. When you bring that up, please bring me some garlic cloves, onions and honey. It will help fight the infection."

"Yessum, Miss Carrie," May responded immediately. "It won't take me long to make it." She spun around to where Matthew was standing, looking helpless. "Go on out to the garden and get me everything for the broth," she barked.

Matthew nodded, obviously relieved to have something to do, and disappeared out the back door.

Rose, Aunt Abby and Janie closed ranks around Carrie as she moved up the stairs.

"You don't have to..."

Aunt Abby held up a hand. "You've done enough alone," she said firmly. "It stops here."

Carrie swallowed back sudden tears as her throat tightened with gratitude. She looked at the three women gazing at her with so much love and compassion. "Thank you," she whispered. Then she turned to run up the stairs to do battle.

It was almost midnight before Robert's fever was completely gone—the result of hundreds of wet rags wrapped around his body, removed when they were hot, and then replaced by cool rags. Even though he was still unconscious, Aunt Abby had managed to get him to swallow several spoons of broth, holding his emaciated body up as tenderly as a baby's to allow him to get it down.

As they worked through the night in tandem, love flowed like a bubbling stream through the room. It chased out despair and replaced it with a relentless hope that pulsated in the air. Carrie could feel it. She knew the others could, too. She almost couldn't believe she could look at Robert and feel such complete peace, but she couldn't deny the reality flooding her heart.

"He's going to be all right," Rose whispered.

Carrie looked up and drew even more hope from the strong light she saw burning in Rose's eyes. "I believe you're right," she said softly, laying her hand on Robert's forehead, happy his breathing was not so shallow, and his skin not so gray.

She had turned back to rinse out some more rags when she heard the bed creak. She spun around, gasping when she saw Robert's eyes were open. Blurred with confusion, they swept the room until they landed on Carrie.

"Carrie..." he whispered hoarsely.

Carrie gave a glad cry and sprang to the side of the bed. "Robert!" She felt his confusion and weakness. Laying her hand on his cheek, she stroked it gently. "You're home, sweetheart. You're *home.*"

Robert's eyes cleared a little more. "Home?" Then his eyes lit with a weak hope. "Oak Meadows?"

Carrie's heart sank. "No," she replied softly. "You're here in Richmond."

She bit back her groan when he turned confused eyes on her. He had no idea where he was. "It doesn't matter," she said, stroking his cheek. "The only thing that's important right now is that you get well. You've been very sick."

Robert continued to stare at her. "The war is over," he mumbled. "We lost."

Carrie controlled the unreasonable desire to laugh hysterically. She was wise enough to know the stress was exacting a toll. She felt Aunt Abby's hand settle on her shoulder and drew the strength she needed to say calmly, "Yes, it's over, Robert. You don't have to fight again."

Robert's eyes burned into her own, and then he sighed. "Good."

Moments later, he was sound asleep.

Carrie straightened and pulled the covers over his body. "He needs sleep now," she said. "He'll sleep through the night. Rest will help him more than anything." She looked at the exhausted faces surrounding her. "Let's go tell everyone the news."

The parlor was full of anxious faces when they arrived. Carrie had a brief thought that Matthew was going to lose his job if he continued to spend every moment at the house, but she was too grateful for his support to encourage him to do anything else.

"Robert will get better," she said, catching the look Rose and Janie exchanged. "He's a little confused right now, but that is the result of the fever. I've seen it in patient after patient. Now that the fever is gone, he'll have a chance to regain his strength. There were things that swirled through his mind during the fever that seem more real right now than reality does. That will go away fairly quickly."

"What does he need?" Matthew asked.

"Quiet," she said. "The only things that will help him are rest and good food."

Matthew opened his mouth to ask another question but closed it again. Carrie knew what was on his mind. "I don't know if he'll come back to his full strength," she admitted reluctantly. "He's been sick for a long time. The body can only take so much." She shook her head. "There is also a good chance he will be the Robert we knew, Matthew. I'm going to believe in that outcome," she finished.

May was standing to the side quietly. "The garden be coming on real good now," she said. "He'll get lots of good food."

"Yes, it is," Carrie agreed, but continued speaking, not even realizing she had made a decision sometime during the long night. "I'm going to take Robert out to the plantation as soon as he can travel. It will be the best place for him to get well." She despised herself for even thinking that she was about to repeat the same experience she had with her mother, walking away from the chance to pursue medical school to care for someone else who was sick. But what kind of doctor would she ever be if she didn't put her patients first—especially the husband she loved with all her heart? She hoped no one in the room could look inside her and see the selfishness lurking there.

"Besides," she added, forcing a light note to her voice, "I promised Father I would be there when he got back. That I would take care of things until he could return."

"Moses and I are going with you," Rose said firmly.

Carrie spun around to look at her. "What? You can't..."

"You're going to need help," Rose said. "None of us will be on the plantation for a long time, but it's where we're going to be until your father returns and until Robert is well. The country will need time to settle down before any more decisions are made."

Carrie wanted to protest further. She was sure she probably should, but she couldn't. The idea of having Rose and Moses with her on the plantation was too wonderful to refuse. She simply reached out and grasped Rose's hand.

"Is now a good time to tell you I'm coming, too?"

Carrie gasped. "Aunt Abby... What... How...?"

Aunt Abby laughed. "Clearly you need me. You're suddenly unable to complete a sentence." She stepped forward and took Carrie's hand.

Carrie's head was spinning, but one thought suddenly broke through the confusion. "I don't even know if the plantation is still there," she gasped, the realization striking her full force. "There may be nowhere to go."

"It's still there, Carrie."

Carrie's head snapped up as Moses walked down the staircase. "You're supposed to be in bed for two more days," she said sternly, happy beyond words to see him standing on his two feet again. He looked weak, but he seemed fine.

"If I stay in that bed one more day, I will go mad," he replied. "You said this morning the infection is clear and the wound is healing nicely. I know I can't do much for a while, but it doesn't mean I can't walk down a flight of stairs."

The room broke into cheers as Moses walked easily into the room and sat down in her father's wingback chair.

Carrie smiled in defeat, and then remembered what he had said. "You said the plantation is still there. How could you possibly know that?"

"Captain Jones was by this morning. He sent some of his men out there to check on it."

"He did?" Carrie was having as much trouble imagining a unit of soldiers being sent out to check on the plantation as she was believing it was still really there. "He must really feel he owes you," she murmured, trying to let the news settle in.

"Actually," Moses responded, "he did this one for you. He's never forgotten the way you escaped the plantation on Granite. He saved it from burning that time because of what you had done, and he wanted to know for himself if it was still standing. He said to tell you he was glad."

Carrie could only stare at him, letting the knowledge the plantation had survived the war when so many had been destroyed sink into her mind.

"So, you see," Aunt Abby teased, "I really do have a place to stay."

"But your business," Carrie protested.

"Poo! What is the point of employees if I can't take some time off when I need to? Rose is right that the country will need some time to settle down and the war to end on all fronts, before I can do much to help down here."

"I hate to miss the party," Matthew said sadly, "but Peter and I have been called out of the city. We're leaving on the sixteenth."

"Just two more days?" Aunt Abby walked over to take his hand. "This time has been so wonderful, like an oasis in the middle of a barren four-year desert. I don't want it to end."

"Clifford and I are leaving for Raleigh in a few days," Janie added, her voice thick with emotion.

Carrie stiffened and turned to her friend, tears filling her eyes. She had known this time was coming but knowing it didn't make it any easier. "Janie..." she whispered, walking over and wrapping her in her arms.

"Don't you start crying," Janie whispered fiercely. "I'm not gone yet."

Carrie stared at her, knowing she had no clue how to say goodbye to the friend who had saved her and become her sister during the last four years.

Aunt Abby moved between them and wrapped an arm around each waist. "You girls have forged a bond nothing will ever break," she said softly. "You may be separated by distance, but nothing will ever break the connection."

Carrie knew that was true. Wasn't she experiencing that truth with Rose and Aunt Abby right now? She took a deep breath and nodded.

"As long as everyone is revealing their plans, I suppose I should ask if there is room for me at the plantation, too," Jeremy said casually.

"The plantation? You're coming, too?" The swing of emotions from loss to excitement was almost more than Carrie could bear.

"I figure it's time to discover the place I was born," Jeremy said easily. "Besides, I haven't spent enough time with my twin yet. If she and Moses are going, I guess I am, too."

Rose gave a glad cry and sprang into Jeremy's arms.

Carrie laughed. "You didn't know?"

Rose shook her head. "It's as much a surprise to me as it is to you."

Carrie looked over at Hobbs. "Are you going home to West Virginia?"

Hobbs nodded solemnly. "I got a letter from my folks yesterday. My dog is waiting to go hunting."

Laughter lightened the atmosphere in the room.

Carrie wasn't done however. She looked at Micah and May standing to the side. "What about you two?"

Micah shrugged. "We like working for your daddy. If he got enough money to hire us when he gets back, both of us would like that. We done talked about it."

"I don't know my father's plans," Carrie said hesitantly, thinking of his lost fortune and not knowing how far the gold hidden upstairs would take him. "I know he plans on going back to the plantation."

"Yessum, I know everything be real mixed up right now," Micah agreed calmly, "but as long as he owns this house, somebody gonna need to care for it. We got a good garden and a place to sleep. That's more than most have. It's enough for right now. We'll see what happens when things settle down."

A sudden knock on the door startled them all. Who was visiting at two in the morning? Micah moved quickly to open it, obviously ready to scold whoever was disturbing them. When he opened it, no one was there.

"Who be out there?" he demanded.

"I need to see Carrie Borden," came a hushed voice from the shadows.

Jeremy and Matthew stepped forward. "Who are you? Why are you here at this time of night?" Jeremy snapped.

Carrie stepped forward. "It's all right," she insisted. "Who could hurt me with all of you here? Who would even think of trying?" She eased out onto the porch. "I'm Mrs. Borden. What can I do for you?"

"I've got a letter for you from your father," the shadow replied as he pressed an envelope in her hand, jumped from the porch, and disappeared into the darkness.

Carrie stared at the envelope in her hand for a long moment and walked back into the room.

"We'll leave you to read it," Aunt Abby said.

"No," Carrie said quickly. "All of you are my family now. I want all of you to hear what he has to say. If any of it is private, I'll leave it out."

Everyone nodded and settled back in their chairs again, expectant looks on their faces.

"When is it dated, Carrie?" Matthew asked.

"April ninth."

He nodded thoughtfully. "He wouldn't have known yet about the surrender."

"He wrote the letter the same day Lee surrendered," Carrie murmured, and then began to read.

> *Dearest Carrie,*
> *I hope this letter finds its way to you. I made it safely to Lynchburg and Granite is safe in a stable. He's already put on a little weight.*

Carrie smiled with relief and continued reading.

> *Governor Smith is quite determined to set up a new Virginia government here in Lynchburg and continue the fight. I also hear President Davis remains committed to the Confederate cause from his new headquarters in Danville.*

"Not anymore," Matthew muttered, and then clarified when everyone stared at him. "We received word before we came over tonight that Davis got notice of Lee's surrender. He is evacuating Danville as well."

"He's on the run," Jeremy commented.

"Yes," Peter agreed. "Lincoln is more than willing to pardon anyone who pledges allegiance to the Union again, but I suspect your president is far from that."

"I suspect that is true," Carrie agreed. She turned back to the letter. Right now, she didn't care about what President Davis was going to do. She was only concerned with her father.

> *I wish I knew what Lincoln's true intentions were. In spite of the determination of both the governor and the president to continue the fight, I*

know it is over. I discover I have no real desire to be on the run. I've heard many plans to escape to Mexico, or Cuba, or even Peru. While I admit to curiosity about those lands, I find I want nothing more than to go home to the plantation.

Carrie's eyes filled with tears as she envisioned her father lonely and alone. "Matthew, do you know what Lincoln intends with government officials?"

Matthew nodded. "President Lincoln wants an easy peace," he said confidently. "He's not looking for hangings and reprisals. He wants a real peace that will allow our shattered country to grow together again." He paused. "I've heard he's hinted that he wished Davis could somehow manage to escape from the United States, and go to some foreign country where vengeance could not reach him. He wants the soldiers to go home and pick up their lives. Lincoln also wants to begin reestablishing civil government in the southern states." He took a breath. "Of course, the war has to end first for all this to happen, but he's fulfilling his vision of sending all the soldiers home as proof of his intentions."

Carrie thought about the numb, aimless soldiers wandering the streets of Richmond. "At least the ones who have somewhere to go," she commented.

"Will the government allow all this to happen?" Rose asked. "There has been a lot of talk that not even all of Lincoln's cabinet agrees with his approach. Add in the Radical Republicans, and there are many who feel the South needs to pay heavily for what has happened. They are demanding martial law."

Matthew shook his head heavily. "Only time will tell. President Lincoln is an astute politician who knows how to wield his power. It won't be easy, but I tremble to think what our country would be like without him at the helm."

"What else does your father say, Carrie?" Janie prompted.

I'm praying you are safe in Richmond, though I cringe to think of you living in a city under Union control. *I know you said you would return to the plantation to wait for me when you are able. I don't know if that is truly possible, but I find the idea of it gives me great comfort.*

I know you and Robert have a life of your own to live. I'm going to do all I can to find my way back home quickly, hoping it is possible for me to live out the rest of my life in peace.

I love you so much, Carrie.
Father

Carrie blinked back the tears stinging her eyes and cleared her throat.

"He's tired," Aunt Abby said quietly. "He's given all he has to give for the Confederate cause, and now he just wants peace."

Carrie nodded. "Yes. There was a time, after Mother died, when leaving the plantation and working in the government was the only thing that gave him peace. Now all that has dissolved around him, and he wants what he spent his life creating." A fierce longing clutched her heart. "I so hope he is allowed to have it," she whispered.

"The war will soon be over," Jeremy said comfortingly. "I truly believe Lincoln wants an easy peace. We'll be out on the plantation soon, and then all of us will have a chance to rebuild our lives."

❦

Three days later, while the sky was still dark, only a faint glimmering revealing that dawn lurked beneath the horizon, a sudden banging on the door reverberated through the house.

Carrie's eyes sprang open in alarm, and she felt Robert shift beside her. "Go back to sleep," she whispered, noting his breathing was a little easier. He still had yet to do more than whisper a few words, but his eyes were getting clearer on a daily basis. He still thought he was at Oak Meadows, but at least he knew who she was.

She could hear Micah shuffle toward the front door, grumbling at the early morning intrusion. Sensing bad news, Carrie jumped up and slipped into a dress, not bothering with her hair.

Rose and Aunt Abby were already at the head of the stairs, eyes wide with alarm when she hurried out of her room. Moses was right behind her.

"What in the world is going on?" Moses growled.

"Mr. Matthew!" Micah's sleepy exclamation rose up the stairway. "What be wrong?"

All of them exchanged looks of deep concern and started down the stairs.

"You need to wake everyone," Matthew said quickly.

"We're awake," Moses assured him.

Janie, Clifford, Jeremy and Hobbs descended down the stairway from the opposite wing of the house.

"What has happened?" Jeremy asked, his eyes heavy with sleep, but his voice clear and full of concern.

"Sit down," Matthew advised in a heavy voice. "This is indeed a dark day for our country."

Carrie sank down along with everyone else, staring at him with fear. "Matthew, you're scaring everyone," she said unsteadily. "What is going on?"

Matthew took a deep breath and looked around the room. "President Lincoln has been assassinated."

There was not a sound as everyone stared at him with complete shock.

Finally the words penetrated Carrie's mind. "He's dead? President Lincoln is dead?" She heard the words come from her mouth but couldn't quite connect them with reality.

"Matthew!" Aunt Abby gasped. "Tell us...what has happened?" she stammered.

Matthew sank down heavily into a chair. "Lincoln was attending the theater with his wife two nights ago. They've identified his killer as a southern actor, John Wilkes Booth."

"Oh my God!" Carrie gasped, horrified by the president's death and also immediately recognizing the consequences that would come from it.

"Booth snuck into his box and shot him point-blank in the head," Matthew said grimly.

Carrie began to weep.

There was not a dry eye in the room as the horror sunk in. Tears flowed freely in a room engulfed in silence.

Carrie was the first to speak. "What will happen now?" she whispered.

Silence was the only answer to her question as they all exchanged lost looks.

Many minutes passed before Aunt Abby rose and walked to the center of the room. "We will be carried forward by hope," she said firmly. She gazed around at all of them, standing in the room like a prophetic angel, her eyes shining. "A terrible thing has happened. Carrie asked what will happen now." She looked around the room again and locked eyes with Carrie. "We will be carried forward by hope."

Carrie allowed the words to burn through her disbelief and horror. She knew Aunt Abby was offering her a rope—a beacon of light in the midst of darkness.

Slowly...very slowly...the atmosphere in the room shifted as Aunt Abby's words sank into their hearts and minds. The sun, just beginning to peak over the horizon, cast a rosy glow into the room.

"You're right," Carrie whispered. "Nothing will change what has happened. We will all have to live through a dark time because of what Booth has done. But we will survive this darkness, just as we have survived the darkness of the last four years. We will create new lives as we reunite our country." Her voice grew stronger as she rose to stand beside Aunt Abby.

"We will be carried forward by hope."

To Be Continued...

Available Now!
www.DiscoverTheBregdanChronicles.com

Would you be so kind as to leave a Review on Amazon?
I love hearing from my readers! Just go to
Amazon.com, put The Last Long Night into the Search
box, click to read the Reviews, and you'll be able to
leave one of your own!

Thank you!

The Bregdan Principle

Every life that has been lived until today is a part of the woven braid of life.

It takes every person's story to create history.

Your life will help determine the course of history.

You may think you don't have much of an impact.

You do.

Every action you take will reflect in someone else's life.

Someone else's decisions.

Someone else's future.

Both good and bad.

The Bregdan Chronicles

Storm Clouds Rolling In
1860 – 1861

On To Richmond
1861 – 1862

Spring Will Come
1862 – 1863

Dark Chaos
1863 – 1864

The Long Last Night
1864 – 1865

Carried Forward By Hope
April – December 1865

Glimmers of Change
December – August 1866

Shifted By The Winds
August – December 1866

***Many more coming... Go to
DiscoverTheBregdanChronicles.com to see how
many are available now!***

Other Books by Ginny Dye

Pepper Crest High Series - Teen Fiction

Time For A Second Change
It's Really A Matter of Trust
A Lost & Found Friend
Time For A Change of Heart

When I Dream Series – Children's Bedtime Stories

When I Dream, I Dream of Horses
When I Dream, I Dream of Puppies
When I Dream, I Dream of Snow
When I Dream, I Dream of Kittens
When I Dream, I Dream of Elephants
When I Dream, I Dream of the Ocean

Fly To Your Dreams Series – Allegorical Fantasy

Dream Dragon
Born To Fly
Little Heart

101+ Ways to Promote Your Business Opportunity

All titles by Ginny Dye
www.AVoiceInTheWorld.com

Author Biography

Who am I? Just a normal person who happens to love to write. If I could do it all anonymously, I would. In fact, I did the first go round. I wrote under a pen name. On the off chance I would ever become famous - I didn't want to be! I don't like the limelight. I don't like living in a fishbowl. I especially don't like thinking I have to look good everywhere I go, just in case someone recognizes me! I finally decided none of that matters. If you don't like me in overalls and a baseball cap, too bad. If you don't like my haircut or think I should do something different than what I'm doing, too bad. I'll write books that you will hopefully like, and we'll both let that be enough! :) Fair?

But let's see what you might want to know. I spent many years as a Wanderer. My dream when I graduated from college was to experience the United States. I grew up in the South. There are many things I love about it but I wanted to live in other places. So I did. I moved 42 times, traveled extensively in 49 of the 50 states, and had more experiences than I will ever be able to recount. The only state I haven't been in is Alaska, simply because I refuse to visit such a vast, fabulous place until I have at least a month. Along the way I had glorious adventures. I've canoed through the Everglade Swamps, snorkeled in the Florida Keys and windsurfed in the Gulf of Mexico. I've white-water rafted down the New River and Bungee jumped in the Wisconsin Dells. I've visited every National Park (in the off-season when there is more freedom!) and many of the State Parks. I've hiked thousands of miles of mountain trails and biked through Arizona deserts. I've canoed and biked through Upstate New York and Vermont, and polished off as much lobster as possible on the Maine Coast.

I had a glorious time and never thought I would find a place that would hold me until I came to the Pacific Northwest. I'd been here less than 2 weeks, and I knew I would never leave. My heart is so at home here with the towering firs, sparkling waters, soaring mountains and rocky beaches. I love the eagles & whales. In 5 minutes I can be hiking on 150 miles of trails in the mountains around my home, or gliding across the lake in my rowing shell. I love it!

Have you figured out I'm kind of an outdoors gal? If it can be done outdoors, I love it! Hiking, biking, windsurfing, rock-climbing, roller-blading, snow-shoeing, skiing, rowing, canoeing, softball, tennis... the list could go on and on. I love to have fun and I love to stretch my body. This should give you a pretty good idea of what I do in my free time.

When I'm not writing or playing, I'm building I Am A Voice In The World - a fabulous organization I founded in 2001 - along with 60 amazing people who poured their lives into creating resources to empower people to make a difference with their lives.

What else? I love to read, cook, sit for hours in solitude on my mountain, and also hang out with friends. I love barbeques and block parties. Basically - I just love LIFE!

I'm so glad you're part of my world!

Ginny

Join my Email List so you can:

- Receive notice of all new books
- Be a part of my Launch Celebrations. I give away lots of Free gifts!
- Read my weekly BLOG while you're waiting for a new book.
- Be part of The Bregdan Chronicles Family!
- Learn about all the other books I write.

Just go to www.BregdanChronicles.net and fill out the form.

51618347R00269

Made in the USA
Lexington, KY
30 April 2016